## A LUX NOVEL
# OBLIVION

D0784016

Jennifer L. Armentrout lives in West Virginia. All the rumors you've heard about her state aren't true. Well, mostly. When she's not hard at work writing, she spends her time reading, working out, watching zombie movies, and pretending to write. She shares her home with her husband, his K-9 partner named Diesel, and her hyper Jack Russell Loki. Her dreams of becoming an author started in algebra class, where she spent her time writing short stories…therefore explaining her dismal grades in math. Jennifer writes Adult and Young Adult Urban Fantasy and Romance.

Find out more at www.jenniferarmentrout.com

Praise for Jennifer L. Armentrout's Lux series:

'An action-packed ride that will leave you breathless and begging for more' Jus Accardo, bestselling author of *Touch*

'An engrossing, sexy, nail-biter! I'm delighted to join the Daemon Invasion' Nancy Holder, bestselling author of *Wicked*

'A riveting story that will keep you turning the pages to the end and then say, "I want more!"' Kate Kaynak, author of the Ganzfield series

'This is the stuff swoons are made of. Fans of *Obsidian* will devour the high-stakes plot and beautifully crafted chemistry' Wendy Higgins, bestselling author of *Sweet Evil*

'The beginning of Armentrout's new Lux series is a thrilling ride from start to finish…This series is guaranteed to hold your attention and have you begging for more' *RT Book Reviews*

'*Obsidian* is fast-paced and entertaining. I couldn't put this one down. Who knew aliens could be sexy?' *YA Fantasy Guide*

'Witty, refreshing and electrifying' Shortie Says

'With a unique and entrancing story, *Obsidian* was action packed, dramatic, captivating, and exciting' A Cupcake and a Latte

'One of those books you get lost in reading and finish in one sitting. Each book is a fast-paced read with a great plot and strong characters. A must-read for young adult book lovers' Hypable.com

'I LOVED *OBSIDIAN*! Get ready to devour this book in one sitting, fall hard for Daemon, and be desperate for book two!' Deborah Cooke, bestselling author of *Dragonfire*

'Take some really hot, sizzling character chemistry, two stubborn love interests who know how to push each other's buttons, and add in some awesome out-of-this-world characters and you've got the makings for one fabulously written story' Mundie Moms

'An incredibly thrilling action packed story from start to finish' @TheBookCafe

'Powerful. Addictive. Wipe away everything you have ever thought about aliens. *Obsidian* sets a new standard' Winter Haven Books

# JENNIFER L. ARMENTROUT

## A LUX NOVEL

# OBLIVION

**HODDER**

First published in the United States of America in 2015
by Entangled Publishing, LLC

First published in Great Britain in 2015
by Hodder & Stoughton
An Hachette UK company

1

Copyright © Jennifer L. Armentrout 2015

The right of Jennifer L. Armentrout to be identified as the
Author of the Work has been asserted by her in accordance
with the Copyright, Designs and Patents Act 1988.

All rights reserved. No part of this publication may be reproduced, stored
in a retrieval system, or transmitted, in any form or by any means without
the prior written permission of the publisher, nor be otherwise circulated
in any form of binding or cover other than that in which it is published and
without a similar condition being imposed on the subsequent purchaser.

All characters in this publication are fictitious and any resemblance
to real persons, living or dead is purely coincidental.

A CIP catalogue record for this title is available from the British Library

Paperback ISBN 978 1 473 62233 3
eBook ISBN 978 1 473 62234 0

Printed and bound by Clays Ltd, St Ives plc

Hodder & Stoughton policy is to use papers that are natural, renewable
and recyclable products and made from wood grown in sustainable
forests. The logging and manufacturing processes are expected to
conform to the environmental regulations of the country of origin.

Hodder & Stoughton Ltd
Carmelite House
50 Victoria Embankment
London
EC4Y 0DZ

www.hodder.co.uk

*This book is for every Daemon Black fan who wanted more of him. I hope you enjoy!*

| LONDON BOROUGH OF HACKNEY LIBRARIES | |
|---|---|
| HK12003083 | |
| Bertrams | 18/12/2015 |
| ARM  TEEN | £7.99 |
| TEEN | 03/12/2015 |

# 1

Faster than any human eye could track, I moved soundlessly among the trees in my true form, racing over the thick grass and the dewy, moss-covered rocks. I was nothing more than a blur of light, speeding along the tree line. Being an alien from a planet thirteen billion light years away was pretty much made of awesome.

I easily passed one of those damn energy efficient cars that was coasting up the main road past my house.

How in the hell was that thing pulling a U-Haul trailer?

Not like that was important.

I slowed down and slipped into my human form, keeping to the thick shadows cast by the oak trees as the car went by the empty house at the start of the access road, and then grinded to a halt in front of the house next to mine.

"Shit. Neighbors," I muttered as the driver's car door opened and a middle-age woman stepped out. I watched as she bent down and spoke to someone else in the car.

She laughed and then ordered, "Get out of the car."

Whoever was with her didn't listen, and the woman eventually closed the car door. She all but bounced up the porch steps and unlocked the front door.

How could this be happening? The house was meant to stay vacant—any house around here was supposed to remain empty of *humans*. This road was the freaking gate to the Luxen colony at the base of Seneca Rocks, and it wasn't like this house went up for sale and those suited assholes didn't realize it.

This could not be happening.

Energy crackled over my skin, humming, and the urge to slip back into my true form was hard to ignore. And that pissed me off. Home was the only place that I—that *we* could be ourselves without fear of discovery, and those assholes—the Department of Defense, the D-O-fucking-D—knew it.

My fingers curled into my palms.

Vaughn and Lane, my own personal government-issued babysitters, had to have been aware of this. It must've slipped their damn minds when they checked in on us last week.

The passenger door of the Prius creaked open, drawing my attention. At first, I couldn't see who got out, but then she walked around the front of the car, coming completely into view.

"Oh shit," I muttered again.

It was a girl.

From what I could see, she was close to my age, maybe a year younger, and as she turned in a slow circle, staring at the forest that crept onto the lawn around the two houses, she looked like she expected a rabid mountain lion to pounce on her.

Her steps were tentative as she neared the porch, as if she was still debating if she really wanted to walk into the house. The woman, who I was guessing was her mom based on the similar dark hair, had left the front door open. The girl stopped at the bottom of the steps.

I sized her up as I drifted silently through the trees. She appeared of average height. Actually, everything about her seemed average—her dark brown hair, pulled back from her face in a messy knot; her pale, roundish face; her average weight—definitely not one of those skinny girls I hated—and her... Okay. Not all of her appeared average. My gaze was hung up on her legs and other areas.

Damn, they were nice legs.

The girl turned around, facing the forest as her arms folded along her waist, just below her chest.

Okay. Two areas in particular were not average.

She scanned the line of trees and her gaze stopped—stopped right where I was standing. My hands opened at my sides, but I didn't move, didn't dare force my lungs to take a breath. She stared *right* at me.

But there was no way she could see me. I was too hidden among the shadows.

A handful of seconds passed before she unfolded her arms and turned, slowly heading into the house, leaving the door wide open behind her.

"Mom?"

My head cocked to the side at the sound of her voice, which was also...average. No real discernible accent or indication of where they came from.

Wherever it was, they must have no sense of personal safety, since neither of them thought to close the door behind them. Then again, around these parts, most humans believed they were completely safe. After all, the town of Ketterman, located just outside of Petersburg, West Virginia, wasn't even incorporated. Deputies spent more time chasing after roaming cattle and breaking up field parties than handling any real crime.

Even though humans did have a nasty habit of going missing around here.

The smirk twisting my lips faded as an image of Dawson formed in my thoughts. Not just humans...

When I thought of my brother, anger bubbled inside me, rushing to the surface like a volcano about to erupt. He was gone—dead because of a human girl. And now there was another damn one moving in *next* door.

We had to...simulate humans, blend among them, and even act like them, but being close to them always ended in disaster.

Always ended in someone missing or dead.

I had no idea how long I stood there, staring at the house, but the girl eventually appeared again. Pulled out of my thoughts, I straightened as she walked to the back of the U-Haul. She dug a key out of her pocket and then opened the metal door.

Or tried.

And tried some more.

She struggled with the lock and then with the lever for what had to be the longest amount of time in history. Her cheeks were flushed, lips pursed. She looked like she was seconds from kicking the back of the U-Haul. Good God, how long did it take one person to open a trailer door? She made it a marathon event. I was half tempted to make myself known and walk my ass over there and open the damn door for her.

Finally, after an eternity, she opened the trailer and pulled down the ramp. She disappeared in and reappeared moments later with a box. I watched her carry it in and then return again. Back up the ramp, she stumbled down it this time, carrying a box that had to weigh more than her by the strained look on her face.

She shuffled around the trailer, and even from where I stood, I could see her arms trembling. I closed my eyes, irritated over…everything. She'd made it to the steps, and I knew there was no way she was going to get the box up that porch without falling and possibly breaking her neck.

I raised my brows.

If she broke her neck, then I guessed that solved the whole "moving in next door" problem.

One foot made it onto the bottom step and she teetered to one side. If she fell then, she would be okay. She made it up another step, and my stomach growled. Damn, I was hungry even though I'd eaten about ten pancakes an hour ago.

She was almost to the top of the steps, and granted, if she fell, she wasn't going to break her neck. Maybe an arm? A leg would be pushing it. As she planted a foot on the next step and then slowly lifted the other foot beside it, I was reluctantly impressed by her sheer determination to muscle that box into the house. When she wobbled dangerously at the top, I muttered a rather obscene list of curse words and raised my hand.

Zeroing in on the box in her hands, I tapped into the Source. In my mind, I focused on raising the box just the slightest, taking the brunt of the weight off her arms. She stopped on the porch just for the tiniest of seconds, as if she recognized the change, and then with a shake of her head, she walked into the house.

Slowly, I lowered my hand, somewhat shocked by what I had done. There was no way she could ever guess that some random dude standing in the woods was responsible for that, but man, that was still a dumbass move on my part.

There was always the risk of exposure whenever we used the Source, no matter how insignificant it was.

The girl reappeared again on the porch, her cheeks bright pink from the work so far, and headed back to the cargo container as she wiped her hands along her denim shorts. Once again, she stumbled out of the trailer with a box of death in her arms, and I had to wonder: where in the hell was her mother?

The girl's step faltered and the obviously heavy box rattled. Glass was inside.

And because I was competing for world's biggest dumbass, I stayed out there, in the trees, stomach grumbling like a damn engine, and helped her carry in box after box without her even knowing.

By the time she/we finished hauling every last item into her house, I was wiped, starving, and certain I'd risked tapping into the Source enough to get my damn head examined. I hauled my tired ass up the steps to my house and slipped inside quietly. No one else was around tonight, and I was too exhausted to cook, so I gulped down half a gallon of milk and then passed out on the couch.

My last thought was of my annoying new neighbor and my too-awesome-to-fail plan to never see her again.

Night had fallen, and thick clouds, dark and impenetrable, blocked out the stars and covered the moon, squelching even the tiniest amount of light. No one could see me. Which was probably a good thing.

Especially considering I was standing outside the once-empty house like a total creeper in one of those true-crime shows—yet again. So much for my never-see-the-chick-again plan.

This was quickly becoming a disturbing habit. I tried to argue with myself that it was necessary. I needed to know more about our new neighbor before my twin sister, Dee, spotted her and decided they were gonna be besties. Dee was all I had left in this world, and I'd do anything to protect her.

Glancing over at my house, I blew out an aggravated breath through my nose. Would it be such a terrible thing if I just, I don't know, just burned the damn house down? I mean, I wouldn't let those…those humans inside burn or anything. I wasn't *that* terrible. But no house, no problem.

Seemed simple to me.

The last thing I needed was another problem—the last thing any of us needed.

A light was on in one of the bedrooms upstairs despite the fact that it was late. It was *her* bedroom. Only a handful of minutes ago, I'd seen the outline of her pass in front of the windows. Sadly, she was completely clothed.

That disappointment took creeper status to a whole new level.

The girl was a problem, a big one, but I had all the working guy parts, which sometimes zeroed out the whole problem thing.

Having someone move next door, someone who was our age, was just too risky. This girl had only been here two days, but it was just a matter of time before Dee saw her. She'd already asked me a couple of times if I'd seen the new neighbors, if I knew who they were. I'd shrugged and said probably just an old couple retiring to the country to ward off her initial enthusiasm, but I knew Dee's excitable personality would be impossible to contain for long.

Speaking of the hyper devil...

"Daemon," a voice whispered from the shadows of my front porch. "What in the world are you doing out here?"

*Debating on whether or not burning down a house next time they head to the store is a reasonable response to getting new neighbors?*

Yeah, I was gonna keep that one to myself.

Sighing, I pivoted around and headed toward the porch. Gravel crunched under my boots. My sister was leaning against the railing, staring at the house next door, a curious expression pinching her face as a soft breeze tossed her long, dark hair around her.

It took unbelievable effort to walk at a normal speed as I joined Dee. Normally, it wasn't something I even attempted when I was home since I could move fast as light, but with the new neighbors, I needed to get back in the habit of appearing...well, human.

"I was out patrolling." I cocked a hip against the railing, my back to the house as if it didn't exist.

Dee raised a brow as she glanced up at me. Bright emerald eyes, the same color as mine, were filled with skepticism. "It didn't look like that."

"Really?" I crossed my arms.

"Yeah." Her gaze flicked over my shoulder. "It looked like you were standing outside that house, watching it."

"Uh-huh."

Her brows knitted. "So, someone has moved in there?"

Dee had been over at the Thompsons' house the last couple of days, which was a freaking blessing even though the idea of her being there with another alien our age, Adam, overnight did not make me a happy camper. But it worked out. She had no idea who had moved in next door, and knowing her, a human girl of her age would be like discovering an abandoned puppy.

When I didn't answer, she sighed heavily. "Okay. Am I supposed to guess?"

"Yeah, some people moved in next door."

Her eyes widened as she whipped back around and leaned out over the railing, eyeing the house as if she could see through it. While our abilities were pretty awesome, we didn't have X-ray vision. "Oh my, they're not Luxen. They're *humans*."

Obviously she would've sensed if they were of our kind. "Yep. They're human."

She shook her head slightly. "But why? Do they know about us?"

I thought of the girl struggling to carry the boxes inside the other day. "I'm gonna go with a no."

"That's so weird. Why would the DOD let them move in there?" she asked, and then immediately added, "Who cares? I hope they're nice."

My eyes drifted shut. Of course Dee wouldn't be worried about it, not even after what happened to Dawson. All she cared about was if they were *nice*. It didn't even occur to her, not for one second, the kind of danger the close proximity of a human posed to us. Not my sister. She was all unicorns puking rainbows.

"Did you see who they were?" she asked, excitement crowding her voice.

"No," I lied, opening my eyes.

Her lips pursed as she drew back from the railing, clapping her hands, and turned to me. We were almost the same height, and I could see delight sparkling in her eyes. "I hope it's a hot guy."

11

I clenched my jaw.

She giggled. "Oh! Maybe it's a girl, like, my age. That would be awesome."

Oh God.

"It would make this summer so much better, especially since Ash is being a you-know-what," she went on.

"No. I don't know what."

She rolled her eyes. "Don't play innocent, you jerk. You know exactly why she's as cuddly as a honey badger right now. She thought you two would be spending all summer together doing—"

"Each other?" I suggested slyly.

"Oh, gross! Seriously. I wasn't going there." She shuddered, and I barely hid my grin as I wondered if Ash had admitted that the doing-each-other part still happened although not in a while. Not often, but it did. "She was complaining about not going wherever you promised to take her this summer."

I had no idea what Dee was talking about.

"Anyway, I really hope whoever is next door is cool." Like a hamster on a wheel, Dee's mind kept on cycling. "Maybe I'll stop over—"

"Don't even finish that sentence, Dee. You don't know who they are or what they're like. Stay away from them."

She placed her hands on her hips as her eyes narrowed. "How will we know what kind of people they are by staying away from them?"

"I'll check them out."

"I don't particularly trust your judgment of humans, Daemon." Her stare turned into a glare.

"And I don't trust yours. Just like I never trusted Dawson's."

Dee took a step back as she drew in a deep, slow breath.

The anger faded out of her expression. "Okay, I understand. I get why—"

"Let's not go there. Not tonight," I said, sighing as I lifted my hand and scrunched my fingers through my hair, making the ends stick up. I needed a haircut. "It's late and I need to make another round before I call it a night."

"Another round?" Her voice had dropped to a whisper. "Do you think…any of the Arum are nearby?"

I shook my head, not wanting her to worry, but the truth was *they* were always nearby and they were our only natural predator—our enemies from the time when our true planet existed. Like us, they weren't from this Earth. They were, in many ways, the exact opposite of us in appearance and abilities. But we didn't kill like they did. Oh no. They derived their use of the Source from feeding off the Luxen they killed. They were like parasites on steroids.

The Elders used to tell us that when the universe was formed, it was filled with the purest light, making those who lived in the shadows—the Arum—envious. They'd become jealous and determined to suffocate all the light. That was how the war started between our two planets.

And our parents died in that war, when our home was destroyed.

The Arum had followed us here, using atmospheric displays to travel to Earth without detection. Whenever there was a meteorite shower or a rash of falling stars, I was on edge. The Arum usually followed such occurrences.

Fighting them wasn't easy. We could either take them out with the Source directly or with obsidian—sharpened into a blade, it was deadly to the Arum, especially after they'd fed. It fractured light. Getting ahold of it wasn't easy, either, but I tried to always keep one on me, usually attached to my ankle. So did Dee.

Never knew when you'd need it.

"I just want to be careful," I said finally.

"You're always careful."

I smiled tightly.

She hesitated and then sprang forward. Stretching up on the tips of her toes, she kissed my cheek. "You can be a demanding jerkface, but I love you. Just wanted you to know."

Chuckling, I wrapped an arm around her shoulders and briefly pulled her in for a hug. "You can be an annoying chatterbox, but I love you, too."

Dee slapped my arm as she stepped back, once again smiling. "Don't be too late."

I nodded and then watched her dart into the house. Dee rarely did anything slowly. She'd always been the one with the endless energy. Dawson had been the laidback one. And I was—I laughed under my breath—the *jerkface* one.

We'd been triplets.

Now we were just twins.

Several moments passed as I stared at the spot my sister had stood in. She was one of the only things left on this planet that I genuinely cared about. I turned my attention back to the house. I wasn't even going to lie to myself about this. The moment Dee realized it was a girl next door, she was going to be all over her like barnacles on a hull—a crusty, seen-better-days hull. And no one could resist my sister. She was a damn fluffy ball of hyped-up sunshine.

We lived among humans, but we didn't get close to them for a metric ton of reasons. And I wasn't going to let Dee make the same mistake that Dawson had. I'd failed Dawson, but that wasn't going to happen to Dee. I would do anything to keep her alive and safe. *Anything*.

**2**

Pressing my forehead against the glass, I cursed under my breath, mainly because I was staring out the window—at that house. Waiting. I was waiting. There were better things to do than this. Like beating my head against cement. Or listening to Dee describe in painful detail every intricate and disturbingly personal attribute of each of those guys in that band she loved.

I forced myself away from the window, yawning as I rubbed my palm along my jaw. Damn near three days later and a part of me still couldn't believe people had moved into the house next door. *Could be worse*, I decided in that moment. Our new neighbor could be a dude. Then I'd have to lock Dee in her bedroom.

Or at least it could have been a girl who looked like a dude. That would've been helpful, but oh no, she didn't look like a guy at all. She was average, I reminded myself, but definitely not a dude.

With a wave of my hand, I turned on the TV and flipped

through the channels until I found a repeat of *Ghost Investigators*. I'd seen this episode before, but it was always fun watching the humans run out of the house because they thought they saw something glowing. I lounged on the couch with my legs on the coffee table and tried to forget about the girl with not-so-average tan legs and a killer ass.

I'd seen her a total of two times before today.

Obviously the day she moved in, when I'd been a dumbass and helped her from afar. I wanted to punch myself in the gonads for that. Sure, she didn't know that I'd lessened the weight of the boxes so she didn't fall right over, but I shouldn't have done it. I knew better.

I'd seen her yesterday. She'd dashed out toward a sedan and grabbed a stack of books out of the car. Her face had lit up with the biggest smile, as if the leaning tower of books were really a million bucks.

It was all very—*not cute*. What the hell was I thinking? Not cute at all.

Man, it was hot in here. Leaning forward, I grabbed the back of my shirt and pulled it over my head. I tossed it to the side and idly rubbed my chest. I'd been walking around shirtless more than ever since *she'd* moved in.

Wait. I'd seen her three times if I counted seeing her through the window last night.

Dammit, I needed to get out and do something. Preferably something that required working up one hell of a sweat.

Before I knew it, I'd stalked across the room and ended up right in front of the window. Again. I didn't want to examine why too closely.

I brushed the curtain aside, scowling. Hadn't even spoken to the girl and I felt like a stalker staring out the window, waiting once more…waiting for what? To catch a glimpse of her? Or to better prepare myself for the inevitable meeting?

If Dee saw me now, she'd be on the floor laughing.

And if Ash saw me right now, she'd scratch out my eyes and blast my new neighbor into outer space. Ash and her brothers had arrived from Lux about the same time as we did, and a relationship just sort of…happened…more from proximity than I could honestly say real emotion. We hadn't dated for months, but I knew she still expected that we'd end up together eventually. Not because she really wanted me, but it was expected of us…so of course she probably didn't want me with anyone else. I still cared for her, though, and I couldn't remember a time without her and her brothers around.

I caught movement out of the corner of my eye. Turning slightly, I saw the screen door on the wide porch next door swing shut. Shit.

I shifted my gaze and caught her hurrying off the porch.

I wondered where she was going. Not much to do around here, and it wasn't like she knew anyone. There hadn't been any traffic next door, with the exception of her mom coming and going at odd hours.

The girl stopped in front of her car, smoothing her hands down her shorts. My lips curved up at the corners.

All of a sudden, she veered toward the left, and I straightened. I fisted my hand around the curtain, and my breath got stuck somewhere in my chest. No, she was not coming over here. She had no reason. Dee didn't even realize there was a girl here yet. No reason…

Oh hell, she *was* coming *here*.

Letting go of the curtain, I backed away from the window and turned toward the front door. I closed my eyes, counting the seconds and reminding myself of the valuable lesson learned at Dawson's expense. Humans were dangerous to us. Just being around them was a risk—getting too close to a human inevitably ended with one of us leaving a trace of the Source on them. And since Dee was obsessed with befriending anything that breathed, it would be especially dangerous for this girl. She lived right next door, and there'd be no way I could control how much time Dee spent with her.

And then there was the fact that I'd been, you know, watching her. *That* could possibly be a problem. I clenched my fists at my sides.

My sister wouldn't have the same fate as Dawson. There was no way I could bear the loss of her, and it had been a *human girl* who had brought him down, led an Arum right to him. Time and time again it had happened with our kind. It wasn't necessarily the human's fault, but the end result was always the same. I refused to let anyone put Dee in danger, unknowingly or not. It didn't matter. Throwing out my hand, I flung the coffee table across the room but caught myself and pulled back just before it crashed into the wall. Taking a deep breath, I settled it back down on four legs.

A soft, almost tentative knock rapped against our front door. Shit.

I exhaled roughly. *Ignore it.* That was what I needed to do, but I was moving toward the door, opening it before I even knew it. A rush of warm air washed over my skin, carrying the faint scent of peach and vanilla.

Man, did I love peaches, all sweet and sticky.

My gaze dropped. She was short—shorter than I'd realized. The top of her head only came up to my chest. Maybe that was why she was staring at it. Or maybe it was the fact I hadn't had the inkling to put on my shirt.

I knew she liked what she saw. Everyone did. Ash had

once said it was the combination of dark, wavy hair and green eyes, the hard jaw and full lips. Sexy, she'd said. I was hot. Might sound arrogant, but it was the truth.

Since she was blatantly checking me out, I figured I could do the same. Why not? She came knocking on *my* door.

The girl... She wasn't cute. Her hair, not really blond or brown, was out of the messy bun, and it was long, hanging over her shoulders. She was short as hell, barely five and a half feet. Still, her legs seemed to stretch forever. Dragging my eyes away from her legs took effort.

Eventually, my gaze landed on the front of her shirt. MY BLOG IS BETTER THAN YOUR VLOG. What in the world did that mean? And why would she have that on her shirt... And the words BLOG and BETTER were stretched taut. I swallowed. Not a good sign.

I lifted my gaze with even more effort.

Her face was round, nose pert, and skin smooth. I bet a million dollars her eyes were brown—big, old doe eyes.

Crazy as hell, but I could feel her eyes as her gaze made the slow perusal from where my jeans hung from my hips, back up to my face. She sucked in a sharp breath, which overshadowed my own inhale.

Her eyes *weren't* brown, but they were large and round, a pale shade of heather gray—intelligent and clear eyes. They were beautiful. Even I could admit that.

And it pissed me off. All of this pissed me off. Why was I checking her out? Why was she even here? I frowned. "Can I help you?"

No answer. She stared at me with this look on her face, like she wanted me to kiss those full, pouty lips of hers. Heat stirred in the pit of my stomach.

"Hello?" I caught the edge in my voice—anger, lust,

annoyance, more lust. *Humans are weak, a risk…Dawson is dead because of a human—a human just like this one.* I kept repeating that over and over again. I placed my hand on the doorframe, fingers digging into the wood as I leaned forward. "Are you capable of speaking?"

That got her attention, snapping her right out of the ogling. Her cheeks turned a pretty shade of pink as she stepped back. Good. She was leaving. That's what I wanted— for her to turn and rush away. Running a hand through my hair, I glanced over her shoulder and then back. Still there.

She really needed to get her cute ass off my porch before I did something stupid. Like smile at the way she was blushing. Sexy, even. And definitely not average. "Going once…"

The flush deepened. Hell. "I…I was wondering if you knew where the closest grocery store is. My name is Katy."

Katy. Her name was *Katy*. Reminded me of Kitty. Kitty cat. Kitten. Look at me, putting all these words together.

"I moved next door." She gestured at her house. "Like, almost three days ago…"

"I know." *I've been watching you for almost three days, like a stalker.*

"Well, I was hoping someone would know the quickest way to the grocery store and maybe a place that sold plants."

"Plants?"

Her eyes narrowed just the slightest, and I forced my face to remain expressionless. She fidgeted some more with the hem of her shorts. "Yeah, see, there's this flower bed in front—"

I arched a brow. "Okay."

Now her eyes were thin slits, and irritation heightened the blush and rolled off her. Amusement stirred deep inside me. I knew I was being an ass at this point, but I was perversely enjoying the spunk slowly igniting behind her eyes, baiting me. And...the flush of anger was sort of hot in a weird, there's-really-something-wrong-with-me kind of way. She reminded me of something...

She tried again. "Well, see, I need to go buy plants—"

"For the flower bed. I got that." I leaned my hip against the doorframe, crossing my arms. This was actually almost fun.

She took a deep breath. "I'd like to find a store where I can buy groceries and plants." Her tone was one that I used with Dee about a thousand times a day. Adorable.

"You *are* aware this town has only one stoplight, right?" And there it was. The spark in her eyes was a blazing fire now, and I was fighting a full-on grin. Damn, she wasn't just cute anymore. She was much, much more, and my stomach sank.

The girl stared at me, incredulous. "You know, all I wanted were directions. This is obviously a bad time."

Thinking of Dawson, my lip curled into a sneer. Playtime was over. I had to nip this in the bud. For Dee's sake. "Anytime is a bad time for you to come knocking on my door, kid."

"Kid?" she repeated, eyes widening. "I'm not a kid. I'm seventeen."

"Is that so?" Hell, as if I didn't already notice she was all grown up. Nothing about her reminded me of a kid, but dammit, as Dee would say, I had piss-poor social skills. "You look like you're twelve. No. Maybe thirteen, but my sister has this doll that kinda reminds me of you. All big-eyed and vacant."

Her mouth dropped open, and I realized that I may have gone a little too far with that last statement. Well, it was for the better. If she hated me, she'd stay away from Dee. It worked with most of the girls. Ah, most of them.

Okay. That didn't work with a lot of girls, but they didn't live next door, so what the hell ever.

"Yeah, wow. Sorry to bother you. I won't be knocking on your door again. Trust me." She started to turn, but not quickly enough that I didn't see the sudden glisten in those gray eyes.

Dammit. Now I felt like the biggest dick ever. And Dee would flip if she saw me acting like this. Stringing together a dozen or so curses in my mind, I called out to her. "Hey."

She stopped on the bottom step, keeping her back to me. "What?"

"You get on Route 2 and turn onto U.S. 220 North, not South. Takes you into Petersburg." I sighed, wishing I'd never answered the door. "The Foodland is right in town. You can't miss it. Well, maybe *you* could. There's a hardware store next door, I think. They should have things that go in the ground."

"Thanks," she muttered and added under her breath, "douchebag."

Did she just call me a douchebag? What decade were we in? I laughed, genuinely amused by that. "Now that's not very ladylike, Kittycat."

She whipped around. "Don't ever call me that."

Oh, I must've hit a sore spot there. I pushed out the door. "It's better than calling someone a douchebag, isn't it? This has been a stimulating visit. I'll cherish it for a long time to come."

Her little hands balled into fists. I think she wanted to hit me. I think I might've liked it. And I think I seriously needed help.

"You know, you're right. How wrong of me to call you a douchebag. Because a douchebag is too nice of a word for you." She smiled sweetly. "You're a dickhead."

"A dickhead?" It would be too easy to like this girl. "How charming."

She flipped me off.

I laughed again, lowering my head. "Very civilized, Kitten. I'm sure you have a wide array of interesting names and gestures for me, but not interested."

And she looked like she did. Part of me was a bit disappointed when she spun around and stomped off. I waited until she yanked open her car door and because I really was an ass...

"See you later, Kitten!" I called out, chuckling when she looked like she was about to race back to the door and kangaroo kick me.

Slamming the door shut behind me, I leaned against it and laughed again, but the laugh ended in a groan. There'd been a moment where I'd seen what flickered behind the disbelief and anger in those soulful gray eyes. Hurt. Knowing that I'd hurt her feelings made the acid in my stomach churn.

Which was stupid, because last night, I'd considered an arson-assisted relocation plan and hadn't felt guilty then. But that was before I saw her up close and all kinds of personal. Before I actually spoke to her. Before I realized her eyes were intelligent and beautiful.

Returning to the living room, I wasn't at all surprised to find my sister standing in front of the TV, her slender arms crossed and green eyes burning. She looked just like that girl's expression—like she wanted to kick me in the nuts.

I gave her a wide berth as I headed to the couch and dropped down on it, feeling a dozen years older than the eighteen I was. "You're blocking the screen."

"Why?" she demanded.

"It's a damn good episode." I knew that wasn't what she

23

was talking about. "The one guy thinks he's possessed by a shadow person or some—"

"I don't give a crap about a shadow person, Daemon!" She lifted her small foot and slammed it down with enough force to rattle the coffee table. Dee took stomping her feet to a whole new level. "Why did you act like that?"

Leaning back, I decided to play dumb. "I don't know what you're talking about."

Her eyes narrowed but not quickly enough that I missed how her pupils gleamed diamond white. "There was no reason for you to talk to her like that. None whatsoever. She came over here to ask for directions and you were a jerk."

Katy's too-bright gray eyes flashed in my mind. I shoved that image away. "I'm always a jerk."

"Okay. That part is sort of true." Her brow wrinkled. "But you're not usually *that* bad."

My stomach churned again. "How much of it did you hear?"

"Everything," she said, stomping her foot again. The TV trembled. "I don't have a doll that is vacant-eyed. I don't have any dolls, you ass."

My lips twitched despite everything, but the humor quickly faded because the memory of those damn gray eyes surfaced again. "It's the way it has to be, Dee. You know that."

"No, I don't. I don't know that and neither do you."

"Dee—"

"But you know what I *do* know?" she interrupted. "She seemed like a normal girl who came over here to just ask a question. She seemed *normal*, Daemon, and you were horrible to her."

I could really do without all the reminders of how shitty I'd been.

"There is no reason for you to act like that."

No reason? Was she insane? Moving as fast as lightning, I came off the couch and was right in front of Dee, bypassing the coffee table in less than a second. "Do I need to remind you what happened to Dawson?"

My sister did not back down. Her chin tipped up stubbornly, and her eyes flashed white. "No. I remember everything about that quite clearly, thank you."

"Then if that's the case, we wouldn't be having this stupid conversation. You'd understand why that *human* needs to stay away from us."

"She's just a girl," Dee seethed, throwing up her arms. "That's all, Daemon. She's just—"

"A girl who lives next door. She's not some chick from school. She lives right there." I pointed out the window for extra effort. "And that is too damn close to us and too damn close to the colony. You know what will happen if you try to become friends with her."

She took a step back, shaking her head. "You don't even know her, and you can't tell the future. And why do you even think we'd become friends?"

Both my brows flew up. "Really? You're not going to try to be her best friend *foreva* the moment you walk out of this house?"

Her lips pressed together.

"You haven't even talked to her yet, but I know you're probably already wondering if Amazon sells friendship bracelets."

"Amazon sells everything," she muttered. "So I'm sure they sell that."

I rolled my eyes, done with this conversation—already done with the most annoying new neighbor, too. "You need to stay away from her," I said, turning and walking back to the couch.

My sister was still standing when I sat down. "I'm not Dawson. When will you realize that?"

"I already know that." And because I really was an ass, I drove the point home. "You're more of a risk than he was."

Sucking in a shallow breath, she stiffened as she lowered her arms. "That...that was a low blow."

It was. I ran my hand down my face as I lowered my chin. It really was.

Dee sighed as she shook her head. "You're such a dick sometimes."

I didn't lift my head. "Don't really think that's breaking news."

Turning away, she stalked into the kitchen and returned a few seconds later with her purse and car keys. She didn't speak as she walked past me.

"Where are you going?" I asked.

"Grocery shopping."

"Oh Jesus," I muttered, wondering how many human laws I'd break if I locked my sister in a closet.

"We need food. You ate it all." Then she was out the door.

Tipping my head back against the couch, I groaned. Good to know everything I'd said had gone in one ear and danced right out the other. I didn't even know why I bothered. There would be no stopping Dee. I closed my eyes.

Immediately, I relived the conversation with my new neighbor, and yeah, I really had been an ass to her.

But it was for the best. It was. She could hate me—she *should* hate me. Then hopefully she'd stay away from us. And that was that. It couldn't be any other way, because that girl was trouble. Trouble wrapped up in a tiny package, complete with a freaking bow.

And worse yet, she was just the kind of trouble I liked.

# 3

It literally took Dee only a handful of hours to take everything I'd said to her, throw it out the window, and run over it with her Volkswagen. She'd come back from the grocery store with bags of crap and a big smile on her face, and I'd known she'd found our neighbor.

When I'd asked her about it, she buzzed past me like a damn hummingbird, refusing to answer any questions about what the hell she was doing, but a little after one, she disappeared out the front door. Being the good older brother—older by a handful of minutes—I'd gone over to the window to make sure everything was okay. But Dee hadn't headed toward her car. Oh no, she had gone straight for the house next door. Not like I was entirely surprised. She had either been on the girl's porch or already in her damn house. It was hard enough keeping an eye on her during the school year, but now this?

Dee avoided me when she finally made her way back over to the house, which was fine by me. I didn't trust myself not to start yelling at her, and even though I was admittedly a grade-A certified asshole, I didn't like losing my cool on my sister.

I'd left home in my SUV that evening, managing to not look at that damn house for one second. Halfway into town, I called up Andrew, Adam's twin and the Thompson brother who matched me in temperament and personality. In other words, we were fucking balls of sunshine.

He was going to meet me at Smoke Hole Diner, a restaurant not too far from Seneca Rocks—the nearby range of mountains that contained beta quartz, a crystal that had this amazing ability to block our presence to what most Luxen considered our only true enemy, the Arum. But even if the beta quartz blocked Luxen, once an Arum saw a human with a trace, they knew Luxen were nearby.

I took my seat in the back, near the massive fireplace that was always cranking during the winter. The diner was pretty cool, with rock formations jutting up among the tables. I kind of dug the whole earthy vibe it gave off.

Andrew was tall and blond and turned heads as he strolled in, walking down the middle of the booths.

I'd had the same effect on the patrons earlier.

Might've come across like I was rocking a healthy dose of arrogance—well, I was—but it was simply the truth. Blending of human and Luxen DNA and the choice we had in the matter typically meant we were *very* blessed in the appearance department. I mean, if you could choose to look like anyone, wouldn't you choose the hottest looks you could? My green eyes were a family trait and my hair tended to curl a bit on the ends whether I wanted it to or not, but my six-foot-something awesome frame and movie-star good looks—well those just fit my stellar personality.

Andrew slid into the seat across from me, his eyes a vibrant blue, just like Adam's and Ash's. He lifted his chin at me in greeting. "Fair warning. Ash knows I was leaving to meet you. Don't be surprised if she shows."

Lovely.

I kept my expression bland out of respect for her and her brother sitting across from me, but a meet-up with Ash was not something I needed right now. "Last I heard, she wasn't very happy with me, so I'd be kind of surprised if she showed up."

He snickered. "You'd be surprised? Really? You've known Ash your entire life. The girl thrives on confrontation."

That much was true.

"So do you," Andrew added, smiling slightly when I lifted a brow. "I don't know what's going on between you two."

"And that's not something I'm really going to talk about with you, Oprah." Besides the fact that they were siblings, so come the hell on, it was also hard to put into words. I liked Ash. Hell, I genuinely cared about her, but I was bored with that whole thing, the expectation of our people that we'd of course end up together. I didn't do predictable.

Andrew ignored that. "But you know what's expected of us." His voice lowered as his gaze met mine. One of the waitresses here was a Luxen, but 99 percent of those around us were human. "There aren't many of our kind around our age, and you know what Ethan wants—"

"The last damn thing I care about is what Ethan wants." My voice was deadly calm, but Andrew stiffened across from me. Nothing pissed me off faster than dealing with the Elder known as Ethan. "Or what any of them expect from me."

His lips curled up on one side. "Something's done crawled up your ass today."

Yeah, and that something had a name that reminded me of a little furry, helpless animal.

"So what's your deal?" he persisted. "Right now you just got this look on your face that said you're either really hungry or you want to kill something."

Shaking my head, I draped my arm along the back of the booth. The Thompsons obviously didn't know about that girl moving in next door, and for some reason I figured it was better if it stayed that way for as long as possible. Not because I cared or anything, but because once they did realize there was a human living next door, I was going to have to deal with them bitching about it.

And I was pissed off enough for all of us already.

We ate and then I headed back home. Andrew's sarcasm had a way of lightening my mood, but I was back to doom and gloom as I pulled up in my driveway again.

It was the Thompsons' night to take patrols, but I was too restless to just sit inside. Our families were the strongest of all the Luxen, hence why the colony was already planning Ash and my nuptials, so it was upon us to run most of the patrols and train the new recruits.

I spent half the night out there, finding nothing to work off the building frustration. Building? Hell. That was laughable. More like constant state of anger that had been present ever since Dawson... Since he'd died. Very few things eased it. Certain things with Ash had, but the peace was always fleeting and it was never worth all the strings attached to it.

I crashed somewhere around three in the morning and woke up way too damn late, near eleven, the pent-up energy still humming in my veins. Dragging myself out of bed, I brushed my teeth, then pulled on a pair of sweats and sneakers.

Dee was already gone when I left the house and stepped out into the muggy summer weather. Her car was in the driveway, but that girl's was gone. Hell. They were together. Of course. My anger hit near stroke levels.

If I could actually have a stroke.

I kicked off the porch steps and started jogging down the driveway. Once I reached the end, I crossed the street and then made my way around the trees. I kept myself running at a human pace so I could burn off as much energy as possible and forced my mind to empty. When I ran, I tried not to think about anything. No Arum. No DOD. No expectations. No Dee. No Dawson.

No girl next door.

Sweat ran down my bare chest and dampened my hair. I had no idea how much time had passed when I finally started to feel a burn in my muscles and I headed back home. By the time I came up the driveway, I could probably eat an entire cow.

And the driveway wasn't empty. *Her* car was back.

I slowed down to a walk as I spied a pile of bags sitting behind the trunk of the car. Frowning, I reached up and shoved my hair off my forehead. "What in the hell?"

They were bags of mulch and soil—heavy-ass bags of mulch and soil.

Stopping, I glanced up at the house with a narrowed gaze. Ah, yes, plants for the flower bed that sort of looked like something straight out of a horror movie. Was Dee seriously with her? A chuckle rumbled out. Dee was going to help with the flower bed? Now that was freaking hilarious. She couldn't tell the difference between crab grass and the real deal, nor was she a fan of dirt under her nails.

I rounded the back of the sedan and then stopped.

Lifting my gaze to the skies, I shook my head and laughed out loud at myself in genuine humor. God, I was pathetic. Thought myself all badass but couldn't seem to walk past a heavy box or bag and not help a girl out. I wheeled back around and gathered up the bags, grunting at their weight. Moving incredibly fast, I deposited them in a neat stack by the pathetically overgrown flower bed and then headed inside to shower.

It was then, as I stood under the steady spray of water, I realized I couldn't remember the last time I'd laughed in real amusement.

Just as I walked out of the shower, my cell went off, ringing from where it sat on the nightstand. I walked over to it, brows rising when I saw it was Matthew.

Matthew wasn't very much older than all of us, but he'd become sort of a surrogate father, since our parents hadn't made the trip here. Like us, he lived outside the colony, and he taught at PHS. I knew without a doubt he would do anything for the Thompsons and us. He wasn't a phone guy, though.

"What up?" I answered, snagging a pair of jeans that I thought might be clean from a pile on the floor.

There was a pause. "Vaughn was just here. Without Lane."

"Okay." I whipped off the towel and tossed it into the bathroom. "You want to add more to that?"

"I was getting ready to," Matthew said as I dragged on the jeans. "Vaughn said they were tracking unauthorized Luxen movement near here. You know what that means."

"Shit," I muttered, snapping the button closed on the jeans. "We have incoming Arum."

After all this time, the DOD couldn't tell the Luxen and Arum apart, and our two kinds really looked nothing alike. Dumbasses. It was probably because they've never actually captured one of the bastards, since we always managed to take care of them before the DOD had a chance to start rounding them up, like they did with us. It was imperative that the government didn't realize there was a difference, because even though the DOD had crawled up our asses, they didn't know what we were fully capable of. It needed to stay that way, but it wouldn't if they realized Arum were an altogether different species.

"Do they know how many?" I asked.

"Sounds like a whole set, but when there is one group of them, you know there's always more."

Well wasn't that wonderful fucking news. My stomach rumbled, reminding me how absolutely starving I was. Outside my bedroom, I took the stairs two at a time and started for the kitchen. Changing my mind at the last minute, I walked outside onto the porch.

And I saw them.

Both girls were hard at work in front of the flower bed, and I had to admit, from where I stood, the thing already looked better. A lot of the weeds and dead plants had been removed, filling the black trash bag by the steps.

Dee looked absolutely ridiculous, delicately tugging the leaves on a new planting as if to turn the plant already stuck in the dirt, and I had no idea what she was attempting to do. Probably trying not to get dirt under her nails. My gaze drifted toward the other girl. She was on her knees, one hand planted in the fresh soil, her back slightly arched with her ass right up in the air. My lips parted, and yeah, my mind immediately went *there*, picturing her roughly in the same position with less clothing.

Which pissed me off, because that was the last place it needed to go. I didn't even find her that attractive for shit's sake. No way. Not at all.

She settled back on her haunches as Dee said something to her, and then she slowly turned her head in my direction.

"Hey," Matthew's voice snapped in my ear.

I dragged away my gaze, frowning as I rubbed my hand over my chest. Shit. No shirt. "What?"

"Are you even paying attention to what I'm saying?" Matthew demanded.

"Yeah." I paused, distracted. I watched the girl turn back to the flower bed, where she started digging furiously with a shovel. "Dee has a new friend. She's human."

There was a sigh on the other end of the phone. "We're kind of surrounded by humans, Daemon."

No shit. "Yeah, but this one moved in next door."

"What?"

"I have no idea why they allowed it." I paused as I glanced over at them. My sister handed her some kind of plant that actually looked like a healthy weed. "But Dee's crawled right up her ass and you know how Dee is. Ever since…Dawson and Bethany, she's been desperate for…" Desperate for everything Dawson had been and I wasn't.

That's the damn truth right there.

"School is one thing," Matthew said, glossing over what I hadn't said but definitely hung between us. "But that close—your home and the colony? What in the world was the DOD thinking?"

"I don't think they *were* thinking." But that didn't seem right. They never did anything without having a reason.

"You need to be careful."

"I'm always careful."

"I'm being serious." Exasperation filled his voice.

"I'll take care of it," I promised. "Don't say anything to the Thompsons yet about her, okay? I don't need to deal with however they're going to react on top of all of this."

Matthew agreed and then ranted on for about thirty minutes, alternating between my new neighbor and the Arum. I was catching bits and pieces of his conversation as I watched the girls from where I stood on the porch. I didn't need Matthew telling me how serious nearby Arum were and the precautions we needed to take, and I think he knew that, too. But that was Matthew, the prophet of doom.

But with confirmation of the Arum moving in, this crap between Dee and that girl needed to end before something happened and drew one of those bastards right to us, like it had with Dawson.

When I got off the phone, I went inside and grabbed a shirt, and then went back outside despite my empty, grumbling stomach. I was hungry and annoyed. Never a good combination.

Dee rose as I crossed the driveway, brushing the grass off her hands, but the girl stayed on the ground, smacking the soil. I dropped my arm over Dee's shoulders, holding her still when she tried to squirm free. "Hey, sis."

She grinned up at me with hope in her gaze. God only knew what she thought about me making an appearance, but I was really going to let her down. "Thanks for moving the bags for us," she said.

"Wasn't me."

Dee rolled her eyes. "Whatever, butthead."

"That's not nice." I tugged her close, smiling down at her when she wrinkled her nose. I felt eyes on us and when I glanced up, I saw that the girl was watching us. The sun had pinked the heights of her cheeks—or something else had. Her hair was pulled up but sweat had dampened the loose tendrils around the nape of her neck. The smile slipped from my face. She was going to be such a problem. "What are you doing?"

"I'm fixing—"

"I wasn't asking you," I said, interrupting her as I directed my attention to Dee. "What are *you* doing?"

The girl shrugged and picked up a potted plant, totally unfazed by me, and my eyes narrowed on her. She acted as if I wasn't even standing there. Unacceptable.

Dee punched me in the stomach. Knowing she could hit a hell of a lot harder than that, I let her go. "Look at what we've done," she said. "I think I have a hidden talent."

I looked over at the flower bed. Yeah, they had done some major work on it. Then again, how hard could it really be, pulling up weeds and planting new shit? I arched a brow when the girl looked at me.

"What?" she demanded.

I shrugged and honestly, I couldn't care less about it. "It's nice. I guess."

"Nice?" Dee all but shrieked. "It's better than nice. We rocked this project. Well, Katy rocked it. I kind of just handed her stuff."

Ignoring my sister, I turned my full attention on the girl. "Is this what you do with your spare time?"

"What—are you deciding to talk to *me* now?" She smiled, and my jaw tightened as she grabbed a handful of mulch. "Yeah, it's kind of a hobby. What's yours? Kicking puppies?"

At first, I wasn't sure why she had said that to me, because *no one* talked back to me. No one was that insane. I tilted my head to the side. "I'm not sure I should say in front of my sister."

"Ew," muttered Dee.

The girl's face flushed even more, and I felt my lips kick up at the corner. What was she thinking? "It's not nearly as lame as this," I added, gesturing at the flower bed.

She stilled. Pieces of red cedar drifted to the ground. "Why is this lame?"

I raised both brows.

The girl wisely retreated, but her jaw jutted out as she returned to spreading the mulch, and my eyes narrowed even farther. I could tell she was forcing herself to keep quiet, and that made me feel like a shark that scented blood in the water.

Dee sensed it, because she pushed me. "Don't be a jerk. Please?"

"I'm not being a jerk." I stared at the girl.

Her brows flew up, and there it was. The attitude. I didn't like it...but I did, and realizing that amped me up. "What's that? You have something to say, *Kitten*?"

"Other than I'd like for you to never call me *Kitten*? No." Running her hands over the mulch calmly, she then stood and grinned at Dee. "I think we did good."

This girl was legit ignoring me.

"Yes." Dee pushed me again, but this time in the direction of our house. "We did good, lameness and all. And you know what? I kind of like being lame."

As I stared at the fresh plants, I still couldn't wrap my head around the fact that she was standing there, pretending like I wasn't even here. This chick was not even one bit intimidated by me. That floored me. I couldn't be reading her right. Yeah, most human girls didn't run from me. They wanted to run to me, but one look would send them scurrying away. This girl was basically like, whatever.

"And I think we need to spread our lameness to the flower bed in front of our house," Dee continued, practically humming with excitement. "We can go to the store, get stuff, and you can—"

"She's not welcome in our house." Annoyed, I knew where this was heading. "Seriously."

Dee's hands balled into fists. "I was thinking we could work on the flower bed, which is *outside*—not inside—the last time I checked."

"I don't care," I snapped. "I don't want her over there."

"Daemon, don't do this." Her voice dropped, and then I saw her eyes turn too bright. "Please. I like her."

Hating the look in her eyes, I exhaled softly. "Dee…"

"Please?" she asked again.

I cursed under my breath as I folded my arms. I couldn't give in to this. There was too much at stake, like her *life*. "Dee, you have friends."

"It's not the same, and you know it." She folded her arms. "It's different."

Glancing over at Katy, I smirked. She looked like she wanted to throw something at me. "They're your friends, Dee. They're like you. You don't need to be friends with someone…someone like *her*."

"What do you mean, someone like me?" Katy demanded.

"He didn't mean anything by it," Dee rushed to add.

"Bullshit," I said. I'd totally meant it. The girl just didn't get what it *really* meant.

Katy looked like she was about to throw down, and if I

hadn't been so damn annoyed, it might've been cute. "What the *hell* is your problem?"

Shock flickered through me as I fully faced her. This girl... Wow. She was kind of prettier than average when her eyes lit with sparks of anger, but I was determined not to care. "You."

"I'm your problem?" She took a step forward, and oh yeah, she wanted to throw down like a mofo. "I don't even know you. And you don't know me."

"You are all the same." And damn, that was the truth. "I don't need to get to know you. Or want to."

Confusion flickered across her face as she threw up her hands. "That works perfectly for me, buddy, because I don't want to get to know you, either."

"Daemon." Dee grabbed my arm. "Knock it off."

I didn't take my eyes off Katy. "I don't like that you're friends with my sister."

"And I don't give two shits what you like," she spat back.

Holy shit. I was not one bit mistaken when I realized she wasn't at all intimidated, and my first, the very immediate response, was that I *liked* that.

And I could not have that.

I moved, faster than I probably should've, but I was there, right in front of her, my gaze locked in on hers.

"How...how did you move...?" She took a step back, her eyes widening as she shuddered.

There it was. Fear. And maybe it made me a complete jackass, but I wanted her afraid, because in my world, fear equaled common sense. "Listen closely," I said, backing her up until she was against a tree, caging her in. She didn't look away from me. "I'm only going to tell you this once. If anything happens to my sister, so help me—" My gaze dropped, and I saw her lips part. Damn, I hadn't noticed how full her lips were until this moment. When I raised my eyes, she had that look again, one that said her mind recognized the danger she was in, but her body was totally not on the same page.

She was attracted to me, even right now, when I'd backed her clear across the yard, and yet she was still attracted to me. And that kicked off something in me that I didn't want to look too closely at.

My lips curled up and I lowered my voice. "You're kind of dirty, Kitten."

She blinked slowly, as if in a daze. "What did you say?"

"Dirty." I let that word hang between us and then added, "You're covered in dirt. What did you think I meant?"

"Nothing." The flush in her cheeks said otherwise. "I'm gardening. You get dirty when you do that."

I resisted a laugh at her poor attempt to explain herself, but she still wasn't cowering in fear, and that was really kind of hot. "There are a lot more fun ways to get…dirty." I caught myself. Where in the hell did that come from? Yeah, I needed to correct that. "Not that I'd ever show *you*."

That…*interesting* flush spread down her throat. "I'd rather roll around in manure than anything *you* might sleep in."

So fucking doubtful.

Part of me wanted to call her on that right here. Lower my head to hers and taste that smart little mouth. I was willing to bet an arm she wouldn't push me away, but the momentary satisfaction wasn't worth it. With one last look, I pivoted around, and as I passed Dee, I yelled out, "You need to call Matthew. Like, now, and not five minutes from now."

That was a lie, but like most lies, it would get the job done.

# 4

My house became a war zone over the next couple of days.

Dee and I argued nonstop about the girl next door, and the words were just wasted time on my end, because she ultimately did what she wanted, no matter how brutally honest I got about the kind of risks befriending her posed.

The only reason I didn't lose my last nerve was the fact that Dee would be leaving Monday, spending a week with the colony, something the damn Elders required at least once a year so that we *did not forget what we were or where we came from* or some kind of bullshit like that. Maybe the week away would wake her up.

Doubtful.

Then on Friday, some of my favorite damn shirts—one of them a *Ghost Investigators*—had turned up missing. I had a strong suspicion the pile of ashes in the kitchen sink I'd discovered later that day had been what was left of my shirts.

Damn Dee.

Fed up with the situation, I'd gone over to the Thompsons',

and Ash had been more than willing to help work off some of the frustration. But it hadn't worked, and when I'd come home in the early hours of Saturday morning, I found myself sitting out on the hood of my SUV, staring at nothing really, with only the stars and the rustling of nearby critters for company.

The idea of even hooking up with Ash had been empty and boring, and nothing happened. Not even a touch. Things like that with Ash had been a take-it-or-leave-it kind of deal for a while, but empty?

Dropping my head, I rubbed at the back of my neck. I could do another patrol, but Matthew was out there and so was Adam. No Arum had been sighted. Yet.

At least my head was quiet at the moment. Except when my head was quiet, I started thinking about what the hell all of us were going to do. When summer ended, we were entering our senior year and all of us—Dee, the Thompsons—would be graduating next spring. What in the hell were we going to do then?

Dee didn't talk about it a lot, not to me at least, but I had a feeling she wanted to leave. Go to college far away from here, and I could sympathize with that. I wanted to get the hell out of here myself, but unlike the teenagers who shared classes with us, it wasn't an easy decision. We'd have to get permission from the DOD. They'd have to approve the relocation, and even if they did, we'd need to find someplace safe, near beta quartz, and it wasn't like there was a wide selection of that available.

And the colony—Ethan—didn't want us to leave at all. He wasn't even happy with us living outside the damn place. He'd be a problem. All the Elders were focused on was the younger generation hooking up and producing more Luxen babies, born and raised on Earth, and yeah, that wasn't in my game plan.

"Hell," I muttered, dropping my hand and lifting my head.

In the quiet moments, I also thought about Dawson, and those thoughts always cycled back to how he could have felt so strongly for a human, had fallen in *love* with one, knowing what it risked. I couldn't wrap my head around it. So many countless, sleepless nights I'd tried to figure it out. In the end, Dawson had given two shits about the danger he posed to his family, but if he truly loved the girl—Bethany— wouldn't he have stayed away from her? The Luxen Elders or the government did not tolerate mixing of our two kinds, and then there was the Arum aspect.

Had love made him that damn selfish? Didn't he realize I'd be lost if anything happened to him?

The stars I stared at held no answers, and as I slowly lowered my gaze, I found myself staring at the bedroom window of the house next door, my new problem. There was a part of me that had accepted there was nothing I was going to be able to do to stop Dee and her from getting closer, but I couldn't just let it go.

I had done exactly that when Dawson had asked me to.

Yeah, these were two different scenarios, but the likelihood of ending the same was high, so I couldn't just walk away from this. I would be keeping an eye on that girl, a very close one.

Monday morning, I woke up before Dee and made her breakfast of W.E.B.—waffles, eggs, and bacon. Even though she was pissed at me, I didn't like the idea of her leaving for a week on those kinds of terms.

And no one, not even my sister, could resist my breakfast skills.

It worked.

At first, I think she was suspicious of my intent, eyeing me warily, but when I didn't mention the girl next door, she was all smiles and hugs from that point on. I followed her outside, carrying her luggage even though she could carry the thing with a pinkie. I popped it in the back of her Volkswagen. The colony could be accessed from the woods, but she would drive the handful of miles and enter through one of the nearly invisible roads leading in. The local humans thought the little village was just full of nature nuts who preferred to live off the grid.

Humans saw what they wanted to see, never what was really right in front of them.

"You sure you don't want me to come with you?" I asked.

Smiling, she shook her head as she walked around the car. "That's the fifth time you've asked."

"The third."

"Whatever." She laughed. "You know if one of the Elders or Ethan saw you, you won't be getting out of there in the foreseeable future. I'll be okay."

I didn't like the idea of it, but I nodded. "Text me when you get there."

"They'd better not try to take my cell phone like they did last time. I'll cut them." Dee turned to me and smiled before climbing in behind the wheel. "Can you do me a favor while I'm gone?"

"Hmm?"

Her expression turned serious. "Try to talk to Katy if you see her."

I arched a brow.

"Actually, how about you make a point to see her, without being a jerk to her so you don't ruin my chances of having one normal friend who is not obligated to like me because we're both freaking aliens. I really like her and it would be great if my *friend* didn't hate my brother," she continued, and I wasn't sure how to feel over the fact that the girl hated me.

Granted, that was the whole point of my being such a dick to her.

"Can you do that for me?" She opened the driver's door. "Make nice with her. Please?"

Her gaze was so earnest that I found myself nodding.

"Really?" she persisted.

I sighed and looked away as I agreed. "Yeah. Sure."

A smile broke out across her face, the kind of smile that had every guy at school tripping all over themselves, and here I was, her brother, most likely lying to her.

But lies…they worked.

I watched her leave and then headed in, going upstairs to take a shower. Afterward, I changed into a pair of jeans and a shirt that hadn't been burned and then puttered around the house, actually picking up after myself. That was a miracle right there.

*Make nice with her.*

I shook my head as I walked over to my trusty stalker window and pulled back the curtain, wondering if — "What in the hell?"

Squinting, I watched the girl next door jump up and down, trying to reach the roof of her car with a sponge with absolutely no success. A slow smile pulled at my lips.

She looked absolutely ridiculous as the minutes ticked by.

Before I even knew what I was doing, I pivoted around and went out the back door, slipping quietly between the houses. I reached the front of the house just in time to see her bend over to pick up the sponge she'd dropped.

I stopped mid-walk, totally admiring the view offered to me. Alien…human… We're all universally predictable it seems.

She straightened as I wandered closer. I thought I heard her curse as she plucked at the sponge before tossing it in the bucket.

"You look as if you could use some help," I said, shoving my hands into the pockets of my jeans.

Jumping, she whipped around with wide, startled gray eyes. There was no mistaking the look of surprise as she eyed me, and it was clear as we stood there staring at each other, she had no idea why I was out there.

Neither did I.

*Make nice with her.*

I swallowed a sigh as I gestured at the bucket with a lift of my elbow. "You looked as though you wanted to throw that again. I figured I'd do my good deed for the day and intervene before any innocent sponges lose their lives."

Lifting her arm, she used it to wipe strands of damp hair out of her face as she watched me. Tension radiated from her. Since she didn't say anything, I walked over to the bucket and snatched the sponge, squeezing out the water. "You look like you got more of a bath than the car. I never thought washing a car would be so hard, but after watching you for the last fifteen minutes, I'm convinced it should be an Olympic sport."

"You were watching me?"

Probably shouldn't have admitted that. Oh well. I shrugged. "You could always take the car to the car wash. It would be a lot easier."

"Car washes are a waste of money."

"True." I walked around the front of her car and knelt, hitting a spot she'd missed. While I was there, I checked out her tires. Jesus. They were in terrible condition. "You need new tires. These are about bald, and winter's crazy around here."

Silence greeted me.

I peered up through my lashes as I rose. She was watching me like I was some kind of hallucination, arms loose at her sides, and damn, the entire front of her shirt was soaked, showing off a very interesting outline I shouldn't even be paying attention to. Turning away, I took care of the roof. When I was done, she was still standing there, absolutely immobile, and that made me grin. "Anyway, I'm glad you were out here." I grabbed the hose and sprayed down the car. "I think I'm supposed to apologize."

"You *think* you're supposed to?" Ahh, she speaks.

I slowly turned around, almost hitting her with the spray of water as I attacked the other side of the car. The slight narrowing of her eyes brought forth a great wealth of satisfaction. "Yeah, according to Dee, I needed to get my ass over here and make nice. Something about me killing her chances of having a 'normal' friend."

"A normal friend? What kind of friends does she have?"

"Not normal."

"Well, apologizing and not meaning it kind of defeats the purpose of apologizing."

I chuckled. "True."

Out of the corner of my eye, I saw her shift her weight from one foot to the other. "Are you serious?"

"Yeah." I worked my way around the car, chasing off the suds as a genius idea struck me. There was no getting rid of this girl, and the likelihood of Dee growing bored with her wasn't going to help. I'd decided Saturday morning I needed to keep a close eye on her and I needed an excuse. There was no way this girl was going to believe I wanted to be around her when I really didn't want to be, but if Dee was going to be her new BFF, I needed to know everything about her, and not just if she could be trusted if something weird went down. "Actually, I don't have a choice. I have to make nice."

She gave a little shake of her head. "You don't seem like a person who does anything he doesn't want to do."

"Normally I'm not." I hit the back of the car with the water as I picked out the first thing I could come up with. "But my sister took my car keys and until I play nice, I don't get them back. It's too damn annoying to get replacements."

I started to grin, because the whole thing was ridiculous. It wasn't like I needed keys to get anywhere. Not like this girl knew that. I made a mental note to text Dee as soon as possible.

She laughed. "She took your keys?"

The small grin slipped off my face as I returned to the side she was standing on. "It's not funny."

"You're right." She laughed again, and it was a nice laugh—throaty. Kind of sexy. "It's freaking hilarious."

I scowled at her. Of course, my keys were on the kitchen counter, but still, she could be more sympathetic to my plight.

Her arms folded across her chest. "I'm sorry, though. I'm not accepting your not-so-sincere apology."

My brows rose. "Not even when I'm cleaning your car?"

"Nope." Her smile grew, and that plain face suddenly wasn't really plain. "You may never see those keys again."

"Well, damn, there went my plan." A reluctant smile broke free. Her attitude was…interesting. Entertaining. "I figured that if I really don't feel bad, then at least I could make up for it."

She tilted her head to the side. "Are you normally this warm and sparkly?"

I walked past her to where the outdoor spigot was. I turned off the water. "Always. Do you usually stare at guys when you stop over, asking for directions?"

"Do you always answer the door half naked?"

"Always. And you didn't answer my question. Do you always stare?"

She blushed a deep pink. "I was *not* staring."

"Really?" I grinned as I turned around. "Anyway, you woke me up. I'm not a morning person."

"It wasn't that early."

"I sleep in. It is summer, you know. Don't you sleep in?"

A piece of hair had snuck free of her bun again and she pushed it out of her face. "No. I always get up early."

Go figure. "You sound just like my sister. No wonder she loves you so much already."

"Dee has taste…unlike some," she said, and there it was again, the attitude. "And she's great. I really like her, so if you're over here to play big, bad brother, just forget it."

God, she was a little firecracker.

"That's not why I'm here." I gathered up the bucket and various sprays and cleaners, and when I glanced over at her, I thought she might be staring at my mouth. Interesting.

"Then why are you here, other than delivering a crappy apology?" she asked.

Placing the supplies on the porch steps, I lifted my arms and stretched as my gaze flickered over to her and stayed. "Maybe I'm just curious why she is so enamored. Dee doesn't take well to strangers. None of us do."

"I had a dog once that didn't take well to strangers," Katy quipped.

For a moment, I didn't move, and then I laughed—a real laugh—and it sounded strange to my own ears. Shit. She was quick.

Her gaze dipped, and then she cleared her throat. "Well, thanks for the car thing."

And she was clearly dismissing me.

I crossed the distance between us—and I hadn't even moved that fast—but based on her soft inhale, I'd caught her off guard. I was right in front of her, and she smelled like peaches again.

"How do you move so fast?" she asked.

Ignoring that loaded question, I let my gaze roam over her face. What was it about her that had my sister bouncing all over the place? Her tongue was sharp as a knife and she came across as intelligent, but there were literally billions of humans like her. I didn't get it. "My little sis does seem to like you."

She opened her mouth and then snapped it shut. A moment passed. "Little? You're twins."

"I was born a whole four minutes and thirty seconds before she was." I lifted my gaze to hers. "Technically she is my little sister."

"She's the baby in the family?" Her voice sounded different as she lowered her gaze.

"Yep, therefore I'm the one starved for attention."

"I guess that explains your poor attitude, then," she shot back.

"Maybe, but most people find me charming." Sometimes.

Her gaze flicked to mine and then stayed. Something shifted in those gray depths. "I have…a hard time believing that."

"You shouldn't, Katy." Her name sounded strange on my tongue and in my thoughts. That damn little piece of hair had fallen free again, brushing her cheek. I caught it between my fingers. "What kind of color is this? It's not brown or blond."

She tugged her hair free of my grasp. "It's called light brown."

"Hmm," I murmured, lowering my gaze. "You and I have plans to make."

"What?" She stepped around me, putting some space between us. "We don't have any plans to make."

I sat down on the steps, stretched out my legs, and leaned back on my elbows. Plans. Plans. I needed plans. My mouth was moving faster than my brain.

"Comfortable?" she snapped.

"Very." I squinted up at her. The front of her T-shirt had dried—the greatest idea known to man and Luxen formed in my thoughts. "About these plans..."

She remained standing. "What are you talking about?"

"You remember the whole 'getting my ass over here and playing nice' thing, right? That also involves my car keys?" I crossed my ankles as I glanced at the tree line. Man, I was such a liar. "Those plans involve me getting my car keys back."

"You need to give me a little more of an explanation than that."

"Of course." I sighed. "Dee hid my keys. She's good at hiding stuff, too. I've already torn the house apart, and I can't find them."

"So, make her tell you where they are."

"Oh, I would, if she was here. But she's left town and won't be back until Sunday."

"What?" She paused. "I didn't know that."

"It was a last-minute thing." Uncrossing my ankles, I started tapping my foot. "And the only way she'll tell me where the keys are hidden is by me earning bonus points. See, my sister has this thing about bonus points, ever since elementary school."

The bonus points thing was true.

"Okay…?"

"I have to earn bonus points to get my keys back. The only way I can earn those points is by doing something nice for you."

She let out a loud laugh, and I looked at her, my eyes narrowing. "I'm sorry, but this is kind of funny."

Her lack of sympathy for my nonexistent problem was amusing. "Yeah, it's real funny."

Her laughter was slow to fade. "What do you have to do?"

"I'm supposed to take you swimming tomorrow. If I do that, then she'll tell me where my keys are hidden—and I *have* to be nice." Totally sounded like something Dee would say. I was rather proud of myself.

Katy stared at me for a moment, and then her mouth dropped open. "So the only way you get your keys back is by taking me swimming and by being nice to me?"

"Wow. You're a quick one."

Her laugh this time was actually quite evil sounding. "Yeah, well, you can kiss your keys good-bye."

I cranked my head back and waited for her to say she was just kidding. "Why?"

"Because I'm not going anywhere with you." Smugness rang in her voice.

"We don't have a choice."

"No. *You* don't have a choice, but I do." She looked over her shoulder at the front door. "I'm not the one with missing keys."

Huh. Perhaps I was a bit too much of a dick the first two times I talked to her. Good thing she didn't know I briefly considered burning her house down. "You don't want to hang out with me?"

"Uh, no."

"Why not?"

She rolled her eyes. "For starters, you're a jerk."

I nodded. "I can be." Not going to disagree with that.

"And I'm not spending time with a guy who's being forced to do it by his sister. I'm not desperate."

"You're not?"

Anger flashed across her face, and again, it transformed her features. "Get off my porch."

Completely committed to my plan, I pretended to consider it. "No."

"What? What do you mean, no?"

"I'm not leaving until you agree to go swimming with me."

She was so going to blow a fuse. "Fine. You can sit there, because I'd rather eat glass than spend time with you."

I was genuinely amused by that statement. "That sounds drastic."

"Not nearly." She started up the steps.

I twisted at the waist and caught her ankle. Damn, her skin was incredibly soft. Fragile. I kept my grip loose. Her gaze lowered to mine, and I forced a smile that had gotten me excused from many school assignments. "I'll sit here all day and night. I'll camp out on your porch. And I won't leave. We have all week, Kitten. Either get it over with tomorrow and be done with me, or I'll be right here until you do agree. You won't be able to leave the house."

She gaped. "You can't be serious."

"Oh, I am."

"Just tell her we went and that I had a great time. Lie."

When she tried to pull her leg free, I held on. "She'll know if I'm lying. We're twins. We know these things." I paused, thoroughly enjoying myself. "Or are you too shy to go swimming with me? Does the idea of getting almost naked around me make you uncomfortable?"

"I'm from Florida, idiot." Grabbing ahold of the railing, she pulled her leg and got nowhere. "I've spent half my life in a bathing suit."

"What's the big deal?" Warmth built under my hand, surrounding her ankle.

"I don't like you." She drew in a deep breath, causing her chest to rise. "Let go of my ankle."

"I'm not leaving, Kitten." Holding her glare, I lifted my fingers, one by one. Screw the whole keeping an eye on her thing. Now this was pure principal. A challenge. "You're going to do this."

Her lips curled back, and I waited, barely able to contain a grin, because I knew she was seconds from laying into me. Maybe even kicking me. But the door opened, stopping her.

I glanced up and saw her mom. There were…bunnies on her pajamas.

"You live next door?" her mom asked.

Seeing my end, I twisted around and smiled broadly. "My name is Daemon Black."

"Kellie Swartz. Nice to meet you." She glanced at her daughter. "You two can come inside if you want. You don't have to sit outside in the heat."

"That's really nice of you." I stood, knocking my elbow into her. "Maybe we should go inside and finish talking about our plans."

"No," she replied immediately. "That won't be necessary."

"What plans?" her mom asked. "I support plans."

I liked her mom.

"I'm trying to get your lovely daughter to go swimming with me tomorrow, but I think she's worried you wouldn't like the idea." I gave her a little love tap on the arm, biting down on my lip when she moved half a foot. "And I think she's shy."

"What? I have no problem with her going swimming with you. I think it's a great idea. I've been telling her she needs to get out. Hanging out with your sister is great, but—"

*"Mom,"* Katy gasped. "That's not really—"

"I was just telling Katy here the same thing." Unable to stop myself, I draped my arm over her shoulders. She stiffened. "My sister is out of town for the next week, so I thought I'd hang with Katy."

Ms. Swartz smiled and her eyes got all big. "That is so sweet of you."

Katy wrapped her arm around my waist and surprise flicked through me. Then I felt it. Her tiny fingers digging into my side. "Yeah, that's sweet of you, Daemon."

Her little nails were freaking sharp. "You know what they say about boys next door…"

"Well, I know Katy doesn't have plans tomorrow," her mom said. "She's free to go swimming."

She dropped her hand and squirmed her way out from under my arm. "Mom…"

"It's okay, honey." Her mom turned, winking at me. "It was nice to finally meet you."

"You, too." I braced myself.

Her mom closed the door, and in a nanosecond, she whirled around and shoved her hands into my chest. I didn't budge. "You jerk."

Knowing when to retreat helped win the war. I backed down the steps. "I'll see you at noon, Kitten."

"I hate you," she spat.

"The feeling's mutual." Pausing, I looked over my shoulder. "Twenty bucks says you wear a one-piece swimsuit."

Katy let out an outraged shriek.

I sort of hoped I would be out twenty bucks tomorrow.

# 5

*U want company today?*

Glancing down at my cell as I tugged a pair of jeans on over the swim trunks, I was at once grateful that Ash knew better than to just show up at our house announced. If she found me heading off to the lake with Katy, she'd go off like a nuclear rocket.

And it wouldn't be because Katy was human, but because I'd never taken Ash to the lake when we'd dated. The lake had been a sanctuary for just Dee, Dawson, and me since we moved here. Part of me couldn't even believe that was the plan I'd come up with to spend the day with Katy. Thinking with the wrong head, most likely.

I reached down, sending a quick text back. *Can't.*

Ash's response was immediate. *What are u doing?*

*Got stuff to do.*

Walking over to my closet to grab a shirt, I smiled slightly when I saw her response. *So? I'm bored. Entertain me.*

*Can't.*

I'd made it downstairs before she replied. *You suck.*

*We have that in common then*, I replied back.

*UR an ass. Whatever. Go do ur STUFF.*

Planned on it. Leaving my phone on the counter, I didn't worry about locking up after I grabbed a towel and then left the house, heading toward…Kat's.

Huh.

I guess she was no longer "that girl" every time I thought of her. For some reason, I didn't like the name Katy. It didn't suit her. Kat did, I decided. So did Kitten. I smirked, recalling how much she hated that nickname.

Last night, I'd texted Dee and let her know what I was doing. Her series of exclamation points and shocked emoticons was a little on the excessive side. She would play along with the whole keys thing, but I wasn't looking forward to the million questions she was going to have when she got home.

I wasn't sure how today was going to end, either. The potential outcomes varied. Maybe I would get lucky and discover something about her that would steer Dee away. What, I had no idea, but damn I was hopeful.

Climbing the porch steps, I knew I was early when I banged on the door with a closed fist, but it amused me to keep her on her toes. A handful of moments passed and the door opened.

Kat appeared, her gray eyes wide as they met mine for a fleeting second.

"I'm a little early," I told her.

"I can see." She sounded like she was about to leave for a dental appointment. "Change your mind? You could always try lying."

"I'm not a liar." I was totally a liar right now.

"Just give me a second to grab my stuff." Then she slammed the door in my face.

I coughed out a laugh. She really was like a prickly, pissed-off little kitten. A part of me actually wanted to show her I could be a nice guy. I hadn't been an ass to her because of who she was—well, other than her being human. While she'd given as good as she'd gotten, though, I'd noticed the flickers of hurt in her eyes at being attacked for no reason. The whole situation was messed up. If I wasn't mean to her, I could be putting us in danger, but being mean to her was upsetting as well. There was no win here for anyone.

She finally reappeared, careful to not brush against me as she stepped outside, closing the door behind her. I wondered what she had on under the shirt and shorts.

"Okay, so where are you taking me?" she asked, not looking at me.

"What fun would it be if you knew? You won't be surprised then."

We stepped off the porch and started down the driveway. "I'm new to town, remember? Everywhere is going to be a surprise for me."

"Then why ask?" I raised a brow.

She bristled as I led her past the cars. "We aren't driving?"

Picturing us trying to drive around the trees, I laughed. "No. Where we're going, you can't drive. It's not a well-known spot. Most locals don't even know about it."

"Oh, I'm special, then."

I looked over at her, studying her profile as we walked down the driveway, and I found that I had a hard time looking away. She was something all right. "You know what I think, Kat?"

She glanced over, catching me staring at her. The tips of

her cheeks flushed. We passed the empty house at the end of the road. "I'm pretty sure I don't want to know."

"I think my sister finds you very special." The next words came out without my really even thinking about it, but once I said them, I figured they were true. "I'm starting to wonder if she's onto something."

A humorless smile appeared on her lips. "But then there's all kinds of *special* now, isn't there, Daemon?"

I jolted at the sound of my name. Was this the first time she had said it? I liked the sound of my name on her tongue. Looking away, I exhaled slowly as I led her across the main highway and into the dense tree line on the other side of the road.

"Are you taking me out to the woods as a trick?" she asked.

I glanced over my shoulder at her, lowering my lashes. "And what would I do out here to you, Kitten?"

She didn't reply immediately. "The possibilities are endless."

I winked. "Aren't they?"

She didn't answer as she tripped through the thick brush, avoiding the mass of vines tangled along the floor of the woods. "Can we pretend we did this?"

*Pretend* to go on a walk with me? I blinked, speechless for probably the first time in like...ever. I was actually being nice right now. She didn't like Dickhead Daemon and she didn't like Nice Daemon? What the hell ever. My God, this girl had me coming and going so much, I didn't know what I was thinking. Did I *want* to be nice to her now? Or was I just being nice to get closer to her and drive Dee away? Jesus, all this thinking about my feelings and hers was probably going to give me a period. "Trust me, I don't want to be doing this, either." I jumped over a fallen tree. Spinning around, I offered her my hand. "But bitching about it isn't going to make it any easier."

"You're such a joy to talk to." Her gaze dropped to my hand and she sucked in her lower lip between her teeth, drawing my attention. The burst of heat low in my gut had nothing to do with aggravation.

She wasn't going to take my hand. She shouldn't.

But she did.

Kat placed her hand in mine, offering a tiny bit of trust, and there was a shock of static from the contact. It happened sometimes, when humans touched us, as if they had dragged their feet along carpet. I ignored it and how incredibly small that hand was in mine. I helped her over the log.

"Thank you," she murmured when I let go.

I ignored how my chest tightened at being her hero, no matter how small. "Are you excited about school?"

"It's not exciting being the newbie. You know, the whole sticking out like a sore thumb. Not fun."

"I can see that."

"You can?" Surprise colored her tone.

She had no idea. "Yeah, I can. We only have a little bit more to go."

"A little bit? How long have we been walking?"

"About twenty minutes, maybe a little longer. I told you it was fairly hidden." A wry grin twisted my lips as she followed me around an uprooted tree. I stepped aside, revealing the clearing we were entering, still a little shocked that I'd actually brought her here. "Welcome to our little piece of paradise."

Kat was silent as she walked past me, her gaze darting all over the place, taking everything in as I felt tension creep into my muscles.

A thin creek cut across the clearing, expanding into a small, natural lake. The water rippled in the soft breeze. Flat, large rocks erupted from the middle. Wildflowers, purple and blue ones, surrounded the lake.

Did she see what I saw? I knew Dee did. Ash, if I'd ever brought her here, would've just been bored. Dawson got it. Matthew might've.

"Wow," she whispered. "This place is beautiful."

"It is." Standing next to her, I raised my hand, blocking the glare of the sun bouncing off the surface of the lake. Peaceful. This place had always been a source of peace. I could come here and escape everything, even if it was just for a few hours. I lowered my hand.

Her soft touch on my arm drew my attention. I looked down to where her hand rested, and then my gaze flicked to hers.

"Thank you for bringing me," she said, and then quickly removed her hand as she looked away.

I didn't know what to say. And that damn tight feeling expanded in my chest a little more.

Kat wandered to the water's edge. "How deep is it?"

"About ten feet in most parts, twenty feet on the other side of the rocks." I ghosted up behind her. "Dee loves it here. Before you came, she spent most of her days here."

Her brows pinched together as she stared at the lake, and then she took a deep breath. "You know, I'm not going to get your sister in trouble."

"We'll see."

"I'm not a bad influence," she stated. "I haven't ever gotten into trouble before."

I walked around her. I could tell she was trying to, well, get past our initial run-ins with each other, but I doubted Bethany ever thought she'd be Dawson's downfall. You could be a weapon without ever realizing you were one. "She doesn't need a friend like you."

"There isn't anything wrong with me," she snapped. "You know what? Forget this."

When she started to turn, I stopped her the best way I could. "Why do you garden?"

Her hands clenched as she faced me. "What?"

"Why do you garden?" I stared at the lake, wondering what in the hell I was really accomplishing by getting to know her, but that question didn't stop me. "Dee said you do it so you don't think. What do you want to avoid thinking about?"

She exhaled roughly. "It's none of your business."

Well then. "Then let's go swimming."

When I glanced at her, she looked like she wanted to strangle me a little. I dipped my chin before she saw the grin, because I doubted that would help. Stepping to the side, I kicked off my sneakers and then reached down, unbuttoning my jeans. I didn't need to look at her to know she was watching. I could feel her gaze on me as I shed my jeans and then my shirt.

And I knew she was really staring when the only article of clothing that remained were the swim trunks.

I didn't look back at her as I stepped to the very edge and then dived in. The rush of cool water immediately scattered all my thoughts, washing them away as I swam underwater. I loved the water. Swimming was a lot like flying, and I could move fast enough that it was damn near close to flying.

When I broke the surface, Kat was still standing there, her face the color of a tomato. I started to tease her, but then decided I really didn't want to have to chase her ass down when she left. "Are you coming in?"

She dragged the toe of her sneaker in the loose soil at the lake's edge as she nibbled on her lower lip. Uncertainty bled out from her as her gaze met mine and then fleeted away. Cute. That was kind of cute.

"You sure are shy, aren't you, Kitten?"

Her foot stilled. "Why do you call me that?"

"Because it makes your hair stand up, like a kitten." Pushing onto my back, I swam a few feet away. "So? Are you coming in?" When she didn't move, I figured I was going to have to motivate her. "I'm giving you one minute to get in here."

Kat squinted. "Or what?"

Twisting around, I moved closer to the bank of the lake, no longer on my back. "Or I come and get you."

Her mouth pinched. "I'd like to see you try that."

"Forty seconds."

Did she really think I wouldn't do it?

"Thirty seconds." I smiled, hoping she didn't do it.

Because I totally would toss her ass into the lake and I would thoroughly enjoy myself.

She snapped into action, muttering under her breath as she reached down with a quick, jerky motion and grabbed the hem of her shirt. She yanked it off and then quickly pulled off her shorts. Then she straightened, her hands on her hips. "Happy?"

Holy shit.

She was not wearing a one-piece, and I got my wish. It was a two-piece red bikini, and yeah, holy shit. All I could do was stare. I don't know what I was expecting, but it wasn't this.

Under the plain shorts and shapeless shirts I'd seen her in, Kat was hiding a…a magnificent body full of the kind of curves that made me want to do stupid things. Fun things, but damn, things that would be really stupid considering everything.

I wasn't staring. I didn't notice how the blood-red bathing suit stretched across her chest, reminding me of the top part of a heart. I didn't notice how her body was reacting to the way I was staring at her, because neither of us was moving, and there was something tangible in that moment, like a physical caress. And I sure as hell didn't count the inch and a half, maybe two inches of skin between her navel and the top of her bottoms.

Aw hell.

Now was a good time to drown myself.

Who was I kidding? I was totally checking her out.

For someone who was so short, her legs appeared incredibly long, but that might've had something to do with the skimpy cut of her bottoms—a cut that displayed the fullness of her hips and the surprising tininess of her waist. Muscles low in my stomach tightened as I dragged my gaze over her soft-looking stomach and then farther north. How that red top was staying on was beyond me, and I didn't know if I should be grateful or disappointed by that.

Average? Had I seriously used the words *average* or *plain* to describe her? Hell, this girl...

The old saying surfaced in my heated thoughts. *Be careful what you wish for.* So true. I wouldn't have wished for this if I had known how intensely my body would've reacted to it, and oh, it was reacting all right.

This plan I'd come up with had to be an all-time dumbass one.

My smile slipped from my face. "I'm never happy around you."

"What did you say?" she demanded, eyes narrowing.

"Nothing. You better get in before that blush reaches your toes." And before I really started considering all the stupid shit I could do right now.

And that blush deepened. She walked stiffly over to the edge of the lake where the water was shallow, giving me a view of her backside, and that really did nothing to help dampen the purely physical response.

Folding her arms along her waist, she dipped her toes into the water. "It's beautiful out here."

Yeah, it was beautiful out here. And it was hot. My gaze dipped to her bent knee and then slid back up, getting hung up on certain areas. My throat tightened. Other parts of me tightened.

Shit.

I dunked myself and when I came back up, it hadn't helped, because now she was wet. She must've gone under while I had. We were only a few feet away, and I was in deeper water, hunched down to where the water lapped at my mouth.

"What?" she asked.

"Why don't you come here?" My heart was pounding in my chest. If she were smart, she wouldn't get anywhere close to me at this moment. Actually, if I were smart, I wouldn't have called her over.

Kat was smarter than me.

She twisted around and dipped under the water, swimming toward the rocks. When she pulled herself out of the water, climbing onto the rock, I swallowed a groan. I wanted to—

"You look disappointed," she said.

God, I *was* disappointed, and I really didn't know what to make out of that. I pushed it aside.

"Well...what do we have here?"

Her legs dangled off the rock, her feet slipping into the water. "What are you talking about now?"

"Nothing." I waded closer to the rock.

"You said something."

"I did, didn't I?"

"You're strange."

"You're not what I expected," I admitted, voice low.

She gave a little shake of her head. "What does that mean?"

I grabbed for her foot, but she moved her leg out of reach. No fun.

"I'm not good enough to be your sister's friend?" she asked.

"You don't have anything in common with her."

"How would you know?" She shifted back as I reached for her other foot.

"I know."

"We have a lot in common. And I like her. She's nice and she's fun." She scooted back this time, completely out of arm's reach. "And you should stop being such a dick and chasing off her friends."

Her words slipped over me, and I laughed outright. "You're not really like them."

"Like who?"

Like any person I'd ever met. Truth was, human and Luxen females treated me the same. Only Ash and Dee mouthed off at me, but we'd grown up together. It was different for them, but others? They pretty much wanted one thing from me. Most of the time I was okay with that, but if I so much as glared in their direction, they scattered like bugs. Not really attractive when you thought about it. But not Kat. She may not have a clue what I was, but she was not scared of me, she wasn't wowed, and as twisted as it was, that turned me on.

That *did* make her dangerous.

I pushed away from the rock, making ripples in the water, and then I slipped under. I swam to the other side of the rock and I stayed under, hoping the icy water would cool down the very inappropriate arousal thing I had going on.

Dammit, I didn't even like the chick, I thought, trying to convince myself.

Yeah, she was amusing. Yeah, even entertaining. And yeah, I wanted to trace her curves with my hands and my mouth. Possibly even my tongue—okay, definitely with my tongue—but she irritated the hell out of me.

And she didn't even like me. She liked *looking* at me, because who didn't, but the distaste went both ways.

I had no idea how much time passed underwater until I was about 92 percent confident I wouldn't do something, and I broke the surface.

"Daemon!"

The sheer panic blanketing the sound of my name caught me off guard. I burst onto the rock, crouching as I scanned the lake, expecting an Arum to be nearby. Those assholes wouldn't blink an eye when it came down to taking out an innocent human.

All I saw was Kat, on her knees, in her damn bikini.

Whelp, there went all the work that cold water had done for me.

She was frozen for a second and then scrambled over the rock, clutching my shoulders. Blood had drained from her face and she was exceptionally pale. "Are you okay? What happened?" Then she let go of my shoulders, hauled back, and smacked my arm. *Hard.* "Don't you ever do that again!"

"Whoa there." I threw my hands up. "What is your problem?"

"You were under the water for so long. I thought you drowned! Why would you do that? Why would you scare me like that?" She jumped to her feet, chest heaving. "You were under the water *forever*."

Oh shit. I'd been under there longer than I'd thought. My body didn't function like hers, and I'd forgotten that. Luxen didn't need to breathe air, but humans weren't supposed to figure that out, dumbass. "I wasn't down there that long. I was swimming."

Her hands were shaking. "No, Daemon, you were down there a long time. It was at least ten minutes! I looked for you, called for you. I…I thought you were dead."

I climbed to my feet slowly, cursing myself every which way from Sunday. "It couldn't have been ten minutes. That's not possible. No one can hold their breath that long."

Her throat worked. "You apparently can."

Damn. I stepped closer to her, my eyes searching hers. "You were really worried, weren't you?"

"No shit! What part of '*I thought you drowned*' don't you understand?" A tremble rocked her.

Hell, she was really upset. Honestly, if I'd drowned, I figured she'd do a little dance on my grave. In her bikini. Shit. Screw the bikini. "Kat, I came up. You must not have seen me. I went right back down."

Taking a step back, she shook her head, and I could see in her steely eyes she didn't believe me. Holy hell, here I was worrying about Dee doing something to expose us, and it was me who did the bonehead thing. *Let it go, Kat. Let it go*. I took a deep breath, thinking maybe if I pissed her off, she would forget what happened in her anger. Better than the other option. "Does this happen often?" I asked.

Her gaze snapped back to mine. "Does what?"

"Imagining things." I gestured at the lake. "Or do you have a horrible issue with telling time?"

"I wasn't imagining anything! And I know how to tell time, you jerk."

"Then I don't know what to tell you." I stepped forward, crowding her. "I'm not the one imagining that I was underwater for ten minutes when it was like two minutes tops. You know, maybe I'll buy you a watch the next time I'm in town, when I have *my* keys back."

She stiffened as she stared up at me and anger clouded over the suspicion in her eyes. "Well, make sure you tell Dee we had a *wonderful* time so that you can get your stupid keys back. Then we won't need a replay of today."

I smiled at her. "That's on you, Kitten. I'm sure she'll call you later and ask."

"You'll have your keys. I'm ready—" She turned, and it happened so fast. Her foot slipped over the wet rock. Thrown off balance, her arms flailed.

I didn't stop to think.

Snapping forward, I reached out and caught her hand just as her feet left the rock. I pulled her forward, and then we were chest to chest. Her skin was warm and dry, mine wet. I clenched down on my jaw as sensation powered through every one of my cells. There was no denying the bolt of lust that shot through me.

Hell, she was so soft in all the right places.

"Careful there, Kitten," I murmured. "Dee would be pissed at me if you end up cracking your head open and drowning."

Kat slowly lifted her head, and her gray eyes met mine. Her lips parted, but she didn't speak, and I was A-OK with that. Words were freaking pointless at this moment, because our bodies were pressed together.

Electricity coursed through my skin, and I had no idea if she felt it, and if she did, if she thought it was just her imagination, but I swallowed a low groan as a light breeze washed over our skin. Her chest rose against mine, and I needed to either let her go or...or what?

There was no other option.

I dropped my arm from her waist, letting my hand slip off her lower back just to freaking torture myself. The skin was soft and smooth, and the near-painful pressure building in me was worth it. "I think it's time we head back."

Officially the smartest decision I had made since first seeing her.

Pathetic.

Kat nodded, and we didn't speak as we made our way back to land, dried off, and dressed, and that was probably a damn good thing, because I was in one hell of a mood for a multitude of reasons.

The walk back was silent and stiff, and when we crested the driveway, my mood went from shit to punch someone when I saw the car in the driveway. Dammit all to hell in a hand basket. Kat glanced up at me, her expression curious.

"Kat, I—"

My front door swung open, banging off the side of my house, and Matthew strolled out like he had every right. He came down the porch steps, not even looking in Kat's direction. "What's going on here?" he demanded.

Man, I cared for Matthew like a brother, but he had no business being in my house like that. I folded my arms. "Absolutely nothing. Since my sister is not home, I'm curious as to why you're in my house?"

"I let myself in," he replied. "I didn't realize that would be a problem."

"It is now, Matthew."

Kat shifted uncomfortably beside me, drawing Matthew's attention. His lip curled up as he shook his head. "Of all people, I'd think you'd know better, Daemon."

Tension poured into the air around us. "Matthew, if you value the ability to walk, I wouldn't go there."

"I think I should go." Kat moved to the side.

For some reason I'll never understand, I stepped in front of Kat, blocking her from Matthew's glare. "I'm thinking Matthew should go unless he has another purpose other than sticking his nose where it doesn't belong."

"I'm sorry," she whispered, voice wavering, and that did a funny thing to my consciousness, made it take notice. "But I don't know what's going on here. We were just swimming."

I squared my shoulders. "It's not what you're thinking. Give me some credit. Dee hid my keys, forced me to take her out to get them back."

Kat sucked in a breath.

Recognition flickered across Matthew's face. "So this is Dee's little friend?"

"That would be me," she said from behind me.

"I thought you had this under control." Matthew gestured at her. "That you'd make your sister understand."

"Yeah, well, why don't you try to make her understand," I retorted, my patience wearing thin. "So far, I'm not having much luck."

Matthew's lips hardened. "Both of you should know better."

And my patience snapped. I was tired. A certain area of my body was aching, and being scolded wasn't going to work for me. Energy crackled over my skin, invisible to the human eye, but it leaked out, charging the air. Thunder cracked. Lightning streaked overhead, bright and near blinding. When the light receded, Matthew's eyes widened for a second and then he spun around, walking back into my house.

Warning received.

I started to turn to Kat, but there was really nothing to say, and so I said nothing as I stalked toward my house. I thought I heard her speak, but it didn't matter.

Nothing that had happened with her mattered.

# 6

Matthew started the moment I walked into the kitchen. "What is going on with that girl, Daemon? You have never acted that way."

I passed him on the way to the fridge, beyond irritated and hungry. "Acted like what?"

He turned to me. "You know what I mean."

Opening the fridge, I eyed everything needed to make a kickass sandwich. Waving my hand, I got all *Beauty and the Beast* up in here and danced the items over to the counter. "Want a sandwich?"

Matthew sighed. "Already ate."

"More for me." I grabbed a plate and moved to the counter.

"Daemon, we need to talk about this."

I snatched up a knife and the jar of mayo. "We don't need to talk about shit, Matthew. I already told you what was going on when we were outside. The story isn't going to get any more interesting."

"You're making sure Dee doesn't get too close to her by hanging out with her?" he asked, disbelief coloring his words. "Swimming together? Is this a new tactic?"

Slapping the slice of bread on the plate, I glanced over to where he stood near the table. My voice was deadly calm. "Let it go, Matthew."

"I can't let it go."

My eyes met his. "You might want to try."

He ran a hand over his short brown hair. "I don't want to argue with you, Daemon."

I almost laughed as I slapped deli meat onto the bread. He was doing a shitty job at not arguing. Tension had stiffened the muscles of my neck and back. Matthew was right about one thing. I'd never acted like I had outside a few minutes ago, not over a human and not against one of my own kind. I don't even know why his presence or his words had grated on me so badly.

Maybe because deep down I knew I passed up the chance to either find out something about Kat I could use against her or scare her off enough that she'd stay away from Dee. I really hadn't done either of those things.

Instead, we'd talked about school and gardening and stupid shit like we...like we were normal.

"This is different," Matthew continued quietly. "We live among the humans, but we don't get close to them, not for any extended period of time. If we do, something always happens. They either find out about us, because we let our guard down, or we trace them and the Arum hunt *us* down. It never ends well. Never."

I faced him, my hands at my sides. "You think I don't know that? What do you expect me to do about her? There's only so much I can do unless you expect me to take her ass out."

Matthew's blue eyes deepened, going from ocean blue to dark skies at dusk. "I don't want to see a young woman harmed, and I don't expect you to be the one who would take care of that if it came to that point. If that girl proves a risk, I will handle it. It won't be like with Bethany, where all of us let it slide until it was too late. I won't let that happen this time."

Energy charged my skin as I stared at him. Realization slipped in and it left me cold. "Her name is Kat," I heard myself say as I stepped toward him, my chin dipping down. "And I will handle her."

"You know I would do anything to protect you all." Matthew planted his hands on the table and took a deep breath. "All of you—you're my family."

Thrusting my hand through my hair, I struggled with my patience. "I know that. We feel the same way, but you do not need to step in here. I will make sure she isn't a risk to us."

His eyes met mine and a moment passed. "You're one of the strongest, if not the strongest, Luxen right now. The Elders know that and so does the DOD, and that means someone is always watching you. You have to be more careful than any of us."

I lowered my hand as the weight of my race settled on my shoulders. There was nothing I could say to that. I was faster and stronger than most Luxen and I could wield more of the Source than any of my kind we knew about. But I didn't take these gifts for granted. I trained harder than anyone. Patrolled more often. And I was determined to stay focused on my duty. Not get lost and vulnerable like my brother had…

Matthew watched me and must have seen something in my eyes. "Your brother wasn't weak."

My head cocked to the side. "He—"

"He wasn't," he interrupted. "He was kinder and he was

more laid back, but he was just as strong as you and you need to remember that. Dawson wasn't weak. He wasn't foolish, and yet, because of a girl, he's gone. Don't follow in your brother's footsteps."

Message received, loud and clear.

*D*on't follow in your brother's footsteps.

That statement was actually laughable.

Just because I wasn't actively trying to run her out of town didn't mean I was going to end up like Dawson. For one thing, Kat and I didn't even like each other. Yeah, there was something physical brewing, but it didn't run deeper than that. Dawson had fallen in love with Bethany. Big difference there.

And my brother—he had been weaker.

Maybe not physically, but when it came to everything else, he was.

It was early evening on Saturday when I saw Kat's mom drive off. Knowing Kat was alone and that Dee would be coming home tomorrow, I knew the last thing I should be doing was what I was doing.

Which was walking my ass over to her house.

After knocking on her door, I ambled to the porch railing and looked up. The sun had a couple of more hours before setting, but a few stars were starting to appear. Shoving my hands in the pockets of my jeans, I waited to see if she'd even answer the door. If I were her, I'd probably never want to see my face again. I couldn't explain my hot-and-cold behavior either. I knew she was bad for Dee, bad for the colony, and especially bad for me. But there was something about her spunk I couldn't shake.

I was a little surprised when the door opened and Kat stepped out onto the porch. "What are you doing?" she asked.

Having no idea how to answer that, I was quiet for a moment and then cleared my throat. "I like staring at the sky. There's something about it. It's endless, you know." Lame.

She stepped closer to me, her movements almost tentative. "Is some crazy dude going to run out of your house and yell at you for talking to me?"

I grinned at that. "Not right now, but there is always later."

Her nose wrinkled. "I'm okay missing 'later.'"

"Yeah." I twisted at the waist, facing her. "Busy?"

"Other than messing with my blog, no."

"You have a blog?" I had to force myself not to laugh. Blogging always seemed like something middle-age moms did, not above-average high school girls.

She folded her arms across her chest, her stance widening as if she were preparing for a battle. "Yeah, I have a blog."

"What's your blog's name?"

"None of your business." Her smile was too sweet.

"Interesting name." One corner of my lips rose when annoyance flashed across her face. Getting her angry was too easy. "So what do you blog about? Knitting? Puzzles? Being lonely?"

"Ha ha, smartass." She sighed. "I review books."

Huh. Books. Should've guessed that. "Do you get paid for them?"

She laughed out loud at that. "No. Not at all."

I frowned. "So you review books and you don't get paid if someone buys a book based on your review?"

"I don't review books to get paid or anything." Her arms unfolded as she seemed to grow more comfortable talking about her blog. "I do it because I like it. I love reading, and I enjoy talking about books."

"What kind of books do you read?"

"All different kinds." She leaned against the railing and looked up, meeting my gaze. "Mainly I prefer the paranormal stuff."

"Vampires and werewolves?" I guessed.

"Yeah."

"Ghosts and aliens?"

"Ghost stories are cool, but I don't know about aliens. ET really doesn't do it for me and a lot of readers."

I raised an eyebrow at that. "What does it for you?"

"Not slimy green space creatures," she replied, and I swallowed a laugh. "Anyway, I also appreciate graphic novels, history stuff—"

"You read graphic novels?" Disbelief flooded me. "Seriously?"

She nodded. "Yeah, so what? Are girls not supposed to like graphic novels and comics?"

I didn't think she wanted me to answer that. Damn, she was always a surprise. "Want to go on a hike?"

"Uh, you know I'm not good with the whole hiking thing." She reached up, tucking a loose strand of hair from her ponytail behind her ear. Did she ever wear her hair down?

Why in the hell was I thinking about her hair?

My gaze followed the movement. "I'm not taking you up on the Rocks. Just a harmless little trail. I'm sure you can handle it."

She pushed off the railing but hesitated. "Did Dee not tell you where your keys were?"

Hell, I'd forgotten all about that. "Yeah, she did."

"Then why are you here?"

How could I possibly explain it to her when I couldn't to myself? I fumbled in my head for an excuse she'd buy and realized I really wasn't that creative. This was probably a sign I should get my ass home and forget all about whatever *this* was. "I don't have a reason. I thought I would just stop over, but if you're going to question everything, then you can forget it." Pivoting around, I headed down the porch steps, totally realizing I was yet again acting like an ass. What could I say? I was good at it.

A moment passed and then, "All right, let's do this."

Surprised, I stopped. "Are you sure?"

She didn't look 100 percent certain when I glanced over my shoulder at her, but she hurried down the steps and followed me. "Why are we going behind my house?" She paused, pointing to the west, at the sandstone mountain still glittering in the fading sunlight. "The Seneca Rocks are that way. I thought most trails started over there."

"Yeah, but there are trails back here that will take you around, and it's quicker," I explained. "Most people here know all the main trails that are crowded. There used to be a lot of boring days out here, and I found a couple of them off the beaten trail."

Her eyes widened. "How far off the beaten track are we talking?"

Cute. I chuckled. "Not *that* far."

"So it's a baby trail? I bet this is going to be boring for you."

"Any time I get to go out and walk around is good." That was true. Luxen naturally had more energy in them, and any physical activity helped. "Besides, it's not as if we'll hike all the way to Smoke Hole Canyon. That's a pretty big hike from here, so no worries, okay?"

She relaxed. "All right, lead the way."

Kat waited outside as I stepped into my house, grabbing two water bottles, and then she followed me across the backyard and into the heavily shaded forest. Something about the fact that she was actually willing to do this struck me wrong. I hadn't been nice to her. That was a big *no shit* there. I wondered if she would do this if Andrew befriended her, just roam right the hell off.

If so, that wouldn't be good.

Andrew would totally be in the Matthew camp, as in he'd have no problem with the idea of preemptively "taking care of her."

"You're very trusting, Kitten," I said quietly.

"Stop calling me that."

I glanced over my shoulder. She was trailing a few steps behind me. "No one has ever called you that before?"

Stepping around a thorny bush, she shot me a bland look. "Yeah, people call me Kitten all the time. But you make it sound so…"

I waited. "Sound so what?"

"I don't know, like it's an insult," she said, and I slowed my longer-legged pace so she was walking beside me now. "Or something sexually deviant."

That knocked a laugh out of me, right along with some of the tension that had carved its way into my neck and shoulders.

"Why are you always laughing at me?"

I shook my head as I grinned. "I don't know, you just kind of make me laugh."

"Whatever." She kicked a rock, apparently deciding that wasn't a good thing. "So what was up with that Matthew dude? He acted as if he hated me or something."

"He doesn't hate you. He doesn't trust you," I muttered.

Her ponytail bounced as she shook her head. "Trust me with what? Your virtue?"

Another laugh burst out of me. "Yeah. He's not a fan of beautiful girls who have the hots for me."

"What?" she blurted out, and then, within a second, she tripped.

I caught her easily, with my arm around her waist, and quickly let go, but I felt the jolt of the brief contact, and my skin hummed.

"You're joking, right?" she asked.

Amused by her inability to watch out for whatever was on the ground, I felt my grin grow even bigger. "Which part?"

"Any of that!"

"Come on. Please don't tell me you don't think you're pretty." When she didn't answer, I sighed. "No guy has ever said you're pretty?"

Her gaze met mine and then skittered away. She shrugged. "Of course."

Huh. "Or...maybe you're not aware of it?"

She shrugged again, and I couldn't believe she didn't see what I... Wait a second. She didn't see what I saw? When had what I saw changed? Because I'd been thinking she was plain as hell. Sometimes above average when she was mad. Or smiling. Or blushing. But, well, mainly she was just average.

As I watched her cheeks pink up even more, I knew I'd been wrong.

Kat wasn't plain. Maybe at first glance, but once you got up close to her, once you spent any amount of time around her, those heather gray eyes, the full lips, and the shape of her face were anything but plain. It ran deeper than the skin, though.

"You know what I've always believed?" I asked, stopping in the middle of the path.

She looked up at me, her eyes wide but not wary. "No."

For a moment, I didn't speak, and the only sound between us was the chirping of nearby birds as my gaze searched hers. "I've always found that the most beautiful people, truly beautiful inside and out, are the ones who are quietly unaware of their effect. The ones who throw their beauty around, waste what they have? Their beauty is only passing. It's just a shell hiding nothing but shadows and emptiness."

Her lips parted, and then she laughed.

Kat laughed.

What in the hell?

"I'm sorry," she said, blinking back tears as a giggle snuck free. "But that was the most thoughtful thing I've ever heard you say. What alien ship took the Daemon I know away, and can I ask them to keep him?"

I scowled. "I was being honest."

"I know, but it's just that was really...wow."

Eyeing her, I shrugged and then started down the trail again. Whatever. "We won't go too far." I paused. "So you're interested in history?"

"Yeah, I know that makes me a nerd." She caught up to me, an extra bounce in her steps.

"Did you know this land was once traveled by the Seneca Indians?"

"Please tell me we aren't walking on any burial grounds?"

"Well...I'm sure there *are* burial grounds around here somewhere. Even though they just traveled through this area, it's not a stretch that some died on this very spot and—"

"Daemon, I don't need to know that part." She lightly pushed my arm.

The ease with which she touched me was unnerving. It took me a moment to get past that.

"Okay, I'll tell you the story and I'll leave some of the more creepy but natural facts out." I grabbed a long branch, holding it back for Kat to duck under. Her shoulder brushed my chest, kicking around my sense of awareness.

"What story?" she asked, thick lashes lowered, shielding her eyes.

"You'll see. Now pay attention... A long time ago, this land was forest and hills, which isn't too different than today with the exception of a few small towns." I pushed the lower branches out of the way for her. At this point, she might impale herself; she was so obscenely unaware of how to walk in the woods. "But imagine this place so sparsely populated that it could take days, even weeks, before you reached your nearest neighbor."

She shivered. "That seems so lonely."

"But you have to understand that was the way of life hundreds of years ago. Farmers and mountain men lived a few miles away from one another, but the distance was all traveled by foot or horse. It wasn't usually the safest way to travel."

"I can imagine." Her response was faint.

"The Seneca Indian tribe traveled through the eastern part of the United States, and at some point, they walked this very path toward the Seneca Rocks." Our gazes glanced off each other. "Did you know that this very small path behind your house leads right to the base of them?"

"No. They always seem so far off in the distance, I never thought of them as being that close."

"If you stayed on this path for a couple of miles, you'd find yourself at the base of them. It's a pretty rocky patch even the most experienced rock climbers stay away from. See, the Seneca Rocks spread from Grant to Pendleton County, with the highest point being Spruce Knob and an outcropping near Seneca called Champe Rocks. Now they are kind of hard to get to, since it usually involves invading someone's property, but it can be worth it if you can scale way beyond nine hundred feet in the sky."

Man, I loved getting up there. Hadn't done it in a while.

"That sounds like fun." Her smile was pained.

I laughed. "It is if you're not afraid of slipping. Anyway, the Seneca Rocks are made out of quartzite, which is part sandstone. That's why it sometimes has a pinkish tint to it. Quartzite is considered a beta quartz. People who believe in…" Hmm, had to proceed carefully. "Abnormal powers or powers in…nature, as a lot of Indian tribes did at one time, believe that any form of beta quartz allows energy to be stored and transformed, even manipulated by it. It can throw off electronics and other stuff, too—hide things."

"Ooo-kay."

I shot her a look and she quieted. "Possibly the beta quartz drew the Seneca Tribe to this area. No one knows, since they weren't native to West Virginia. No one knows how long any of them camped here, traded, or made war." I slowed my steps, nearing the small stream. "But they do have a very romantic legend."

"Romantic?" She followed me around the stream, her ponytail bouncing with each step. It was sort of distracting.

"See, there was this beautiful Indian princess called Snowbird, who had asked seven of the tribe's strongest warriors to prove their love by doing something only she had been able to do. Many men wanted to be with her for her beauty and her rank. But she wanted an equal."

I wasn't normally a chatty Cathy. Most people who knew

me would probably be checking my temp by now, I'd strung so many sentences together in a row. But Kat was riveted. I liked that.

"When the day arrived for her to choose her husband, she set forth a challenge so only the bravest and most dedicated warrior would win her hand. She asked her suitors to climb the highest rock with her." The path narrowed and I slowed down. "They all started, but as it became more difficult, three turned back. A fourth became weary and a fifth crumpled in exhaustion. Only two remained, and the beautiful Snowbird stayed in the lead. Finally, she reached the highest point and turned to see who was the bravest and strongest of all warriors. Only one remained a few feet behind her and as she watched, he began to slip."

Stepping around an outcropping of rocks, I waited until Kat had passed them. "Snowbird paused only for a second, thinking that this brave warrior obviously was the strongest, but he was not her equal. She could save him or she could let him slip. He was brave, but he had yet to reach the highest point like she had."

"But he was right behind her? How could she just let him fall?" She sounded almost panicked and, yeah, cute again.

"What would you do?" I asked, genuinely curious.

"Not that I would ever ask a group of men to prove their love by doing something incredibly dangerous and stupid like that, but if I ever found myself in that situation, as unlikely—"

"Kat?"

She squared her shoulders. "I would reach out and save him, of course. I couldn't let him fall to his death."

"But he didn't prove himself," I reasoned.

"That doesn't matter." Her gray eyes flashed like storm clouds. "He was right behind her and how beautiful could you truly be if you let a man fall to his death just because he slipped? How could you even be capable of love or worthy of it, for that matter, if you let that happen?"

I nodded slowly. "Well, Snowbird thought like you."

A wide smile broke out across her face. "Good."

"Snowbird decided that the warrior was her equal and with that, her decision had been made. She grabbed the man before he could fall. The chief met them and was very pleased with his daughter's choice in mate. He granted their marriage and made the warrior his successor."

"So is that why the rocks are called Seneca Rocks? After the Indians and Snowbird?"

"That's what the legend says."

"It's a beautiful story, but I think the whole climbing several hundred feet in the air to prove your love is a little excessive."

I chuckled. "I'd have to agree with you on that."

"I'd hope so or you'd find yourself playing with cars on an interstate to prove your love nowadays." Her features tensed, and then a flush raced across her cheeks.

"I don't foresee that happening," I said quietly.

"Can you get to where the Indians climbed from here?" she asked.

"You could get to the canyon, but that's serious hiking. Not something I would suggest you doing by yourself."

Kat laughed, and the sound was light and almost free. "Yeah, I don't think you have to worry about that. I wonder why the Indians came here. Were they looking for something? It's hard to believe that a bunch of rocks brought them here."

"You never know." Who knew why they came, but there had to be a reason. "People tend to look on the beliefs of the past as being primitive and unintelligent, yet we are seeing more truth in the past every day."

She looked at me in a long, assessing way. "What was it that made the rocks important again?"

"It's the type of rock..." I turned to her, my gaze sliding across her face and then over her shoulder. Oh shit. My eyes widened. "Kitten?"

"Would you stop calling me—?"

"Be quiet," I whispered, gaze fixed over her shoulder as I placed my hand on her bare arm. "Promise me you won't freak out."

"Why would I freak out?" she whispered back.

Well, most people would freak out over a three-hundred-pound bear only several feet away, and it was a big one. Energy began building in me. I tugged Kat closer to me and her hands flew to my chest, above my heart. "Have you ever seen a bear?" I asked.

"What? There's a bear—?" She pulled out of my grasp and spun around.

Kat stiffened against me.

The bear's ears twitched, picking up on our breathing. I willed Kat to remain still. There was a good chance the bear would just mosey on past us. Or at least I hoped it would, because if that sucker rushed us, I was going to have to do something to scare it off.

Something that would not be easy to explain.

"Don't run," I told her.

She gave a jerky nod.

My hands settled on her arms again, and I don't even think she felt it. Then, without any provocation, the bear huffed out a low growl as it rose onto its hind legs. Massive jaws opened and it roared, pawing at the air.

Oh shit.

Letting go of Kat, I stepped away from her and started waving my arms, shouting at it, but the bear dropped onto its paws, shoulders shaking and fur coat twitching. It charged right at Kat.

Cursing, I shot back toward her. She was frozen, eyes squeezed shut and face drawn and pale. I didn't stop to think. I lifted my hand and blinding white light, tinged in red, swirled down my arm, snapping into the air. A bolt of light, very much like lightning, slammed into the ground, no more than a foot in front of Kat, startling the bear.

All of it happened so fast.

Scared, the bear reared back and shifted its heavy body, running off in the opposite direction just as the light receded. The burst of energy bounced, and I saw Kat's legs fold and her head tip to the side. And she went down.

I snapped forward, catching her before she hit the ground and lifting her up in my arms, cradling her close to my chest as I kept my eyes on the area the bear had disappeared to. I doubted she'd passed out due to fright. She'd been too close to the Source. God only knew what the charge had done to her heart or nervous system.

"Shit shit shit," I muttered, calming only slightly when I heard her heartbeat still pounding in her chest.

When I was sure the bear wasn't coming back, I looked down at her. Pressure clamped down on my chest. Oh no. Dammit. No...

A faint white glow surrounded Kat, almost like an aura or like the space around her was glowing with a supernatural light humans couldn't see. But it would be visible to any Luxen...*and* to any Arum.

I'd traced her.

# 7

**K**at seemed incredibly small and delicate in my arms, her weight so slight I pressed her closer. Oddly, her head fit perfectly against my shoulder, as if she'd placed it there and fallen asleep instead of passing out.

I couldn't believe I'd inadvertently knocked her out.

In a twisted way, it was a blessing in disguise. Most likely I wouldn't have to come up with some whacked-out excuse for why it seemed like lightning had shot from my fingertips and scared a bear off.

Above, dark clouds rolled in. A storm was brewing—a common consequence of too much charged power. Something to do with the electrical fields affecting the weather and blah blah blah.

But even if Kat woke up and believed the incoming storm had something to do with scaring the bear off, I'd traced her. Which was equivalent to putting a bull's-eye on her back, especially when there might be Arum around.

Shit.

Here I was, ranting at Dee over how dangerous it was getting close to Kat, and I'm the one who was bored and coaxed her into a walk, who had endangered them all.

The trace should fade in a couple of days. As long as she stayed home and no one other than Dee saw her, then it shouldn't be a problem.

I laughed drily, almost bitterly. Not going to be a problem? Dee was never going to let me hear the end of it.

Heading back down the trail, I forced my gaze to stay forward instead of on what I carried, focused on the scenery. Trees—lots of trees and maple-shaped leaves, pine needles, a few shrubs…birds hopping from limb to limb, shaking out their feathers. A squirrel shimmied up the trunk of a tree.

I glanced down.

Thick lashes fanned paler-than-normal cheeks. I kind of thought she looked like Snow White. Good God, that sounded lame. Snow White? But her lips were parted perfectly, and they were rosy even without makeup.

Thunder cracked and the scent of rain rolled in. Checking to make sure she was still out like a little kitten, I picked up the pace and flew down the trail. Even as fast as I moved, the storm was unpredictable, and the skies opened up, drenching us. And still, she slept.

She reminded me of Dawson. An atomic bomb wouldn't have woken my brother.

After reaching the porch steps, I slowed down and shook my head, sending droplets of rain flying in every direction. I stopped at the door and frowned. Had she locked it before she left? Dammit, I couldn't remember. If so, she probably had a key in her pocket, but that would mean going into her pocket and getting it. How else would I explain how I unlocked her door?

My gaze dipped and ran over her legs. Legs unbelievably long for someone so short...and those shorts were short. Tiny pockets, too.

Yeah, I was not going after that key.

Well past time to deposit her little butt on the swing and get the hell out of here.

Sighing, I went over to the swing and started to put her down, but she snuggled closer. I froze, wondering if she was awake. A quick check told me she wasn't. Again, I went to lay her down, but I stopped this time. What would she think if she woke up here alone?

Why did I care?

"Dammit," I muttered.

Searching the porch frantically as if it held the answers, I finally rolled my eyes and sat, placing her beside me. It made sense that I would stay. I had to know if she had seen me shoot a lightning bolt out of my hand, I reasoned. I kept my arm around her, because knowing my luck, she'd slip out of the swing and crack her head open. Then Dee *would* kill me.

I tipped my head back and closed my eyes. Why had I come over here today? Was it really just boredom? If that was the case, I could've watched the episodes of *Ghost Investigators* I had DVRed. I hadn't really considered what I was doing until I was knocking on her door and it was too late to think about it.

I was an idiot.

Kat murmured something and wiggled closer, pressing her cheek against my chest. She was molded to the entire right side of my body: thigh to thigh. Her hand curled below my hip and I started counting backward from a hundred. When I got to seventy, I found myself staring at her lips.

I really needed to stop staring at her lips.

Her brow wrinkled, lids flickering as if she was having a bad dream. Some ridiculous part of me responded to that—to the minute distress pinching her features, tensing her body. My thumb started to move along her lower back, tracing idle circles. Seconds passed, and she settled right down, her breathing deep and steady.

How long would she sleep? Part of me wasn't bothered by the prospect of sitting here for hours. There was something calming about holding her, but it was also the exact opposite, because every inch of my body was aware of how she fit to my side, of where her hand was, the rise and fall of her chest.

This was peaceful *and* torturous.

Some time later, after what felt like forever and yet not enough time at all, Kat stirred awake. It was a slow process that began with her muscles tensing, relaxing, and then tensing again when she realized what...*who* she was lying on.

My hand stilled, but I didn't move it away. Wasn't like she was going to fall on her face now, but I...I just didn't, and I wasn't at all okay with that. I clenched my jaw.

Kat lifted her head. "What...what happened?"

Oh, you know, shot a pure bolt of energy at a bear and you wilted like a delicate flower at my feet. Then I carried you back like a true gentleman and sat here for God knows how long and just stared at you.

Yep, so not going there.

I pulled my arm free. "You passed out."

"I did?" She scooted back, brushing a mass of hair out of her face. It was then that I realized her hair had come undone at some point. My gaze dropped briefly. As expected, her hair was long and thick, falling over her shoulders.

"I guess the bear scared you," I told her. "I had to carry you back."

"All the way?" She looked disappointed, which made me curious. "What…what happened to the bear?"

"The storm scared it. Lightning, I think. Are you feeling okay?"

Lightning lit the porch, startling her. "The bear was scared of a storm?"

"I guess so."

"We got lucky, then." She glanced down, brows knitting, and when those lashes lifted, I had to force myself to keep breathing normally. There was a quality to those gray eyes—a glimmer that sucked me right in. "It rains here like it does in Florida."

I nudged her knee with mine. "I think you may be stuck with me for a few more minutes." Really, that was a stupid excuse for not leaving. I needed something better—no, what I needed was to leave. Get up and leave. But then she spoke again.

"I'm sure I look like a drowned cat."

I'd almost prefer the drowned cat. "You look fine. The wet look works for you."

She scowled. "Now I know you're lying."

I was a lot of things, but until recently, a liar wasn't one of them. And apparently, I was as unpredictable as the weather, so much so that I had no idea what I was doing until I shifted and wrapped my fingers around her chin, tilting her head toward me.

"I wouldn't lie about what I thought," I said, and that was the truth.

Kat blinked slowly, and my gaze dropped to her lips again. I really, really needed to stop looking at her lips. Muscles tightened at the thought of tasting them. She'd probably clock me in the face and then lay into me with that razor-sharp tongue of hers. Which made me want to grin.

I leaned forward. "I think I understand now."

"Understand what?" she whispered.

My unwilling fascination with her—I got it. She didn't put up with any of my crap. I was surrounded by people who looked to me to have all the answers, to protect them, to never show fear. And so I put on a big front and swaggered around like nothing frightened me. It was exhausting sometimes. But Kat, she saw right through all my bluster and kept me honest. And I liked that...a lot.

A pink flush stained her cheeks. I chased that color with my thumb. "I like to watch you blush."

She sucked in a tiny breath, and it undid me. Pressing my forehead against hers, I pushed it to the limit. This was insanity, but she smelled of peaches and her skin was soft and her lips looked even softer.

I was caught up in a web there really was no escaping. A web of Kat... One I damn guarantee she had no idea she weaved. A naive beauty, and I'd seen a lot in my eighteen years to know that was a rarity. Something to be cherished.

Lightning struck again, and Kat didn't jump at the thunder this time. She was focused in a way that pleased me, pulled at my control, and teased me with what I could never have. Shouldn't even want, but I wanted... God, did I ever want. And if we continued where we were heading, it would get messy. I already knew what happened when Luxen and humans mixed. I had too much responsibility to be fooling around with her. Too much going on...

But I still wanted.

My fingers slipped along the curve of her cheek as my head tilted. I was going to regret this—holy crap was I ever, but I wasn't stopping. Our lips were only a breath away...

"Hey, guys!" Dee called out.

I jerked back, sliding in one fluid movement and putting distance between us on the swing while Kat turned a fierce shade of red. I'd been so absorbed in her, I hadn't heard my sister's car or noticed the storm had passed and the sun was out, shining and all.

Great.

Dee came up the steps, her smile fading as her gaze bounced between us and then narrowed. No doubt she was seeing the faint trace around Kat and wondering how the hell that happened. Then she seemed to focus on what she'd just interrupted.

Her mouth dropped open.

It wasn't often that I surprised her…like this. I grinned. "Hey, there, sis. What's up?"

"Nothing," she said. "What are *you* doing?"

"Nothing," I replied, jumping from the swing. I glanced at a silent, dazed-looking Kat. Her gray eyes were still hazy and wide. Freaking beautiful. Damn, I needed to nip this in the bud right now, before something worse than just a trace happened. I met her gaze. "Just earning bonus points."

Kat went ramrod straight, her eyes flashing and hands curling in her lap as my words sank in.

Ah, there it was—there was the kitten coming out, claws sharpening. The warm, cuddly creature was gone in an instant. I'd done that. Taken her up and slammed her right back down to earth, to reality. That was all me.

I wasn't proud, but at least this way she'd live. We'd all live.

I spun toward the steps, leaving her with my sister, who was staring at me in confusion. I felt like the biggest ass on the planet.

Hell, in the universe.

The sun had set when my bedroom door burst open and Dee whirled in like a tornado, dark hair streaming from behind her and eyes gleaming with excitement.

"What in the world did I interrupt?" she demanded.

I closed the lid on my Mac before Dee could see what I was looking at. "You're back from the colony early."

She danced over to the bed, rising up on the tips of her toes. "Not like that's really important, but if you must know, I think Ethan was just getting super annoyed with me and decided to let me leave." She paused, grinning mischievously. "Plus, they're having some kind of dinner reception for the females who are getting married Tuesday night and I said I'd come back...with Ash."

My brows rose. "Uh, does she know that?"

"Yes. And she's totally ticked off at me, but she can't say no. But that's not important!" She clapped her hands as she rocked back and forth. "What were you doing on the porch with Katy?"

I sat the Mac on my nightstand. "I was sitting out there with her."

Dee's eyes narrowed. "Yeah, duh, but you weren't just doing that. Don't play with me."

Had Kat said more? The urge to ask rushed to the tip of my tongue, but I mentally punched myself in the face. Wasn't going to go there. "I'm not playing with you, sis."

"That's poppycock!"

"Poppycock," I repeated slowly and then laughed. "Are you high?"

She lifted her hand and flipped me off. "You looked like you were about to kiss her."

A muscle thrummed along my jaw as I leaned back

against the headboard, folding my arms behind my head. "I think you are projecting or something."

"While I think Katy is hot, I don't want to make out with her." She winked.

"Glad to hear that," I muttered.

"Ugh, why can't you just admit you were about to do something!" She threw herself onto the bed, shaking the entire frame. Girl looked small but she was like a damn train. "You were going in for the kiss. Your hand was on her chin."

Closing my eyes, I decided the last thing I needed was a blow-by-blow description of how close I came to complete disaster.

"And then add in the fact you made up some lame excuse about keys and bonus points?"

"The bonus points thing wasn't a lie. You used to make me do that all the time," I reminded her.

She punched my leg, causing me to grunt. "Yeah, when I was, like, five years old."

My lips twitched.

"So why did you make up an excuse to hang out with her?" she persisted.

I sighed. "Like I told you when I texted you, I haven't been particularly nice to her and I needed an excuse. Otherwise she would've said no." The last part was definitely not a lie. If I hadn't virtually blackmailed her into going to the lake with me, she would've said no. Tonight? I really hadn't had to say anything. Interesting.

"But why—?"

"Dee," I growled, opening my eyes to find my sister lying on her stomach with her chin in her hands. She was grinning up at me. "Shouldn't you be focused on something a little more important."

She batted her lashes. "I think I am focused on something super important."

I resisted the urge to knock her off the bed. "You can't tell me you didn't notice the trace on her."

"Oh! Yeah. *That*." She tapped pale blue nails against her cheek. "How did that happen?"

For a moment, all I could do was stare at her. Obviously, she wasn't that concerned, which made me fear for her well-being. "We went on a walk—"

"How romantic," she cooed.

My lips turned down at the corners. "It wasn't romantic."

"I think it is," she went on happily. "When Adam and I take walks it always ends with us—"

"If you want Adam to stay alive, I suggest you don't finish that sentence."

She rolled her eyes. "Anyway, so you went on a totally not romantic walk and…"

I was going to knock her off this bed. "And we happened across a bear. It charged us and I had to do something. I didn't think you'd be happy with me if I let a bear maul her to death."

"Gee, you think?"

I mouthed a not very nice four-letter word that included "you" at her.

She giggled. "So how did you explain that one off?"

"Well, the energy kind of knocked her out, and I blamed it on the storm—lightning." I exhaled loudly. "I was lucky."

"*Katy* was lucky."

My gaze shot to her. "How so?"

Dee moved in one fluid motion, sitting cross-legged in less than a second. "That you were there to save her."

It seemed too obvious to point out the fact that she

wouldn't have needed me to protect her if I hadn't dragged her out into the woods in the first place.

"Can I ask you something?" Dee poked my knee with her fingers of death.

I arched a brow. "Do I really have a say in that?"

"No." She flashed a quick grin. "Do you...do you like Katy?"

Every single part of me locked up. My sister waited while a hundred different responses ran through my head. Did I like her? What in the hell kind of question was that? I lowered my arms and sat up a little, throwing one leg off the bed.

"Daemon?"

I didn't look at my sister as I stood. "No."

"What?" she whispered.

"You heard me." I rubbed my palm over my jaw, sighing as I walked over to the dresser and picked up the remote. "Look, I'm sure she's a great girl and friend, and if she wasn't...human, she'd be about three thousand times awesome, but no, I don't like her." Dee was quiet as I returned to the bed, and she didn't look up when I sat back down. Her lips were pursed, and now I felt like shit. "Want to watch a movie?"

"Sure." She smiled, but it didn't reach her eyes, and I wished I hadn't even looked at her. "Do you think she'll be safe at least? With the trace?"

"Yeah. I've got this." The pressure was back on my shoulders, and I flipped on the TV. "As long as she stays put for the next couple of days, she'll be fine."

Dee moved until she was sitting against the headboard, shoulder to shoulder with me. After a moment, she pulled her knees to her chest and wrapped her arms around her legs. I started flipping through On Demand and she sighed morosely.

I opened my mouth and then closed it. Another moment passed and I lowered the remote. "I lied."

She turned to me. "About what?"

"The first question you asked." I didn't look at her as I shook my head, staring at the list of movies on the screen. "I lied, just a little."

# 8

**"I** was beginning to wonder if you were becoming a recluse or something." Andrew sat on the narrow railing surrounding the raised deck, his legs dangling into empty space. A near-empty bottle of beer was perched on the railing beside him, and if he'd been human, he would've been the poster child for the dangers of underage drinking. "Or if you just didn't like us anymore."

Sitting in a chair with my feet kicked up on the patio table, I smirked. "It would be the latter."

Andrew snickered. "You're a jackass."

I didn't disagree with that statement.

Across from me, Adam mirrored my same position, except he was staring out into the woods, a thoughtful expression on his face. Sometimes being around the brothers was hard, because it reminded me of how it used to be with Dawson.

Andrew and Adam were identical in physical appearance, both tall and strong, blue eyed and blond, but their personalities couldn't be any more different. They really were like Dawson and I used to be. I was the hothead. Dawson was the calm one. Andrew was the asshole and Adam was the peacekeeper.

Not that I'd ever tell Dee, but I was glad it was Adam she appeared to be taking more seriously. I really didn't know how much their relationship had progressed, and I tried not to think about it, but yeah, I was glad. Andrew was too much like me.

As I watched Andrew finish off his beer, my mind wandered. Coming over to their place Tuesday evening didn't feel right, not when Kat had a trace on her, but Andrew had been right. I hadn't seen the guys in a while and Dee had told me that Kat was staying home. She would be okay there, since it was doubtful an Arum would get that close to the colony, and as long as she wasn't out running around publically with Dee, endangering her, I really shouldn't care.

I *didn't* care.

Dee's question had been haunting me. *Do you like her?* I'd said no, and I had lied a little. What I felt for Kat was complicated and twisty. I liked her, but I didn't. I also liked wolves, but I didn't want one as a pet.

Picking up my bottle of water, I took a long swig of it as Adam glanced over at me. "Do you know when the girls are getting back?"

I raised one shoulder. "Don't know."

"Ash was pissed." Andrew chuckled as he looked over his shoulder. "She said she was leaving as soon as Dee finished stuffing her face with food."

"Gotta love a girl with an appetite," Adam murmured, lips tipping up at one corner.

My eyes narrowed on him.

Adam's grin faded. "Or not."

"Sounds about right," I commented, idly spinning the bottle of water.

Andrew leaned backward and flipped over, landing on his feet like a damn cat. He twisted around, picking up the empty bottle. "I need another drink." He looked over in my direction. "You?"

"I'm good."

"Pansy ass."

I flipped him off.

He chuckled as he disappeared into the house, closing the door behind him. My gaze traveled behind the deck, to the heavy edge of the forest. From our vantage point, I could see the tips of Seneca Rocks. I liked it out here. Like where Matthew lived, there really weren't any other houses nearby, and it was almost always quiet. The only noise came from the wildlife, and as night was steadily falling, the hum of crickets increased. I looked up. Darker storm clouds were starting to roll in.

"I know," Adam announced.

Frowning, I looked over at him. "Know about what?"

He glanced at the door before he continued. "I know about the girl who moved in next door."

The foot I'd been moving stilled. "I'm going to take a wild guess and say Dee told you?"

Adam nodded as he leaned back, folding his arms. "Dee really likes her."

"Hmm."

"I haven't said anything to Ash or Andrew. Not planning to, because you know how they're going to react. I'm guessing Matthew knows?" When I nodded, his thoughtful expression returned. "Got to admit, though, I'm kind of surprised you haven't said anything."

I sat the bottle on the table. "Don't know why you'd think I'd actually bring it up. Not like I sit around and think about the girl."

Adam cocked his head to the side, his grin slow to appear. "Well, I wasn't insinuating that you sit around and think about her, but normally, you'd be bitching to anyone who'll listen about Dee making friends with a human girl."

A muscle flexed in my jaw. "It's not important."

"It kind of is," he replied.

"And I don't sit around bitching about things."

Adam's shoulders shook with a silent laugh, and I started to tell him exactly what I thought about that when my phone vibrated in my pocket. Stretching to the side, I yanked it out of my pocket. Dee's name flashed across the screen.

I answered it. "You done with that dinner thing already?"

Adam perked up across from me, and I decided I really didn't like that. "I think we have a problem," Dee started, her voice pitched high.

Pulling my feet off the table, I tensed. "What kind of problem?"

"Is there any chance that Kat is with you?" she asked, sounding hopeful.

A ball of dread settled in my stomach like lead. "No. No chance in hell."

"Oh no. I just got back to the house and her car is not in the driveway. So I stopped over to just be sure she wasn't there and no one answered." She paused, her breath ragged over the phone. "She's left the house, and she has a trace on her."

I was standing without even realizing it, walking over to the edge of the deck. My voice was low. "You said she was staying in tonight."

"I know." Her voice rose. "That's what she told me, but she didn't."

"Dammit." My hand tightened around the phone. "Of course she didn't."

"Is everything okay?" Adam asked from behind me.

I ignored him as Dee spoke up. "Don't be mad at her, Daemon. She doesn't know it's not safe for her out there right now. She has no idea. This isn't her fault."

Her fault or not didn't matter. It was still a huge pain in my ass.

"I'm going to go and see if I can find her. I bet she's at the library and I will—"

"No, you won't. You aren't going anywhere. You keep your butt at home." Anger rushed over me, but underneath that, dread was expanding. "I'll take care of it."

"Daemon—"

"I'll text you as soon as I find her." I resisted the urge to turn the phone into a missile. "I'm sure she's fine. Just...just stay home and don't worry."

Hanging up, I dropped the phone back in my pocket. "I've got to go."

Adam stood, concern etched into his features. He already had his phone in his hand, and I hoped like hell Dee knew to keep the whole trace thing to herself. "Is everything okay?" he asked.

"Yeah." I placed my hands on the railing. "Tell Andrew I'll catch up with him later."

I vaulted over the railing, dropping a good fifteen feet below, landing in a crouch. I rose and took off toward the front of the house. I almost started to go past my SUV, because I could get to the library faster on foot, but how would I explain that to Kat when I found her?

Hell.

Pivoting around, I hurried toward my car and climbed in. Turning the engine on, I threw the SUV into reverse, navigating it around the cars and trees. The drive into town felt like it took an eternity, and I had to have gotten behind every slow-moving ass on the highway. Fat drops of rain splattered off the windshield. Since it started raining, it appeared no one could drive more than twenty miles an hour. My hands clenched the steering wheel until my knuckles bleached white. Anger rolled through me like the storm brewing outside.

I was angry at Kat for not staying put, furious with myself for putting her in a position where I was going to have to search her ass down and come up with some lame-ass reason why I was there.

And pissed off that I hadn't been home to catch her ass leaving.

When I made it into Petersburg, I was ready to run over a small village with my SUV, and since parking was a bitch in the evening and I wasn't in a hurry or anything, I ended up having to leave the car three blocks over, parked behind a diner.

There was a lot of traffic on the main streets, so I had to watch myself. The rain was tapering off and the street lamps were flickering on as I headed down the sidewalk, toward the town library. My mood was dark, matching the clouds ahead, and when I spied the library and didn't see her car, I was ready to destroy something.

Either she had already left or she'd never been here. There was only one other place to check, a less trafficked side road that was behind the library. I picked up my pace, cutting across the narrow lawn in front of the building, and rounded the side.

An icy chill exploded along the base of my neck and powered down my spine, kicking my instinct to shift into my true form into overdrive. The dread exploded like a buckshot.

I could feel *them*, tainting the air and the ground, cloaking the narrow street in unnatural, thick shadows. My brain clicked off and I picked up speed, becoming a blur as I cleared the side of the library. I spotted Kat's car. A light was on inside, but I didn't see her.

The presence of an Arum grew stronger.

Shooting across the road, I came up on her car and I felt it—the oily thickness in the air nearly choking me. Then I saw it in its human form, but the edges of it were shaded out, transparent like dark smoke. I didn't see Kat, but it had something—*someone*—on the ground, and I knew without seeing her that it was Kat.

And it could already be too late.

This…this was my fault.

The rage and dread whirled through me like a hurricane, and I had no idea how I managed to stay in my human form as I grabbed the Arum by its shoulder. My hand sunk a few inches into it, and then I had ahold of its bone and muscle. I yanked back hard, lifting the Arum into the air and tossing it several feet to the side. I caught a brief glimpse of Kat, and my fury tasted like death in the back of my throat.

The thing twisted in midair, turning to nothing more than shadows before consolidating rapidly into a human mass as it landed on its feet. I shot toward it, catching the bastard in the stomach with my shoulder. It cried out and then pushed back, shoving its hand toward my chest. A curse exploded out of me as I staggered back a step. The arm turned transparent, and I knew what it was going to try to do. Feed.

Yeah, not going to happen.

I spun out of the way, avoiding its grip. Moving as fast as a cobra striking, I grabbed ahold of the Arum and tossed him over my shoulder. He landed near Kat, stunned for a moment.

A soft whimper rattled me. Kat was hurt.

Before I could process this new fear, the Arum popped to its feet. The combination of blond hair and pale skin washed the thing out, and as it charged me, dark shadows blossomed under the thin layer of skin. I caught the Arum by the throat, lifting him into the air.

A series of coughs came from the direction of Kat, and I cursed as I power-bombed the asshole into the road. Asphalt cracked. Tiny rocks that were knocked loose flew into the air.

Hatred bled into the pale blue gaze that met mine, so much cold hatred. We rolled farther away, into the shadows. He landed a punch. I landed more. Taking out the Arum in public like this was risky, but I needed to end this and I needed...I needed to check on her.

Lifting my arm, I brought my hand down onto the Arum's chest as I summoned the Source. Energy, pure and raw and as powerful as a solar flare, burned down my arm. An intense whitish-red light erupted from my hand, flowing into the Arum.

Time froze for a moment as the light washed over the creature, seeping into its chest cavity, beyond its skin, and invading every cell. Bright white light washed over its eyes, chasing after the shadows lurking under its skin.

I rocked off the Arum, just in the nick of time, too. The pale skin disappeared, replaced by a smooth onyx shell. The creature stilled for a moment, its mouth hanging open in a silent scream, and then it exploded into a million wispy fragments that floated up, disappearing into the sky.

The charge backed up into the environment around us. Streetlamps exploded, casting the entire street into darkness. Breathing heavily, I took a step back and looked over to Kat. She was lying on her stomach awkwardly, nearly facedown in the road. Something about that ripped through me.

I crossed the distance between us in a heartbeat, kneeling beside her as I reached out, placing my hand on her shoulder. A soft moan radiated from her, and that tearing feeling deep inside me increased.

"It's okay. He's gone. Are you okay?" Damn. That was a stupid question. She started to lift her head, and I saw the angry red mark on her cheek, like a bright strawberry. Her left eye was swelling. Anger punched through me. She was hurt and in pain, that much was obvious, and her breathing didn't sound right. There was a concerning wheezing quality to it. I wasn't a doctor, but it didn't sound good.

"Everything is okay," I told her, and that was a lie, because as I spoke those three words, I did something so incredibly reckless I might as well have thrown myself in front of a speeding truck.

She was hurt, and instinctively, I knew I could fix some of it, even all of it. I'd never done it before. It was so forbidden, so taboo for our kind it was barely spoken of. One of our most remarkable attributes, the one thing that the Arum could not assimilate after feeding, was our regenerative ability. We healed rapidly from almost all injuries…and we could heal others.

I reached out to the Source, pulled it down inside myself, and then I pushed it into Kat, guiding the light to her chest and her raspy lungs. If anyone walked by right now, they'd see our bodies lit up like a lightbulb, and I counted myself ten kinds of foolish, but I didn't stop. Her eyes were closed, but as the energy began to crackle along her skin, her lashes fluttered as if to open, and I ran my hand gently across her eyes and down her cheek, and she relaxed.

Her breathing evened out a little as she slowly turned her head toward me. "Thank you for…" She trailed off.

"Kat," I called to her, concerned. "Are you still with me?"

"You," she whispered.

"Yes, it's me." I moved my hand to her wrist. She jerked her arm back, and I reached for her again. Since I was in for a penny, I might as well go for the whole screwed-up pound. "I can help you."

"No!" she cried out.

I considered ignoring that as I glanced down at her wrist. She was still hurt, but the worst of her injuries, whatever had been affecting her breathing, had healed. I released the Source and stood, exhaling roughly. A thousand thoughts spun through me, all circling back to what in the hell had I done? "Whatever. I'll call the police."

The last thing I wanted to involve was the police, but Kat needed to be looked at by actual medical professionals. Taking a step back, I pulled out my phone and did just that, keeping a wary eye on her. She struggled to sit up, and I stopped myself from helping her. There was a good chance if I touched her again, I'd end up healing her some more, since my impulse control was so awesome at this point.

"Thank…you," she said, voice hoarse after I hung up the phone.

I winced. The trace on her before had been a soft glow, but after healing her, she was lit up like a fucking neon sign. "Don't thank me." I shoved my hand through my hair and then lowered it to my side. Both hands formed fists as I watched her finally sit up. The mark on her face, the swelling in her eye, made me wish the Arum were still alive so I could kill it all over again. "Dammit, this is my fault."

She stared up at me, confusion and something else I couldn't quite pinpoint etched into her face. Frustration doubled inside me. This was my fault. Like a dumbass, I'd traced her on Saturday. I knew there was a chance there were Arum nearby, and I hadn't made sure she stayed home. Then she was attacked, because the Arum saw that damn trace and knew she could lead it back to us—what it really wanted.

"Light—I saw light," she whispered, lowering her gaze.

"Well, they do say there is light at the end of the tunnel."

She shrank back, cringing.

Shit. That was possibly the most asshole thing I could say. I crouched down. "Dammit, I'm sorry. That was thoughtless." I paused. "How bad are you hurt?"

"My throat... It hurts." She lifted a shaky hand and pressed it to her throat, wincing. "So does my wrist. I'm not... sure if it's broken. But there was a flash...of light."

My gaze zeroed in on her wrist. The skin was quickly deepening in color, becoming a purplish red. I didn't think it was broken. There was a good chance I'd fixed that, but she couldn't know that. No one could know that. I drew a deep breath. "It might be broken or sprained. Is that all?"

"All? The man... He was trying to kill me."

"I understand that. I was hoping he didn't break anything important." I glanced at the top of her disheveled head. "Like your skull?"

"No...I don't think so."

"Okay, okay." I stood, looking around. I needed to do damage control. "Why were you out here anyway?"

"I...wanted to go to the library." She paused for a moment. "It wasn't that...late. It's not...like we are in a crime-ridden…city. He said he needed help…flat tire."

My eyes widened as I turned back to her. "A stranger approaches you for help in a dark parking lot and you go and help him? That has to be one of the most careless things I've heard in a long time. I bet you think things through, right? Accept candy from strangers and get into vans with a sign that reads 'free kittens'?"

She made a soft sound as I began to pace.

"Sorry wouldn't have been helpful if I didn't come, now would it?" I said.

"So why were…you out here?"

I stilled, running a hand over my chest. "I just was."

"Geez, I thought you guys were supposed to be nice and charming."

I frowned. "What guys?"

"You know, the knight in shining armor and saving the damsel in distress kind."

Shaking my head, I lowered my hand. "I'm not your knight."

"Okay…" she whispered, pulling her legs up and resting her head on her knees. Everything about her movements looked painful. "Where is he now?"

"He took off. Long gone by now." I started toward her. "Kat…?"

She lifted her head, and when I didn't speak, she lowered her good arm to the ground and started to stand.

"I don't think you should stand." I kneeled again. "The ambulance and police should be here any minute. I don't want you passing out."

"I'm not going…to pass out." As if on cue, the sound of sirens could be heard.

"I don't want to have to catch you if you do." I glanced

down at my hands. The skin had been scraped, but it had already healed "Did...did he say anything to you?"

Her brows knitted as she grimaced "He said...I had a trace on me. And he kept asking...where they were. I don't know why."

Hell. Lowering my chin, I looked over my shoulder. "He sounds like a lunatic."

"Yeah, but...who did he want?"

My attention snapped back to her. "A girl stupid enough to help a homicidal maniac with his *tire*, maybe?"

Her lips thinned. "You're such an ass. Has...anyone ever told you that?"

In that moment, I decided that if she was calling me an ass, she was going to be okay. "Oh, Kitten, every single day of my blessed life."

She stared at me, but I couldn't tell what she was thinking. "I don't even know what to say..."

"Since you already said thank you, I think nothing is the best way to go at this point." I stood. "Just please don't move. That's all I ask. Stay still and try not to cause any more trouble."

Kat frowned and looked like she wanted to say something, but praise all the higher beings in the universe, she remained quiet. The relief was short-lived, because when I glanced down at her, she was shaking so badly her teeth had to be rattling. It was then I realized she was soaked from the rain and shock was probably kicking in.

Pulling off my shirt, I found myself kneeling beside her again. My shirt wasn't the best thing, but it was better than nothing. I carefully pulled it on over her head, keeping the material away from her bruised cheek. I got her limp arms through the holes, and the noodle quality to those arms worried me a little. I glanced up quickly. Her eyes were closed, thick lashes fanning the tops of her cheeks.

"Kat?"

Too late.

She toppled over to the right, and I caught her before she face-planted onto the cement. Her head lolled to the side and her hair, half up and half down, fell across her one unmarred cheek. Holding her against my chest with one arm, I brushed the hair back from her face. My fingers lingered along her jaw just below her ear. The sound of sirens grew closer, but I concentrated on each breath she took, her chest rising and falling steadily.

Kat was out cold.

"Hell," I muttered, staring down at her as I shifted her so the back of her head was cradled in the crook of my arm.

This was becoming a disturbing trend.

# 9

There were few places in this world that I hated as much as hospitals. Luxen didn't get sick—no colds or cancers, no heart disease or strokes. Bumps and bruises could be healed with a touch of a hand. So I avoided these places at all costs.

Tonight it was unavoidable.

I stayed as out of the way as *in*humanly possible, leaning against the wall while Kat's mother flipped her shit. The pea-green curtain fluttered every time someone roamed into the room and back out. The deputies had come and gone, talking to both of us. Robbery gone wrong. I was in the right place at the right time. The police would do everything to try to locate the offender, but good luck there, because there was nothing left of the shithead, but what could I say? I just smiled and nodded and waited for the moment I could get the hell out of here. Actually, I could've already left, but it didn't feel right to do so.

I needed time to think.

My gaze drifted over to the narrow bed. Kat looked tired

when my eyes found her. She was looking out the window, her pale face drawn and weary. The splash of red on her cheek wasn't easy to look at. Neither was her swollen eye. It could've been worse. My touch had sped up the healing process there and most likely repaired more serious injuries related to the imprint on her throat, remarkably similar to fingers. It was faint, but it was hard to look at.

Her arm was in a cast. Torn tendon or something. If she hadn't pulled her arm away, I could've fixed that, too. I mean, why not at this point? The trace was still around her, stronger than before, and I had a feeling it wouldn't be fading anytime soon.

Why in the hell hadn't they given her something for the pain yet?

Kat appeared incredibly small in that bed. Alone with me for a few seconds, she glanced over, and I raised a brow. Her gaze immediately flicked away.

Her mom had disappeared in search of a doctor and returned with a middle-age man, graying at the temples, who was vaguely familiar. The doc—Dr. Michaels—started reading off her chart, telling us things we already knew. He looked in my direction, and again, I was struck with this odd sense that I knew him from somewhere.

Probably around town. It was that small.

Dr. Michaels left after handing over some pain meds, and it was about damn time someone gave her something. Her mother hovered by her bed, and my jaw flexed when I saw the wetness gather in Kat's eyes. The girl… Yeah, she was tough stuff. She'd been holding it together this whole time. I started to close my eyes when I sensed my sister's presence. I'd called her on the way in, and no amount of reasoning had convinced her to stay at the house.

Dee rushed right past me. I chuckled. Glad to see that she was worried about me, because you know, I didn't just fight an Arum or something. "Oh no, Katy, are you okay?"

Kat lifted the injured arm, and damn if she didn't offer a weak smile. "Yes. Just a little banged up."

Dee stared at Kat and then whipped around to me. "I can't believe this happened. *How* could this have happened? I thought you—"

"Dee," I warned.

She straightened, cheeks flushing as she received the silent message. Exhaling raggedly, she turned back to Kat, approaching her bed slowly. "I'm so sorry about this."

"It's not your fault," Kat replied.

My sister sat down, perched on the edge of the bed, distraught and seconds from getting up and kicking me, I'm sure, because she thought this was my fault.

It was.

But not for the same reasons as Dee believed. She was upset that I hadn't gotten to Kat in time, but the truth was, if I'd listened to my own advice and stayed away from her, I never would've traced her in the first place.

They started talking among themselves, and I let my eyes drift closed. Tonight had been... There really weren't any words when it came to the amount of FUBAR that had gone down, and fighting that Arum had drained me. I heard Dee talking about taking Kat home if her mom couldn't, which probably meant I would be the one taking them home.

Ms. Swartz returned, and although Kat was released, there was a huge accident out on one of the highways. Being the nurse on call that night, her mom couldn't leave, but Dee convinced her that we would not only take her home but watch out for signs of a concussion.

Thanks, Dee.

To be honest, I was...okay with that. I really didn't want either of them out there alone right now. Not until that trace was gone. My jaw tightened.

Because if there was one Arum, there were always three more. Luxen were always born in sets of three, so Arum always hunted in fours.

Dee left the ER room to grab a snack, and when I opened my eyes, Kat's stare was fixed on me, but something was off about it. Her eyes were glassy. Pain meds must be kicking in.

I pushed off the wall, making my way toward her. She closed her eyes. "Are you going to insult me again? Because I'm not up to...pear for that."

My lips twitched. "I think you mean par."

"Pear. Par. Whatever." Those heavy lashes lifted.

The bruises and red marks kept drawing my attention. "Are you really okay?"

"I'm great." She yawned. "Your sister acts as if this is her fault."

"She doesn't like it when people get hurt," I said quietly, and then as an afterthought, "and people tend to get hurt around us."

Her unsteady gaze met mine. "What does that mean?"

Dee returned at that moment, grinning. "We're good to go, with the doctor's orders and all."

Thank God.

I moved to Kat's bed, gingerly getting an arm behind her shoulders, helping her stand. The look she sent me, one of dazed bewilderment, was kind of cute. "Come on, let's get you home."

She shuffled two steps and then swayed unsteadily. "Whoa, I feel buzzed."

I glanced at Dee, who raised her brows and said, "I think the pills are starting to work."

"Am I...slurring yet?" Kat asked.

"Not at all." Dee laughed.

Kat hobbled a couple more steps, and I saw this going nowhere fast. Sighing, I scooped her up and then deposited her gently in a wheelchair just outside the ER room. "Hospital rules."

She just stared at me.

We stopped long enough to fill out some paperwork, but Kat wasn't much of a help by that point. The nurses thankfully put most of it aside for her mom to fill out later. Once we got to Dee's car, I picked Kat up and placed her in the backseat.

"I can walk, you know."

I carefully buckled her in, making sure I didn't jar the arm that was in the cast. "I know." Closing the door, I sent Dee a look as I walked around to the other side of the backseat and climbed in. By the time Dee had turned the engine, Kat's head was on my shoulder.

Stiffening, I glanced down at her and then up. Dee wasn't looking at me as she was pulling out of the parking spot. Then I glanced back at Kat. This couldn't be entirely comfortable. It sure as hell wasn't for me. Taking a deep breath, I lifted my arm and placed it around her shoulders. She immediately snuggled up, like a little kitten, with the good side of her face.

This was weird.

There were more moments of us being total asshats to each other than there were of us being actually decent, but the fact she'd do this and that I'd let her, actually aid in the process, was very...yeah, weird.

Her breathing deepened, and one of her hands fell to my

thigh, the fingers slowly uncurling. "Kat?" I whispered.

No response.

"Is she awake?" Dee asked from the front.

"Out cold."

Dee let out a shaky breath. "She's going to be okay, right?"

I stared down at Kat, and even in the dark of the car, I could see her scratched-up cheek. "Yeah, she'll be fine."

"She said she was going to stay at home… I could still see it," she said.

"I know." We'd both known the trace was still there, and no one was kicking their own ass more than me. I paused. "Don't worry. I'm not going to let anything happen this time. I swear."

"It's not your fault. I shouldn't have said that in the ER. You didn't know this was going to happen."

I didn't know exactly, but it hadn't come out of left field either. We all knew there was a chance. It was why Dee had tried to convince her to stay home tonight.

"You did something, didn't you?" Dee asked quietly. "It's stronger now."

"I didn't…mean to." A few strands of Kat's hair fell across her cheek. I brushed them back. "It just happened. Shit."

Dee didn't speak again until she hit the highway. "Be honest with me. How badly was she hurt?"

"I don't know." I watched Kat's hand twitch against my leg. "I think… I think it was pretty bad. She seemed to have trouble breathing. That Arum was going to kill her."

"Oh God," Dee whispered.

Looking out the window, I watched the darkened trees blur past, broken up every few moments by headlights. "We…

I just need to be more careful."

Dee didn't respond for a long moment. "Adam called. He knew something was up when you left the house. I told him—"

"I know you told him about Kat. He said something tonight." I dragged my gaze from the window, finding Dee's in the rearview mirror. "I'm going to have to tell them."

She sucked in a sharp breath. "Adam doesn't care, but…"

Yeah, she didn't need to elaborate. Ash and Andrew would most definitely have a problem with it, but I'd killed an Arum tonight. Couldn't keep the lid on this jar of shit any longer.

We didn't speak the rest of the way, and Kat didn't wake up when we pulled in front of the house. She only stirred, murmuring under her breath when I unbuckled her and carefully drew her out of the car, once again in my arms and tucked against my chest.

"I got her purse and keys," Dee announced, closing the driver's door. "I'm going to unlock the door. You got her?"

"Of course."

Dee's gaze met mine, and I didn't want to know what she was thinking in that moment, but she whirled around and darted across the driveway, toward Kat's house. Twisting at the waist, I kneed the car door shut. I turned, shifting Kat in my arms.

She stirred, sliding her hand up my chest to my shoulder. A shiver rushed over my skin. Wrong as hell. Her lashes lifted, and I stopped a few feet from the car as the corners of her lips lifted up, too. Silvery moonlight glanced over her cheek. "Hey," she whispered.

"Hey."

Her unfocused gaze drifted over my face. "You…you are really pretty."

A surprised laugh burst out of me. "Thanks, Kitten."

Yeah, she was totally high and out of it, but her smile widened as her eyes closed. I wasn't high or out of it when I whispered back to her, "So are you."

'd never been in Kat's house before, and I don't even know why it felt weird to be inside. Maybe it was because she was passed out. I hadn't investigated the house as I followed Dee into a similar foyer and through a doorway to the right. Dee had turned on a lamp, and soft yellow light enveloped the living room.

Books.

Books were everywhere.

Stacked by the corner of the couch, in a neat pile of five, spines facing out. Two were on the coffee table. One had a shiny bookmark poking out of the top. Three more were on the end table. Another was on the TV stand, and it too had a bookmark shoved in it. Was she reading two books at once? More?

I could barely read one at a time.

"I think we should stay down here," Dee said, sitting in a worn recliner by the window. "Just in case something is wrong."

Looking at Dee, I turned and stared at the couch, the only other available seating. I carried Kat over to the couch and laid her down. I sat beside her, my gaze crawling up to the slow-moving ceiling fan.

Dee talked for a little while, but she quickly fell asleep,

virtually leaving me solely responsible for Kat, which was a bad idea in general, since I was doing a real bang-up job of that.

I dropped my elbow on the arm of the couch and rested my cheek in my palm, watching Kat's shoulders rise and fall steadily. I could've turned on the TV, but I didn't want to wake her or my sister.

Flicking my wrist, I managed to turn off the lamp without destroying it with a quick zip of energy. As the darkness surrounded us, the image trying to stir formed in my thoughts. I doubted I would ever get the scene of that Arum standing over a broken Kat out of my head or forget the raspy sound of panic in her voice when she hadn't realized it was me at her side.

Yeah, tonight was going to linger.

I must've dozed off at some point, because daylight now filtered through the living room as Kat snuggled her way closer. Her head ended up in my lap, and that wasn't entirely comfortable. I shifted her carefully, but damn, I may not be human, but I *was* a guy.

Kat slept soundly, her injured arm curled against her chest and her lips slightly parted. I lifted my head, working a kink out of my neck. It was then that I realized my hand was resting on her curved hip.

Huh.

I had no recollection of doing that. Must've been in my sleep. I didn't move my hand, though. My entire being focused on that hand—which was only slightly better than focusing on where her head was. Through the thin denim of her jeans, the curve of her hip was soft. Warm. I imagined that this was what couples did, though Ash and I were never like this. She could get touchy. So could I, but this? Nah, I don't think we'd ever done anything like this.

Why was I even thinking about that with Kat?

Lack of sleep was getting to me.

Kat suddenly stiffened, and my gaze flew to her face. Her lashes were up. I couldn't see her eyes, but her chest rose sharply. Was she in pain? "You okay, Kitten?"

"Daemon?" Her voice was hoarse, throaty with sleep and sort of, okay, really kind of sexy. "I... Sorry. I didn't mean to sleep on you."

"It's okay," I told her and helped her sit up. Her face was too pale and the purplish bruise around her eye pissed me off. I didn't even want to check out her neck at this point. "Are you okay?" I repeated, eyeing her closer.

Her gaze found mine. "Yeah. You stayed here all night?"

"Yeah." Seemed pretty obvious.

Kat looked at Dee and then swallowed. She lifted the arm in the cast but lowered it back to her lap as she slowly refocused on me. I couldn't zero in on what she was thinking. She looked shocked. Confused. Sleepy. Cute.

Goddammit with the cute shit.

I needed to focus. "Do you remember anything?"

She nodded and then winced. "I was attacked last night."

"Someone tried to mug you." I resisted the urge to ask if she was okay yet again.

Her brows knitted. "He wasn't trying to mug me."

Hell. "Kat—"

"No." She started to stand up, but I circled my arm around her waist, keeping her in place. I didn't want her standing too quickly and falling, cracking her head open, and bleeding all over her precious books. "He didn't want my money, Daemon. He wanted *them*."

Dammit. I stiffened, thoughts racing. "That doesn't make any sense."

"No shit." She frowned down at her injured arm. "But he kept asking about where *they* were and about a trace or something."

"Clearly the guy was insane," I said, keeping my voice low while I willed her to brush it off as such. "You realize that, right? That he wasn't right in the head? Nothing he said means anything."

"I don't know. He didn't seem crazy."

"Trying to beat the crap out of a girl isn't crazy enough for you?" I asked, shaking my head. "I'm curious what you think is crazy."

Her frown deepened. "That's not what I meant."

"Then what did you mean?" I twisted toward her, careful not to jar her arm. "He was a random lunatic, but you're going to make it bigger than it is, aren't you?"

Kat drew in a sharp breath. "I'm not making this anything. Daemon, that wasn't a normal lunatic."

Frustration thinned my patience. The thing was, she was right. There had been nothing normal about the "man" who had attacked her, but I couldn't let her know that. I needed her to drop this. "Oh, you're an expert on crazy people now?"

"A month with you and I feel I have a master's degree in the subject." She glared at me as she scooted away. She swayed a little.

"You okay?" I touched her good arm. "Kat?"

She shook my hand off, good and angry. "Yeah, I'm okay."

I looked away, tense. She didn't need my shit right now. Obviously she wasn't up for a throw-down between us, and I was actually, legitimately worried about her. She looked worn the hell out, but I had to shut this down. "I know you're probably messed up after what happened last night, but don't make this into something it's not."

"Daemon—"

"I don't want Dee worried that there is an idiot out there attacking girls." My jaw hardened and my voice turned icy. "Do you understand me?"

Her lower lip trembled, and seeing that was like taking a kick to the gut. Yeah, I was an ass. I sucked at empathy and sympathy. The whole assimilation into human society the DOD had forced us into really hadn't worked out that well for me, but that didn't mean I enjoyed kicking someone when she was down.

I started to get up, but when I lifted my gaze from her mouth, our gazes locked. In that moment, I wished I had the ability to change someone's thoughts. That was also probably terrible, but I would remove the memory of the assault. Not just to protect what we were and my family, but to also erase those shadows that lingered in her gray eyes. What happened last night was going to haunt her for a long time, I could tell.

From the recliner, Dee yawned loudly, obnoxiously so.

Kat jerked back, looking over at my sister, who apparently had been awake for a while.

"Good morning!" She chirped like a bird and all but slammed her feet onto the floor. "Have you guys been awake long?"

I sighed heavily. "No, Dee, we just woke up and were talking. You were snoring so loudly we couldn't stay asleep any longer."

She snorted like a little pink pig. "I doubt that. Katy, are you feeling…okay this morning?"

"Yeah, I'm a little sore and stiff, but overall okay."

Dee's smile was forced as she reached up, pushing the disheveled waves of hair out of her face.

"I think I'm going to make you breakfast." Without waiting for an answer, she sprang onto her feet and bolted into the kitchen. Doors opened. Pots clanged off one another.

I sighed again.

"Okay," Kat murmured.

Standing, I lifted my arms and stretched, loosening the taut muscles. More pots banged around in the kitchen. Knowing what I had to do, I lowered my arms and faced Kat. "I care more about my sister than I do anything in this universe. I'd do anything for her, to make sure she's happy and she's safe. Please don't worry her with crazy stories."

Kat flinched as pain splashed across her face, and I knew that glimpse of hurt had nothing to do with her physical injuries but everything to do with the coldness radiating from my words. "You're a dick, but I won't say anything to her," she said, her voice barely above a whisper. "Okay? Happy?"

Happy? Our gazes held once more, and I spoke the truth. "Not really. Not at all."

# 10

Kat could no longer be trusted with the whole staying home thing, so when we called a little impromptu meeting of the Luxen kind Thursday night, we did it at our house just to make sure Kat didn't roam off into a snake pit or something.

Dee had spent Wednesday with her, and I continued my creeper status that night by keeping watch over Kat's house. At least I did it from my front porch this time.

Darkness had fallen when the Thompsons and Matthew arrived, everyone piling into the living room. All the lights next door were off, but I knew Kat's mom was home. I was hoping that meant there was little to no trouble Kat could get herself into.

Talking to the Thompsons about Kat was the last thing I wanted to do. Damn. Throwing myself repeatedly off the top of Spruce Knob would be more fun, because this was going to go over like a pile of shit-covered bricks.

I stood in the center of the room, arms folded across my chest, bracing myself. Dee was perched on the edge of a recliner, her hands folded in her lap. Adam was leaning against its arm, and the tense pull of his expression told me he knew why he was here.

Ash was sitting on the couch beside Andrew. Her blonde hair brushed her shoulders as she tipped her head to the side, sighing loudly. My lips twisted into a wry grin. She had no problem letting people know when she was bored or unhappy. Matthew sat on the arm of the couch, back stiff and shoulders straight.

"So what's going on?" Andrew asked, glancing up from the cell in his hand. "The last time we were called together like this, someone died."

My eyes narrowed. Of course, he was talking about Dawson. Not cool.

Ash turned her head to him, blonde brows arched. "Really?"

One shoulder rose. "And?"

Adam sighed. "We need to work on improving your sensitivity later, brother."

"Whatever," muttered Andrew, glancing back at his phone. His finger scrolled across the screen.

Matthew gave a little shake of his head. "What did you want to discuss, Daemon?"

He knew about Kat and he also knew where this conversation was heading, but he was wrangling the convo back to the point at hand. Had to give him props for that. "There is a girl named Kat—"

"Who is incredibly awesome," Dee interjected. "And super nice and smart and—"

"She moved in next door." I cut her off, because frankly none of that mattered. Andrew's fingers stilled over the screen and he looked up, his mouth opening. I went on. "I don't know why the DOD allowed that. Yesterday I had my normal check-in with Vaughn and Lane. I asked them, and Vaughn was the one to answer, giving some lame reason about the government not wanting the house to sit empty for so long. That it was too suspicious."

Ash's gaze sharpened. "Why didn't you tell us about her sooner?"

"Didn't see the point at the time." A muscle along my jaw began to tick, because the look on Ash's face pretty much summed up the amount of BS associated with that statement. "We're talking about it now."

She looked over at Dee. "And let me guess. You're her new best friend?"

Dee met her stare. "So what if I am?"

"I really shouldn't have to explain all the problems with that," Ash retorted. "And I'm sure Daemon has pointed out every one of them."

I had.

"Katy and I are friends," Dee replied, leaning forward in the chair. Beside her, Adam tensed. "That's not going to change, and I'm not going to sit here and let you give me crap about it. It is what it is."

Ash turned wide blue eyes on me. "Daemon—?"

"You heard her." I grinned when Ash's hands curled into fists. Her head was about to spin. "I've been keeping an eye on Kat, getting to know her so we know what we're dealing with."

Andrew snickered. "I bet you have."

I drew in a deep breath and let it out slowly. Didn't work. "You got something to say, bud?"

He raised a shoulder. "I just think 'keeping an eye on her' is code for something else."

"Keeping an eye on her means exactly what it is," Matthew explained, sending Andrew a look of warning. "The fact that the DOD allowed humans to move next door is suspicious. Daemon is smart by trying to gauge if she or her mother is a risk."

Dee frowned. "Are you trying to say that she could somehow be planted there by the DOD?"

"We don't know," Matthew simply said, and while he had a good point, I didn't think that was the case. More like his general paranoia talking. "Anything is possible, is all I am saying."

My sister's frustration was evident in the stubborn line of her jaw. "Katy is not some kind of government spy."

"Well, if she was, we'd be screwed, since I traced her last week." I dropped that bomb, and everyone but Dee reacted as expected. There were curses. Matthew nearly had the Luxen version of a stroke. Ash looked downright murderous.

Adam sat down on the arm of Dee's chair. "How did that happen?"

"There was a bear. It was charging her." I left out the fact we'd gone on a walk, since no one really needed to know that. "I used the Source to scare the animal off. Kat didn't see me do it. She thought it was lightning." I paused. "I didn't have any other option."

"Yeah, you did." Andrew frowned as he placed his cell on the coffee table. "You could've just let the bear eat her ass. Problem solved."

Ash nodded her agreement.

I didn't even bother responding to that. "The point is, she was traced, and the DOD isn't banging down our doors and locking us in cages. Vaughn and Lane acted yesterday like nothing had changed, but I thought you all should know what happened."

"We should have known about this girl when she first moved in," Ash said, voice thinned with anger.

Dee rolled her eyes. "It wasn't your business."

"It's all of our business," Andrew corrected. "The Elders aren't cool with us living outside the colony as it is. After what happened with Dawson, we have to be careful. In other words, don't run around *tracing humans*, dickhead."

I slowly lifted my hand and flipped him off.

Andrew smirked as he leaned back against the couch, shaking his head. "This is just unbelievable. First it's Dawson and—"

"Don't finish that sentence, Andrew. For real," I warned, my chin dipping down. "I'm not Dawson. This isn't the same thing."

When Andrew opened his mouth, his brother wisely stepped in. "Shut it, Andrew. I really don't want to end the night picking you off the floor."

It was my turn to smirk.

Matthew eyed me closely. "Is that all?"

I shook my head as I kept an eye on Andrew. "No. Kat was attacked by an Arum Tuesday night."

"Damn," Matthew muttered, running a hand through his cropped brown hair. "I... Is she okay?"

Surprise flicked through me. I hadn't expected Matthew to care. "Yes. She's okay." The memory of her struggling to get air into her bruised throat surfaced. "She's going to be okay. I killed the Arum, and she doesn't know what it was. She thinks it was a mugger."

Ash stood fluidly and moved to the window overlooking the porch. She didn't say anything, but she was antsy and that was never a good thing.

"The trace is still on her. It should fade in a couple of days, but we need to be on the lookout for the other Arum."

The conversation steered toward patrolling and how Matthew was going to notify the Elders that we had confirmation of Arum in the vicinity. We needed to train some new recruits to help with the doubled patrols, which was my, Adam, and Andrew's job. Yay us. It wasn't long before everything cycled back to Kat and what we were going to do about it.

"I'm handling it with her," I said, pretty much over this conversation.

Andrew looked like he wanted to say something smart, but one look from his brother shut him up. It was Dee who ended up bringing our little meet-and-greet to a screeching halt. "Why don't we just tell her the truth?" she asked.

I stared at her, unsure I had heard correctly.

Matthew stood, turning to Dee. "You cannot be serious."

"Why not?" Dee raised her hands, her expression earnest. "She's a good person, and she's logical. She's not going to freak out or call the media. Frankly, who would believe her? She'll understand. Trust me."

"Dee," Adam said quietly, kneeling beside her. "You can't tell her what we are."

Anger flashed across her face, deepening the hue of her eyes. "I'm telling you, Adam, she can be—"

"Okay, Dee. Let's say she can be trusted and that she doesn't tell anyone," I said, meeting my sister's gaze. "She takes this shit to her grave, but that's not the only problem. You might trust her. That doesn't mean everyone in this room does."

"Namely me," Andrew commented.

"And what do you think will happen if the Elders find out

about Kat knowing the truth?" I persisted, hoping to reason with Dee on a different level. Ash finally faced us again, her expression blank as she watched us. "Or what do you think the government will do? They don't know her. They have no reason to trust her. She'll disappear. Hello. Bethany, anyone?"

Dee sucked in a sharp, audible breath at the reminder of our brother's human girlfriend who "disappeared" along with him last year.

"You don't want to put her in that position, do you?" I asked. "Because that's what you're also risking by telling her the truth."

For a moment, she held my gaze but then lowered it. She shook her head. "No. I wouldn't want to risk that."

A little bit of relief coursed through me. At least I didn't have to worry about her telling Kat the truth.

Ash folded her slender arms across her chest. "I can't believe you."

Dee glanced up. "What?"

"You have no problem risking our safety, but you worry about hers? Like we mean absolutely nothing?"

"That's not what I feel or what I've said," Dee argued as she glanced back and forth between us. "We can take care of ourselves. And Katy wouldn't throw us in front of a bus. That's all I was trying to say."

I didn't step in as they continued to argue, because Dee needed to wise up. She needed to hear what Ash was saying. Not that it really changed anything. I trusted that Dee wouldn't tell Kat the truth, but she wouldn't stay away from her.

I walked the Thompsons out while Matthew remained inside, talking to Dee. Probably lecturing her, so there was a good chance I was going to be out here a while. Standing on the porch, I watched Adam and Andrew cross the lawn toward their car. The latter was eyeing Kat's house like he wanted to nuke it.

Andrew might be a problem.

"Daemon?"

Twisting around, I found Ash standing there. "Hey."

"I'm sorry about being such a bitch to your sister in there."

I grinned. "No you're not."

She glanced up and to the right, and then laughed. "Okay. You're right. I'm not. She needed to hear it." Two car doors shut. The brothers were waiting for her. "But I'm surprised. I never thought you'd be the one to mess up."

"Well, if I was perfect all the time, no one else would have a chance."

Ash arched a brow and ignored what I said. "How exactly have you been keeping an eye on her?"

Warning bells started going off. I knew what she was getting at, but what the hell? Ash and I had broken up a while ago. Sure, we messed around like exes do from time to time, but she knew the score and even set the rules. "Not sure what you mean by that question?"

Her smile was sugary sweet and sharp as glass. "I think you know exactly what I mean." There was a pause, and I pictured her sharpening her fangs on my bones. "You haven't come around in a couple of weeks. I'm betting if I asked Dee when that girl moved in, it's going to fall around that same time. What do you have to say about that?"

Laughing under my breath, I looked away, my gaze narrowing on the car. "What do I have to say about that? Well, if it were actually your business when it came to what I do, which it's not, I'd have to say you are way off the mark when it comes to why I haven't been around. The reasoning hasn't changed. You know that."

She appeared to mull that over. "Yeah, you don't see us long-term, but that's never stopped us from spending some one-on-one time together."

"She has nothing to do with that."

Ash stopped at the top of the porch steps, half turned away. She wasn't smiling anymore as she looked over her shoulder at me. Challenge burned in her cobalt gaze.

A challenge I had no intention of meeting.

"Prove it," she said.

I stared at the two Luxen males who rarely ventured out of the colony. They weren't very much older than me, but they stood in front of me like two fresh recruits about to enter the marines.

"We're r-ready to begin patrolling," one said, looking everywhere but at my eyes. Yeah, I was going to have to do a hard pass on this guy being ready.

Beside me, Adam chuckled as he eyed the two guys. "An Arum would eat you alive, spit you back out, and then suck you down like a smoothie."

The other Luxen blanched, and I thought he might hurl.

I sighed.

Helping prepare these two asshats on how to patrol for Arum and not get killed in the process was not how I wanted to spend my afternoon.

Especially when Kat was with Dee, and even though I'd asked Dee to make sure they stayed home, since Kat was virtually a glow stick, I knew that my sister ultimately did whatever she wanted.

As did Kat.

But stepping in and making sure members of the colony were able to help with the doubling of patrols would keep them both alive, so I was going to have to deal. And really, it wasn't that bad if I was being honest with myself. I got to be in my true form, and damn, that was like stripping off clothes on a too-hot day. There was nothing like the wind glancing off your essence when you hit speeds that broke the sound barrier. Superman had nothing on a Luxen.

Just thinking about it got my heart pumping.

"This is boring," muttered Andrew.

I smirked.

It had also been damn amusing to drag Adam and Andrew along to help out. Neither wanted to be there. Adam stayed relatively quiet as we ran the newbies around the whole damn mountain, pushing them to run harder and faster. Andrew bitched the entire time. No big surprise there.

The one who looked like he was going to puke stepped forward. I think his name was Mitchell. Maybe Mikey. I was going to go with Mitchell. "I know we're not as strong or fast as any of you, but we are ready."

"Yeah, you're about ready to die," Andrew replied, snorting.

I shot him a warning look. "Way to be motivational."

He flipped me off. "Whatever."

Stepping forward, I clapped my hand on Maybe Mitchell's shoulder. "It's not just about being fast and strong. It's about focusing and preparing for the worst. It's about outsmarting the enemy and anticipating their next move."

"But being fast and strong helps," Andrew chimed in, and I thought maybe I should've left his ass back at the house. "Like I'm stronger than Daemon."

"What?" I dropped my hand and turned around, arching a brow. "Are you on drugs?"

"High on life, man." He winked. "And I'm totally stronger than you."

I chuckled. "If you sincerely believe that, then you *are* high."

"Huh." Andrew shot Adam a look as he swaggered up to me. I watched him snatch up a small rock. "You see that tree over there?" He pointed at an ancient oak several yards away. "I bet I can throw this rock right through the middle."

"And you think I can't?"

"I know you can't." Andrew turned to Maybe Mitchell and his nameless buddy. "What do you think, guys?"

They looked nervous, not wanting to answer.

"I bet Andrew can do it," Adam said, shoving his hands into the pockets of his jeans. "And I bet you can't."

They were out of their damn minds. "You're going to make me embarrass you."

"I'll take that risk." Andrew tossed the rock up and caught it. "It's a bet, then?"

Why the hell not? I nodded and waved my hand toward the distant tree. "By all means."

"Perfect." Andrew took several steps back and squinted at the huge oak. A second later, he slipped into his true form and let the rock fly.

He didn't throw that rock like a human would. Using the Source, he turned it into a damn missile. It flew through the air faster than the eye could track. Bark splintered when the rock made contact and embedded deep.

Maybe Mitchell let out an exclamation of wonder.

Andrew grinned as he faced me. "Beat that."

I snorted as I picked up a rock that was smaller than my palm. "Easy. And I can do it without even switching forms."

"You know what Dee was telling me the other day?" Adam asked as I stepped back. "It's real interesting."

Ignoring him, I lifted my right arm. The two tools from the colony exchanged looks. The Source rippled down my arm.

Adam continued. "She was saying that Katy ran into Simon, that footballer at school, at the store and thought they made a cute couple. She thinks he'll ask Katy out, too, and you know what happens after a date with that Romeo jock... Someone will be getting—"

I looked at him sharply as I let go of the rock. Adam better not be suggesting what I was pretty sure he was. The only thing Simon looked good with was my fist, sure as hell not Kat.

The twist of Adam's lips told me he was lying. Kat hadn't run into that dumbass.

Glancing back at the tree, I cursed. That tiny moment of distraction cost me and screwed up my aim. The rock had zoomed past the tree, missing it by a mile. Dammit.

Adam laughed as he elbowed his brother. "See, guys, focus actually is as important as strength."

I lifted my hand and flipped them off. Both burst into laughter, and I rolled my eyes as I bent, picking up another rock. This one was about the size of my hand. I turned to them. "I'm not going to miss this time, and I won't be aiming for the trees."

My threat made them laugh all the harder. I scowled as I

turned away. At least the two asshats from the colony weren't laughing. They looked scared. A heartbeat passed and then I spun, throwing the rock.

Adam darted to the left, narrowly avoided taking a direct hit. "What the hell?" he shouted, eyes narrowed. "You could've messed up this gorgeous face."

Tipping my head back, it was now my turn to laugh. "I think you need to look in the mirror if you think that's gorgeous."

"Ha," Andrew said, grinning.

"We're identical." Adam shook his head at his twin. "He's insulting both of us, you idiot."

Grinning, I wiped my hands on my jeans, but the humor quickly faded as realization set in, slamming into me with the force of a speeding bullet. The mere mention of Kat's name had distracted me, pulled away my focus. This time it was just a stupid bet, but what if it had been something more serious, like if an Arum had been around?

People could die.

Closing my eyes, I swore under my breath. This thing with Kat…it was getting ridiculous, and it was unacceptable.

Completely unacceptable.

# 11

I saw Kat on and off over the next couple of days, usually when I was heading out to my car, and each time, the trace was getting fainter and fainter—thank God.

Whenever she saw me, she seemed to want to speak to me. She would stop or head in my direction, but we didn't talk. Mainly because I wasn't having that. I needed to keep an eye on her to make sure another Arum didn't snatch her up or endanger her, but there needed to be distance between us. That day at training had proven how just the mention of her name could put everyone at risk. She made me weak.

So, *obviously*, that was the only reason I'd gone to Smoke Hole Diner on Sunday afternoon. The trace on Kat had been pale, like a flickering candle creating a whitish glow, so there had been no stopping Dee. From what I'd gathered, she'd dragged Kat into town, loaded her up with school supplies, and then introduced her to Smoke Hole Diner.

I followed them. I wasn't taking any more chances.

Dee had appeared surprised by my presence and Kat had

been… Well, she had been annoyed that I had provoked her, and then she had tried to thank me. That was the last thing she needed to do, since the cast on her arm and the bruises on her face would've never happened if I hadn't taken her for a walk that day.

My time at the diner had been short-lived. I'd also been followed. By Ash, who for some reason had been under the impression that we were supposed to meet there. Guess I missed that memo. None of that had turned out well. The moment Ash realized Kat was *that* Katy, I ended up having to drag her fired-up butt out of the diner and had spent the better part of Sunday talking Ash off the ledge.

Ash was still pissed on Monday, according to Andrew.

Needless to say, I wasn't in the greatest mood when I left my house early Tuesday evening and went for a run in the nearby woods. I stayed out there in the muggy August weather until sweat slicked my skin and I'd burned off as much energy as possible.

On the way back, I decided I could go for a gallon of ice cream. I doubted there was any in the house. The moment ice cream was brought in, Dee consumed it like she was starving.

Jogging up the driveway, I slowed as the houses came into view. My gaze went straight to Kat's house. The porch wasn't empty. I reached into my pocket and pulled out my phone, tapping the screen to turn off the music blaring through the earbuds.

Kat was sitting on the swing, her head bowed and her features pinched. In her hands was a thick hardcover book. A light breeze tossed into her face a strand of her hair that wasn't clipped back. She absently knocked it out of her way. The sun hadn't set yet, but the light was waning and it was still as humid as a bath in hell. Reading couldn't be easy in those conditions, but she was oblivious to the world as I wrapped the headphones cord around my phone.

She had no idea I was even there. I could easily slip into my house unnoticed. She was safe out here. The trace was barely visible now, having faded even more in the hours since I'd last seen her. There was no reason for me to stop or hang around outside. Distance. There needed to be an ocean's worth of distance between us.

So of course I walked my ass right to her house.

Kat glanced up when I reached the steps to the porch, her gaze widening when she spotted me.

"Hey," I said, sliding my phone in my pocket.

She didn't immediately respond. Oh no, she was too busy checking me out, which pleased me to hell. Her gaze dropped, wandering over my bare chest and stomach. Her throat worked as she looked away, cheeks turning pink, and she tilted her head to the side and gave a little shake. "Hey."

Leaning against the railing, I folded my arms. "You reading?"

Her hands tightened around the edges of the book. "You running?"

"Was," I corrected.

"Funny," she said, pulling the book to her chest. The cast on her arm stood out starkly. "I *was* reading."

"Seems like you're always reading."

Her nose wrinkled. Cute. "How would you know?"

I lifted a shoulder. "I'm surprised Dee isn't with you."

"She's with her...her boyfriend." The corners of her lips slipped down. "You know, I had no idea she had a boyfriend until today. She never mentioned him before."

That made me laugh. "That will do wonders for Adam's self-esteem."

"Right?" Her grin was a flash and it was fleeting. "It's weird."

"What is?"

She cuddled the book closer, like it was a security blanket. "I've spent all this time with Dee and I had no idea she was seeing someone. She never mentioned it. It's just weird."

"Then maybe you're not as good of friends as you think."

Her eyes narrowed as she cut me a look. "Wow. That was nice of you to say."

I shrugged again. "Just pointing out the obvious."

"How about you go point out the obvious elsewhere," she snapped, lowering her book. "I'm busy."

A grin appeared on my lips. The claws were out. "Reading does not equate to being busy, Kitten."

The bow-shaped lips parted. "You did not just say that."

My grin spread.

"That is… It's *sacrilegious*."

I chuckled as I unfolded my arms. "I don't think that's what that word means."

"It is to book lovers all around the world!" Kat narrowed her eyes. "You don't understand."

"Nope." I lifted myself up and sat on the railing.

She sighed. "And you are also not going anywhere."

"Nope."

Looking down at her book, she slowly pulled a bookmark out of the front and marked the page she'd been reading. Kat closed the book and lowered it to her lap. She stared at it like it would somehow make me disappear. Not likely.

"So…" I drew the word out, turning my head to hide my grin when she sighed loudly. "How's your blog going? Still talking about cats or something?"

"Cats? I don't talk about cats. I talk about books."

I totally knew that. "Huh. I thought you spent all that time on the Internet talking about cats."

"Whatever."

"It makes sense." I looked at her then.

Her gray eyes sparked. "I cannot wait to hear this explanation. And if you can't tell, that was sarcasm."

"I thought it sounded like excitement, but anyway, spending all day on the Internet talking about cats is kind of like preparing to become the crazy cat lady when you're older."

The skin around her mouth tightened. "I would throw this book at you, but I respect the book too much to do that."

Tipping my head back, I laughed.

"Only you would find that funny."

"It *is* funny." Lowering my chin, I saw her fighting a grin. Our gazes collided and held. Silence stretched out between us, thickening the already sultry air.

"So." She drew the word out this time, and I raised my brows as she looked away. "That girl who was at the diner. Ash? She was really…lovely."

"Uh-huh." Another feminine minefield. These girls were crafty as hell.

She pushed the swing with her toes. "You two are seeing each other?"

"We used to date." I tilted my head, curious by the direction of the conversation. "And I'm sure Dee pointed out the fact that we used to date. She would've been all about clarifying that."

Her cheeks darkened in color, and I knew I had been right. "Ash didn't act like things were in the past."

"That's on her."

Kat eyed me. "And that's all you have to say?"

"Yeah." I lifted a brow. "Why would I have to say anything

else? Especially to you." I was teasing her, but I was so bad at it, so out of practice, it totally came out dickish. I knew it, but this conversation was quickly turning into a train wreck I was powerless to stop watching.

Her shoulders stiffened and her expression turned impassive. "Why are you over here, Daemon?"

Damn. That was a good question. And one I'd been asking myself over and over since she first moved in.

She continued, her gray eyes cold. "Because if you've come over just to be ignorant, you can turn back around."

I felt myself smile, and I was sure that confirmed just how twisted I was. "But I don't want to turn back around."

"Too bad," she replied, sliding off the swing. "You know what, you can just sit out here and be a jackass with no audience. How about that?"

Kat started past me, and I pushed off the railing and was in front of her before she could even take a breath. Damn, I hadn't meant to move so quickly. She jerked back, pressing the book to her chest. "Holy crap, how do you move so fast?"

"I don't move that fast." I looked down at her. She barely reached my chest, but her personality, her attitude, was so much taller. That piece of hair was loose again, brushing her cheek. "Are you still nervous about school?"

Her brows furrowed. "What?"

I decided to ask the question slowly. "Are. You. Still—"

"No. I heard you." She shifted her weight to her other foot. "But why...why do you care? Why would you—?"

That piece of hair was getting to me, so I reached up and caught it between my fingers. The texture was soft as silk. Her breath caught, and my gaze flicked to Kat's. Up close, those eyes were really amazing, a startling shade of gray, and the pupils were black and large. Carefully, so I didn't brush the skin of her cheek, I tucked the piece of hair back behind her ear. The swelling in her eye really had gone down, and the skin had mostly healed from the night she'd been attacked, but the patch was pinker than the rest, as if her arm wasn't enough of a reminder.

In a second, I saw her once more, lying on the road, not moving and absolutely helpless. My chest tightened painfully. I pushed the image aside, wondering when I would stop seeing it.

Kat appeared to be holding her breath. Her question cycled around my thoughts. *Why do you care?* I shouldn't. I didn't.

"Daemon?" she whispered.

The sound of my name, spoken without rancor, was a rarity, and it had an electrifying effect. Those pretty pink lips spoke my name perfectly. I wanted to know what my name tasted like on her lips and tongue. Had I thought about kissing her before? I must've, because the sudden need, the almost overwhelming desire to claim her mouth didn't surprise me.

Would she let me kiss her?

Probably not.

Should I kiss her?

Probably not.

If I went ahead and did it, would it blow up in my face?

Yep.

I dropped my hand and took a step back. When I dragged in the next breath I really didn't need, the scent of peaches and...and vanilla surrounded me.

I didn't say anything as I turned around and walked off the porch. And Kat didn't stop me. I didn't look back, but I also didn't hear a door close. I knew she was standing there, watching me.

And I also knew that there was a part of me that cared.

Later that night, long after Dee was home and asleep, I sat in bed with my laptop open. My finger drifted along the touch pad as I scrolled through the blog.

*Katy's Krazy Book Obsession.*

I laughed under my breath.

Good name.

This wasn't the first time I'd checked it out. The night Dee had returned from the colony, I'd been taking a look at it. Since then, Kat had added ten more reviews. How in the world had she read that many books in that short period of time? Plus she did these other things. Something called Teaser Tuesdays, which were really just a few lines from some book she was reading. There was In My Mailbox, where she filmed herself talking about the books she had either bought, borrowed, or received from a publisher.

I'd watched five of those damn videos.

And every time she picked up a book, her entire face transformed into a wide, brilliant smile, the kind I had yet to see in person and probably never would. She loved those books. No doubt about it.

I clicked on a sixth video, one that was filmed before she moved here, and was shocked to see a different Katy. She was the same, of course, but there was a light in her eyes that seemed to be out now. I wondered what had turned off Katy's inner light. I swallowed. It was probably me, treating her like an asshole, interfering in her life and almost getting her killed.

I closed out the tab and winged my laptop across the room. Before it slammed into the wall, I lifted my hand, stopping the shiny metallic piece of crap before it shattered into thousands of dollars' worth of tiny pieces. It hovered in the air as if an invisible hand caught it before I slowly lowered it to my desk. I exhaled roughly.

This evening I had wanted to kiss Kat. There was no fooling myself. And it hadn't been the first time. Knew it wouldn't be the last time. I'd already accepted that I was attracted to her, so wanting to act on it made sense. No BFD there.

Wanting something and doing it were two different things.

Wanting something and *really* wanting it were also two different things.

Kind of like how you can want someone when you don't even like them?

Then again, that wasn't entirely the truth. I did like her. Reluctantly. She was smart. The nerdiness was cute. Her fiery attitude was admirable.

But I hadn't been lying when I said that things weren't like they were for Dawson and Bethany. Those two had…they had been in love with each other and neither of them had stopped for one damn second to think about the consequences.

The consequences were all I thought about. The memory of Kat in that last video haunted me, telling me more clearly than all of my arguments that I was just no good for her.

Too bad my body wasn't getting the message.

This was going to be a long night, I thought, as I slipped my hand under the sheet and closed my eyes. A very long night.

# 12

The first day of school wasn't exciting to me. For Dee, it was a big deal. The first day of our last year of high school at PHS—that was what she yelled at me when my alarm had gone off for the third time, and we had forty minutes to get ready, eat something, and get to class.

To me, it was stupid that we started school on a Thursday, had two days of classes, and then had the weekend off. Why didn't they just start on a Tuesday?

I barely made it, lucky that I found a pair of jeans and a shirt that was clean. Hell, I was happy that I found a notebook in the back of my car.

PHS was a small high school compared to most. Only a couple of floors, it was beyond easy to get from one class to the next. Through homeroom and first period, I wondered how Kat was doing. Being the new kid had to suck, especially when you moved to such a small town where everyone had grown up together. Kids around here were friends since they were in diapers.

It was when I walked into trig class that I saw Kat near the back of the classroom. I spotted a couple of seats empty on the other side of class and knew that's where I should go.

Instead, I switched my notebook to my other hand and headed straight down the aisle where she was seated. She kept her eyes glued to her hands, but I knew she was aware of me. The faint blush along the tips of her cheekbones gave her away.

Remembering how her breath caught the other night on her porch, I grinned.

But then my gaze slid to the awkward splint covering her slender arm, and my grin faded. Potent rage swept through me at the reminder of how close she'd come to becoming an Arum's play toy. My teeth gnashed as I stalked past and fell into the seat behind her.

Images assaulted me of how she'd looked after the Arum attack—shaken, terrified, and so tiny in my shirt as we waited for the useless police to show up. If anything, this should've served as a reminder to get my ass up and move to a different seat.

I pulled a pen out of the spiral ring on my notebook and poked her in the back.

Kat glanced over her shoulder, biting her lip.

"How's the arm?" I asked.

Her features pinched, and then her lashes swept up, her clear eyes meeting my stare. "Good," she said, fiddling with her hair. "I get the splint off tomorrow, I think."

I tapped my pen off the edge of the desk. "That should help."

"Help with what?" Wariness colored her tone.

Using the pen, I gestured to the trace surrounding her. "With what you've got going on there."

Her eyes narrowed, and I remembered she couldn't see what I could. I could've clarified, made something up right then, but it was so much fun getting a rise out of her. When it looked like she was two seconds from smacking me upside the head with her splint, I couldn't help myself.

I leaned forward, watching her eyes flare. "Fewer people will stare without the splint is all I'm saying."

Her lips thinned in disbelief, but she didn't look away. Kat met my stare and held it. Not backing down—never backing down. Reluctant respect continued to grow inside me, but underneath that, something else was developing. I was two seconds from kissing that pissed-off look right off her face. I wondered what she'd do. Hit me? Kiss me back?

I was betting on the hitting part.

Billy Crump let out a low whistle from somewhere off to the side of us. "Ash is going to kick your ass, Daemon."

Kat's eyes narrowed with what looked a lot like jealousy. I smiled, thinking about how she'd asked about Ash and me. I might just need to change my bet. "Nah, she likes my ass too much for that."

Billy chuckled.

I tipped my desk down and leaned forward even farther, bringing our mouths within the same breathing space. A flash of heat went through her eyes, and I so had her. "Guess what?"

"What?" she murmured, her gaze dropping to my mouth.

"I checked out your blog."

Her eyes shot back to mine. For a second they were wide with shock, but she was quick to smooth her expression. "Stalking me again, I see. Do I need to get a restraining order?"

"In your dreams, Kitten." I smirked. "Oh wait, I'm already

starring in those, aren't I?"

She rolled her eyes. "Nightmares, Daemon. Nightmares."

I smiled, and her lips twitched. Dammit, if I didn't know better, I'd think she liked our little fights, too. Maybe she was just as twisted as I was. The teacher started calling out roll, and Kat turned around. I sat back, laughing softly.

Several of the kids were still watching us, which kind of knocked the sense back into me. Not that I was doing anything wrong. Teasing her wouldn't bring the Arum to us or put her in danger—or my sister. When the bell rang, Kat bolted from the class like she was afraid of catching something. Two girls were right behind her. I thought their names were Lea and Cassie. Something like that. Shaking my head, I grabbed my notebook and headed out into the throng of students.

During a class exchange an hour later, I ran into Adam, who fell in step beside me. "There is talk."

I arched a brow. Damn. That sounded ominous. "Talk about what? How everyone drives trucks around here? Or how cow tipping really is a pastime? Or how my sister is never, ever going to seriously get with you?"

Adam sighed. "Talk about Katy, smart-ass."

Schooling my features, I stared straight ahead as we navigated the crowded halls. Both of us were a good head or so taller than most. We were like giants in the land of humans.

"Billy Crump's in your—"

"Trig class? Yeah, I know that already."

"He was talking in history about you flirting with the new girl," Adam said, sliding past a group of girls who were openly staring at us. "Ash overheard him."

With each passing second, my annoyance was hitting an all-new high.

"I know you and Ash aren't seeing each other anymore."

"Yep." I grit my teeth.

"But you know how she gets," Adam continued quickly. "You better be careful with your little human—"

I stopped in the middle of the hall, two seconds from throwing Adam through a wall. Kids shuffled around us as I spoke barely above a whisper. "She's not my little human."

Adam's gaze was unflinching. "Fine. Whatever. Out of everyone, I don't care if you took her into the locker room and did her, but she's glowing...and so are your eyes," he added, voice low. "And all of this is familiar."

Shit. On. A. Brick. My eyes were doing the diamond thing? Great. Glowing eyes were one step away from a Luxen shifting into their true form. Wouldn't that be fun if I turned into a glowing alien in the middle of a high school hallway? Striving for patience I wasn't known for, I started walking, leaving Adam behind.

I needed to get my shit together.

This back-and-forth crap had to stop. I was beginning to wonder if I had a split personality. Jesus. I needed to stay the hell away from Kat. And that would keep her away from the rest of the Luxen, namely Ash.

When was the moment Katy became different from the herd—from the rest of the humans? Someone I wanted to know? The day at the lake? When we went for a walk? The night the Arum got a hold of her? Or one of the many times she told me off?

Shit.

Adam was right. All of this was familiar, except we'd had this conversation with Dawson over Bethany.

Dammit. This was not happening.

I glided through the rest of my classes bored out of my

freaking mind. Many times last year, I tried to convince Matthew to get me a forged high school diploma. No such luck there. The DOD probably thought school was a privilege for us, but what they taught couldn't keep my interest. We learned at an accelerated rate, leaving most humans in the dust. And the DOD would have to approve my request to go to college if that's what I decided. Hell, I wasn't even sure I wanted to go to college. I'd rather find a job where I got to work outside—something that didn't include four small walls.

When lunch rolled around, I was half tempted to call it a day. School wasn't the same without Dawson. His exuberance for everything, even the mundane, had been contagious.

Not hungry, I grabbed a bottle of water and headed to our regular table. I sat beside Ash and leaned back, picking at the label on the bottle.

"You know," Ash said, leaning against my arm, "they say what you're doing is a sign of sexual frustration."

I winked at her.

She grinned and then turned back to her brother. That was the thing about Ash. Even though we'd dated on and off for years, she could be cool…when she wanted to be. Truth was, I think she knew deep down that she really wasn't that into me either. Not like Dawson and Bethany had felt about each other.

God, I was thinking a lot about him today.

He should be here, the first day of our last year. He should've been here.

Lifting my eyes, I immediately found Kat in the lunch line. She was talking to Cassie—no, *Carissa*—the quieter of the two girls in trig. My gaze dropped down to her flip-flops and slowly worked my way back up.

I think I loved those jeans. Tight in all the right places.

It was amazing really—how long Kat's legs looked for someone so short. I couldn't figure out why it seemed that way.

Ash's hand dropped to my thigh, drawing my attention. Warning bells went off again. She was so up to something. "What?" I asked.

Her bright eyes fixed on mine. "What are you looking at?"

"Nothing." I focused on her, anything to keep her interest off Kat. As feisty as the little kitten was, Kat was absolutely no match for Ash. I set the bottle aside, swinging my legs toward her. "You look nice today."

"Don't I?" Ash beamed. "So do you. But you always look yumtastic." Glancing over her shoulder, she then turned back and slid into my lap faster than she should have in public.

A couple of the boys at a neighboring table looked like they would've traded in their moms to be in my position.

"What are you up to?" I kept my hands to myself.

"Why do you think I'm up to anything?" She pressed her chest against mine, speaking in my ear. "I miss you."

I grinned, seeing right through her. "No, you don't."

Pouting, she slapped my shoulder playfully. "Okay. There are some things I miss."

About to tell her that I had a good idea of what that thing was, Dee's jubilant shriek cut me off. "Katy!" she yelled.

Cursing under my breath, I felt Ash stiffen against me.

"Sit," Dee said, smacking the top of the table. "We were talking about—"

"Wait." Ash twisted around. I could picture the look on her face. Lips turned down, eyes narrowed. All that equaled bad, bad times. "You did not invite her to sit with us? Really?"

I focused on the painting of the PHS mascot—a red-and-black Viking, complete with horns. *Please don't sit down.*

"Shut up, Ash," Adam said. "You're going to make a scene."

"I'm not 'going to make' anything happen." Ash's arm tightened around my neck like a boa constrictor. "She doesn't need to sit with us."

Dee sighed. "Ash, stop being a bitch. She's not trying to steal Daemon from you."

My eyebrows shot up, but I kept up the prayer. *Please don't sit down.* My jaw locked. *Please don't sit here.* If she did, Ash would eat her alive out of pure spite. I'd never understand girls. Ash didn't want me anymore, not really, but holy hell if she'd allow someone else to go there.

Ash's body started to vibrate softly. "That's not what I'm worried about. For real."

"Just sit," Dee said to Katy, her voice tight with exasperation. "She'll get over it."

"Be nice," I whispered in Ash's ear, low enough for only her to hear. Ash smacked my arm hard. That'd leave a bruise. I pressed my cheek into her neck. "I mean it."

"I'll do what I want," she hissed back. And she would, too. Worse than what she was doing now.

"I don't know if I should," Kat said, sounding incredibly small and unsure.

Every stupid, idiotic thought in my head demanded that I dump Ash out of my lap and get Kat out of here, away from what surely was going to end up being horrible.

"You shouldn't," Ash snapped.

"Shut up," Dee said. "I'm sorry I know such hideous bitches."

"Are you sure?" Kat asked.

Ash's body trembled and heated up. Her skin would be too warm for a human to touch without realizing something was different, wrong even. I could feel her control slipping away. Exposing herself wasn't likely, but she appeared mad enough to do some damage.

I turned my head to look at Kat for the first time since I'd seen her in the line. I thought about the conversation on the porch, when she grinned at me. I thought about how she reacted when I'd told her about the legend of Snowbird. And I already knew I was going to hate myself for what I was about to say, because she didn't deserve this. "I think it's obvious if you're wanted here or not."

"Daemon!" My sister's eyes filled with tears, and now it was official. I was irrevocably a dick. "He's not being serious."

"Are you being serious, Daemon?" Ash twisted toward me.

My gaze held Kat's, and I clamped down on every confusing and contradictory thought I was having. She needed to leave before something shitty happened. "Actually, I was being serious. You're not wanted here."

Kat opened her mouth, but she didn't say anything. Her cheeks had been pink—the way I liked them—but the color faded quickly. Anger and embarrassment filled her gray eyes. They glistened under the harsh lights of the cafeteria. A sharp pierce sliced through my chest, and I had to look away— because I had put that look in her eyes. Clenching my jaw, I focused over Ash's shoulder on that stupid mascot again.

In that moment, I wanted to punch myself in the face.

"Run along," Ash said.

A few snickers sounded and anger whipped through me, heating my skin. It was ridiculous that I was pissed over other people laughing when I'd already embarrassed her and hurt her more than anyone.

Silence fell over the table, and relief was imminent. She had to be leaving now. There was no way—

Cold, wet, and sloppy stuff plopped on the top of my

head. I froze, aware enough not to open my mouth unless I wanted to eat…spaghetti? Did she…? Sauce-covered noodles slid down my face, landing on my shoulder. One hung off my ear, smacking me against the neck.

Holy shit. I was dumbfounded as I slowly turned to look at her. Part of me was actually…amazed.

Ash leaped from my lap, shrieking as she shoved her hands out. "You… You…"

I plucked one of the noodles off my ear and dropped it on the table as I peered up at Kat from underneath my lashes. The laugh came up before I could stop it. Good for her.

Ash lowered her hands. "I will end you."

My humor vanished. Jumping up, I threw an arm around Ash's waist. "Calm down. I mean it. Calm down."

She pulled against me. "I swear to all the stars and suns, I will destroy you."

"What does that mean?" Kat balled her hands, glaring at the taller girl like she wasn't afraid of her one bit, and she should've been. Ash's skin was scorching hot, vibrating just beneath the surface. At that moment, I really started to doubt she wouldn't do something stupid and reveal us in public. "Are you watching too many cartoons again?"

Matthew stalked over to our table, his eyes connecting with mine for a moment. I'd hear about this later. "I believe that's enough," he said.

Knowing not to argue with Matthew, Ash sat down in her own seat and grabbed a fistful of napkins. She tried to clean up the mess, but it was pointless. I almost laughed again when she started stabbing at her shirt. Sitting down, I knocked a clump of noodles off my shoulder.

"I think you should find another place to eat," Matthew said to Katy, voice low enough that only the people at our table could hear. "Do so now."

Looking up, I watched Kat grab her book bag. She hesitated, and then she nodded as if in a daze. Turning stiffly, she stalked from the cafeteria. My gaze followed her the whole way out, and she kept her head held high.

Matthew turned from the table, probably off to do some damage control. I wiped the back of my hand down my sticky cheek, unable to stop myself from laughing softly.

Ash smacked me again. "It's not funny!" She stood, hands shaking. "I can't believe you think that was funny."

"It was." I shrugged, grabbing my water bottle. Not like we didn't deserve it. Looking down the table, I found my sister staring at me. "Dee…"

Tears built in her eyes as she stood. "I can't believe you did that."

"What did you expect?" Andrew demanded.

She shot him a death glare and then turned those eyes on me. "You suck. You really freaking suck, Daemon."

I opened my mouth, but what could I say? I did suck. I'd acted like an ass, and it wasn't like I could defend that. Dee had to understand that it was for the best, but when I closed my eyes, I saw the hurt in Kat's eyes and I wasn't so sure I'd done the right thing…at least the right thing by her.

# 13

**D**ee was giving me the cold freeze. Not that I was surprised. I deserved it after what had gone down during lunch, but getting chewed out was better than the baleful stare sent in my direction as I headed out to patrol.

There was no way I was getting the spaghetti sauce out of my shirt.

I headed out into the dusk, crossed the backyard, and entered the woods. I waited until I was several feet into the dense forest before I started running—and not that human version of it. I picked up speed, dissolving into a form made of only light, racing over the fallen trees and boulders, moving farther and farther away from home. The feeling of running in my true form was like lightning—powerful and fast and exhilarating. It required incredible focus, too, or else I could end up running straight through a tree. I'd done that once and was still picking the bark out of my skin a week later.

*You're not wanted here.*

Hell. As the unwanted thought broke my concentration,

I skidded to a stop several miles in, kicking up loose soil and pebbles.

Closing my eyes, I settled back into my human form and stretched my arms above my head. Loosening my muscles, I emptied my thoughts. It was harder this time. Then, a handful of seconds later, I shed my human form. White light tinged in red flickered over the shadowed tree trunks and grass.

Freedom washed over me again.

I moved forward, seeing the world around me in crystal clarity. Heat rolled off me, and I was careful not to linger in one area too long. I moved silently through the woods, covering miles in minutes. Soon I was near town, where I'd most likely pick up on an Arum.

Combing the county, I couldn't help but think of the time Dawson had been out here. It had been during the winter, right before Bethany had shown up and it all went to hell. He'd found an Arum and had almost been taken out by it.

Dawson would've been drained dry of everything that made us what we were if I hadn't shown up. I hadn't been there when it really counted, though. Saving his life before didn't mean shit when he ended up losing it in the end.

I stayed out until it was late, slipping back into my human form just before I left the woods and returning home well after midnight. Instead of heading in through the back door, I walked around the front and glanced up at the house beside mine.

The bedroom light was on.

Kat was up late.

She probably had her nose stuck in a book, living in a pretend fantasy world while I was actually out there living in the real fantasy world.

There couldn't be two more different people.

People?

I laughed, but it was dry and lacked humor. We weren't even of the same damn species, and yet in that moment, while I walked up the porch steps, knowing she was awake, I felt closer to her than I had to anyone in a very long time.

God, that was a huge problem.

I needed to seriously end this. I needed to get her to stay away from Dee, and I needed to stay away from her.

I knew what I had to do.

Stepping off the porch the next morning on the way to school, I stopped as I heard the engine of Kat's car groaning as it turned over without starting up. The sound was familiar. Battery was dead. Knowing her, she probably left a light on or something.

The hood popped as she unlocked it from the inside. Kat threw open the driver's door and walked around to the front of her car. The faded denim jeans she was wearing should be illegal.

Reaching down to wrap her fingers around the edges, she tensed and then looked over in my direction.

Smirking, I lifted my hand and wiggled my fingers at her.

Her eyes narrowed. "What?"

"Nothing."

She stared at me a moment longer and then turned back to her car, lifting the hood and hooking it into place. Then she stepped back, put her hands on her hips and stared at the engine.

My grin spread.

She reached into the engine and wiggled wires like that was going to do something beneficial, her ponytail bouncing with the effort. Sort of cute. Desperate. But cute. She then clasped her fingers around the hood and leaned in. The cast on her arm was a huge freaking eyesore.

Of course my gaze zeroed right in on a certain asset of hers.

I managed to pull my gaze away before I gave myself a damn eyestrain. Walking toward my car, I opened the passenger door and tossed my books on the seat. I closed the door and then walked across the small patch of grass and onto her driveway.

Kat stiffened but ignored me as I walked up the side of the car. "I don't think wiggling wires is going to help."

Letting go of the hood, she glared in my direction with stormy eyes. "Are you a mechanic or something? A special hidden car talent I know nothing about?"

I laughed under my breath. "You actually don't know anything about me."

Her lips pursed. "I count that as a blessing."

"I bet you do," I murmured as I stepped closer to the front of her car, forcing her to take a step back.

She sighed. "Hello. I was standing there."

I winked at her. "You're not standing there anymore." Using my body to shield what I was doing, I ran the tips of my fingers along the battery, sending a jolt of high-powered energy into it. "Anyway, can you try turning it on one more time?"

"Why?"

"Because."

"It's not going to work."

Turning to her, I smiled tightly. "Just try it, Kitten."

Her cheeks flushed. "Don't call me that."

"I wouldn't call you that if you were sitting in your car, turning it on," I replied reasonably.

"Oh my God," she griped and then pivoted. She stomped around to the driver's side. "Whatever."

I arched a brow as she all but threw herself into the car and turned the ignition. The battery sparked to life and the engine turned over, starting the car. Too bad the hood blocked the windshield, because I would've paid good money to see her face. That being said, I really didn't have time for this crap. This was not part of "the plan" I'd devised last night to push her even further away.

I sighed and lowered the bar, closed the hood, and locked it into place.

Kat was staring out the windshield, lips parted.

"See you at school." I paused, unable to resist adding, "Kitten."

I grinned as I heard her shriek.

When I moseyed on into trig later that morning, the first thing I noticed was that her hair was down where it had been up earlier that morning, and the fact that I noticed the change didn't even register on the screwed-up scale. I liked her hair down. It was long and a little wild-looking, like her hair was constantly in a state of rebellion.

I really needed to stop thinking of her hair as if it had a personality.

Kat was whispering with the two girls—Carissa, and the

curly-haired one was *Lesa*. Yeah, those were their names. Their mouths clamped shut, all three of them, the moment they saw me.

Interesting.

Kat bit down on her lip as she sank into her chair.

Even more interesting.

I made my way past her and the girls, taking my seat right behind Kat. Carissa spun around, facing the front, while Lesa kept peeking over her shoulder.

Hmm.

I had a plan when it came to dealing with Kat. I needed to stick to said plan.

Pulling the pen out of my notebook, I poked Kat in the back. She stiffened, but didn't turn around, so I poked her again, this time with a little more effort. She whipped around, her long dark hair flying out around her. "What?"

I smiled at the irritation in her tone. Behind her, I could see that everyone was watching us. They were probably worried she was going to whip out another plate of food, maybe syrupy pancakes this time, and dump it on my head.

Tipping my chin down, I lowered my gaze. "You owe me a new shirt."

Her jaw came unhinged.

"Come to find out," I continued, voice low, "spaghetti sauce doesn't always come out of clothes."

Kat's pink lips parted. "I'm sure you have enough shirts."

"I do, but that was my favorite."

"You have a favorite shirt?" Her nose wrinkled. Cute.

Dammit. Not cute.

"And I also think you ruined Ash's favorite shirt, too," I pointed out.

She tilted her head to the side. "Well, I'm sure you were

there to comfort her during such a traumatic situation."

"I'm not sure she'll recover," I replied drily.

Kat rolled her eyes and then started to turn around.

The plan—stick to the plan. "You owe me. Again."

The warning bell rang as she stared at me. "I don't owe you anything."

Tipping the desk down, I leaned in. Scant inches separated our mouths. "I have to disagree." And then, because apparently I sucked at keeping to the plan, I said, "You're nothing like I expected."

Her gaze dropped to my mouth. "What did you expect?"

A hundred things that she wasn't. "You and I have to talk."

"We have nothing to talk about."

I watched her lips form those words, and then I lifted my eyes to hers. "Yes. We do. Tonight."

The tip of Kat's tongue darted out, wetting her upper lip. Holy crap, that got me in a lot of areas. My fingers tightened around the edge of the desk. She nodded and then turned around slowly. Satisfaction flooded me, and I smiled tightly.

And then noticed the teacher and the class were staring at us. Oh well. I lowered my desk back onto all four legs. Someone cleared their throat. The teacher began calling names. I lifted my fingers, one by one off the edge of the desk.

As plain as day, the edge of the desk was sunken along eight different areas. Melted, as if it been too close to an extreme heat. Without even testing it out, I knew the indents would match my fingers.

After school, I ended up getting waylaid by Matthew. He'd wanted to know how I was handling the situation between Ash and Kat. He was actually worried that Ash would do something to harm Kat and potentially expose us.

I wasn't so sure about that.

If Kat had dumped food on Ash somewhere more private, yeah, there would've been a good chance that Ash would've tried to fry her. And Ash had the potential to make Kat's life a living hell at school, but I liked to think that she realized Dee wouldn't stand for it.

I wouldn't stand for it.

What went down in the cafeteria, though, reinforced the likelihood of bad stuff going down the more Kat was around us. She'd already been targeted by an Arum, and that could— that would—happen again. It wasn't necessarily Kat's fault. Actually, it wasn't her fault at all. She didn't understand the dynamics or what she was getting herself into.

Dee had human friends before, but they were more like acquaintances, people she wasn't entirely close to. Kat was different. If she didn't live next door and so close to the colony, then maybe she wouldn't pose such a problem.

Maybe I wouldn't think twice about her.

But none of that was either here or there. With school back in session, there were other people that Kat could buddy up with. Dee would eventually get over it. And everything would go back to being normal.

Time for me to stop screwing around with this.

It was close to eight when I knocked on Kat's door. Her mom's car was gone from the driveway, and for some reason, as I walked over to the porch railing, I wondered if that was why Kat was so into reading. With her mom never around, I imagined she had to be lonely.

Or maybe she just enjoyed reading that much.

The door opened, and Kat stepped out. I opened my mouth, but immediately closed it. Kat had changed since school. And it wasn't just the missing cast, which was thankfully off her arm now. She also had a dress on—a pale blue dress with tiny straps and a lacy hem that showed off her legs and the slope of her shoulders.

Her hair was still down, cascading down her back, and as she closed the door behind her, I had a hard time focusing on what the hell I was doing over here.

She walked over to me, and moonlight sliced over her cheek as she lifted her gaze to mine. "Is Dee home?"

"No." I glanced up at the stars blanketing the sky. Dee would be home soon, though. "She went to the game with Ash, but I doubt she will stay long." I turned to her. "I told her I was going to hang out with you tonight. I think she'll come home soon to make sure we haven't killed each other."

Kat looked away, but I saw the grin. "Well, if you don't kill me, I'm sure Ash will be more than glad to do so."

"Because of spaghetti-gate or something else?" I asked.

She shot me a long look. "You looked mighty comfy with her in your lap yesterday."

"Ah, I see." I pushed off the railing. "It makes sense now."

"It does?"

"You're jealous."

"Whatever." She laughed as she turned away, walking down the steps. "Why would I be jealous?"

I followed her, enjoying the view. "Because we spent time together."

"Spending time together isn't a reason to be jealous, especially when you were forced to spend time with me." She paused and then shook her head. "Is this what we need to talk about?"

I shrugged. "Come on. Let's take a walk."

Her hands smoothed over her dress. I wondered if she wore that for me. "It's kind of late, don't you think?"

"I think and talk better when I walk." Meeting her gaze, I held out my hand. "If not, I turn into the dickhead Daemon you're not very fond of."

"Ha. Ha." Her gaze flickered to my outstretched hand. "Yeah, I'm not holding your hand."

"Why not?"

"Because I'm not going to hold hands with you when I don't even like you."

"Ouch." I placed my hand over my chest. "That was harsh."

She snorted. "You're not going to take me out in the woods and leave me there, are you?"

I grabbed my chest as if wounded. "Sounds like a fitting case of revenge, but I wouldn't do that. I doubt you'd last very long without someone to rescue you."

"Thanks for the vote of confidence."

I grinned at her, but it quickly faded. There would be no more grins between us after tonight. We walked in silence, crossing the main road and into the woods, where the moonlight barely cut through the thick trees. We walked side by side, and it was hard not to be aware of her.

"Ash isn't my girlfriend," I said finally, and I don't know why I was telling her this. "We used to date, but we're friends now. And before you ask, we're not *that kind* of friends even though she was sitting on my lap. I can't explain why she was doing that."

"Why did you let her?" she asked.

"I don't know, honestly. Is being a guy a good enough reason?"

"Not really." She was watching where she walked.

"Didn't think so." I stepped around a broken tree limb. "Anyway, I'm...I am sorry about the whole lunch thing."

Kat tripped.

My hand snapped out, catching her good arm. Once she was upright, she backed off, folding her arms across her waist. Her expression was shadowed but pained.

"Kat?"

She glanced in my direction. "You embarrassed me."

"I know—"

"No, I don't think you do know." She started walking, her hands cupping her elbows. "And you pissed me off. I can't figure you out. One minute you aren't bad and then you are the biggest ass on the planet."

I stared at her retreating back for a moment. All of this would be so much easier since she was mad at me. I deserved that anger, but none of it settled well on me.

"But I have bonus points." I easily caught up to her, keeping an eye out for rocks and exposed roots. "I do, right? Bonus points from the lake and our walk? Did I get any from saving you that night?"

"You got a lot of bonus points for your *sister*," she said. "Not for me. And if they were my bonus points, you've lost most of them by now."

"That blows. It really does."

She stopped walking. "Why are we talking?"

"Look, I am sorry about that. I am." I let out a long breath. "You didn't deserve the way we acted."

In the increasing darkness, she studied me. A moment passed. "I'm sorry about your brother, Daemon."

I stilled, caught completely off guard. I never talked to her about Dawson. Obviously Dee would have at

172

some point, but I knew Dee wouldn't have told her everything. How I should have warned him to stay away from Bethany. How it was all my fault for not keeping my brother safe. "You don't have any idea what happened to my brother."

"All I know is that he disappeared—"

My hand opened and closed at my side. Disappeared? Was that what Dee had told her? It didn't matter. "That was a while ago."

"It was last year." Her voice was gentle. "Right?"

"Oh, yeah, you're right. Just seems longer than that." I cast my gaze to the slices of dark sky peeking between the thick branches. "So how did you hear about him?"

There was a moment before she responded. "Kids were talking about it at school. I was curious why no one ever mentioned him or that girl."

So Dee hadn't brought it up? Interesting. "Should we have?"

"I don't know." Her response was quiet. "Seems like a pretty big deal that people would talk about."

I started walking again, my movements stiff. "It's not something we like to talk about, Kat."

"I don't mean to pry—"

"You don't?" Familiar frustration rose. I knew I shouldn't take my anger out on Kat, but maybe this was the perfect lead-in to pushing her away for good. "My brother is gone. Some poor girl's family will probably never see their daughter again, and you want to know why no one told *you*?"

"I'm sorry. It's just that everyone is so…secretive. Like, I don't know anything about your family. I've never seen your parents, Daemon. And Ash hates my guts for no reason. It's weird that there are two sets of triplets that moved *here* at the same time," she continued, proving that someone had been talking to her. Probably the girls in trig. "I dumped food on your head yesterday, and I didn't get in trouble. That's plain weird. Dee has a boyfriend she's never mentioned. The town—it's odd. People stare at Dee like she's either a princess or they're afraid of her. People stare at *me*. And—"

"You sound like those things have something in common."

"Do they?"

"Why would they? Maybe you're feeling a little paranoid. I would be if I'd been attacked after moving to a new town."

"See, you are doing it now!" she all but shouted as she followed me deeper into the woods. "Getting all uptight because I'm asking a question, and Dee does the same thing."

"Do you think maybe it's because we know you've been through a lot, and we don't want to add to it?" I threw back at her.

"But how can you add to it?"

I slowed down, taking a deep breath as we hit the clearing and the lake came into view. This was all going way off track. "I don't know. We can't."

Kat shook her head as she stared at the water. Stars reflected off the still surface, and I hated that I brought her here to do this. No longer would I look at this place as a haven of comfort or peace.

"The day at the lake." My voice was low. I wanted her to know this. Not that it would matter when this was over, but I needed her to know this. "There were a few minutes when I was having a good time."

She twisted toward me. "Before you turned into Aquaman?"

My shoulders tensed as I lifted my gaze to the sky. For the first time in a long time, I thought about home, our real home, and how different things would be—should be. "Stress will do that, make you think things are happening that aren't."

"No, it doesn't," she said firmly. "There is something…odd here."

"Other than you?"

Irritation rolled off her. "Why did you want to talk, Daemon?"

I lifted my arm and clasped the back of my neck. It was time to get this over with. "What happened yesterday at lunch is only going to get worse. You can't be friends with Dee, not like the kind of friend you want to be."

Kat stared at me. "Are you serious?"

I lowered my hand. "I'm not saying you have to stop talking to her, but pull it back. You can still be nice to her, talk to her at school, but don't go out of your way. You're only going to make it harder on her and yourself."

A long moment passed. "Are you threatening me, Daemon?"

Lowering my gaze to hers, I braced myself. "No. I'm telling you how it's going to be. We should head back."

"No," she said. "Why? Why is it wrong if I'm friends with your sister?"

My jaw tensed. This was a mistake, because I didn't like this—no, I hated doing this. I had a mean streak the size of the equator, but this…this wasn't me. Frustration rolled into a burst of heated energy, stirring the fallen leaves and tossing Kat's hair.

"You aren't like us," I said, and then I really went there. I crossed every line that I knew to drive the point home. "You are *nothing* like us. Dee deserves better than you, people that are like her. So leave me alone. Leave my family alone."

Kat jerked as if I'd delivered a physical blow, and truth was, what I had done was far worse than anything physical. She took a step back, blinking rapidly.

Then I sealed the deal. "You wanted to know why. That's why."

"Why...?" Her voice cracked. "Why do you hate me so much?"

My control slipped for a moment, and I flinched. I didn't hate her. God, I wished I did, but I didn't, and seeing the tears building in her eyes killed me.

And then, because she was anything but weak, she rallied. "You know what? Screw you, Daemon."

I looked away, my jaw working "Kat, you can't—"

"Shut up!" she hissed. "Just shut up."

She stalked past me, heading back down the path we'd taken. It was too dark for her to make it without busting her ass. "Kat, please wait up."

Unsurprisingly, she didn't listen.

"Come on, Kat, don't walk so far ahead. You're going to get lost!"

She picked up her pace, and then she was running. The urge to go after her was hard to ignore, and I would've easily caught up, but it didn't take a genius to figure out she wanted as much space between us as possible.

I'd hurt her, really hurt her this time, cutting deep. Anything I'd said to her before was nothing compared to what I'd said this time. I had a feeling I'd finally accomplished my mission, but I didn't feel a single ounce of satisfaction.

I heard her stumble up ahead and grunt. Concern flared to life, and I picked up speed. "Kat!"

She ignored me once more and rushed forward. The road was up ahead, and she broke into an all-out run. I was closer to her now, only a few feet behind, and I saw her lift her hands and wipe them across her face.

Kat was crying.

I'd made her cry.

She hit the road and my heart stopped. I shouted her name, but there was no way she'd be able to react fast enough. It was too late.

Kat had stepped out in front of a truck.

# 14

Two bright headlights enveloped Kat's form, and the truck's loud roar filled my head. Her arms were thrown up, as if she was trying to shield herself. I saw her in my mind, broken and destroyed on the hot asphalt. The fire and life in her gray eyes dulled forever, and rage enveloped me.

I didn't hesitate.

Summoning the Source, I shattered every rule of our kind in a nanosecond. For Kat.

The burst of energy was so powerful and raw, it heated the air around us. Thunder cracked, reverberating through the valley. And the truck stopped. Everything about the vehicle and inside it simply *stopped*, suspended in time. The ground shivered under my feet and traveled outward.

Strained, I held the vehicle back, calling on everything inside me. Tiny bursts of light sparked around the truck. The driver was frozen. Time was frozen except for me and Kat.

My body began to tremble with the effort, and the world took on a whitish tint.

Kat lowered her hands and slowly turned around. Her eyes were wide as she lifted her hand to her chest. She took a step back. "Oh my God…"

I couldn't continue holding the truck back while in my human form. I knew my eyes were glowing by then, iridescent. I had a choice. Any second now I was going to lose control and the truck would continue its original path and barrel into Kat. Or I could endanger Kat and Dee and my race even more by exposing us. But at least Kat would still be alive, for however long she survived the Arum. I didn't hesitate in my choice.

The shift happened almost immediately, starting with my veins first. Intense white light filled them and then washed over me, replacing my clothing and human skin. The tremble moved past my arms, over my chest, and down my body. Power rippled out, gliding over to her.

And then I was completely in my true form, lighting up the whole damn road.

Kat was seeing me for what I really was.

Off in the distance, I heard Dee shouting, but I couldn't afford to lose focus. Not until after I got Kat out of the path of certain death.

Kat looked back at the truck. The vehicle was shaking, as was the driver. I wouldn't be able to hold it back much longer or keep the driver suspended. He would be traced—hard-core traced. So would Kat. I couldn't worry with the driver, though. His out-of-state tags meant once he was unfrozen, he'd be long gone.

The engine in the truck screamed, trying to push through, and I reached out for even more of the source. As the energy coursed through my form, a ball of intense heat grew in my belly, threatening to burn through me. Our kind could channel energy in the form of light, but even we had limits.

Just when I thought I was surely going to lose control, Kat came unstuck. She spun around and took off. I pulled the Source back and it slammed into me, knocking me back a step as the truck roared past and sapping the last of my energy. The street was empty.

Shit.

Kat was running up the drive. I had to… God, I didn't even know what I was going to do. Thinking was pointless now, especially since I hadn't actually thought about what I was doing from the moment she stepped one foot onto the road. I ran after her. Halfway up the driveway, Dee appeared, but Kat dodged her and kept running, right into the woods.

"Stay back," I shouted at Dee.

"But—"

"I mean it, Dee. Stay back!"

For once, she read the warning in my voice and saw the severity in the situation. She backed off with a look of horror on her face. What happened tonight was what I'd been warning her about this whole time.

Except it had been me who had exposed us.

Branches smacked at me and snagged my shirt as I raced after Kat. Spying her up ahead, I called out, but she didn't stop, and I wasn't going to chase after her all night. I dropped the human speed BS and within a heartbeat, I was on her.

I caught Kat from behind, my arms around her waist. We went down in a tangle of legs. I twisted before we hit the ground, absorbing the brunt of the fall. I rolled, pinning her down in the mossy grass under me.

Kat went crazy.

She slammed her hands against my chest and pushed. "Get off!"

I grabbed her shoulders, forcing her back before she hurt herself. "Stop it!"

"Get away from me!" she screamed, wiggling and trying to use her hips to throw me off.

Any other time, her rough movements would've firmly placed my head in the wrong place. Not now. "Kat, stop it! I'm not going to hurt you!"

Her wild gaze connected with mine, and she stilled underneath me, only her chest rising and falling erratically. Neither of us moved for what felt like an eternity. Panic filled her gaze, mingling with unshed tears.

That cut me. "I won't hurt you. I could never hurt you."

Kat wasn't thrashing anymore. She was staring at me with those wide, beautiful eyes. Some of the panic eased off, but she was still frightened. Her body trembled as she looked away, pressing her cheek to the grass as she squeezed her eyes shut.

What was I going to do?

I couldn't let her tell the world about us. There were only two options at this point. I took care of her, as in what Matthew had volunteered to do. Or I somehow convinced her to keep quiet. I hadn't risked everything to save her from that demon truck to harm her myself now.

Slowly, so I didn't startle her, I placed my finger under her chin and gently turned her head to mine. "Look at me, Kat. You need to look at me right now."

She kept her eyes tightly closed.

I shifted up, bracing my weight on my legs as I clasped her cheeks. Her skin was smooth and too cool. My fingers smoothed over the line of her jaw, and I saw that my hands trembled slightly. I didn't know if I could make her understand, but I had to try. I had to stop the bullet heading straight for her head.

"Please," I whispered.

Her chest rose sharply, and then her lashes swept up. Her gaze tracked over my face, and I knew she was trying to reconcile what she saw now versus what she'd seen by the side of the road. The pale moonlight broke through the trees, gliding over her cheekbones and mouth.

"I'm not going to hurt you," I tried again. "I want to talk to you. I need to talk to you, do you understand?"

She nodded.

I closed my eyes, letting out a sigh. Weariness invaded me. "Okay. I'm going to let you up, but please promise me you won't run. I don't feel like chasing you anymore right now. That last little trick nearly wiped me out." I opened my eyes, finding her watching me closely. "Say it, Kat. Promise me you won't run. I can't let you run out here by yourself. Do you understand?"

"Yes," she whispered hoarsely.

"Good." Leaning back, I slipped my hand down her cheek and then moved to the side. Crouched on my heels, I watched her scoot away until her back was pressed against a tree. I waited for a few seconds, to see if she was going to freak out. When she didn't, I sat down in front of her. I shoved my hand through my hair, swallowing a month's worth of curses. "Why did you have to walk out in front of the truck? I was trying everything to keep you out of this, but you had to go and ruin all of my hard work."

She pressed a shaking hand to her forehead. "I didn't do it on purpose."

"But you did." I dropped my hand to my lap. "Why did you come here, Kat? Why? I—we were doing well and then you show up and everything is thrown to hell. You have no idea. Shit. I thought we'd get lucky and you'd leave."

"I'm sorry I'm still here." She pressed even further against the tree, tucking her legs to her chest.

I wanted to punch myself. "I'm always making this worse." Shaking my head, I tried again. "We're different. I think you realize that now."

She placed her forehead on her knees for a moment and seemed to collect herself. She lifted her head. "Daemon, what are you?"

Smiling ruefully, I rubbed my palm along my temple. "That is hard to explain."

"Please tell me. You need to tell me, because I'm about to lose it again." Her voice rose.

I met her gaze and spoke the truth. "I don't think you want to know, Kat."

Her breath caught as she stared back at me. Understanding crept into her expression. If she asked me what I knew she wanted to, everything would change. Everything *had* already changed, but if she asked, I would tell her the truth. I would give her enough information to prove that we could trust her.

Or for her to hang herself with.

There were simply no other choices.

Kat exhaled softly. "Are you…human?"

I barked out a short laugh. "We're not from around here."

"You think?"

"Yeah, I guess you've probably figured out we're not human."

She drew in a shaky breath. "I was hoping I was wrong."

I laughed again, even though none of this was funny. "No. We're from far, far away."

Her arms tightened around her legs. "What do you mean

by 'far, far away'? Because I'm suddenly seeing visions of the beginning of *Star Wars*."

Why was I not surprised by the fact that she went there? "We're not from this planet."

Kat's mouth opened and then closed. "What are you? A vampire?"

My eye roll was so epic I was afraid my eyes would get stuck there. "Are you serious?"

"What?" Frustration rose in her voice. "You say you're not human, and that limits the pool of what you can be! You stopped a truck without touching it."

"You read too much." I exhaled slowly. "We're not werewolves or witches. Zombies or whatever."

"Well, I'm glad about the zombie thing. I like to think what's left of my brains are safe," she muttered, and I glanced at her sharply. "And I don't read too much. There's no such thing as that. But there's no such thing as aliens, either."

I leaned forward quickly, curving my hands over her bent knees. Her eyes widened as they locked with mine. "In this vast, never-ending universe, do you think Earth—this place—is the only planet with life?"

"N-no," she stammered. "So that kind of stuff...that's normal for your... Hell, what do you call yourselves?"

After a beat of silence, I leaned back and tried to figure out what the best way to go about this was. I'd never had to tell anyone about us before. This was a first. And she looked like she was seconds away from laughing hysterically. Not necessarily good.

"I can tell what you're thinking," I admitted. "Not that I can read your mind, but it's written all over your face. You think I'm dangerous."

She wetted her lips. "This is crazy, but I'm not scared of you."

"You're not?" Surprise shuttled through me.

"No." She laughed, and it had a concerning edge to it. "You don't look like an alien!"

I arched a brow. "And what do aliens look like?"

"Not…not like you," she sputtered. "They aren't gorgeous—"

"You think I'm gorgeous?" I smiled.

Her eyes narrowed. "Shut up. Like you don't know that everyone on this planet thinks you're good-looking." She grimaced. "Aliens—if they exist—are little green men with big eyes and spindly arms or…or giant insects or something like a lumpy little creature."

I let out a loud laugh. "ET?"

"Yes! Like ET, asshole. I'm so glad you find this funny. That you want to screw with my head more than you guys have already screwed with it. Maybe I hit my head or something." She started to push to her feet.

"Sit down, Kat."

"Don't tell me what to do!" she fired back. There was my Kitten. I let out a sigh of relief. If she could yell at me, she wasn't as afraid as I'd feared. We might just make it through this shit storm.

I stood fluidly, keeping my arms at my sides while I allowed my eyes to change. "Sit. Down."

Kat stared at me—stared at what was likely my green eyes glowing surreally. She sat down. And saluted me.

She literally just saluted me with her middle finger.

Wow. How could I not appreciate that kind of backbone? I grinned even wider. This girl could slay me if I let her.

"Will you show me what you really look like? You don't sparkle, do you? And please tell me I didn't almost kiss a giant brain-eating insect, because seriously, I'm gonna—"

"Kat!"

"Sorry," she muttered.

Closing my eyes, I struggled for patience and calm. When I was sure I could shift without accidentally burning half the forest, I shed my human skin. I knew the moment the transformation was complete because I heard her say, "Holy shit."

To her, I would look like a man made out of light, which wasn't too far from what we really were. I opened my eyes. Kat had a hand up, shielding her eyes. The light I threw off was intense, turning night into day.

When I was in my true form, I couldn't speak in a language that Kat would understand, so I did something I'd only ever done with those of my kind. This was also forbidden. But so was everything I was doing right now, so really, might as well go the whole nine yards.

Luxen had the ability to transfer our thoughts telepathically to one another. We could communicate that way if we were in our true forms, which wasn't often, but humans could not respond back. We couldn't pick up on their thoughts.

*This is what we look like.*

Kat gasped.

*We are beings of light. Even in human form, we can bend light to our will.* I paused. *As you can see, I don't look like a giant insect. Or...sparkle.*

"No," she whispered.

*Or a lumpy little creature, which I find offensive, by the way.* I lifted my arm, stretching out my hand to her, palm up. *You can touch me. It won't hurt. I imagine that it's pleasant for humans.*

She swallowed as she glanced at my hand and then up toward the general vicinity of where my eyes were. The she reached out. Her fingers brushed mine. A jolt of electricity, totally safe, transferred from my hand to hers. Whitish-red light danced up her arm. I smiled as her eyes widened.

Gaining courage, she wrapped her fingers around mine, causing little wisps of light to whip out and circle her wrist. My light enveloped her hand.

*Figured you'd like it.*

Truth was, I liked it, too. In my true form, I was hypersensitive to, well, everything. I liked her touch. Probably a little too much.

Pulling my hand free, I stepped back. My light slowly faded, and then I returned to the form she was more familiar with. "Kat."

She stared at me, slowly shaking her head.

Perhaps I should've waited on the whole show-and-tell thing. "Kat?"

"You're an alien," she whispered as though trying to convince herself.

"Yep, that's what I've been trying to tell you."

"Oh…oh, wow." She curled her hand, holding it to her chest. "So where are you from? Mars?"

"Not even close." I laughed. "I'm going to tell you a story. Okay?"

"You're going to tell me a story?"

I nodded as I dragged my fingers through my hair. "All of this is going to sound insane to you, but try to remember what you saw. What you know. You saw me do things that are impossible. Now, to you, nothing is impossible." I waited for that to sink in. "Where we're from is beyond the Abell."

"The Abell?"

"It's the farthest galaxy from yours, about thirteen billion light years from here. And we're about another ten billion or so. There is no telescope or space shuttle powerful enough to travel to our home. There never will be." As if our home still existed, I thought as I stared at my open palms. "Not that it matters if they did. Our home no longer exists. It was destroyed when we were children. That's why we had to leave, find a place that is comparable to our planet in terms of food and atmosphere. Not that we need to breathe oxygen, but it doesn't hurt. We do it out of habit now more than anything else."

Recognition flared across her features, and I bet she was thinking about the day at the lake. "So you don't need to breathe?"

"No, not really." I shrugged. "We do out of habit, but there are times we forget. Like when we're swimming."

"Go on."

I waited for a moment, wondering if she could handle all of this, and then decided to go for it. I refused to acknowledge the part of me that wanted her to know everything. The part that wanted to desperately know what she'd think if she knew the real me. "We were too young to know what the name of our galaxy was. Or even if our kind felt the need to name such things, but I do remember the name of our planet. It was called Lux. And we are called Luxen."

"Lux," she whispered. "That's Latin for light."

"We came here in a meteorite shower fifteen years ago, with others like us. But many came before us, probably for the last thousand years. Not all of our kind came to this planet. Some went farther out in the galaxy. Others must've gone to planets they couldn't survive on, but when it was realized that Earth was sort of perfect for us, more came here. Are you following me?"

Her stare was blank. "I think. You're saying there're more

like you. The Thompsons—they're like you?"

I nodded. "We've all been together since then."

"How many of you are here?"

"Right here? At least a couple hundred."

"A couple hundred," she repeated. "Why here?"

"We…stay in large groups. It's not…well, that doesn't matter right now."

"You said you came during a meteorite shower? Where's your spaceship?" Her nose did that cute wrinkle thing.

I arched a brow. "We don't need things such as ships to travel. We are light—we can travel with light, like hitching a ride."

"But if you're from a planet billions of light years away and you travel at the speed of light… It took you billions of years to get here?"

Did she really just do that math in her head? "No. The same way I saved you from that truck, we're able to bend space and time. I'm not a scientist, so I don't know how it works, just that we can. Some better than others."

She nodded slowly, but I had a feeling that was just for show. She wasn't freaking out, so that was good news at least.

I continued as I sat back down. "We can age like a human, which allows us to blend in normally. When we got here, we picked our…skin." She winced, and I shrugged. What could I do? It was the truth. "I don't know how else to explain that without creeping you out, but not all of us can change our appearances. What we picked when we got here is what we're stuck with."

"Well, you picked good then."

I grinned as I ran my fingers over the grass. "We copied what we saw. That only seems to work once for most of us. And how we grew up to look alike, well, our DNA must've taken care of the rest. There are always three of us born at the same time, in case you're wondering. It's always been that way." I watched her sit back down, no more than a foot or so in front of me. "For the most part, we're like humans."

"With the exception of being a ball of light I can touch?"

My grin spread. "Yeah, that, and we're a lot more advanced than humans."

"How advanced is a lot?" she asked quietly.

"Let's say if we ever went to war with humans, you wouldn't win. Not in a billion years."

She was frozen, and then leaned back from me. Probably should've kept that little piece of knowledge to myself. "What is some of the stuff you can do?"

I met her gaze. "The less you know is probably for the best."

Kat shook her head. "No. You can't tell me something like this and not tell me everything. You…you owe that to me."

"The way I see it, you owe me. Like three times over," I pointed out.

"How three times?"

"The night you were attacked, just now, and when you decided Ash needed to wear spaghetti." I ticked them off my fingers. "There better not be a fourth."

Confusion marked her expression. "You saved my life with Ash?"

"Oh yeah, when she said she could end you, she meant it." I sighed as I tipped my head back. "Dammit. Why not? It's not like you don't already know. All of us can control light. We can manipulate it so that we're not seen if we don't want to be. We can dispel shadows, whatever. Not only that, but we can harness light and use it. And trust me when I say you don't ever want to be hit with something like that. I doubt a human could survive."

"Okay..." She twisted her hands together, a movement she appeared to be unaware of. "Wait. When we saw the bear, I saw a flash of light."

"That was me, and before you ask, I didn't kill the bear. I scared it off. You passed out because you were close to the light. I think it had an effect on you. Not sure why it affected you then and not now. Anyway, all of us have some sort of healing properties, but not all of us are good at it," I continued, lowering my chin. "I'm okay at it, but Adam— one of the Thompson boys—can practically heal anything as long as it's still somewhat alive. And we're pretty much indestructible. Our only weakness is if you catch us in our true form. Or maybe cut our heads off in human form. I guess that would do the trick."

"Yeah, cutting off heads usually does." Her hands slid to her face and she sat there, cradling her head. "You're an alien."

I raised my brows at her. "There is a lot we can do, but not until we hit puberty, and even then we have a hard time controlling it. Sometimes, the things we can do can get a little whacked-out."

"That has to be...difficult."

"Yes, it is."

She lowered her hands, pressing them to her chest. "What else can you do?"

I eyed her. "Promise not to take off running again."

"Yes," she said, and then nodded. Very cute.

"We can manipulate objects. Any object can be moved, animated or not. But we can do more than that." I reached over and picked up a fallen leaf. I held it between us. "Watch."

Tapping into the Source, I let the heat whip down my

arm to the tips of my fingers. Smoke wafted from it, and then a tiny spark flew. Flames, bright and orangey, burst from my fingers, licking up over the leaf. In the time it took for the heart to beat, the leaf was gone.

Kat rose onto her knees and inched closer. I watched her, surprised. Flames crackled over my fingers. She lifted her hand, placing her fingers near the flames. When she pulled her hand back, her eyes were wide with wonder. "The fire doesn't hurt you?"

"How can something that's a part of me hurt?" I lowered my hand, shaking it so the flames were extinguished. "See? All gone."

She scooted even closer. "What else can you do?"

I watched her for a second, and then I smiled before I moved quicker than she could track. One second I was sitting in front of her, and the next I was leaning against the tree, several feet away.

"How…in the world—wait! You've done that before. The creepy, quiet moving thing. But it's not that you're quiet." She sat back, dazed. "You move that fast."

"Fast as the speed of light, Kitten." I darted forward and then slowly sat down. "Some of us can manipulate our bodies past the form we chose originally. Like shift into any living thing, person or creature."

She glanced down and then back up. "Is that why Dee fades out sometimes?"

What the hell? "You've seen that?"

"Yes, but I figured I was seeing things." Leaning to the side, she uncurled her legs, stretching them out. Of course, that drew my attention, because of…well, legs. "She used to do it when she was feeling comfortable, it seemed. Just her hand or the outline of her body would fade in and out."

I dragged my gaze from her legs and nodded. "Not all of us have control over what we can do. Some struggle with their abilities."

"But you don't?"

"I'm just that awesome."

She rolled her eyes but then popped up straight. "What about your parents? You said they work in the city, but I've never seen them."

I returned to feeling up the grass. "Our parents never made it here."

"I'm…I'm sorry."

"Don't be. It was a long time ago. We don't even remember them."

"God, I feel so stupid," she said after a moment. "You know, I thought they worked out of town."

"You aren't stupid, Kat. You saw what we wanted you to see. We are very good at that." I sighed. "Well, apparently not good enough." When I looked at her again, she had this far-off look on her face. "You're handling this better than I expected."

"Well, I'm sure I'll have plenty of time to panic and have a mini breakdown later. I will probably think that I have lost my mind." She bit down on her lip. "Can…can you all control what others think? Read minds?"

I shook my head. "No. Our powers are rooted in what we are. Maybe if our power—the light—was manipulated by something, who knows. Anything would be possible."

Anger sparked in her eyes, and she bristled up like a little angry kitten. "This whole time I thought I was going crazy. Instead, you've been telling me I'm seeing things or making shit up. It's like you've given me an alien lobotomy. Nice."

My eyes narrowed as I stared at her. "I had to. We can't

have anyone knowing about us. God knows what would happen to us then."

Kat exhaled roughly, and I could tell she was struggling to let it go. "How many…humans know about you?"

"There are some locals who think we're God-only-knows-what," I explained. "There's a branch of the government that knows of us, within the Department of Defense, but that's about it. They don't know about our powers. They can't," I nearly growled, meeting her eyes. "The DOD thinks we're harmless freaks. As long as we follow their rules, they give us money, our homes, and leave us alone. So when any one of us goes power-crazy it's bad news for several reasons. We try not to use our powers, especially around humans."

"Because it would expose what you are."

"That, and…" I rubbed my jaw, suddenly tired. I didn't want to admit that I'd been putting her in danger. "Every time we use our power around a human, well, it leaves a trace on that person, enables us to see that they've been around another one like us. So we try not to ever use our abilities around humans, but you…well, things never went according to plan with you."

"When you stopped the truck, did that leave a… *trace* on me?" When I didn't answer, she started to put it together. "And when you scared the bear away? That's traceable by others like you? So the Thompsons and any other alien around here know I've been exposed to your… alien mojo?"

"Pretty much," I said. "And they aren't exactly thrilled about it."

"Then why did you stop the truck? I'm obviously a huge liability to you."

Damn, wasn't that a loaded question? Andrew and

Matthew both would probably demand the same thing if I told them about Kat knowing what we were, and I was really hoping that conversation would never happen. I really didn't know how to answer that question.

Or maybe I did, and I just didn't want to speak it out loud.

Kat drew in a deep breath. "What are you going to do with me?"

I lifted my gaze. "What am I going to do with you?"

"Since I know what you are, that makes me a risk to everyone. You…can light me on fire and God knows what else."

I couldn't believe what she was saying. I knew I'd been a dick to her, but come on. She had to sense there was something more between us. Didn't she? Shit. Maybe not. Maybe I was so good at my douchebag skills, as she called them, she had no clue how I was really starting to feel about her. I pondered telling her everything. How just being around her made me smile more than I had in years. How I admired her spunk and the way she stood up for herself, and especially the way she stood up to me and my bullshit. As a warm feeling started to grow in my chest, I nipped that shit in the bud pronto, with an image of my dead brother and the human he'd fallen for squaring my jaw. No, it was still better if we went our separate ways, but that didn't mean I couldn't ease her fears at least. "Why would I have told you everything if I were going to do anything to you?"

Her lips pursed. "I don't know."

Moving toward her, I reached out, but stopped short when she flinched from me. My stomach sank as my fingers curled around empty air. "I'm not going to do anything to you. Okay?"

She nibbled on that lower lip. "How can you trust me?"

Another loaded question that was hard to answer. This time when I reached out, she didn't pull away. I curved my finger under her chin, holding her gaze to mine. "I don't know. I just do. And honestly, no one would believe you. Plus, if you made a lot of commotion, you'd bring the DOD in, and you don't want that. They will do anything to make sure the human population isn't aware of us."

Kat seemed to process that, and for a moment, our gazes held. We were connected by not just the physical touch but also the truth. When she pulled away from me, I didn't particularly like it.

And I didn't like that I didn't like it.

"So that's why you said all those things earlier?" she asked, her voice small. "You don't hate me?"

My gaze fell to my hand as I lowered it. My tongue worked around the words. "I don't hate you, Kat."

"And this is why you don't want me to be friends with Dee, because you were afraid that I'd find out the truth?"

"That, and you're a human. Humans are weak. They bring us nothing but trouble." Yeah, that came out harsher than I'd intended, but that's probably for the best. She needed to know what was at stake—for all of us.

Her eyes narrowed. "We aren't weak. And you're on *our* planet. How about a little respect, buddy."

Amusement flooded me. "Point taken." I looked her over. "How are you handling all of this?"

"I'm processing everything. I don't know. I don't think I'm going to freak out anymore."

Happy to hear that. I pushed to my feet. "Well then, let's get you back before Dee thinks I killed you."

"Would she really think that?" she asked slowly as though she were afraid of the answer.

196

I watched her from where I towered over her and when she met my gaze this time, I knew she saw the coldness in it. "I'm capable of anything, Kitten. Killing to protect my family isn't something I'd hesitate over, but that's not what you have to worry about."

"Well, that's good to know," she murmured.

I cocked my head to the side. "There are others out there who will do anything to have the powers that the Luxen have, especially mine. And they will do anything to get to me and my kind."

"And what does that have to do with me?"

Crouching down, I glanced around us. "The trace I've left on you from stopping the truck can be tracked. And you're lit up like the Fourth of July right now."

Her breath caught.

"They will use you to get to me." I reached out, pulling a leaf from her hair. Then I touched her cheek, where her skin had been torn from the night she'd been attacked. "And if they get a hold of you...death would be a relief."

# 15

Kat was quiet most of the walk back. The trace around her was vibrant, like an all-white disco ball. That was going to be so incredibly problematic.

As the trees cleared, she spoke. "Can I...can I see Dee?"

I kept my steps slow so she didn't have to struggle to keep up with me. "I think waiting until tomorrow would be a good idea. I need to talk to her, explain to her what I've told you."

Her gaze turned woeful as we neared the houses, but she nodded. I followed her up the porch steps where light was on, casting a soft glow over Kat's bowed head. Through the windows, I could see that her house was dark. Her mom was at work, as usual. After everything that had gone down, I didn't think her being alone tonight was a good thing.

What if she woke up in the middle of the night and started calling everyone under the sun? Okay. That wasn't exactly probable. Kat wasn't stupid, but she could wake up and freak out. That would be understandable.

I held open the screen door for her as she reached for the

main door. "Do you want to spend the night at my place?"

Kat stopped and turned to me slowly. One eyebrow rose. "Come again?"

A chuckle rumbled out from me. "Get your mind out of the gutter, Kitten."

Her lips pinched. "My mind is not in the gutter."

"Uh-huh." I gave her a half grin. "You can stay at *our* house if you'd like. Then in the morning, Dee will be right there."

She didn't speak as her gaze searched mine, and then she nodded. "Okay. I just…I need to grab a few things."

I nodded. "I'll wait for you downstairs."

Again, she studied me like she was trying to figure me out, and then she pushed open the main door. As she walked in, she flipped the light on in the foyer. Glancing over her shoulder, she looked back but didn't meet my stare. "I'll be right back."

"I'll be here."

Kat darted up the staircase, her flip-flops smacking off the steps. While she was upstairs, I didn't stay put. The layout of the house was the same as ours, so when I roamed off to my left, I entered the kitchen. I flipped on the overhead light and scoped out the place. I wasn't really looking for anything. Mostly, I was just curious.

But what I saw tipped up the corners of my lips.

Everywhere I looked, there were books, just as it had been in the living room. Two were on the counter, near a toaster. One was on the fridge, and I had no idea why there'd be one there. There were three on the kitchen table, stacked next to two unopened packages.

How in the world could someone have so many books?

I heard her moving around upstairs. I turned off the light

and returned to the foyer. A few seconds later, she started down the stairs, carrying a small tote bag. "I'm ready."

Kat locked up, and then we headed toward my house. On the way, she kept peeking in my direction. I could tell she had more questions. Who wouldn't after finding out they were living next door to aliens? But I figured she had to have a breaking point, and I really didn't want to be the one to push her over the edge. That was one reason I didn't want her talking to Dee.

But I also needed to make sure we were on the same page, that Kat realized what she'd just stepped in and the consequences of knowing what she did.

When we reached the front door, I stopped and faced her. There was no light on, and we stood in the dark. "There's something I just need to make sure of, okay?"

She held the tote close to her body. "All right?"

I lowered my voice just in case Dee was hovering inside the door. She was somewhere in the house. I could feel her. "What I've told you? What you know? I can't stress enough how much of a big deal this is. This goes beyond a normal level of trust. It's my life—our lives—you're holding in your hands," I told her. "I don't expect you to care too much about tossing me under a speeding bus, but you'd also be tossing Dee under it."

Kat stepped closer, so close, her tote bag brushed against my stomach. "I do get that, Daemon. Honestly? What you said earlier was true. No one would believe me. They'd think I was crazy, but I would never do anything to betray Dee." She paused, exhaling softly as she tipped her chin up. "And even though you're a giant douchebag, I wouldn't do that to you, either."

My lips twitched. "Well, that's good to hear."

"I'm serious," she insisted. "I'm not going to tell anyone."

Some of the icy unease faded off, but the thing was, only time would tell if Kat could seriously be trusted. I hoped so. Not just for Dee's sake or mine, but for her own.

I led her into the house and took her upstairs. She was looking around, her gaze bouncing off everything, and I realized this was the first time she'd been in our house. I figured Dee was in her bedroom, and I half expected her to jump out at any movement.

I walked Katy to a guest bedroom almost never used and opened the door. Flipping on the light, I stepped into the stale, cold air of the room. "You can stay in here." I walked toward the bed. It was made. "There're extra blankets in the closet there."

Kat turned slowly, eyeing the closet.

"There's a bathroom right across from this room. My bedroom is next door," I explained as I rubbed my palm over my chest. "Dee's bedroom is down the hall. Just let...let it all go for tonight. She'll still be here in the morning."

She nodded.

My gaze flickered to hers. Dark smudges of exhaustion had formed under her eyes. I suspected she'd be out cold the moment her head hit that pillow. "Do you need anything else?"

"No."

I stood there for a moment, feeling like there was something else I needed to say, but I couldn't grasp on to any words, so I nodded and then turned toward the door.

"Daemon?"

Stopping, I twisted around.

She was nibbling on her lower lip. "Thank you for saving my life tonight. I would be a pancake if you hadn't."

I didn't respond to that, because there was really wasn't a reason for her to thank me.

"And…" She stepped forward, lowering the tote. "And thank you for telling me the truth. You can trust me with it."

My lashes lifted and I met her earnest stare. I wanted to believe her. "Prove it."

It wasn't lost on me as I left the room, closing the door behind me, that I had parroted Ash's words. Heading down the hall, I stopped at Dee's door and gently rapped my knuckles on it.

The door flew open, and my sister was standing there, eyes shining. "Does she hate me?" she whispered.

"What?" I frowned, stepping inside and closing the door. "God. No. She doesn't hate you."

Dee folded her hands together. "Are you sure? I've been lying to her, and how can she like me when all I've done—"

Wrapping my arm around her shoulders, I drew her in for a hug. "She understands why you couldn't be honest, Dee. She doesn't hate you for it."

She face-planted in my chest, and when she spoke, her voice was muffled. "You told her?"

"Yeah." I lowered my cheek to the top of her head and quickly told her what had happened with the truck. "I didn't have a choice."

Dee was quiet for a moment. "Yeah. Yeah, you did, Daemon."

I knew what she was referencing, and I hated that Dee believed if it had come down to it, that I would do that.

"I also think it's nice you brought her over here," she continued.

No response to that.

"She thinks I'm a freak, doesn't she?" she muttered.

I laughed as I pulled back. "No. She doesn't."

She didn't look like she believed me. "Kat's tired. She's barely standing on her feet. Give her till tomorrow and then you can jump all over her, okay?"

Dee relented, and after chatting with her for a few moments, I headed back to my bedroom. Burned the hell out, I changed into a pair of sleep pants and was about the throw myself on the bed but was dying of thirst.

I really needed to put a small fridge up here.

Sighing, I walked out of the room. The hallway bathroom light was on as I headed downstairs. I grabbed a bottle of water and made my way back up, my brain strangely empty of all concerns, which proved just how tired I was.

As I neared my door, the bathroom door opened and Kat stepped out in the hallway. She froze. I froze. Shit. I became a damn statue.

Kat clutched a toothbrush and toothpaste in her hands. Her hair was up in a messy knot and the thin wisps around her face were damp. She'd washed her face, and looked like she'd gotten more water on the dark blue shirt she wore than she did her face. Speaking of that shirt…

It was all that she was wearing. And it was thin. And I was getting an eyeful that I very much appreciated.

The visual packed an intense punch and there was no stopping the way my body, which could be so freaking human at times, reacted. The shirt was loose and bulky, ending at midthigh, and good Lord, those thighs…

Who knew a shirt could be so damn sexy?

Her face was as red as a ripe tomato, but she…she was checking me out in the same way I was checking her out. Her eyes were most definitely not on my face, so I didn't feel too much of an ass for staring at certain areas of her. Not when her gaze was trained on my stomach and then my chest...and then back down to where the pajama bottoms hung.

Kat sucked her lower lip in between her teeth.

Aw, hell.

I swallowed a groan, and she must've heard the noise, because her gaze flew to my face, and that blush deepened like a sunburn. She darted for the extra bedroom. "G-Good night."

"Night," was all I managed.

I walked into my bedroom and quietly closed the door behind me. Making it to the bed, I flopped down on it and stared at the ceiling.

It was going to be another long night.

It was weird, how I felt after telling Kat the truth. I thought I'd be more ill at ease. I'd never told a human before, and it had been bad enough when Dawson told Bethany the truth. I don't know why I wasn't as pissed off or panicked this time around.

Instead, I was more...relieved. I didn't have to pretend anymore or hide what I really was around her. I didn't have to be the constant douchebag she liked to call me. Sure, I needed to keep her at a distance, but at least I could explain the stakes in a way she could understand now. Home had once again become the sanctuary it had been before Kat moved in next door.

Like I said, it was weird.

I'd stayed MIA Saturday morning while Dee talked to

Kat. I figured they needed their time to work through the big discovery, and when Kat finally headed next door sometime that afternoon, Dee explained that she'd actually shown Kat one of Dee's strongest abilities.

In her true form, Dee had a knack at mirroring the image of another person. Most of us could do it, but for only short times. Dee could hold the mirror image for a hell of a lot longer than all of us.

Dee had apparently made herself look like Kat.

I kind of felt bad for Kat at that point.

I stood in the kitchen, rinsing off plates before placing them in the dishwasher as Dee bounced around. Excitement buzzed in her voice as she went over every detail from her talk with Kat. I couldn't hide my grin, just like Dee couldn't hide her relief.

"I told her that you can do just about anything," she said. "She asked what you could do after I mirrored her."

My grin spread. I bet Kat loved hearing that.

"I totally reinforced the fact that the government doesn't know about all our abilities and how important it is that they never find out." She bounded over, grabbing the plate out of my hand and placing it in the dishwasher. "It didn't seem like you told her much about the Arum."

The grin on my face started to slip.

Dee closed the dishwasher door and danced over to the kitchen table. "I explained what happened to our planet and how the government doesn't realize that the Arum are a totally different species."

I slowly turned around. "What else did you tell her?"

"I elaborated on the whole trace thing." Her forehead scrunched. "She didn't seem surprised by that, so I'm guessing you talked to her about some of it. I told her she didn't have to worry. We would keep an eye on her, and now since she knows what she's dealing with, I think it will be easier to keep her safe."

"Yeah." I shoved my fingers through my hair. I didn't mind that Dee had talked to Kat about this stuff. After all, I had started the conversation last night, but I wondered how Kat was handling all of this.

"She can really be trusted," Dee continued on as I lowered my hand. She picked up the jug of tea and walked it to the fridge. "She knows what will happen if the DOD finds out that she knows about us. She's not going to say anything, Daemon."

I nodded as I folded my arms across my chest. "No one else needs to know that she knows the truth. Not even Adam."

Dee opened her mouth.

"I mean it, sis. Adam is a good guy. He's not like Andrew, but you know this is a big deal, especially after… after Dawson and Bethany. The others will worry, especially Matthew. We can't take the risk that one of them will panic and report Kat."

Her eyes widened as she closed the fridge door. "Do you think one of them would do that?"

I considered that question. "I don't know. I want to say no, but…anything's possible. And there's always the risk that one of them might accidentally say something in front of the other Luxen. We just need to be careful."

Dee fiddled with the hem of her shirt. "Okay. No one else needs to know."

Pushing away from the sink, I started toward the stairs and then changed my mind. "I'm going to go check on Kat. You want to come?"

She started to speak and then smiled broadly. "Nah. I think I'll stay here for now. I'll see her later."

I narrowed my eyes. "Why are you smiling like you're high?"

"No reason." She rocked back on her feet, smiling so wide I thought her face might crack. "No reason at all."

Frowning, I shook my head and pivoted around. I made it to the door before Dee called out, "Take your time."

I shot her a dark look over my shoulder, and she burst into a fit of giggles. Whatever. I crossed the front yard and saw Kat through the kitchen window. Well, I saw the white glow around her... I headed for the back door and knocked.

The door swung open, and unfortunately she wasn't wearing only the shirt like last night. Actually, that was probably a good thing. But that trace on her. Damn. The others were going to see it first thing Tuesday morning, after Labor Day, and I was going to have to come up with one hell of an excuse.

"Hey?" she said, sounding unsure.

I nodded in response.

Wariness flickered over her face. "Um, do you want to come in?"

Not feeling down when it came to enclosed spaces and Kat, I shook my head. "No, I thought maybe we could go do something."

Her brows flew up, and I almost laughed. "Do something?" she asked.

"Yeah. Unless you have a review to post or a garden that needs tending."

"Ha. Ha." She started to close the door.

I lifted my hand, stopping the door without touching. Shock replaced the irritation, and I grinned. "Okay. Let me try that again. Would you like to do something with me?"

She hesitated. "Where did you have in mind?"

I pushed away from the house, walking backward as I shrugged. "Let's go to the lake."

"I'll check the road before I cross this time," she said, and I turned around. "You're not taking me out in the woods because you changed your mind and decided your secret is not safe with me, are you?"

I busted out laughing. "You're very paranoid."

She snorted. "Okay, that is coming from an alien who apparently can toss me into the sky without touching me."

"You haven't locked yourself in any rooms or rocked in any corners, right?"

Her eyes rolled when I glanced over at her. "No, Daemon, but thanks for making sure I'm mentally sound and all."

"Hey." I raised my hands in mock surrender. "I need to make sure you aren't going to lose it and potentially tell the entire town what we are."

"I don't think you need to worry about that for several reasons," she replied drily.

I gave her a pointed look. "You know how many people we've been close to? I mean, really close to?"

She wrinkled her nose, and I wondered where her mind went, and that made me chuckle. "Then one little girl goes and exposes us. Can you see how hard that is for me to... trust?"

"I'm not a little girl, but if I could go back in time and do it all over I wouldn't have stepped out in front of that truck."

"Well, that is good to know."

"But I don't regret finding out the truth. It explains so much. Wait, can you go back in time?" Her expression was serious. "The possibility hadn't crossed my mind before, but now I honestly wonder."

I sighed, wanting to laugh. "We can manipulate time, yes. But it's not something we'd do, and only going forward. At least I've never heard of anyone being able to bend time to the past."

"Jesus, you guys make Superman look lame."

I smiled as I dipped my head to avoid a low-hanging branch. "Well, I'm not telling you what our kryptonite is."

A moment passed. "Can I ask you a question?"

I nodded as our feet kicked at the leaf-covered ground.

"The Bethany girl who disappeared—she was involved with Dawson, right?" she asked.

I tensed. "Yes."

"And she found out about you guys?"

Several seconds passed before I could decide how to answer this question. "Yes."

Kat glanced at me. "And that's why she disappeared?"

"Yes." More or less, that was the truth.

"Did she tell someone? I mean, why did she...have to disappear?"

"It's complicated, Kat."

"Is she...dead?"

When I didn't answer that question, she stopped. I looked back, and she was digging a pebble out of her sandal. "You're just not going to tell me?"

I grinned at her.

"So why did you want to come out here?" She shook the rock out and placed the sandal back on. "Because it's fun for you to be all evasive?"

"Well, it is amusing to watch your cheeks get all pink when you're frustrated."

Her cheeks burned brighter.

I winked and started walking again. Her questions were valid, and I was being a jerk about it, but there really weren't easy answers to those questions. The lake came into view. "Besides the twisted fact that I like watching you get all bent out of shape, I figured you'd have more questions."

"I do."

"Some I won't answer. Some I will." I glanced over at her, and she didn't look upset at me. I felt like I needed to take a picture to capture that moment. "Might as well get all your questions out of the way. Then we don't have a reason to bring any of this up again, but you're going to have to work for those questions."

She arched a brow. "What do I have to do?"

I glanced out over the lake and smiled. "Meet me on the rock."

"What? I'm not wearing a bathing suit."

Kicking off my shoes, I turned my smile on her. She blinked once and then twice before quickly looking away. "So? You could almost strip down—"

"Not going to happen." She crossed her arms.

That was a damn shame.

"Figured," I replied. "Haven't you ever gone swimming in your clothes before?"

Her lips pursed. "Why do we have to go swimming for me to ask questions?"

My gaze zeroed in on that mouth for way too long before I lowered my gaze. "It's not for you, but for me. It seems like a normal thing to do." I shifted my weight. "The day we went swimming?"

"Yes." She took a step toward me.

Lifting my gaze, I met her stare. I took a deep breath. "Did you have fun?"

Kat tilted her head to the side. "When you weren't being a jerk and if I ignore the fact that you were bribed into it, then yes."

Smiling, I looked away. One of these days, maybe, I'd tell her that I hadn't been bribed. "I had more fun that day than I can remember. I know it sounds stupid, but—"

"It's not stupid." Her response was immediate and genuine. Then she shocked the hell right out of me. "Okay. Let's do this. Just don't go underwater for five minutes."

Relaxing, I laughed. "Deal."

While I pulled off my shirt, she slipped off her sandals. I could tell she was watching me from under her lowered gaze. I waited for her to change her mind, but she grinned at me, and I...shit. There was a weird tugging in my chest as I watched her walk up to the water's edge and dip her toes in.

"Oh my God, the water is cold!" she shrieked.

I could do something about that.

"Watch this." Winking at her, I turned back to the lake. I let go of my human form. White light spread out from my chest and over my form. I shot off the ground, moving incredibly fast. To her, I probably looked like nothing more than a fiery ball. I hit the center of the lake. In my true form, heat radiated off me, warming the lake as I whipped around, under the water.

As I neared the rocks, I shifted back into the form Kat was more comfortable with as I hauled myself up on the rocks.

"Alien powers?" she asked.

Water sluiced off my skin as I leaned over the edge of the rock, motioning her forward. "Come in, it's a little warmer now."

She didn't look like she believed me when she placed her

foot in. Her body jerked as she glanced up at me, her eyes wide. "Any other cool talents?" she asked as she waded over to the rocks.

"I can make it so that you can't even see me."

When she reached the side of the rocks, she placed her hand in mine. I pulled her up easily, and once she gained her footing, I let go and scooted back, giving her room.

She shivered as she sat on the sunbaked rock. "How can you do things without me seeing?"

Leaning back on my elbows, I stretched out my legs. "We're made of light. We can manipulate the different spectra around us, using them. It's like we're fracturing the light, if that makes any sense."

"Not really."

"You've seen me turn into my natural state, right?" When she nodded, I went on. "And I sort of vibrate until I break apart into tiny particles of light. Well, I can selectively eliminate the light, which allows us to be transparent."

She tucked her knees against her chest. "That's kind of amazing, Daemon."

I smiled as I folded my arms behind my head and lay back. "I know you have questions. Ask them."

Kat slowly shook her head. "Do you guys believe in God?"

"He seems like a cool guy."

She blinked. "Did you guys have a god?"

"I remember there was something like a church, but that's all. The Elders don't talk about any religion," I explained.

"What do you mean by 'elders'?"

"The same thing you'd mean. An old person."

She scrunched her nose.

That made me grin. "Next question?"

"Why are you such an ass?"

I laughed under my breath. "Everyone has to excel at something, right?"

"Well, you're doing a great job."

Closing my eyes, I welcomed the sun soaking into me. "You do dislike me, don't you?"

Kat didn't respond right off. "I don't dislike you, Daemon. You're hard to…like. It's hard to figure you out."

"So are you," I admitted and then decided to rock this whole honesty thing. "You've accepted the impossible. You're kind to my sister and to me—even though I admit I've been a jerk to you. You could've run right out of the house yesterday and told the world about us, but you didn't. And you don't put up with any of my crap." I laughed. "I like that about you."

"You like me?"

"Next question?" I said smoothly.

Kat leaned in closer. "Are you guys allowed to date people—humans?"

I shrugged one shoulder as I glanced over at her. "'Allowed' is a strange word. Does it happen? Yes. Is it advised? No. So we can, but what would be the point? Not like we can have a lasting relationship when we have to hide what we are."

She appeared to consider that. "So, you guys are like us in other, uh, departments?"

I sat up, arching a brow. "Come again?"

Her cheeks flushed in the sunlight. "You know, like sex? I mean, you guys are all glowy and stuff. I don't see how certain stuff would work."

Like sex?

She was legit asking me if we could have sex?

The question made me want to laugh. It also made me want other things that had to do with what she was thinking, and the fact that I physically responded that way so quickly was a bit disconcerting.

It was also interesting.

And I was also an idiot.

My lips curled up in a half smile and before I could really think about what I was doing, I moved, rolling her onto her back before she could blink an eye. She sucked in a soft breath. I hovered over her, my wet hair falling forward as I braced my weight on my hands. A droplet of water sneaked free, landing on her cheek. She didn't even notice it.

"Are you asking if I'm attracted to human girls?" I lowered myself, and our bodies met in all the areas that counted. With our wet clothes, it felt like there was barely anything between our skin. She was amazingly soft under me, and I could feel her shallow breaths. As close as we were, I saw the way her eyes dilated. I shifted my hips just the slightest and I felt her gasp in every part of me. "Or are you asking if I'm attracted to *you*?"

Our eyes met and held. Silence stretched out between us, and I knew she had her answer.

And I also knew I needed to get off her before I engaged in total dumbassery.

Taking more effort than it should have, I rolled off her. When I spoke, there was no mistaking the change in my voice. "Next question."

Kat didn't sit up. "You could've just told me, you know?" She turned her head toward me. "You didn't have to *show* me."

True dat.

"And what fun would there be in telling you?" I turned *my* head toward her. "Next question, Kitten?"

"Why do you call me that?"

"You remind me of a little fuzzy kitten, all claws and no bite."

Her lips twitched. "Okay, that makes no sense."

I shrugged.

A moment passed. "Do you think there are more Arum around?"

That was a tough one. I tipped my head back, studying her to determine how real she wanted me to get. "They are always around."

"And they're hunting you?" Her voice dropped.

I flipped my gaze to the sky. "It's the only thing they care about. Without our powers, they are like…humans, but vicious and immoral. They're into ultimate destruction and whatever."

"Have you…fought a lot of them?"

"Yep." I rolled onto my side, facing her. "I've lost count of how many I've faced and killed. And with you lit up like you are, more will come."

Her gaze momentarily lifted. "Then why did you stop the truck?"

"Would you have preferred I let it pancake you?" I asked, referencing what she had said that night.

"Why did you?" she persisted.

I clenched my jaw. "Honestly?"

"Yes."

"Will it get me bonus points?" I asked softly.

Her chest rose with a deep breath, and then she lifted her hand. She brushed back the strand of hair that had fallen across my forehead. Her fingers grazed my skin, and I stilled, closed my eyes briefly. Such a soft, innocent touch, but it hit me hard.

"Depends on how you answer the question," she said.

When I opened my eyes, her features were tinged in white. She pulled her hand back, exhaling softly. I eased onto my back, my arm against hers. "Next question?"

Kat folded her hands together over her stomach, and she didn't pull away. "Why does using your powers leave a trace?"

Much safer ground. "Humans are like glow-in-the-dark T-shirts to us. When we use our abilities around you, you can't help but absorb our light. Eventually, the glow will fade, but the more we do, the more energy we use, the brighter the trace. Dee blurring out doesn't leave much of anything. The truck incident and when I scared the bear, that leaves a visible mark. Something more powerful, like healing someone, leaves a longer trace. A faint one, nothing big so I'm told, but it lingers longer for some reason.

"I should've been more careful around you," I continued. "When I scared the bear, I used a blast of light, which is kind of like a laser. It left a large enough trace on you for the Arum to see you."

"You mean the night I was attacked?" Her voice was hoarse.

"Yes." I scrubbed my hand down my face. "Arum don't come here a lot, because they don't think any Luxen are here. The beta quartz in the Rocks throws off our energy signature, hides us. That's one of the reasons why there are a lot of us here. But there must have been one coming through. He saw your trace and knew there had to be one of us nearby. It was my fault."

"It wasn't your fault. You weren't the one who attacked me."

"But I basically led him to you," I pointed out.

As my words sank in, she paled. Fear filled her gaze. I hated that, and like earlier, I was concerned with how much of this information she could handle.

"Where is he now? Is he still around?" she asked. "Is he going to come back? What—"

Reaching between us, I found her hand and squeezed gently. "Kitten, calm down. You're going to have a heart attack."

Her lips parted slowly. "I'm not going to have a heart attack."

"Are you sure?" Her hand felt warm and small inside mine.

"Yes." That earned me another epic eye roll.

"He isn't a problem anymore," I explained.

She turned her head more fully toward me. "You...you killed him?"

"Yeah, I kind of did." I wasn't trying to scare her, but she needed to know I would kill anyone who threatened my family...and now her.

"You kind of did? I didn't know there was any 'kind of' in killing someone."

"Okay, yes, I did kill him." I heard the startled catch in her breath. "We're enemies, Kitten. He would've killed me and my family after absorbing our abilities if I didn't stop him. Not only that, he would've brought more here. Others like us would've been in danger. *You* would've been in danger."

"What about the truck? I'm glowing brighter now," she said. "Will there be another?"

When there was one Arum, there were usually three more. Maybe we'd get lucky this time. "Hopefully there are none nearby. If not, the traces on you should fade. You'll be safe."

"And if not?"

"Then I'll kill them, too." And that was the truth. "For a while, you're going to need to stay around me, until the trace fades."

"Dee said something like that." She bit down on her lip. "So you don't want me to stay away from you guys anymore?"

"It doesn't matter what I want." I glanced down at our hands. It struck me then that I'd been tracing the alphabet on her hand. I had no idea. "But if I had my way, you wouldn't be anywhere near us."

Kat yanked her hand free. "Gee, don't be honest or anything."

"You don't understand," I said. I was determined that she understand the danger not staying away from us originally had put us all in. I didn't want to be cruel, but she had to know what was at stake. "Right now, you can lead an Arum right to my sister. And I have to protect her. She's all I have left. And I have to protect the others here. I'm the strongest. That is what I do. And while you're carrying the trace on you, I don't want you going anywhere with Dee if I'm not with you."

Sitting up, she turned toward the shore. "I think it's time I head back."

Aw hell, she really wasn't getting it. When she started to stand, I caught her arm. Her skin immediately warmed under my palm. "Right now, you can't be out there by yourself. I need to be with you until the trace fades."

"I don't need you to play babysitter." Her jaw jutted out stubbornly. "I'll stay away from Dee until it fades."

"You're still not getting it." God, I wanted to shake her. "If an Arum gets a hold of you, they aren't going to kill you. The one at the library—he was playing with you. He was going to get you to the point that you'd beg for your life and then force you to take him back to one of us."

"Daemon—"

"You don't have a choice. Right now, you're a huge risk.

You are a danger to my sister. I will not let anything happen to her."

Anger flushed her face. "And then after the trace fades? Then what?"

"I prefer that you'd stay the hell away from all of us, but I doubt that's going to happen. And my sister does care for you." I let go of her elbow and leaned back, beyond frustrated. "As long as you don't end up with another trace, then I don't have a problem with you being friends with her."

Her hands balled into fists. "I'm so grateful to have your approval."

I forced a smile. How much more clearly did I need to put it out there for her? She was in danger and she was a risk. This...this wasn't personal. "I've already lost one sibling because of how he felt for a human. I'm not going to lose another."

"You're talking about your brother and Bethany," she stated.

"My brother fell in love with a human...and now they're both dead."

# 16

Sometimes Kat was as open as a picture book. Everything she thought and felt plainly visible on her face. I watched as the irritation eased away, replaced by sympathy I wasn't comfortable seeing.

"What happened?" she asked quietly.

Part of me wanted to ignore the question. To say something ignorant and distract her, but there was another half of me that wanted to...to talk about it, to really talk about it. That part won out. "Dawson met Bethany, and I swear to you, it was like love at first sight. Everything for him became about her. Matthew—Mr. Garrison—warned him. I warned him that it wasn't going to work. There was no way we can have a relationship with a human."

I stared over her shoulder, at the tree line. "You don't know how hard it is, Kat. We have to hide what we are all the time, and even among our own kind, we have to be careful. There are many rules. The DOD and Luxen don't like the idea of us messing with humans. It's as if they think we're animals, beneath them."

"But you're not animals," she said, a bit fiercely. It was kind of cute watching her come to my defense for once, even though I probably didn't deserve it.

"Do you know any time we apply for something, it's tracked by the DOD?" I shook my head, disgusted. "Driver's license, they know. If we apply for college, they see it. Marriage license to a human? Forget it. We even have a registration we have to go through if we want to move."

"Can they do that?" Shock flooded her voice

I laughed drily. "This is your planet, not ours. You even said it. And they keep us in place by funding our lives. We have random check-ins, so we can't hide or anything. Once they know we're here, that's it. And that's not all. We're expected to find another Luxen and to stay there."

Her gaze sharpened. "That doesn't seem fair."

"It's not." I sat up, draping my arms over my bent knees. "It's easy to feel human. I know I'm not, but I want the same things that all humans want—" What was I saying to her? I cleared my throat as my jaw worked. "Anyway, something happened between Dawson and Bethany. I don't know what. He never said. They went out hiking one Saturday and he came back late, his clothing torn and covered with blood. They were closer than ever. If Matt and the Thompsons didn't have their suspicions before, they did then. That following weekend, Dawson and Bethany went out to the movies. They never came back."

Kat closed her eyes.

"The DOD found him the next day in Moorefield, his body dumped in a field like garbage. I didn't get to say good-bye. They took his body before I could even see him, because of the risk of exposure. When we die or get hurt, we resort back to our true form."

Her voice was soft when she spoke. "Are you sure he's... dead then, if you've never seen his body?"

"I know an Arum got him. Drained him of his abilities and killed him. If he were still alive, he would've found a way to contact us. Both his and Bethany's bodies were taken away before anyone could see. Her parents will never know what happened to her. And all we know is that he had to have done something that left a trace on her, enabling the Arum to find him. That's the only way. They can't sense us here. He *had* to have done something major."

"I'm sorry," she whispered. "I know there's nothing I can say. I'm just so sorry."

Lifting my chin, I gazed up at the sky. The weight of losing Dawson was like a hundred-pound ball of lead settling in my stomach. It hurt. Still hurt like it was yesterday. Still woke up some nights and found myself in his bedroom, wishing I could just see him one more time.

"I...I miss the idiot," I said raggedly.

Kat didn't say anything, but she leaned over, wrapping her arms around me. I stiffened out of surprise. She didn't seem to notice, because she squeezed me tight, and then she let go, pulling away.

I stared at her, shocked to my very core. After the things I said to her a handful of minutes ago, she did this? Hugged me?

She lowered her gaze to her hands. "I miss my dad, too. It doesn't get any easier."

The breath I let out was harsh. "Dee said he was sick but not what was wrong with him. I'm sorry...for your loss. Sickness isn't something we're accustomed to. What was it?"

"It was brain cancer. It started off with just headaches.

222

You know? He'd get these terrible headaches and then he started having vision problems. When that happened, he went in for testing and he had cancer." She glanced up at the sky, her brows knitting together. "It seemed like it happened so fast after that, but I guess, in a way it hadn't been. I got time with him before he..."

"Before what?" I watched her, unable to do anything but that.

Her smile was sad. "He changed toward the end. The tumor affected things. That...that was hard, you know?" Shaking her head, she lowered her chin. "But I have all the memories of the good times, like when we worked out in the garden together or went to the bookstore. Every Saturday morning we did the garden thing. And then every Sunday afternoon, since I could remember, we went to the bookstore."

I was beginning to see why she loved gardening and reading so much. It kept her close to her father. We'd both suffered so much loss. "Dawson and I...we used to go hiking together all the time. Dee's really never been big on that."

She grinned a little. "I can't really picture her climbing a mountain."

I chuckled at that. "Agreed."

As daylight turned to dusk, and stars started to fill the sky, we...we just talked. I told her about the first time Dawson morphed into someone else and got stuck. She talked to me about how her friendships fell apart after her father got sick. I found it interesting that she took the blame for that. We talked until the air took on a chill, and it was time for us to head back.

Truth be told, I really didn't want to return to reality. I enjoyed this. Kat. Me. Talking. Never thought I would, but I did. I really did.

Comfortable silence surrounded us as we walked back to our houses. There was a light on in the living room of Kat's house, so her voice was low when she turned to me. "What happens now?"

I didn't answer.

I had no idea what happened now.

I spent most of Sunday listening to Dee and Kat talk about books and how book boyfriends were universally better than real boyfriends while they sat in the living room. And since I was a guy, maybe not human, I really wanted to disagree with that statement, but once they started listing the attributes of some of these dudes in the books Kat carried around with her, there was no way anyone could compete with that.

I felt like I needed to warn Adam or something.

Matthew was having a cookout on Labor Day, which Kat had found hilarious that aliens were celebrating Labor Day... up until Dee was leaving. For a multitude of obvious reasons, Kat couldn't go with Dee. She tried not to show it, but the smile she wore while she sat on our front porch didn't reach her gray eyes.

"I don't have to go over there," Dee said, sensing what I did. "I can stay—"

Kat opened her mouth, but I jumped in. "You've gone every year. You have to go this year or it's going to look strange."

She worried on her lower lip as she glanced at Kat. "Are you going to be okay here?"

"Why wouldn't she be?" I demanded, folding my arms.

Kat shot me a glare.

"Her mom has to work today, so she's spending the day alone," Dee answered before Kat could reply.

I cocked a brow. "How is that different from any other day?"

Kat's lips pursed.

"Don't be a jerk." Dee's eyes narrowed. "It's different, because today is a holiday."

Kat opened her mouth again.

"It's Labor Day," I pointed out drily. "It's not like it's Thanksgiving or Christmas. I'm not even sure it's a real holiday."

"Oh, it's real. It's on calendars and stuff," Dee insisted. "It's a holiday."

I rolled my eyes. "It's a stupid holiday. Kat is—"

"Is right here, in case you all forgot that." Kat stood, dusting off the back of her jeans. She shot me a baleful glare before turning to Dee. "I'll be okay. Daemon, and God knows I hate saying this, is right. It's just Labor Day. It's no big deal. Adam is going to be there, right?"

Dee nodded while I eyed Kat.

She smiled again. "Go have fun with him."

By the time my sister finally got her butt in her car and left, I had been prepared to Hail Mary throw her all the way to Matthew's house. I wasn't sure I'd make it, but I was willing to try.

As Dee's tires crunched over the gravel, Kat moseyed on past me, and my gaze tracked her, riveted by the way her hips swayed. Did she realize how she walked? Jesus.

"Where are you going?" I asked, lashes lowered.

She stopped on the porch steps. "Um, going next door."

"Huh," I murmured, leaning against the side of the house.

Her lips turned down at the corners. "Aren't you going to the cookout?"

I shook my head. "That's never been my thing."

"Really? A cookout has to be a 'thing' to do?" she challenged.

"Whether it's my thing or not, it's kind of irrelevant. Someone needs to be here with you."

Those full lips dipped into a scowl. "I don't need a babysitter—"

"Yeah, you kind of do."

Kat faced me, and it became obvious that she was ready to fully engage. It took a Herculean effort not to smile. After yesterday, the time spent at the lake, something shifted between us. A connection I wasn't sure how to handle had been forged.

"I do not need a babysitter, Daemon." Her hand closed over the railing. "I'm just going over to my house and I'm—"

"Going to read a book?"

Fire was seconds away from shooting out of her eyes. Maybe even her mouth, too. "What if I am? There's nothing wrong with reading."

"I didn't say that there was." I smiled.

"Whatever." She pivoted and stomped down the steps.

I should've let her go. As long as she stayed here, when I was around, she would be safe, and the bonus was Dee wasn't with her. But as I watched her stalk toward her house—her empty house—I cursed under my breath and pushed off from where I was standing.

"Hey," I called out, unfolding my arms.

Kat kept walking.

Sighing, I shot off the deck. She didn't see me, not until I appeared in front of her. Jerking back, her hand flew to her chest. "Holy crap," she gasped. "A warning would be nice."

I shoved my hands into the pockets of my jeans. "I called out."

"And I ignored you!" Lowering her hand, she drew in a deep breath. "What do you want?"

"Not to be ignored."

Her head tilted to the side. "Really?"

My lips twitched. "Yes."

She shook her head as a warm breeze tossed loose strands across her face. "For some reason, I don't think that's the case."

"Maybe not." I stepped toward her, slowly this time. "I have some cow meat in the fridge. We could make hamburgers."

"Cow meat?" Kat caught the strand of hair and tucked in behind her ear. "That…is a gross way of saying hamburger meat."

"It is, isn't it?" I started past her, bumping her arm with my elbow. "We can have our own little cookout. I've got a grill."

Kat stared straight ahead as I kept walking.

"Are you coming or not?"

Her back was to me, and for a long moment I thought she was going to ignore me, and well, that would be really awkward. Especially if I had to go back to her, throw her over my shoulder, and force her to eat my grilled cow meat, because I would do it. No one should eat cow alone, I'd decided. Plus, I really wasn't going to analyze why I didn't want to think of her spending the holiday alone.

Kat turned around, catching that piece of hair again and wrapping it behind her ear. "Do you have cheese?"

I arched a brow. "Uh. Yes."

She folded her arms across her chest. "Swiss cheese?"

"Yeah, I think so."

A second passed and then she smiled, flashing straight, white teeth. "Okay. Only if you make me a Swiss cheese hamburger and you don't refer to it as cow meat."

Dipping my chin, I felt the corners of my lips quirk up. "Deal."

Dee ended up taking the fall for why Kat looked like she was lit up like the Vegas Strip. It had been her decision, and it had made sense, since I wasn't sure anyone would've believed I'd make the same mistake twice.

As expected, Matt wasn't thrilled about it. None of them were. I didn't blame them.

And also, as expected, when I told Kat she had plans that evening, as in sticking around so I could keep an eye on her, she stated she had other plans. Everyone and the lamppost knew she didn't have other plans.

Kat was just being stubborn.

After school on Tuesday, I followed Kat home. She'd gone to the post office first, which pissed me off. The girl looked like a lightbulb to the Arum. She knew that, and still moseyed her sweet behind to the post office to pick up an armful of packages.

Packages that contained *books*.

As if she needed more books.

When I had pointed that out to her in the parking lot, she

stared at me like I'd kicked a small child into oncoming traffic and had stated quite firmly, "You can never have too many books."

Then on the way home, she brake-checked me when I'd ridden up her bumper too close to get her to drive faster than I could walk. Didn't she get that every minute out here we were exposed? I worried every day until I could get her home, next to me, where I could protect her.

I blew my horn at her several times. It was either that or ramming the back end of her busted-ass Camry.

It had taken forever to get to her house, and the moment I parked my SUV, I was the poster child for impatience. I got up and went to her driver's side. Apparently, I had moved too fast.

"Jesus!" She rubbed her chest. "Would you please stop doing that?"

"Why?" I rested my arms on the open window. "You know about us now."

"Yeah, but that doesn't mean you can't walk like a normal human being. What if my mom saw you?"

I grinned. "I'd charm her into believing she was seeing things."

Opening the door, she barely waited for me to step back as she shoved past me. "I'm having dinner with my mom."

I popped in front of her.

Kat squeaked and took a swing at me. "God! I think you like to do that to piss me off."

"Who? Me?" I widened my eyes. "What time is dinner?"

"Six." She stomped up the steps. "And you are not invited."

"Like I want to eat dinner with you."

She raised her hand, flipping me off.

I grinned. "You have until six thirty to be next door, or I'm coming after you."

"Yeah. Yeah."

Spinning around, I smiled as I headed over to my house, wondering if she realized she had left all those precious books in her car.

Dee showed up a little after four, but it wasn't until it was close to the time when Kat was supposed to be here that she opened up the freezer and flipped out.

"Where is the ice cream?" Her voice was strained.

I leaned against the counter. "What ice cream?"

"What ice cream?" she repeated slowly, disbelief ringing in her voice. "The half a gallon of rocky road ice cream that was in the freezer yesterday!"

"Huh."

"I can't believe you ate all the ice cream, Daemon!"

"I didn't eat all of it."

"Oh, so it ate itself?" Dee's shriek could burst eardrums. "Did the spoon eat it? Oh wait, I know. The carton ate it."

"Actually, I think the freezer ate it," I responded drily. Dee whipped around and threw the empty carton at me, turning the damn thing into a speeding baseball. It smacked off my arm, stinging. I caught it before it hit the floor. "Ouch. That wasn't very nice."

She glared at me as I tossed the carton in the trash. It was then that I heard someone in the living room. Turning around, I headed for the room. It was Kat. I glanced at the clock and my lips twitched. It was a couple of minutes after six thirty. Leaning against the frame of the door, I crossed my arms and waited for her to realize I was there.

When she saw me, all she did was stand there and…stare. Her gaze moved over me like she hadn't seen me before, and

I found that interesting. I raised a brow. "Kat?"

She looked away quickly. "Did you get hit by an ice cream carton?"

"Yes."

"Damn. And I missed that."

"I'm sure Dee would love to do a replay for you."

Kat grinned at that.

"Oh, you think this is funny." Dee burst into the living room, car keys in hand. "I should be making you go to the store and get me rocky road, but because I like Katy and value her well-being, I'm going to get it myself."

Kat's eyes widened. "Can't Daemon go?"

I smiled at her.

"No. If the Arum comes around, he's only going to see your trace." Dee grabbed her purse. "You need to be with Daemon. He's stronger than me."

Kat sighed heavily, and if I had feelings, I'd be offended. "Can't I go next door?"

"You do realize your trace can be seen from the outside?" I pushed out of the doorway. "It's your funeral, though."

"Daemon," Dee snapped. "This is all your fault. My ice cream is not your ice cream."

"Ice cream must be very important," Kat murmured.

"It is my life." Dee swung her purse at me but missed. "And you took it from me."

I rolled my eyes. "Just get going and come right back."

"Yes, sir!" She saluted me. "You guys want anything?"

Kat shook her head, and when Dee walked to the door, I shot over and gave her a quick one-armed hug. "Be careful."

"As always." She waved good-bye and darted out the door.

"Wow," Kat said. "Remind me never to eat her ice cream."

"If you do, even I wouldn't be able to save you." I flashed a grin at her. "So, Kitten, if I'm going to be your babysitter for the evening, what's in it for me?"

Her eyes narrowed. "First off, I didn't ask you to babysit me. And you made me come over here. And don't call me Kitten."

I laughed. "Aren't you feisty tonight?"

"You ain't seen nothing yet."

Grinning, I walked into the kitchen. "I can believe that. Never a dull moment when you're around." I paused when I realized she was still standing in the middle of the living room. "Are you coming or not?"

"Going where?"

"I'm hungry."

"Didn't you just eat all of the ice cream?"

"Yeah, still hungry."

"Good Lord, aliens can eat."

I glanced over my shoulder, finding that she still hadn't moved. "I have this strong inclination that I need to keep an eye on you. Where I go, you go." I waited for her to move and when she didn't, I winked at her. "Or I can forcibly move you."

"All right," she huffed and then stomped past me, plopping down at the kitchen table.

I grabbed a plate of leftover chicken from the fridge. "Want some?"

Kat shook her head and then rested her cheek on her hand as she watched me move around the kitchen. Whenever I glanced over at her, she had a thoughtful look on her face.

I brought my plate to the table and sat across from her. Yesterday, during the little impromptu cookout, we really hadn't talked. Strangely, it hadn't been an awkward silence between us. It had been...nice. "So how are you holding up?"

She dropped her gaze. "I'm doing okay."

"You are." I took a bite of the cold chicken. "You've accepted all of this. I'm surprised."

"What did you think I'd do?"

I shrugged. "With humans, the possibilities are endless."

She chewed on her lower lip. "Do you think that we are somehow weaker than you because we're human?"

"It's not that I think you're weaker, I know you are." I eyed her over my glass of milk. "I'm not trying to be obnoxious by saying that. You are weaker than us."

"Maybe physically but not mentally or...morally," she argued.

"Morally?"

"Yeah, like, I'm not going to tell the world about you guys to get money. And if I was captured by an Arum, I wouldn't bring them back to you all."

"Wouldn't you?"

An emotion I couldn't read flashed across her face as she leaned back in the chair. "No. I wouldn't."

"Even if your life was threatened?" Disbelief colored my tone.

Kat shook her head as she laughed. "Just because I'm human doesn't mean I'm a coward or unethical. I'd never do anything that would put Dee in danger. Why would my life be more valuable than hers? Now yours...debatable. But not Dee."

I didn't want to believe her, but I realized I did as I went back to eating.

"So how long will it take for this trace to fade?"

Looking up, our eyes met. I picked up my glass of milk

and took a long drink. The hollows of her cheeks flushed. "Probably a week or two, maybe less." I squinted, checking out the glow. "It's already starting to fade."

"What do I look like? A giant lightbulb or something?"

I laughed, because she kind of did. "It's a soft white glow that's around your body, kind of like a halo."

"Oh, well that's not too bad. Are you done?" When I nodded, she grabbed my plate and stood, surprising me. She walked over to the sink, placing the plate there. "At least I don't look like a Christmas tree."

I followed her, bending my head down next to hers when I spoke. "You look like the star atop the tree."

Kat gasped and spun around, her eyes wide. Of course, she hadn't heard me move. She leaned back, gripping the edge of the counter behind her. "I hate it when you do that alien superspeed thing."

As I stared down at her, I smiled. Her cheeks were flushed prettily again. Didn't take a genius to know our proximity affected her, and not in a bad way. "Kitten, what are we going to get into?"

Her eyes darted over my face and then she blurted out, "Why not hand me over to the DOD?"

Caught off guard, I took a step back. "What?"

"Wouldn't everything have been easier for you if you handed me over to the DOD? Then you wouldn't have to worry about Dee or anything."

Damn, that was a good question. One I had asked myself over and over again. A question I knew everyone would ask if they ever found out that Kat knew about us. "I don't know, Kitten."

"You don't know?" she asked. "You risk everything and you don't know why?"

Irritation pricked at my skin. "That's what I said."

The widening of her eyes clearly spelled out the disbelief she was feeling. I didn't have a good enough reason for not turning over her. The DOD would love all over me if I had, and as much as I hated them, it worked to all of our benefits to keep them happy. There had to be a reason and I—

I cut off that thought. This conversation was leading to something far too serious. I didn't have time for that.

Leaning in, I dropped my hands on either side of her hips and lowered my chin. "Okay. I do know why."

Her breath caught. "You do?"

I nodded. "You wouldn't survive a day without us."

"You don't know that."

"Oh, I know." I tilted my head to the side, and while I was teasing her, I was also telling her the truth about what would happen if she ended up with the DOD. "Do you know how many Arum I have faced? Hundreds. And there have been times I barely escaped. A human doesn't stand a chance against them or the DOD."

"Fine. Whatever. Can you move?"

I grinned.

And Kat quickly lost her patience. She planted her hands in my chest and pushed—pushed hard. I didn't budge. My grin turned into a smile. "Asshole," she muttered.

She made me laugh. I really should have moved out of the way, but she was just so much fun to tease and I hadn't laughed this much in a very long time. I think deep down, neither had she. "You have such a mouth on you," I told her. "Do you kiss boys with that thing?"

Her cheeks turned bloodred. "Do you kiss Ash with yours?"

"Ash?" My smile disappeared. "You would like to know that, wouldn't you?"

Kat smirked. "No, thank you."

I didn't believe her for one second. I leaned in until only a few inches separated us. The scent of peaches and vanilla surrounded me. "You aren't a very good liar, Kitten. Your cheeks get red whenever you lie."

My brain clicked off when her cheeks turned an even brighter color. Before I knew it, my hand was wrapped around her arm. I wasn't gripping her. No. I was *holding* her, and her skin was warm under mine. I dragged my gaze to hers, and I couldn't look away.

Energy coursed through my body, causing my skin to hum. Tension practically crackled between us, and damn, it was hard to ignore that.

Part of me didn't want to. "I have a strange idea that I should test this out."

Her gaze slipped to my mouth. "Test what?"

"I think you *would* like to know." I grazed my hand up her arm, swallowing a groan when I felt her shiver. I stopped at the nape of her neck, under the heavy veil of hair. In the kitchen light, her hair was a deep brown, but I knew out in the sun, it was streaked with red. "You have beautiful hair."

"What?"

Yeah, that kind of came out of nowhere. Weird.

"Nothing." I slowly worked my fingers through the strands, and hell, they were as soft as I imagined. And yep, I'd imagined how it felt before. An ache filled me.

When my eyes made their way back down, I saw that her rosy lips had parted. She looked like she was waiting for a… for a kiss, and God, she was…

Damn. Kat was…she was beautiful.

A beautiful pain in my ass.

It took every ounce of energy I had to not lean down and

kiss her. But that would be a bad idea on so many levels, I couldn't count them all.

Slipping my hand out from her hair, I reached behind her and picked up a bottle of water I'd left there earlier. Her eyes widened as she slumped against the counter.

I turned back to the kitchen table before she could see me smiling. "What was it that you were asking, Kitten?"

"Stop calling me that."

I took a drink as I faced her. "Did Dee pick up a movie or something?"

"Yeah," she said, rubbing her hands up and down her arms. "She mentioned it earlier in class."

"Well, come on. Let's go watch a movie."

Kat actually listened and followed me into the living room; she lingered in the doorway while I found a DVD near Dee's schoolbag. Picking it up, I saw what it was and flipped it over. "Whose idea was this?"

Kat shrugged.

I read the description and then muttered, "Whatever."

She cleared her throat as she inched into the room. "Look, Daemon, you don't have to sit and watch a movie with me. If you have other things you want to do, I'm sure I will be fine."

Glancing up from the movie, I shrugged. "I have nothing to do."

"Okay." She hesitated for a moment and then walked over to the couch.

I popped the movie in and then sat on the other end of the couch. The TV came on, and Kat's sharp glance brought a smile to my face. My smile spread when I looked over at her a few seconds later and found her staring at me. "If you fall asleep during this movie, you'll owe me."

She frowned. "Why?"

"Just watch the movie."

Kat's gaze flipped to the TV, and after a few moments, I shifted to get comfortable. It was hard, because I was so damn aware of her sitting right there. I'd already forgotten what the movie was about by the time the first scene appeared on the screen.

And that was about how long I lasted without finding myself staring at Kat.

# 17

I didn't sleep well Tuesday night, so after snagging the obsidian blade off my dresser, I'd ended up doing patrols at three in the morning. There had been no sign of Arum nearby, but I knew it was only a matter of time before another one was seen. I wanted to catch it before it caught us.

Or Kat.

Wednesday morning was a blur, and for the most part, I was too distracted to put much effort into annoying Kat. She got one pen poke from me and that was all. My mind was in a dozen or so different places. Last night I had thought a lot about Dawson. I had thought a lot about Dee and how I knew she wanted to leave this area. I had thought a lot about what the Thompsons or Matthew would do if they found out about Kat. I thought a lot about *her*.

As I went through the morning, I felt a hell of a lot older than I should, than I was.

Things didn't improve for me when I strolled into the cafeteria and spotted Kat in the lunch line. She wasn't alone.

That asshole was with her—Simon Cutters. I didn't like the dude—never had. He was a touchy punk, and I didn't think he was all talk and no action when it came to the girls. And of course, he was sniffing around Kat.

A god-awful, unfamiliar emotion swirled inside me. I didn't want to put a name to it, didn't want to even acknowledge it, but all of a sudden I wanted to beat the ever-living crap out of Simon. I wanted to show him that he wasn't even worthy of speaking to Kat.

Simon waited for her at the end of the line.

Oh hell no, I was not okay with this.

I stalked past the line, to where Simon was standing in front of Kat.

She was staring at her plate. "We have a test next week, right?"

Simon nodded. "Right before the game, too. I think Monroe does that—"

Coming right up on Simon, I crowded him as I reached for a drink, forcing him to take a step back from her. Kat's chin jerked up as surprise flickered across her face.

I grabbed a carton of milk off the cart, flipping it in my hand as I turned toward Simon. We were the same height, but he was bulkier than me, and because of that, the idiot probably thought he could take me. I really hoped he wanted to find out.

"How you doing, Simon?" I asked, flipping the milk.

Simon took a step back, blinking as he cleared his throat. "Good—doing good. Heading over to my—uh, my table." Apparently he didn't want to see if he could take me. Shame. "See you in class, Katy."

Kat frowned as she watched Simon scuttle off, then she looked up me. "Okay?"

"Are you planning on sitting with Simon?" The question came out of my mouth before I could stop it.

"What? No." She laughed. "I was planning on sitting with Lesa and Carissa."

"So am I." Dee bounded in from nowhere, balancing a plate in one hand and two drinks in the other. "That is if you think I'd be welcome?"

That ugly, weird feeling settled heavy on my chest. Not waiting to hear Kat's response, because of course Dee would be welcome, I pivoted and headed back to where I saw the triplets sitting with a couple of others.

"Hey," Adam said as I dropped into the seat next to him. I lifted my chin in response, which earned me a low, "O—kay."

I sat my history text on the table and cracked it open.

"Someone is in a mood," Andrew said under his breath.

Without looking up, I muttered, "Someone wants to die."

Andrew laughed, unaffected by the statement. "What were you doing talking to Simon?"

I shrugged. "Just saying hi."

Beside me, Adam sent me a long look. "That's...odd."

"It's nothing," I said, and then started flipping the pages of my textbook. A few moments later, I felt holes being burned into the top of my head and glanced up, finding Ash scowling at me. "What?"

"Why are you being a dick?"

I raised my brows. That really didn't even warrant a response. About to turn back to whatever the hell I was looking at in the textbook, I found myself searching the tables until I saw a certain gray-eyed human girl.

Kat was smiling as she picked up her drink, her pink lips moving as she said something to Lesa. The girls laughed. Kat picked up the slice of pizza as Dee angled her body slightly, and then Kat's gaze roamed over our table and our eyes collided—met and then held.

Space separated us, but it didn't feel that way. I waited for her to look away. She didn't. I knew I should before Ash or Andrew noticed, because they would, but I didn't look away, either. Oh no, I continued eyeballing her, thinking of last night in my kitchen, how she had been waiting for me to kiss her. I knew that she had been.

And I knew that she wouldn't have stopped me.

Even from where I sat, I could see her lips part and her cheeks turn pink.

"You are really starting to bother me," Ash said, voice low, and when I didn't respond, her foot slammed into my shin. "Hello. Am I invisible?"

Frowning, I dragged my gaze away from Kat and looked at Ash. Her eyes burned like sapphires. "How could you ever be invisible?"

Her lips curled up in a tight smile. "I don't know. I'm feeling like I am right now."

"Huh," I murmured, taking a drink of my milk.

The small smile faded. "Don't sound too concerned," she said drily. "Wouldn't want you to stress yourself out over there."

I didn't reply as I placed the carton of milk down and returned to…chapter oh-who-the-hell-cares? I lasted about three minutes before I looked up and was staring at Kat again. Just like last night.

Screw me.

"**H**ow are things going with your new neighbors?"

Leaning against the side of my SUV, I stared down the empty back road several miles from the base of Seneca Rocks. Officer Lane had been waiting for me when I left school Thursday afternoon. With one flash of the Expedition's headlights, I knew he wanted me to go to our regular meeting place.

The only thing not regular was the timing of the check-in and the fact that Vaughn wasn't with him. Couldn't be too disappointed about Vaughn. Maybe he fell off the face of the earth.

I raised one shoulder in response to Lane's question, keeping it casual even though I didn't like the line of questioning. Wasn't the first time I'd been asked, but it was usually Vaughn doing the asking. "It's going. They seem pretty cool."

"No problems then?" Dark glasses shielded Lane's eyes.

Defining the word "problem" would be interesting. "Nope."

"That's good." Lane looked down the road. "I was worried."

Unease stirred in my gut. "Why?"

"You don't like humans," he answered honestly. "And with one moving in right next door, I figured you'd be pissed about that."

I snorted at Lane's frank honesty. Can't say I actually liked Lane, but he was better than Vaughn. When Dawson... when he died, Lane had seemed genuinely upset, unlike Vaughn, who obviously hadn't cared. "I wasn't happy. You knew that when I asked you and Vaughn about why they were allowed to move in, but what can I do?"

"Nothing," replied Lane. He folded his arms as his chin turned toward me.

I shrugged again. "Where's your buddy?"

"Vaughn?" One side of Lane's lips curled, almost like the idea of him being friends with Vaughn disgusted him. I knew there was a reason I tolerated Lane. "He's off doing something with Husher."

Now it was my turn. My lips curled in revulsion. Nancy Husher. Man, I disliked that woman. Didn't trust her, which was bad, because she was pretty high up there in the DOD, but luckily, we didn't have to deal with her often.

"A couple of weeks ago, there was an abnormal burst of energy around here," Lane stated, changing the subject to something else I didn't want to talk about. "It was tracked back to the main access road outside of your house."

I was betting "a couple of weeks ago" was code word for Kat stepping in front of a speeding truck.

Lane shifted his weight, which was slight. "You all playing football again?"

I almost laughed. Dee had made that up the last time we'd been asked about unusual activity. We didn't play any Luxen form of football and we sure as hell didn't toss around balls of energy, but it had been the perfect excuse. I nodded. "With the Thompsons. We got a little out of hand."

"Your new neighbors didn't see this, did they?"

I clenched my jaw. "We're not stupid. They weren't home."

Lane nodded. "Good to hear."

Pushing off the side of my SUV, I unfolded my arms. "Anything else?"

Officer Lane shook his head.

I opened the driver's door and was about to climb in when he stopped me. "Be careful, Daemon. With your new neighbors, it's not just going to be me or Vaughn keeping an eye on you. You might want to lay off the football."

Saturday evening was going to be the night that I locked Kat in her house. Swear to God, deities, and whoever else, it was going to happen.

"You're going to let me do this," she said, her eyes a stormy gray as she glared at me. "Because I'm not just going to sit here and do nothing."

"I never said you have to sit here. I don't want to sit here, either."

Her chin raised a notch. "No one is making you stay here, then!"

"Really?" Derision dripped from my voice. "I think you know why I'm here."

Kat tossed her head back and groaned. "I just want to go to this bookstore Carissa was telling me about. It's in town."

I knew which one she was talking about. Not like it was hard. There was only one bookstore in town. It was a used one, and the owner sometimes had no idea what they had in their store or its value. "And while the last thing I want to do is spend Friday night in a bookstore, all I'm saying is that I'm going with you."

Her little hands balled into fists. "Can't you see why I don't want you to go? You don't want to, and you're going to make it a terrible experience."

I rolled my eyes. "I will not."

She crossed her arms and stared at me pointedly.

"Seriously."

Looking over my shoulder, toward the woods, Kat sighed heavily. "Look, I get that I shouldn't go by myself. That it's—"

"Dangerous and stupid," I supplied helpfully.

The line of her jaw hardened, and a moment passed. "Yeah, I get that it's dangerous, but—"

"That should be the end of the conversation right there."

Kat lowered her frustrated gaze to mine. "But it's Friday evening, and Dee went to the movies with Adam, and I'm... I'm stuck here with—"

"With me?" I raised both brows as I crossed my arms, mirroring her stance.

She sighed again. "I don't want to sound like a jerk, but I don't...you don't even like me most of the time. I mean, one minute you're really cool and are actually fun to be around and the next—like the last couple of days—you have been such a jerk."

I hadn't been the friendliest since the day in the cafeteria. I didn't like the shit with Lane and the questions he'd been asking. I didn't like the shit with Simon. I didn't like that I didn't like the shit with Simon. I didn't like the shit with the Thompsons, namely Andrew and Ash, who were not at all secretive about their growing contempt when it came to Kat. I didn't like the shit with Matthew, whose paranoia was damn near contagious. I didn't like the shit with Dee, because she acted like nothing was wrong and everything was unicorns vomiting rainbows.

I didn't like the shit with Kat in general.

Needless to say, my mood was *shit*.

The center of Kat's cheeks were slightly pinker than the rest of her face, and even though her gaze was steady, I knew my mood swings affected her. The girl was mentally strong— an emotional powerhouse—but I wasn't easy on her. No way, nohow. And even though it was her who moved into this house and it was her who walked out in front of that truck, none of this was her fault.

Rubbing my palm along my jaw, I met her gaze. "I promise I'll behave."

She cocked her head to the side. "I don't believe you."

"You really don't have to." Reaching into the pocket of my jeans, I pulled out my car keys. "Come on. I know what bookstore Carissa was talking about. If you want to see it, we're going to have to leave now before it closes."

Kat didn't move.

"You're gonna want to see it." I jumped off the porch, landing nimbly in front of the steps. "They have like a bunch of books they sell for like fifty cents a piece." Her eyes lit up like the faint glow around her.

I backed up toward my driveway. "If you're lucky, the actual owner will be there."

She uncurled her arms. "Why would that make me lucky?"

"Because he looks like Santa Claus."

Kat blinked, and then a surprised laugh burst out of her. The sound did a weird thing to my chest, something I ignored as I opened the driver's car door. "You're coming, right?"

Finally, after what felt like forever, she got into the SUV and immediately turned up the radio, the universal sign that indicated "don't talk." The ride into town was quiet, and I kept my mouth shut as we walked into the tiny used bookstore that smelled like dust and old pages.

Unfortunately, the owner wasn't working, but Kat didn't seem to care. The moment she stepped inside, it was like Christmas morning to her. A smile appeared and it didn't leave as she buzzed from one overstocked shelf to the next, oblivious to the clouds of dust she stirred up every time she pulled a book out of a pile. There was no one else in the narrow shop besides the older lady behind the register, who had her nose in a book.

I stood back, out of her way, and I'd pulled out my phone,

opening up *Candy Crush*, but I wasn't paying attention to the game. Hell, I was still on the damn candy trail. I was watching her. I couldn't help it. Especially when she bent over, scanning the lower shelves.

Uncomfortable, I shifted my legs. Didn't help. Images flooded me. Kat starred in all of them. The costar was the red bikini. Heat moved under my skin, and I ground my molars. I needed to think about something—anything else.

Kat stretched up, reaching for a book several shelves above her, and the shirt she wore rode up, revealing a thin slice of skin above her jeans.

Aw, hell…

She clutched a book to her chest, and I was really, really envious of that book.

I shifted again. Still didn't help.

She spun around, heading for a wire bin full of small paperbacks covered with bare-chested men and women in fancy, old-school dresses. She dug around until she stacked a pile of them on the outside and then looked at me. "Can you help me?"

Slipping my phone in my pocket, my walk toward her was a bit…awkward. "What's up?"

"Hold your arms out, please."

I did what she asked.

And a few moments later, I was holding a pile of romance books.

I had no idea how my life veered so far off track that this was what I was doing on a Friday night, but a part of me wasn't all that upset. Which of course upset me even more.

Kat ended up leaving the store with more books than any human needed, and the whole way home she smiled that… that beautiful smile I rarely ever saw. She chattered about the books, and even though I didn't respond to anything she said, she kept going on.

She was actually happy.

I knew the moment I opened my mouth I was going to ruin that, like I always did. I thought about the fact that I knew none of this was her fault. And I thought about the fact that this whole time Dee had been careful around her and I hadn't. In my attempts to keep Dee safe and Kat in the dark, I put Dee at risk and exposed what we were.

In reality, I was the problem.

And my attraction to Kat didn't help the situation. Made it all the more dangerous.

Kat's trace was going to fade soon, less than a week. After that, I needed to keep my space. For real this time. No more broken record shit.

No more *shit*.

# 18

Days became shorter, and with each day that passed, the warm breeze swirling through the valley chilled. Leaves turned into bright shades of gold and red before sifting to the ground, announcing the arrival of autumn.

By mid-October, Kat's trace had completely faded. It had done so four days after our trip to the used bookstore in town, and I'd done what I told myself I needed to do.

With the exception of seeing her in class and whenever Dee had her over at the house, I stayed away from her. Of course, I still annoyed the hell out of her when I had a chance. Because really, there were very few things that amused me as greatly as poking her with my pen in trig and watching her gray eyes turn stormy.

I was really beginning to wonder if the pen was subconsciously symbolic for something else. That "something else" didn't amuse me. Oh no, it did something else.

I knew she was spending more time with the girls from our class. Therefore so was Dee, and while it irked me that my sister was becoming more and more involved with humans, there was nothing I could do to stop that.

The reality was, unless she eventually moved into one of the colonies, she would always be surrounded by humans. She would always grow close to one of them. Hell, if Adam and her didn't work out, she could end up...falling for one.

Just thinking about *that* made me want to punch a hole through the ozone.

There was one other thing that made me want to do that.

Simon Cutters.

The over-touchy jackass was getting on my bad side, and I might have lost my cool just a tad bit when he started talking to Kat in trig class. His backpack took a trip to the floor, and being the good guy that I was, I tried to warn Kat about Simon. That conversation hadn't ended well.

Kat had accused me of being jealous. *Me*? Of *Simon*? Was she insane? There was no way I was jealous of any human. Whatever. If she wanted to help the guy most likely voted to knock someone up on prom night *study*, then it was her planned parenthood. Not mine.

Up until Dee had informed me between classes, with a downright devilish gleam to her eyes, that Simon had asked Kat to homecoming and she had accepted. Fire coated the inside of my mouth as my sister bounced away, so pleased one would think she was just awarded a lifetime supply of rocky road. Why would she be happy about that? Everyone knew how Simon was and no one, not even Kat, could be that naive.

There were more important things I could focus on, like if there was a new episode of *Ghost Investigators* this week or not, but when I spotted Kat walking all the way to the back of the parking lot after school, near the football field and track, I couldn't let it go. "Kat!"

She turned around, squinting as a gust of chilled air blew the long strands of dark hair across her face. I approached her slowly, realizing that this was the first time in...in weeks that we were actually somewhat alone.

The strap on her bag was twisted, cutting into her shoulder. I reached out and fixed it, straightening the strap. "You know how to pick a parking spot."

A moment passed before she responded. "I know."

We walked to her car, and while she placed her bag in the backseat of her Camry, I waited with my hands in my pockets and tried to come up with a nice, non-jerk way of saying she needed to change her mind when it came to Simon. The "are you insane?" argument didn't seem like it would be very helpful, but that was what my brain kept cycling back to.

Closing the door, she faced me. "Is everything okay? It's not...?"

"No." I shoved my fingers through my hair. "Nothing... uh, cosmic-related."

"Good." She leaned against the car, her hands clasped together. Her keys dangled from her fingers. "You scared me there for a second."

When I twisted toward her, it left only a few inches between us. "I hear you're going with Simon Cutters to the dance."

Kat brushed a strand of hair out of her face. The wind tossed it right back. "News travels fast."

"Yeah, it does around here." I snagged the piece of hair this time and tucked it back behind her ear. My knuckles brushed against her cheek, and what felt like electricity danced from her skin to mine. "I thought you didn't like him."

"He's not bad," she said, shifting her gaze to the people on the track. "He's kind of nice, and he asked me."

Kind of nice? "You're going with him because he asked you?"

Her gaze sharpened as it returned to mine. She nodded as she fiddled with the keys. "Are you going to the dance?"

I hadn't been planning on it. Shifting my stance caused my leg to brush her thigh. "Does it matter?"

Her lips pursed. "Not really."

"You shouldn't go with someone just because he asked you."

She glanced down at her keys, and I had the feeling she wanted to stab me with them. "I don't see why this has anything to do with you."

"You're my sister's friend, and therefore it has something to do with me." My reasoning was total bunk.

And Kat knew that, because she gaped at me. "That is the worst logic I have ever heard." Whipping around, she headed toward the driver's door, stopping in front of the hood. "Shouldn't you be more concerned with what Ash is doing?"

"Ash and I aren't together."

Shaking her head, she started walking again. "Save your breath, Daemon. I'm not backing out because you have a problem with it."

Did she always have to be so damn stubborn? I cursed under my breath as I trailed after her.

"I don't want to see you get into any kind of trouble."

"What kind of trouble?" She yanked open the car door.

Catching the door, I arched a brow. "Knowing you, I can't even begin to imagine how much trouble you'd get in."

She glared up at me. "Oh yeah, because Simon's going to leave a trace on me that attracts killer cows instead of killer aliens. Let go of my car door."

"You are so frustrating," I snapped. Although there were

some cows around these parts that could probably take her out. "He has a reputation, Kat. I want you to be careful."

For a moment, she stared at me, and I thought she got what I was saying. "Nothing is going to happen, Daemon. I can take care of myself."

I was wrong. "Fine."

What happened next could only happen to someone like Kat. I let go off the door at the same exact second she was yanking it back. "Kat—"

The door caught her fingers, and her yelp of pain was like being doused with cold water. Bright red blood appeared on her pointer finger, and the rest were a deep red. "Christ!" she squeaked. "That hurt."

My hand was wrapped around her palm before I even realized what I was doing. Heat flashed from my hand to hers, and she inhaled softly.

"Daemon?" she whispered.

The redness faded from her bruised fingers. I lifted my gaze to hers. Our eyes locked. Her pupils were dilated in shock, and what I was doing sank in—what I had done.

I had healed her.

Dropping her hand, I gave a little shake of my head. "Shit…"

"Did you…is there another trace on me?" she asked as she wiped the blood off her finger, revealing completely healed skin. "Holy crap."

I couldn't believe what I'd done.

Kat hadn't been seriously injured. Just a scratch and some sore fingers. She would've been fine. I swallowed as I scanned her. A barely-there white glow surrounded her. It wouldn't be that noticeable, probably not even to others. "It's faint. I don't think it will be a problem. I can barely see it, but you might—"

"No! It's faint. No one will see it. I'm fine. No more babysitting." Her eyes widened as she drew in a shallow breath. "I can take care of myself."

Denials formed on the tip of my tongue, but she…she was right. Kat was a hundred percent right. I straightened, stepping back from the car. "You're right. Obviously you can, as long as it doesn't involve car doors. You've lasted longer than any human that's known about us."

Kat opened her mouth, but I turned around, stalking back toward the middle of the parking lot. Anger boiled inside me, but not at her. The first time I'm around her alone for a handful of minutes, I ended up healing a very minor injury like a freaking idiot.

Apparently I needed to work on my self-control.

Glancing over to the right, I laughed drily when I spotted Simon on the field. He was carrying his helmet as he jogged toward the center, where a group was huddled together.

My eyes narrowed as I lifted my finger on my right hand.

The helmet flew out of his hand, knocking into his shoulder pads. Caught off guard, he stumbled to the side and then went down on one leg, staring at the fallen helmet like it was a pit viper. The guys in the huddle laughed. My lips twisted into a wry grin.

Yeah, I really needed to work on my self-control.

Slapping the mayo on the piece of bread, I hummed under my breath, as loudly as I could to drown out the conversation from the kitchen. It wasn't working.

"He's going to think you're the hottest chick there," Dee said, her voice pitched obnoxiously loud.

I glanced up at the ceiling, exhaling loudly through my nose.

"Um, that's good." Kat cleared her throat. "I guess."

Picking up the lid, I nearly broke the mayo jar as I screwed it back on.

"You guess?" Dee laughed. At this point, I'd swear she was yelling. "Girl, he's not going to be able to keep his hands *off* you."

I smushed the slice of bread down, my jaw grinding until there was a good chance I was going to crack my molars.

"I'm pretty sure the same thing can be said about Adam when he sees you in the dress you got," Kat replied.

Dee giggled. "That's what I'm hoping for."

Oh for the love of everything in this world and the universe...

There was a pause. "You sure about the dress, though? It's kind of low-cut."

I closed my eyes, swallowing a groan.

"Oh, I'm sure," Dee assured her. "I'm *so* sure."

All but slamming the sandwich down on my plate, I was seconds from tossing myself out the kitchen window, but then I heard Kat saying she was heading back home and a few seconds later, the door shut.

I moved silently to the window by the table that overlooked the front yard. Kat appeared in the waning light, her backpack bumping off her lower back as she crossed the driveways. That ponytail of hers swayed with each step. As did her hips. My gaze dropped.

It was a couple of days after the day at her car and the tiny trace wasn't at all visible. Thank God. But I still worried and I—

"What are you doing?" Dee asked.

So caught up in being...well, sort of creepily watching Kat, my sister had sneaked up on me. That never happened. I turned around slowly. "Nothing. What are you doing?"

The look on her face screamed she didn't believe me. "Nothing."

I arched a brow.

She mirrored the gesture. "My 'nothing' means I'm not checking someone out from the kitchen window."

My eyes narrowed.

"You know," she continued, walking over to the counter. "You could've come into the living room and stared at her in person. You didn't have to hide in your bedroom and then in the kitchen."

"I wasn't hiding."

"Uh-huh." She spotted my turkey sandwich. "Did I tell you—"

"That's my sandwich. Don't..." Too late. I sighed as I watched her take a huge bite. "Help yourself."

"Thank you," she said as she chewed. "You make awesome sandwiches."

"I know," I grumbled.

Dee grinned as she leaned against the counter. "Did I tell you about the awesome dress Katy bought?"

Pulling out the kitchen chair, I dropped down in it and stretched out my legs. "Why would you tell me about her dress?"

"I didn't, but I'm sure you heard us talking about it."

"People in the next state heard you talking about it, Dee."

She ignored that. "It's stunning and Katy looks amazing in it."

My jaw was starting to ache again.

"Like she's going to look so hot at the dance, so hot." Dee paused, taking another huge bite of *my* sandwich. "Oh, and did I tell you Simon is taking her out?"

I counted to ten before answering. "Yes, Dee, you told me, and I think you're a crappy friend for allowing her to go with him."

"I am not a crappy friend!" She stomped her bare foot and rattled the chairs. "I know Kat isn't in trouble with him. She'll be fine. *Anyway*, did you know about the party after the dance?"

"Everyone knows about the party after the dance."

She waved the sandwich like she was saluting me with it. "Well, since you know everything, smart-ass, then you know Simon invited Kat."

I stilled. "She's not going with him to that damn field party."

"Oh. Yes." Dee smiled broadly and downright evilly. "Yes, she is."

No way. All anyone did at the party was get drunk and get laid, namely Simon. If he was taking her there…

My stomach churned.

"Don't worry, Adam and I are going. She'll be okay there." She finished off the sandwich, not even saving me a tiny piece. Then again, I didn't have much of an appetite right now. "Too bad you're not going to see Kat in her dress since you're too cool to go to homecoming."

"I never said I wasn't going."

Dee plastered a blank look on her face. "You didn't? Huh. I was pretty sure you said something like…" She deepened her voice. "'I'd rather punch myself in the nuts then go to that stupid dance.' Or something like that."

My lips twitched. "That was last year."

"When you were dating Ash."

I said nothing.

"So you're going to the dance?" she asked, flipping the long wavy black hair over her shoulder. When I said nothing, the blank look faded. "I bet you're going to that damn field party, too."

I smiled tightly. "What color is Kat's dress?"

Dee struggled to keep her expression bland and failed. Her eyes glimmered. "You're going to love it. That's all I'm going to say. You're just going to have to wait and see."

Adjusting my tie, I stepped out of the SUV and grabbed my tux jacket off the backseat, slipping it on. Immediately, I wanted to strip the damn thing off.

Homecoming.

Practically the last place on earth I wanted to be. A night of watching sweaty, gawky human teenagers paw all over each other wasn't my idea of a fun night. But I had little choice.

I glanced over at Ash. Standing beside her brother, dressed in a white gown, she really did look great. Too bad it was never, ever going to work between us. Our feelings for each other, even if she refused to admit it, had morphed into a more familial thing.

Andrew looked over at me as he messed with his cuff links. His brows inched up. "I don't even know why you're coming to this, man."

His sister made an impatient noise in her throat. "I have to agree, but can we move this conversation inside?" She waved a slender hand at the school. "I have people I need to make jealous."

I smiled. "Do tell?"

"My dress." She twirled around, and I swore it was see-through for a second. I squinted. Yep. It was definitely see-through in certain areas.

I couldn't help it. My smile spread, especially when Andrew looked away, his face paler than it was a few seconds before.

"My dress could feed a small village for a year, which means these…people haven't ever seen the likes of such beauty and perfection," Ash continued.

Shaking my head, I laughed. Ash…well, she was an acquired taste.

As the three of us headed in, I knew they'd never believe me if I told them why I really was here.

It had to do with one sweaty, gawky human teenager pawing all over one human in particular. The conversation I had with Kat a week ago, when we had been by her car, had replayed over and over in my head. Granted, the whole healing-her-hand thing had veered me off track, and even though we hadn't talked about her homecoming date since then, I hadn't forgotten about it. Definitely not after learning that Kat might've agreed to go to the damn party in the field afterward.

There was no way I could stay home. Instinct was screaming that she was going to need me. Or it was a really messed-up territorial need to…to do what?

Go in there, beat the crap out of Simon, and claim my girl?

Uh, no, because beating the crap out of humans would probably end in death, and she wasn't my girl. No way in holy hell was Kat my girl.

Ash disappeared into a flock of several girls who were already squawking and squealing about her dress. Forcing myself to breathe and not zoom around the room, popping all the balloons that probably took an entire day to blow up, I found the nearest empty table and sat. Following suit, Andrew did the same. He started talking about some football game I could give two craps about, and I zoned him out.

And waited.

And waited some more.

And then I saw Simon's jock–douchebag friends head toward the door, and I knew that meant Kat was here. Leaning back in my chair, I casually looked over my shoulder. Something unexpected happened to my chest. It felt like someone had walked right up to me and socked me in it. I might have stopped breathing. Right there, surrounded by humans, in front of Andrew, who was still running his mouth about some game.

"Oh Mary, mother of baby Jesus," I muttered, eyes narrowing.

Kat stood by the door, her hands clasped around a tiny clutch as her gaze bounced around the gymnasium nervously. The dress…aw man, that dress should be illegal. Tight around the breasts and waist, then flowing over her hips like a river of crimson silk. Her hair was up, revealing a long, graceful neck I'd never really noticed before. That was weird, because her hair was always up it seemed, but then again, that amount of cleavage was never showing before. Except when she wore that bikini. Speaking of red…

Red.

Red was my favorite color.

Dee had been so right about the damn dress.

Kat wasn't cute. She wasn't even sexy. She was beautiful—absolutely breathtakingly beautiful. Not that I hadn't noticed that before, but now? Now was something entirely different.

I watched her bolt as soon as she spotted Lesa, and an approving smile spread over my lips. *That's right, Kitten,* I thought, *stay away from Simon. He so doesn't deserve to be in the same time zone as you.*

I had no idea how long I watched her, but I eventually lost sight of her in the crowd. Part of me wanted to get up, punch Andrew in his mouth to shut him up, and go find her. But that would raise eyebrows, so I remained there, gripping the back of my chair so hard it groaned under the pressure.

Then she reappeared with my sister, skirting the dance floor. She stopped, twisting gracefully until her gaze landed on my table as if she'd been looking for me. Something inside me roared a male approval.

Our eyes locked, and there was that sucker-punch feeling again, except it moved lower, into my stomach. I was mesmerized, enthralled. Her lips parted and—

And Simon pushed through the crowd, blocking her from me. Every muscle in my body locked up as a primal urge rushed through me. I started to stand, but at the last moment, forced myself to sit back down.

A few seconds later, Ash arrived at the table. She was saying something, but I didn't really hear her. Then Andrew leaned over, snapping his fingers in my face. "Man," he said. "What's your deal?"

"Shut up."

"Nice." Andrew got up. "I'm getting something to drink."

"Peace out," I murmured, keeping an eye on Simon…and

Simon's hands. I did not like them.

"Do you want to dance?" Ash asked, surprising me. I'd thought she'd left. "Or do you want to sit here and glower?" When I didn't answer, she huffed as she stood. "Whatever. You're boring."

I barely acknowledged that she'd actually left that time and that I was sitting at a table alone, like a dork. My gaze was trained on the couple. Couple? God. It was insulting to Kat to even refer to her and Simon as a couple.

But I could deal. What Kat was doing really wasn't any of my business. In reality, she could do whatever she wanted. If that meant dancing—

Simon's hand glided down the front of her dress, causing Kat to jerk back. Her angry expression was lost in a sea of faces and...well, that was it. I was on my feet before I even realized it, moving between dancers, my hands curling into fists.

I stalked up to them, stopping behind Kat. "Mind if I cut in?"

Simon's eyes shot wide, and he must've seen his impending doom in my face, because he dropped his arms and took a step back. "Perfect timing. I needed to get a drink anyway."

I arched a brow and then turned to Kat, dismissing the idiot. "Dance?"

She stared back a moment, then carefully placed her hands on my shoulders. "This is a surprise."

Damn if it wasn't. We really hadn't talked since the day at her car. Like I'd said then, the trace was so faint it hadn't been recognizable. Didn't mean I hadn't kept an eye on her when she went into town, with and without Dee. She just didn't know that I was there.

I wrapped an arm around her waist and took one of her hands in mine. And damn if she didn't feel right in my arms, perfect actually.

Stupid and oddly wishful thinking.

Her incredibly long lashes swept up, and eyes warm but wary searched mine. A pretty flush spread across her cheeks and down her throat. I'd do something terrible to know what she was thinking. I pulled her closer.

Confusion and a...richer emotion marked her features. "Are you having a good time with...Ash?"

"Are you having a good time with Happy Hands?"

She sucked in her lower lip, and I bit back a groan. "Such a constant smart-ass."

I laughed, and she shivered in my arms. "The three of us came together—Ash, Andrew, and me." Why was I telling her this? My hand slipped to her hip and I cleared my throat, looking over the top of her head. "You...you look beautiful, by the way. Really too good to be with that idiot."

Her eyes widened. "Are you high?"

"Unfortunately, no I'm not. Though I am curious why you would ask."

"You never say anything nice to me."

"Good point." Damn, I was a dick sometimes. Well, most of the times. I lowered my chin, and she jumped when my jaw grazed her cheek. "I'm not going to bite you. Or grope you. You can relax."

She was silent, so I took that as a good thing. Acting on instinct, I guided her head to my chest and then placed my hand on her lower back. Dancing like that was normal. Nothing for anyone to freak over, including me.

Breathing in that peachy scent of hers, I closed my eyes and let the music guide us. There was something strangely intimate about slow dancing. Not the bumping and grinding kind that left little to the imagination, but this—two bodies melded together, drifting to the same beat, touching in all the right places. Intimate.

Okay, maybe I was high.

My hand curled against her back. "Seriously, how's your date going?"

When I glanced down, she was smiling. "He's a little friendly."

"That's what I thought." I searched for him in the crowd, wanting to knock him out. "I warned you about him."

"Daemon," she said, sighing. "I have him under control."

I snickered. "Sure looks like it, Kitten. His hands were moving so fast I was beginning to question if he was human or not." She stiffened in my embrace. "You should sneak out of here and go home while he's distracted. I can even get Dee to morph into you if need be."

Kat pulled back, and I immediately missed the way she felt in my arms. "It's okay if he gropes your sister?"

Well no, but... "I know she can take care of herself. You're out of your league with that guy."

We'd completely stopped dancing by this point. A storm was brewing, and it had a name: Kitten. I almost smiled.

"Excuse me?" she said. "I'm out of my league?"

Didn't she get it? "Look, I drove here. I can let Andrew and Ash catch a ride with Dee, and take you home." Sounded like a good plan to me, but the look on her face said it was no-go. "Are you actually considering going to the party with that idiot?"

"Are you going?" She pulled her hand free.

"It doesn't matter what I'm doing." And I wasn't ready to let her go yet. "You're not going to that party."

"You can't tell me what to do, Daemon."

Frustration whipped through me. Didn't she get that I was trying to look out for her? This wasn't a "who is the boss of me" contest. "Dee is taking you home. And I swear, if I have to throw you over my shoulder and carry you out of here, I will."

Her hand fisted against my chest. "I'd like to see you try."

I smiled. "I bet you would."

"Whatever. You're the one who's going to cause a scene carrying me out of here."

I made a sound low in my throat, but she actually smiled up at me, a mixture of smugness and innocence. "Because your local alien teacher is watching us as we speak. What do you think he's going to believe when you toss me over your shoulder, buddy?"

Son…of a biscuit. She was talking about Matthew.

"Thought so," she said.

I was still seriously considering throwing her over my shoulder and carrying her out of here with the whole school watching. I think I also wanted to kiss her…with the entire school watching. Probably do things that would make that flush turn a deeper shade of red.

Her glare turned defiant, and damn if a part of me didn't really, really like that.

A smile formed on my lips. "I keep underestimating you, Kitten."

266

# 19

The field where all the keg parties were held was roughly two miles outside of Petersburg and was accessed by a beaten-down dirt road that most would miss unless they knew it was there. I parked near the road, so I didn't end up blocked in.

Climbing out of the car, I slipped my keys into my pocket as I scanned the lines of vehicles haphazardly parked. Off in the distance, the orangey glow from the bonfire beckoned as I closed the door. The scent of gasoline and burning, damp wood was strong. Shadows moved around the fire. Laughter rang out, mingling with shouts. Music blared from speakers.

I'd left the dance a few minutes after Kat walked out with Simon. Ash and Andrew were still back at the school, and I wasn't sure if they would end up here or not. Field parties weren't their thing. I'd been to a few, with...with Dawson. I wasn't really keen on Dee being here, even with Adam, but she wasn't who I was worried about.

I knew Kat could handle herself. Deep down, I knew that.

How could I not? But that didn't mean she didn't need help or that she wasn't in over her head with someone like Simon.

Walking around the cars, trampled cornstalks crunched under my steps. As I neared the bonfire, a girl stumbled out from behind a truck, blocking my path. A red Solo cup dangled precariously from her fingers as she teetered on heels. Dark brown hair was piled up and clumps of dried grass and cornhusks clung to her silvery dress.

The girl, whom I vaguely recognized, couldn't have been older than fifteen. Her chin lifted, and her glazed eyes roamed over me. "Daemon?"

Unable to figure out her name, I nodded. "Are you okay?"

"Yep." She giggled, raising her cup to her lips. "Why you ask?"

I arched a brow. "You have dirt and pieces of corn all over your dress."

Another giggle echoed out of her. "I might've fallen a time…or four. These shoes—" She lifted her leg to show me and wobbled suddenly. My hand snapped out, catching her arm and steadying her as she continued to lift her heeled foot. "These shoes are ah-mazing, but they are not suited for field parties."

"No doubt," I murmured, letting go of her arm when I was sure she wasn't going to face-plant on the car next to her. "Are you here with someone?"

"Uh-huh. I'm here with Jon. He's my boyfriend," she explained, grinning as she swayed forward. "Unless you wanna be here with me, then I'm not here with anyone. Jon doesn't exist. Nope."

I smiled slightly. "Sorry, babe, but I'm here for someone else."

"For shame!" She smiled broadly and then whispered,

"That was bad of me to say Jon doesn't exist, right? He's really nice. Can it be our secret?"

Amusement flickered through me. "It'll be our secret."

"Yay!" She hobbled unsteadily as she clapped her hand against her cup. Beer sloshed over the side.

I could've left the girl there, roaming aimlessly for whatever reason between cars, but that seemed wrong for a multitude of reasons. "Let's go find Jon."

Turned out Jon wasn't in much better shape when we found him sitting by the fire. Based on what the girl had said, they hadn't even made it to the dance. When I deposited her with Jon, he stared at me like he half expected me to dropkick him into next week.

Scoping out the groups huddled around the fire, unease formed in my gut when I didn't see Kat or Simon among them. I headed to my right, eyeing the smaller groups near the thick outcropping of trees. Couples. Lots of couples. If Kat was among them, I'd...

What would I do?

I stopped walking right then, standing in front of the truck with its doors open, blasting music. What would I do if I saw Kat with Simon, doing those things the couples were doing in the shadows of the bare trees? What could I do? She had every right to be with him. She wasn't...

Kat wasn't mine.

Acid churned in my gut as I wheeled around. Dee was standing there, the light from the fire reflecting off the angles of her face. Her eyes were unnaturally bright. "Have you seen Kat?" she asked.

The unease exploded. "You haven't?"

"I saw her about five minutes ago. She was heading over to me, but then I lost track of her. She was with

Simon, but…" Her nose wrinkled. "I just need to find her."

My hands curled into loose fists. "I thought you weren't worried about Kat being with Simon."

Adam appeared at Dee's side. "I don't think there will be a problem—we don't think that, but Simon is pretty trashed, so…"

I didn't like what I was hearing. "Where did you see her last?"

"She was over there." Dee pointed to the other side of the fire, closer to the woods. "But she's not there anymore."

No shit.

We split up at that point and it took a couple of minutes to find someone who was about 70 percent certain that they had seen Kat head into the woods with Simon. That little piece of knowledge made me want to bang my head off the rough tree bark. I wanted to shake my sister. Whatever happened to the all-touted girl code? Wasn't it some kind of unspoken law that required them not to let one another roam off with questionable dudes?

I followed a worn man-made trail, preparing myself for the fact that I just may find Kat and she might not want to be found. Actually, that was the high likelihood here. Just because Simon was a touchy jackass who was currently trashed, didn't mean Kat needed rescuing or that she wanted rescuing.

If she was fine, I was going to walk away. She didn't even need to know that I was here. If she was okay, I needed to—

"Simon, *stop*!" Kat's shriek cut through the muted hum of music.

Instinct flared and I shot off like a bullet. A second was too long, but I found her and rage erupted inside me like a violent volcano. The son of a bitch had her pinned against a tree. His hands were on her. His *body*. His *mouth*.

They didn't hear me or see me, but that bastard *felt* me when I slammed my hand down on his shoulder and tore him away from her. Cocking back my arm, I nailed him in the face. His feet left the ground and for a very happy moment he was airborne. He hit the ground, legs and arms sprawled, with a not so satisfying *thud*.

I bent over him, grabbing the collar of his wrinkled dress shirt. "Do you have a problem understanding simple English?"

"Man, I'm sorry," Simon slurred, grasping my wrist. "I thought she—"

"You thought what?" I hauled him up with little effort, recognizing and enjoying the flare of fear in the human boy's eyes. I wanted to rip the motherfucker apart, limb from limb. Then I wanted to piece his ass back together. Rinse and repeat about a half a million times. "That no meant yes?"

"No! Yes! I thought—"

Close to absolutely destroying him, I raised my hand and froze him. Simon was a statue, his hands in front of his face. Blood pooled under his nose. Eyes wide and unblinking. Stepping back, I dragged in a deep breath.

"Daemon," Kat said from behind me. "What...what did you do?"

I glared at the frozen idiot. "It was either this, or I'd kill him."

Out of the corner of my eyes I saw Kat step around me. Her back was to me as she poked Simon's arm. "Is he alive?"

"Should he be?" I asked.

Kat looked over her shoulder at me, her eyes shadowed, but I saw what she was thinking in that moment, and I wanted to murder his ass. It didn't matter that I had warned her about him. This wasn't her fault. She didn't ask for it. Those things shouldn't be crossing her mind.

I tensed. "He's fine. Right now, it's like he's sleeping."

"God, what a mess." She backed up, wrapping her arms across her chest. "How long will he stay like this?"

"As long as I want. I could leave him out here. Let the deer piss on him and the crows crap on him."

A laugh choked out of her. "You can't...do that, you know that? Right?"

I shrugged.

"You need to turn him back, but first, I'd like to do something."

While I waited to see what she wanted to do, she unfolded her arms and walked right up to Simon. Without saying a word, she kicked him right between the legs.

"Whoa." I let out a strangled half laugh. "Maybe I should've killed him."

Kat shot me a look.

Frowning, I waved a hand, unfreezing Simon. He doubled over, cupping his hands between his legs as he moaned, "Shit," over and over again.

I pushed Simon back a few steps. "Get the fuck out of my face, and I swear if you so much as look at her again, it will be the last thing you do."

The idiot wiped a hand under his bloodied nose as he looked over at her. "Katy, I'm sorry—"

He had a death wish.

"Get. Out. Of. Here," I warned, taking a threatening step forward.

Simon spun around and took off, stumbling and limping over bushes. A white glow burned around him. He was traced. I didn't give a shit. Dead silence fell between us. Even the music seemed to have disappeared. I took a few precious seconds to calm myself down. It wasn't working. I started walking, a couple of feet between us because my fury was too close to the surface. I knew my eyes were glowing at this point, and I knew there was a good chance Simon had seen that briefly.

Something shimmery on the ground caught my attention. Kat's shawl.

Snatching it off the ground, I turned around and headed back to where Kat still stood. It was the first time I was getting a good look at her. Curls had slipped free, falling around her face. Her eyes were bright, even in the darkness. My gaze dropped. The front of her red dress was torn.

I was going to kill Simon.

Cursing under my breath, I handed the shawl to her. She took it with shaking hands.

"I know," she whispered, pressing the shawl to the front of her ruined dress. "Please don't say it."

"Say what? That I told you so?" Disgust dripped from my tone. "Even I'm not that much of an ass. Are you okay?"

She nodded and drew in a deep breath. "Thank you."

I watched her shiver. The shawl hid nothing, covered nothing. Shrugging off the tux jacket, I stepped around her and draped it over her shoulders. "Here." My voice was rough. "Put this on. It will…cover up everything."

Kat looked down at herself, and her shoulders tensed. She shoved her arms into my jacket and then tugged the edges together. Pressing her lips together, she fiddled with it, not looking at me, not looking at anything.

I was so going to kill Simon.

Besides murdering him very slowly, I also wanted to…I wanted to gather Kat close. I wanted to hold her, and the urge was intense and entirely unfamiliar to me. I wasn't even sure she'd want my comfort. I wasn't even sure I could give it.

But I hated seeing her like this.

Placing the tips of my fingers against her cheek, I smoothed back some of the wild strands of hair. Her gaze lifted. Those beautiful gray eyes were full of tears.

"Come on," I whispered. "I'm taking you home."

Her gaze searched mine, and then she nodded. She took one step before she said, "Wait."

Was she really going to argue with me now? "Kat."

"Won't Simon have a trace on him, like me?"

"He does."

"But—"

"It's not my problem right now." I took her hand, steering her down the worn path. Truth was, the trace on Simon was strong enough to attract the attention of an Arum, and I knew it made me terrible, but I didn't care. Not right now.

We reached my car, and I opened the passenger door for her. She peeked over at me and then climbed in. I closed the door and headed around the front of the SUV while I pulled out my phone. I texted Dee, letting her know I was taking Kat home. I didn't mention what happened. That was up to Kat if she wanted to go into detail.

Once inside, I passed a short look in Kat's direction. "I let Dee know I was taking you home. When I got here, she said she saw you but couldn't find you."

She nodded as she yanked on the seat belt. The jerky motion caused the belt to get stuck. Frustration poured out of her. "Dammit!"

Leaning over the center console, I gently pried her icy fingers off the strap and tilted my head as I pulled on it. My jaw grazed her cheek and then my lips, and I liked to think that last part was accidental. But I wasn't sure. I locked down those thoughts, ignoring the rush of sensations the brief touches conjured. The seat belt was twisted, and I set about straightening it. As I flipped the strap over, the back of my knuckles brushed across her chest. The jacket I'd given her had gaped open, probably while she struggled with the restraint, and there was nothing between the back of my hand and the swell of her chest.

That *hadn't* been on purpose.

I jerked my hand back as I lifted my gaze to hers.

Holy shit, when did we get this close?

There was maybe an inch between our mouths, and her sweet breath danced over my lips. The back of my damn hand tingled like I'd shoved it into an electric socket—a really soft electric socket. As if compelled, my gaze lowered to her parted lips. I wanted...

What I wanted was wrong, way wrong. Kat had almost been assaulted, for Christ's sake.

I clicked her seat belt in and then returned to my side of the SUV, turning the key. Reaching over, I kicked on the heat, then I clutched the steering wheel, damn near cracking it as I navigated my way out of the field strewn with cars.

We didn't talk.

Thick, strained silence filled the inside of the car. I glanced over at Kat several times during the drive. Her head was resting back against the seat and her eyes were closed. I didn't think she was asleep. Not when her hands were so tightly balled in her lap.

I had no idea what she was thinking, but if she was thinking half of what was going through my head, she had to be going crazy over there. Because I was still thinking about killing Simon. I was thinking about how Kat looked standing there, her eyes filling with tears. I thought about the front of her dress torn and how close…how close she came to something horrific happening. And I wanted to kill Simon more. I was also thinking about those moments when we first got in the car and how close our mouths had been.

I was thinking about the fact that I wanted to kiss her.

And I shouldn't want that. I couldn't want that.

Halfway to the house, I decided I needed to hear her voice, to know that she was okay over there. "Kat?" She didn't respond. Her eyes remained closed, and I figured she was ignoring me. For some reason, I sensed that—

Then I felt it.

As if the air conditioner had suddenly been cranked on high, a blast of iciness slammed into me. My gut clenched. Several feet ahead, a black shadow formed in the center of the road.

"Shit!" I slammed on the brakes.

Kat jerked in her seat, her hands landing on the dashboard as the SUV skidded to a halt. A second later, the car turned off, engine, lights—everything.

Well, hell…

The shadow contorted, taking shape. Within a heartbeat, a man stood where the shadow had been. Dressed in dark jeans and a leather jacket, I thought it looked pretty damn stupid wearing sunglasses at night. This one was identical to the one I killed the night at the library.

And he brought his brothers.

A shadow slipped from the side of the road, and then another. Two more joined the one in the center of the road. Three of them.

"Daemon," Kat whispered. "Who are they?"

My vision tinted with a fierce white light. "Arum."

# 20

Normally I would've welcomed this throw-down, especially after dealing with Simon. I had some pent-up aggression I really wanted to beat out of something, but not with Kat nearby. I didn't want her exposed to these creatures. They could kill her with a snap of their wrists.

Kat needed to get out of here.

That was the priority.

Keeping my eyes on the Arum, I reached down and yanked up my pants leg. My fingers brushed the leather binding around one end of the obsidian blade and I pulled it free.

"This is obsidian—volcanic glass." I placed it in her shaking hands, wrapping her fingers around the fashioned handle. "The edge is wicked sharp and will cut through *anything*. It's the only thing on this planet, besides us, that can kill the Arum. This is their kryptonite."

Kat stared at me, shaking her head silently.

"Come on, pretty boy!" yelled the Arum in the front, his

voice sharp as razors and guttural. "Come out and play!"

Such clichéd assholes.

Ignoring them, I cradled her cheeks, forcing her terrified gaze to mine. "Listen to me, Kat. When I tell you to run, you run and you don't look back no matter what. If any of them—*any*—chase you, all you have to do is stab them anywhere with the obsidian."

"Daemon—"

"No. You run when I tell you to run, Kat. Say you understand."

Her chest rose and fell heavily. "Please don't do this! Run with me—"

"I can't. Dee is at that party." I held her gaze. "Run when I tell you."

Kat's lips trembled, and I let my gaze soak in her features for one more second, committing the height of her cheekbones to memory, along with the bow shape of her lips and those endless gray eyes. Then I let go and opened up the car door. I rounded the grille on the SUV, smiling at the three Arum. "Wow. You guys are uglier as humans than in your true form. Didn't think that was possible. You look like you've been living under a rock. See the sun much?"

The one in the center bared his teeth like a wild animal. "You have your arrogance now, like all Luxen. But where will your arrogance be when we absorb your powers?"

"In the same place as my foot." My hands balled into fists.

The middle Arum tilted his head in confusion.

It was never fun when I had to explain what I meant. "You know, as in up *your ass*." I smiled and the two Arum hissed. "Wait. You guys look familiar. Yeah, I know. I've killed one of your brothers. Sorry about that. What was his name? You guys all look alike to me."

Their forms started flickering in and out, turning from human to shade and back again. My goal was to get them really pissed and a hundred percent focused on me so that Kat could slip away. It appeared to be working.

"I'll rip your essence from your body," the Arum growled, "and you will beg for mercy."

"Like your brethren did?" I retorted. "Because he begged—he cried like a wounded animal before I ended his existence."

And that was it. The Arum bellowed in unison, the sound of howling winds and death. I threw up my hands, summoning the Source. It rose inside me, powerful and all-consuming, and then spread outside of me, tapping into the tiny particles of energy that existed inside everything on this planet. The very air around me heated, causing a series of loud cracks.

God, it felt *real* good to let loose.

An earthy scent filled the air as the nearby trees lifted. Dirt clung to their thick roots. I flicked a finger. The closest tree, a large elm, slammed into the back of an Arum, knocking him several yards down the road. Trees flew into the road, one by one, but the other two Arum were just a little bit smarter than the one peeling himself off the cracked asphalt.

I pulled on the Source again. Chunks of asphalt cracked and gave way along the shoulder of the road. Pieces of it lifted in the air, spinning as it turned a bright orange, heated like lava. I winged those suckers at the Arum as the two blinked in and out, avoiding the branches from the trees. One of the Arum threw his hand back.

Then they were done playing. So was I.

As the smell of burned tar filled the air, I shifted into my true form. One of them rushed me as I slammed my hands together. The Source rippled out, hitting the nearest

Arum. The blast spun him up in the air, a direct and lethal hit, momentarily knocking him into his human form. Dark sunglasses shattered. Pieces floated in the air, suspended. Another clap followed, and the Arum exploded in an array of dazzling lights that fell like a thousand twinkling stars.

I threw out my arm again, and the other Arum flew back several feet, spinning and tumbling through the air, but he landed in a crouch.

It was time for Kat to go.

*Run.* I spoke to her in my true form. *Run now, Kat. Don't look back. Run!*

All I heard was the car door open and then everything was lost in the sound of the Arum howling. The other one was back and the remaining one was circling me. I darted to the right as one of them released a dark essence, a ball of shadow-filled energy that would be fatal if it hit me. I spun out as it shot over my shoulder. Like a thick glob of oil, when it smacked into one of the fallen trees, the energy ripped it in two.

Damn.

Pulling the Source, I formed a ball of iridescent light in the palm of my hand and then hurled the plasma ball right back at them.

The Arum weren't as fast as me, but they were avoiding the balls, and I knew, in my bones I knew what they were doing—wearing me down, tiring me out, like we were boxing. We all were moving, darting back and forth. My hold on my true form flickered.

The Arum seized that one moment of weakness.

One rushed me from the front and, as I braced myself for a full-body attack, the other sped up. I twisted, trying to keep it in sight. A second where I took my eyes off one, and I made a huge mistake. Twisting at the waist, I threw out another blast of energy, but it fizzled out before reaching the Arum, skidding across the road in a shower of sparks.

Shadowy arms went around my neck from behind, immediately chilling. Ice drenched me as I reached up, allowing fingers to form. I wrapped them around the arm choking me, but he brought me down to one knee.

"Ready to beg?" the Arum in front of me taunted, taking human form. "Please do. It would mean a lot to hear the word 'please' leaking from your lips as I take everything from you."

Light crackled all around me as I lifted my head. Still in my true form, I called on the Source one last time.

"Silence to the end, eh? So be it." The Arum stepped forward, lifting his head. "Baruck, it is time."

Baruck forced me to stand. "Do it now, Sarefeth!"

There was no way I was going down like this. No way in hell. Dee was at that party with Adam. They'd find her. And Kat was out there, somewhere and too close. Hell no. This wasn't happening. This wasn't going to happen to my sister. This wasn't going to happen to Kat. Energy built and expanded just as the one in front of me—Sarefeth—shifted into his true form, nothing more than smoke. I drew on the power as he slammed his hand against my chest, *into* my chest. My back bowed as I ground down. Pain exploded in every cell, startling me. Never had I felt anything like that. It seized every part of me, forcing a scream out of me as I briefly shifted into my human form.

Without any warning, the Arum in front of me, the one named Sarefeth, jerked his hand free from me and spun away. Pain still rippled throughout me, causing me to shift back and forth between forms, but I...I had to be hallucinating, because I saw her.

Kat was standing a few feet behind Sarefeth, like some

kind of warrior princess, hair wild and red dress torn, the obsidian blade glowing red in her hand. Then Sarefeth exploded, breaking into pieces and floating up to the sky.

Baruck released me as I shifted back into my true form. I tried to push past the pain of the feeding as Baruck started toward Kat, but the Arum changed course, shifting into nothing more than a shadow, pulling the darkness into him, fleeing toward the other side of the road like a coiled snake and disappearing into the night.

Then Kat was at my side, on her knees. "Daemon—Daemon, please say something."

My light flared, throwing off heat that had to be too intense for Kat. I slowly became aware of my hands pressing into the cracked and burned pavement. I thought I heard Kat cry, and that—*that* forced me to pull it together. I shifted into my human form and reached out, grabbing her arm as she started to scuttle away.

"Daemon, oh God, are you okay?" She was back at my side, her palm pressed to my cheek. The feeling of her hand... *God.* "Please tell me you're okay? Please!"

Slowly, I lifted my head and placed my other hand over hers, the one against my cheek. "Remind me to never piss you off again. Christ, are you secretly a ninja?"

Kat laughed and sobbed in the same breath, and then she threw herself at me. I caught her and barely stopped myself from tumbling over backward. My hand delved deep into the mass of hair that had fallen free, and I held her just as tightly as she clung to me. She pressed herself to me like she was trying to become one with me, and even though my skin felt raw, the pain was nothing compared to the feeling of her right in that moment.

I pressed my forehead against her shoulder. "You didn't

listen to me."

"I never listen to you." She squeezed me hard before pulling back. Her gaze roamed over my face. "Are you hurt? Is there anything I can do?"

"You've already done enough, Kitten." Gathering my strength, I pushed to my feet, bringing her along with me. I took in the destruction around us. "We need to get out of here before anyone comes."

Stepping back, I summoned the Source one last time and lifted my hand. Trees lifted off the road and rolled to the sides, clearing a path, and then we made our way back to the car. It roared to life as soon as I turned the key. I glanced over at Kat. She was shaking in the seat. "Are you okay? Hurt in any way?"

"I'm okay. It's just…a lot, you know?"

A lot? I coughed out a laugh, but there was no humor to it. I hit the steering, frustrated. "I should've known there would be more coming." I should've been more prepared. "They travel in fours. Dammit!"

"There were only three of them," she said.

"Yeah, 'cuz I killed the first one." Leaning back, I pulled out my cell. I needed to call Dee. The others needed to be warned that there was still one more out there, and since three of his brothers had just been killed, he was going to be seeking some nasty revenge.

Kat concerned me.

What she had just witnessed would bring a grown man to his knees in terror and shock. But she was quiet as I called Dee and then Matthew, and remained so on the trip home. Whenever I glanced over at her, I'd see a tremor make its way through her, but she wasn't freaking out.

Kat blew me away.

This human girl was strong, with a core made out of steel. She was holding it together. Not only that, she had most definitely saved my life. I was man enough to admit that. If she hadn't intervened when she did, I don't know if I would've broken Baruck's hold. I owed her my life. I could've died out on that road, and there would be two Arum and not one gunning for my family—for Kat.

Because she was lit up like the moon again.

The houses were dark when I pulled into the driveway. Turning off the engine, I looked over at Kat as I opened the car door. The overhead light was triggered, casting a soft light against her pale cheeks. She didn't move. "Kat?"

Blinking slowly, she turned her cheek toward me. "Yes?"

Asking if she was okay seemed stupid. My gaze dropped to her hand. She was still holding the obsidian blade. I reached over, gently easing it out of her grasp. Her eyes rose to mine. "I want you to stay the night at our place," I said. "You're traced again, and even though I doubt the Arum will find his way here, I'd rather be safe than sorry."

Her lips parted. "But if I'm traced, isn't it more of a risk that I'm in the house with you—with Dee."

My jaw tightened. "If an Arum tracks you to your house, we're right next door. It's virtually the same. Plus Dee is with Matthew and Adam right now. Andrew is there, too."

"But it's not," she reasoned quietly. "If he—if it—

comes after me, then at least you—"

"I want you in my house," I cut in, ignoring her logic. "Okay?"

Kat stared at me for a long moment and then nodded. She climbed out, and I followed her into her house. Once the foyer light flipped on, I realized she was missing a shoe and her knees were a scratched, dirty mess. All of her was. I opened my mouth to say something, anything, but she limped ahead, pulling herself upstairs.

My eyes drifted shut as my hand tightened around the leather binding on the obsidian. My shoulders sagged with fatigue.

When I had talked to Matthew, he asked if Kat had seen what had gone down. There was no way I could lie or hide the truth. I'd answered with a yes.

"We're going to have to talk about this later," he'd replied.

And I knew later was going to come real quick.

Opening my eyes, I saw Kat appear at the top of the steps, carrying a tote. She was still dressed in her ruined gown, my jacket swallowing her. Exhaustion clung to her every step, and she walked as if she was ready to sit down and take a nap.

Kat had saved my life.

No matter what Matthew or the Thompsons ended up thinking or saying, I was going to have her back. She had mine.

I met her halfway, taking the tote from her, and then after she locked up, we headed over to my house.

"I told my mom I was staying with Dee," she said, clearing her throat. "I called when I was upstairs."

"Cool." I opened the front door, and a rush of cold air

greeted us. Kat shivered. "Sorry. We keep it pretty cold at night."

"I remembered," she murmured, glancing at the stairs leading to the second floor. The skin across her cheekbones was drawn and pale. "It's okay."

Once we were in the guest room, Kat groaned as she peered into the tote. "I'm such an idiot. I brought regular clothes with me. Nothing to sleep in. I'm going to have to go back over."

"I'll find you something. Just give me a second." I went to Dee's room and grabbed a pair of bottoms and an old shirt, knowing she wouldn't mind. When I returned, Kat had shrugged off my jacket and laid it across the dresser. She held the front of the dress together as I placed the borrowed clothes on the bed.

Again, I wanted to say something to her, but nothing of any value came to mind. Kat gathered up the clothes and shuffled into the bathroom in the hallway. I went into my room, took a shower in the bathroom attached, and then quickly changed into a pair of sweats and a T-shirt. I checked my phone, scrolling through the texts from Dee and then Andrew, who had heard about what happened via Adam. Dee was coming back home, as soon as they found Ash. Matthew would make sure of it.

I found myself back in the hallway, near the bathroom. The water was turned off, and as I stood there, I thought I heard her laugh. It wasn't a happy laugh. Concern ratcheted up.

"Are you okay in there?" I said to the closed door.

There was a pause and then, "Yeah."

I hesitated and then wheeled around, walking into the guest bedroom. I sat on the edge of the bed. Kat could probably use some space right now, but I… *Shit.* I reached up, rubbing the center of my chest, where the Arum had got me. I didn't want her to be alone right now.

I didn't want to be alone right now.

A few minutes passed and Kat walked in, and I lifted my gaze. Her hair was damp, darkening the shoulders of the gray shirt I'd found. Shadows had formed under her eyes, and she was still too pale, but she was so…so not plain. Not average. Not like anyone I'd ever known. Realizing that was like taking a direct hit from an Arum. I didn't know what to do with it.

Kat stopped a few feet from the bed. "Are you okay?"

I nodded, lowering my hand, sort of shocked that she was asking about my well-being. "Whenever we use our powers like that, it's like…losing a part of ourselves. It takes a bit to recharge. I'll be fine." I paused. "I'm sorry you had to go through any of this. I didn't say thank you. You should've run, Kat. They would've…killed you without thinking twice. But you saved my life. Thank you."

Her mouth opened and then closed as she rubbed her arms. It seemed to take her a moment to respond. "Will you stay with me tonight?" She then added in a rush, "I'm not coming on to you. You don't have to, but—"

"I know." I felt the same way. I just wanted to hold her, reassure myself we were both okay. I stood, and it felt like my stomach dropped to my feet. "Just let me check the house again, and I'll be right back."

Before I left the room, she was already in the bed, and when I glanced back at her, she had the covers tugged up to her chin and was staring at the ceiling. A small smile pulled at my lips as I made quick work of double-checking the doors. Then I grabbed my phone out of my room. Dee would be home soon, and if I was smart, I could've just told Kat that. Sit up with her and wait until a more appropriate bedmate appeared, but that's not what I did.

I returned to the guest bedroom and got a little stuck in the doorway when I saw her in the bed again. She should be in *my* bed. As soon as that mess of a thought entered my head, I pushed it right back out, blaming the night's drama. Shutting the door behind me, I went to the large bay windows overlooking the front yard.

Kat scooted over to the edge of the bed as I walked around to the other side, and I hid my smile. You'd think we were sharing a tiny bed based on how far she moved over. I climbed in beside her, leaving the comforter at my waist. My temperature ran way higher than hers.

Neither of us spoke.

Both of us lay there, side by side, staring at the ceiling. If anyone said a year ago I'd be lying in a bed with a human girl like this, I would've told them to get off drugs.

Biting down on my lip, I turned my head toward hers. A handful of seconds passed before she looked over at me. I grinned at her.

Kat laughed, and yeah, I liked that sound. "This…this is so awkward."

My grin spread. "It is, isn't it?"

"Yes." She giggled.

It sounded crazy to laugh after everything, but my laughter joined hers. This was ridiculous. Everything. Ninety percent of the time we lived to annoy the crap out of each other. I knew that went both ways, but I'd saved her life in the past. She saved mine tonight. And here we were, sharing a bed for no real reason. At least on my side, the shit was funny.

And Kat was…there were no words.

I reached over, catching the tiny tears that had coursed down her cheeks. They weren't sad tears. Our eyes locked as I lowered my hand. "What you did back there? It was sort of amazing," I murmured.

One side of her lips twitched up. "Right back atcha. Are you sure you're not injured?"

I grinned. "No. I'm fine, thanks to you." Shifting away from her, I turned off the lamp on the nightstand the good ol'-fashioned way—the human way.

The room was plunged into darkness. "Am I glowing?" she asked.

Well, duh. She'd gotten a dose in the field and I'd lit that street up with the Source like a carnival. "Like a Christmas tree."

"Not just the star?"

I rolled onto my side, close enough to her that my hand brushed her arm. "No. You're super bright. It's kind of like looking at the sun."

She held up her hand, and that was cute. "It's going to be hard for you to sleep then."

"Actually, it's kind of comforting. It reminds me of my own people."

"The whole obsidian thing?" She looked over at me. "You never told me about that."

"I didn't think it would be necessary. Or at least I'd hoped it wouldn't be."

"Can it hurt you?"

"No. And before you ask what can, we don't make a habit of telling humans what can kill us," I replied evenly. "Not even the DOD knows what's deadly to us. But the obsidian negates the Arum's strengths. Just like the beta quartz in the Rocks throws off a lot of the energy we put off, but with obsidian, all it takes is a piercing and...well, you know. It's the whole light thing, the way obsidian fractures it."

"Are all crystals harmful to the Arum?"

"No, just this type. I guess it has something to do with the heating and cooling. Matthew explained it to me once. Honestly, I wasn't paying attention. I know it can kill them. We carry it whenever we go out, usually hidden. Dee carries one in her purse."

She shuddered. "I can't believe I killed someone."

"You didn't kill *someone*. You killed an alien—an evil being that would've killed you without thinking twice. That was going to kill me." I absently rubbed at my chest. "You saved my life, Kitten."

Kat didn't respond, and I knew it was going to be hard for her to understand.

"You were like Snowbird," I said after a few moments.

"How do you figure?" she asked.

I smiled slightly. "You could've left me there and run, like I said. But instead you came back and you helped me. You didn't have to."

"I...I couldn't leave you there." The next breath she took was audible. "It wouldn't have been right. And I would've never been able to forgive myself."

"I know." I stifled a yawn. "Get some sleep, Kitten."

She was quiet for all of five seconds. "But what if the last one comes back?" I paused, realizing a new fear. "Dee's with Mr. Garrison. He knows I was with you when they attacked. What if he turns me in? What if the DOD—"

"Shh," I murmured, finding her hand with mine. I ran my fingers over the top of hers. "He won't come back, not yet. And I won't let Matthew turn you over."

"But—"

"Kat, I won't let him. Okay? I promise you. I won't let anything happen to you."

This time it was her soft inhale that I heard, and I knew my promise was bold and it was a big deal, but it was one I wouldn't break.

# 21

I wasn't sure if I was dreaming, but if I was, I didn't want to wake up. The scent of peach and vanilla teased me, invaded me.

Kat.

Only she smelled that wonderful, of summer and all the things I could want and never have. The length of her body was pressed against mine, with her hand resting on my stomach. The steady rise and fall of her chest became my entire world, and in this dream—because it had to be a dream—I felt my own chest matching her breaths.

Every cell in my body sparked and burned. If I were awake, I'd surely take on my true form. My body was on fire.

Just a dream, but it felt real.

I couldn't resist sliding my leg over hers, burrowing my head between her neck and shoulder, and inhaling deeply. Divine. Perfect. Human. Breathing became more difficult than I'd ever imagined. Lust swirled through me, heady and consuming. I tasted her skin—a slight brush of my lips, a flick of my tongue. She felt perfect underneath me, soft in all the places I was hard.

Moving over her, against her, I loved the sound she made—a soft, wholly feminine murmur that scorched every piece of me. "You're perfect for me," I whispered in my own language.

She stirred under me, and I dreamed her responding, wanting me instead of hating me.

I pressed down, sliding my hand under her shirt. Her skin felt like satin underneath my fingertips. Precious. Prized. If she were mine, I'd cherish every inch of her. And I wanted to. Now. My hand crept up, up, up. Her skin was so smooth, so soft.

Kat gasped.

The dreamy cloud dissipated with the sound I felt all the way through me. Every muscle locked up. Very slowly, I pried my eyes open. Her slender, graceful neck sloped before me. A section of skin was pink from the stubble on my jaw...

The clock on the wall ticked.

Shit.

I'd felt her up, in my sleep.

I lifted my head and stared down at her. Kat watched me, her eyes a smoky, wonderful gray and questioning. Double shit.

"Good morning?" she said, her voice still rough with sleep.

Using my arm, I pushed up and even then, knowing that none of it had been a dream, I couldn't look away from her, didn't want to. An infinite need was there, in her, in me. Demanding that I kneel to it, and I wanted to—dammit, did I ever want to.

The only thing that got to me, that cleared the layers of lust and idealistic stupidity out of my head, was the trace shimmering around her. She looked like the brightest star.

She was in danger. She was a danger to us.

With one last look, I shot across the room with inhuman speed, slamming the door behind me. Every step away from that room, from that bed, was painful and stiff. Rounding the corner, I almost ran into my sister.

Dee studied me, eyes narrowed.

"Shut up," I muttered, heading past her.

"I didn't say anything, jerk-face." Amusement betrayed her words.

"Don't say anything," I warned.

Once inside my bedroom, I quickly changed into a pair of sweats and slipped on my sneakers. Running into my sister cooled most of me down, but there was a raw edge to my nerves, and I needed to be out of this house, away from her.

Not even bothering to change my shirt, I picked up speed, shooting through the house and out the front door. The moment my sneaks touched the porch, I took off and darted into the woods in a burst of speed. Overhead skies were gray and bleak. Drizzle pelted my face like a thousand tiny needles. I welcomed it, pushing and pushing until I was deep in the woods. Then I shed my human skin, taking my true form as I shot among the trees, moving until I was nothing more than a streak of light.

I wanted that—I wanted Kat.

That wasn't an entirely new thought or realization. From the moment I saw those legs, I'd pictured said legs wrapped around me, tangled with mine, more than a time or two. And then she'd rocked that red bikini? Wanting her wasn't new, but the intensity of what I felt this morning was.

I wanted Kat so badly it neared physical pain.

Had it been because of last night? Her saving me? Or had

it been earlier, seeing her with Simon and that dress? Or had it been building from day one? None of it mattered.

This was wrong.

Think of Dawson. Look at what had happened to him. Did I want to take the same risk? Leave Dee all alone? But even now I could feel her skin, taste it—sweet and sugary like candy. Hear that wonderful sound she made over and over again, haunting every mile I put between us.

An idea began to form—one that Dee would hate, but I didn't see any other option. I could go to the DOD and request a move to one of the other communities. We'd be giving up our home, leaving behind our friends and Matthew, but it would be for the best. It was the right thing to do. Dee would be safe.

It would keep Kat safe.

Because Dee couldn't stay away from her, and neither could I. But no matter where I went, what I was running from would still be with me—Kat. She wasn't just back in the house, in that bed. She was with me now, inside me. And there was no outrunning that.

When I returned from my run, everything felt under control. I had a plan, one I would act on. I entered the house, determined.

Andrew's car was parked outside, and I really hoped the whole clan wasn't here already. Then again, I knew the inevitable confrontation with Matthew and the Thompsons would happen fast.

Dee was waiting for me in the living room. She opened her mouth.

"Where's Kat?" I asked, and then mentally punched myself in the nuts. Asking about her right off the bat didn't seem like I had everything under control.

My sister cocked a brow. "She went next door a few minutes ago. Her mom is home, but she's coming back over in a few minutes." She took a deep breath. "Daemon—"

Adam roamed out from the kitchen, an apple in his hand. "Andrew and Ash are pissed."

Lifting my forearm, I wiped the sweat beading across my forehead. "And that's different from any other day?"

He smirked. "Well, they can't believe you guys kept this a secret—the whole Kat knowing about us. They're on their way over here now."

"With Matthew." Dee folded her arms across her waist. Worry filled her gaze. "He's also not very happy, Daemon. I'm afraid he's going—"

"He's not going to do anything." I pinned Adam with a hard look. "You're not pissed?"

"Not really." He raised a shoulder as he bit into the apple, chewing thoughtfully. "I mean, she's known for a while, right? Dee made it sound like she has and she hasn't said anything yet, so why would she now?"

"She won't," Dee and I responded at the same time.

I shot my sister a wry look while she grinned. "I'm taking a shower." I turned, starting for the stairs.

Glancing over her shoulder at Adam, Dee trailed after me. "Kat is coming back over here, like in ten minutes."

"Okay."

"Everyone else is coming over here," she added.

I was halfway up the stairs when it hit me. Twisting

around, I stared down at Dee.

"Kat knows that they know and that they are coming over. She wants to be here, and I think it's a good idea."

I came down a step as my brows rose. "Having her here with three Luxen who disliked and distrusted her already is a good idea how? Unless we're considering making it easier for them to try to fry her a good idea."

"Andrew and Ash are a lot of talk. You know that," Adam said from the foyer. "They won't hurt her."

"I won't let them."

Dee's eyes widened, and yeah, I'd thrown that right out there. God only knows what Dee thought anyway, especially after this morning. She blinked. "*Anyway*, I think it's a good idea for them to actually see her—to see that she can be trusted. I'm not worried about Ash or Andrew. It's Matthew who needs to be convinced. You know that."

That was true. I wasn't willing to believe that Ash and Andrew were all talk, but they wouldn't go to the DOD or the Elders. Matthew would, but he was also a fair and logical person. If he was convinced that Kat wouldn't run her mouth, then he would back down, and having Kat here for them to see that she would keep quiet was probably the only way to convince Matthew. Plus, I would be here to make sure Kat stayed safe during the initial face-off.

"Okay," I said, turning back around to grab a quick shower first. I made it to my bedroom with Dee right behind me.

She closed the door and waited for me to face her. "What's going on between you and Katy?" she asked.

Immediately, I thought of Kat this morning, her soft body tucked under mine. "Nothing is going on, Dee."

Doubt crossed her face. "You slept with her last night."

I almost choked on my own spit as I toed off my sneakers. "I didn't sleep with her."

"You were in the same bed with her, so that's sleeping together even if it's not *sleeping* together." She narrowed her eyes. "I want to know what's going on."

Part of me wanted to tell her it was none of her business, but all that would do was increase her suspicions. "Look, she was stressed out last night and scared. Between what happened at that damn field party and then coming face-to-face with three Arum, she needed someone with her. I was that someone. That's it. It's not a big deal."

Dee was silent as she twisted her hair in her hands. "It is a big deal." Then she smiled broadly while I stared at her. "It's a *very* big deal."

After a quick shower and change of clothes, I headed downstairs. Kat was there, glowing like a damn star. She looked up when I entered the room. Her gaze moved from mine and then down, way down, and a pink flush swept across her cheeks. I watched it spread down her throat and disappear under her collar. I wondered just how far that blush traveled.

Hell.

"They're here," Adam said, heading for the front door.

Kat stiffened, but remained quiet and alert. As the crew rolled in, I sat down on the arm of the recliner she was sitting in. My position was clearly noted by everyone.

Dee smiled like she'd just figured out the key to life.

When Ash and Andrew spotted the traced Kat and where I was sitting, their faces slipped into scowls so deep I wondered if they'd be stuck that way.

Matthew looked like he wanted to vomit. He came to a complete stop in the middle of the room. "What is she doing here?"

"She's lit up like a freaking disco ball," Ash said accusingly. "I could probably see her from Virginia."

Kat's eyes narrowed.

"She was with me last night when the Arum attacked," I explained. "You know that. Things got a little...explosive. There was no way I could cover what happened."

Matthew ran a hand through his hair. "Daemon, of all people, I expected you to know better, to be more careful."

My brows furrowed together. "What the hell was I supposed to do exactly? Knock her out before the Arum attacked?"

Ash arched a brow. The look on her face said she totally supported that idea.

"Katy has known about us since the beginning of school," I said. "And trust me when I say I did everything possible to keep her from knowing."

Andrew sucked in a sharp breath. "She's known this entire time? How could you allow this, Daemon? All of our lives have been in the hands of some human?"

Dee rolled her eyes. "Obviously she hasn't said a word, Andrew. Chill out."

"Chill out?" Andrew's scowl matched his sister's. "She's a stupid—"

"Be careful with what you say next." My skin started to hum. "Because what you don't know and what you can't possibly understand will get a bolt of light in your face."

Ash swallowed thickly as she looked away, shaking her head. Silence fell as my message was read loud and clear.

"Daemon," Matthew said, stepping forward. "Threatening one of your own for her? I didn't expect this from you."

My shoulders stiffened. "It's not like that."

"I'm not going to tell anyone about you guys." Kat spoke for the first time. "I know the risks to you and to me if I did. You all don't have anything to worry about."

"And who are you for us to trust?" Matthew asked. "Don't get me wrong. I'm sure you're a great girl. You're smart and you seem to have your head on straight, but this is life or death for us. Our freedom. Trusting a human is not something we can afford."

I didn't like where this was heading already. "She saved my life last night."

Andrew laughed. "Oh, come on, Daemon. The Arum must've knocked you around. There is no way a human could've saved any of our lives."

"What is it with you?" Kat snapped, fiery as ever. "You act like we're incapable of doing anything. Sure, you guys are whatever, but that doesn't mean we're single-celled organisms."

A choked laugh came from Adam.

"She did save my life," I repeated, wrangling everyone's attention. "There were three Arum that attacked, the brethren of the one I killed. I was able to destroy one, but the two overpowered me. They had me down and had already begun reaching for my powers. I was a goner."

"Daemon," Dee whispered, paling. "You didn't tell us any of this."

Doubt colored Matthew's voice when he spoke. "I don't see how she could've helped. She's a human. The Arum are powerful, amoral, and vicious. How can one girl stand against them?"

"I'd given her the obsidian blade I carry and told her to run."

"You gave her the blade when you could've used it?" Ash sounded stunned. "Why?" Her eyes darted to Kat. "You don't even like her."

Kat frowned.

"That may be the case, but I wasn't going to let her die because I don't like her," I replied, and the words didn't sit well with me. This wasn't the time to piss Ash off even more by disagreeing. I didn't look at Kat to see her response. I didn't want to know.

"But you could've been hurt," Ash protested. Fear thickened her voice. "You could've been killed because you gave your best defense to her."

I sighed. "I have other ways to defend myself. She did not. She didn't run like I told her. Instead she came back, and she killed the Arum who was about to end me."

Reluctant pride shone in Matthew's eyes. "That is... admirable."

"It was a hell of a lot more than admirable," Dee interjected, turning a wide stare on Kat. "She didn't have to do that. That has to account for more than being admirable."

"It's courageous," Adam said quietly, staring at the throw rug. "It is what any of us would've done."

"But that doesn't change the fact that she knows about us," Andrew shot back, casting his triplet a scornful look. "And we are forbidden from telling any human."

"We didn't tell her," Dee said, stirring restlessly. "It kind of happened."

"Oh, like it happened last time." Andrew rolled his eyes

as he turned to Matthew. "This is unbelievable."

Matthew shook his head. "After Labor Day weekend, you told me that something occurred but you took care of it."

"What happened?" Ash demanded. "You're talking about the first time she was glowing?"

"I walked out in front of a truck," Kat muttered.

Ash stared at me, her blue eyes growing to the size of saucers. "You stopped the truck?"

I nodded.

The anger washed away from her face as she blinked rapidly. "Obviously that couldn't be explained away. She's known since then?"

"She didn't freak out," Dee said. "She listened to us, understood why it's important, and that's it. Until last night, what we are hasn't even been an issue."

"But you lied to me—both of you." Matthew leaned against the wall, between the TV and overflowing bookcase. "How am I to trust you now?"

Out of the corners of my eyes, I saw Kat lift two fingers to her temple.

"Look, I understand the risk. More than any of you in the room." I rubbed the heel of my palm where my chest still ached from where the Arum had gotten me. "But what is done is done. We need to move forward."

"As in contacting the DOD?" Andrew asked. "I'm sure they'd know what to do with her."

My voice was low and calm, but that was not how I felt. "I'd like to see you try that, Andrew. Really I would, because even after last night, and I'm not yet fully charged, I could still kick your ass."

Matthew cleared his throat. "Daemon, threats aren't necessary."

"Aren't they?" I challenged.

A heavy silence fell in the room, broken only when Matthew spoke again. "I don't think this is wise. Not with what...with what happened before, but I'm not going to turn you over." He looked at Kat, sighing heavily. "Not unless you give me reason to. And maybe you won't. I don't know. Humans are such...fickle creatures. What we are, what we can do, has to be protected at all costs. I think you understand that. You're safe, but we aren't."

Andrew cursed under his breath and Ash looked ready to throw something, but it was Matthew's call. He was like our very own Elder. All of us knew that. A bit of relief eased the tension in my muscles. At least I wasn't going to have to fight those I'd grown up with and considered family.

"You said there was one Arum left?" Adam asked, shifting the conversation. "What's the plan? He knows there are Luxen here obviously. He's going to come back."

"He won't wait. They're not known for being patient." Matthew moved over to the couch and sat down next to Dee. "I could contact the other Luxen, but I'm not sure if that would be smart. Where we may be more confident in her, they won't be."

"And there's the problem that she's a megawatt lightbulb right now," Ash added, her upper lip curling. "It doesn't even matter if we don't say anything. The moment she goes anywhere in town, they are going to know that something big happened again."

"Well, I don't know what I'm supposed to do about that," Kat replied.

"Any suggestions?" I asked. "Because the sooner she's not carrying a trace, the better all of this is going to be."

"Who cares?" Andrew rolled his eyes. "We have the

Arum issue to worry about. He's gonna see her no matter where we put her. All of us, right now, are in danger. Any of us near her are in danger. We can't wait around. We have to find the last Arum."

Dee shook her head. "If we can get the trace off her, then that will buy us time to find him. Getting rid of the trace should be the first priority."

"I say we drive her out to the middle of nowhere and leave her ass there," Andrew muttered.

"Thanks." Kat rubbed at her temples with her fingers. "You're so very helpful with all of this."

He smiled back at her. "Hey, just offering my suggestions."

"Shut up, Andrew," I said.

Andrew's eyes rolled once more.

"Once we get the trace off her, she'd be safe," Dee insisted as she tucked her hair back, face pinched. "The Arum don't mess with humans, really."

"I have an idea," Adam said. Everyone looked at him. "The light around her is a by-product of us using our power, right? And our power is concentrated energy. And we get weaker when we use our powers and use more energy."

Matthew's gaze sparked with interest. "I think I'm following you."

"I'm not," Kat muttered, and my lips twitched.

"Our powers fade the more we use them, the more energy we exert." Adam turned to me. "It should work the same with our traces, because the trace is just residual energy we are leaving on someone. We get her to exert her own energy; it should fade what's around her. Maybe not completely, but get it down to levels that aren't going to draw every Arum on Earth to us."

Matthew nodded. "It should work."

I rubbed at my chest. "And how are we going to get her to exert energy?"

Andrew grinned from across the room. "We could take her out to a field and chase her around in our cars. That sounds fun."

Kat dropped her feet onto the floor. "Oh, fuc—"

My laugh cut her off, earning me a dark look from one very pissed-off little kitten. "I don't think that's a good idea. Funny, but not a good idea. Humans are fragile."

"How about I shove my fragile foot up your ass," she retorted, and that made me grin...up until when she pushed me clear off the arm of the chair. "I'm getting a drink. Let me know when you guys come up with anything that won't potentially kill me in the process."

I watched her hurry out of the room, smiling faintly. Man, she was not a happy camper right now. Couldn't blame her. Refocusing on the room, my gaze collided with Ash's. Aaand there was another person who did not appear to be feeling warm and fuzzy.

"This could work," Dee said, smoothing her hands over her legs. "We just get her to exert energy, and that's not that hard. Running will do it. Jumping jacks. Jogging in place. Sit-ups—"

"Sex," Andrew supplied.

Everyone looked at him. The last thing I needed to think about was the words "sex" and "Kat" in the same sentence.

"What?" He chuckled. "I'm not suggesting anyone have sex with her—"

"Dear God," Matthew muttered, pinching the bridge of his nose.

"But you all were listing things that burn energy, and sex will do that."

Dee was staring at the carpet. Adam looked oddly embarrassed, and Ash pushed to her feet and started to walk. "That's disgusting for a list of reasons that have nothing to do with her being a human." She stopped beside me and stared with an icy glare. "You can do better than that."

"She could do better than us," I replied without even thinking, and damn, it was the truth.

Shock splashed across Ash's face, and then she started past me, heading toward the kitchen. I caught her arm and met her stare. "Don't do anything that's going to make me unhappy."

"Everything makes you unhappy," she spat back.

"I mean it, Ash." I ignored her comment. "If I have to come in there and break you two up, I'm not going to like it."

Her lips curled. "What do you think I am? Geez." She pulled her free. "I'm not going to hurt her. I just want something to drink."

Part of me felt like I should follow Ash, but Matthew was already eyeballing me like I was seconds away from making babies with a human, which wasn't even something I was sure could happen. There weren't any screams or shouts of rage coming from the kitchen, but I kept one ear out for just that as the conversation continued around me.

This had actually gone better than I thought it would, almost too easy. Unease sprouted like a noxious weed and it continued to grow, making me restless. I stood and walked over to the window. Pulling the curtain back, I peered outside even though I wasn't sure what I was looking for.

Matthew announced that he would speak to the DOD and the colony. The destruction that had been caused to the road last night would've already been discovered, and the DOD would be monitoring the display of energy already.

Luxen against Luxen throw-down. That's what we were going with. While the DOD didn't know exactly what we could do, the full extent of our powers, they did know we had greater strength than humans. It was probably likely they'd buy that two of us could have wreaked that havoc. Maybe. If we were very, very lucky they would.

Kat returned to the room, a bottle of water in her hand. Our gazes met and then held for a brief moment. She looked away quickly, sitting on the edge of the recliner. She was pale as she sucked her lower lip in between her teeth, and when Ash reappeared with nothing in her hands, I could only guess what she had said to Kat in the kitchen.

"Can we talk for a moment?" Matthew asked in a low voice.

I nodded and then glanced over at Dee. She smiled, obviously getting the message I didn't need to say. She would keep an eye on Kat for me. Matthew and I stepped outside. "What's up?" I asked even though I already knew where this conversation was heading.

"Let's take a walk," he suggested.

I followed him off the porch and in the opposite direction of Kat's house. I decided to not beat around the bush. "I know you're worried about Katy, but she's not going to say anything," I said, shoving my hands into the pockets of my jeans as we reached the first outcropping of trees. "I know that's hard to believe, but she's had plenty of chances to say something. And what I said about her saving my life last night? I wasn't exaggerating, Matthew. I was able to take out one of the Arum, but two of them tag-teamed me. The one she killed had been feeding on me."

Matthew sucked in an unsteady breath. "You came too close, then."

"I did," I admitted quietly, ducking my head under a low-hanging branch. "It won't happen again."

He didn't respond immediately, so I continued on. "You should've seen her, Matt. I told her to run and to hide, but she came back. Like a freaking ninja," I said, barking out a short laugh. I could still see her standing there. "Stabbed the Arum with the obsidian blade like she'd done it a million times. It was…yeah, it was amazing."

"Sounds like it." He walked side by side with me. "Not many humans would've done that. She's a brave girl."

"Yeah." I smiled slightly. "Yeah, she is."

Matthew's steps slowed to a stop. "It's not her I'm worried about, Daemon."

Frowning, I stopped and looked at him. "It's not?"

His expression was open. "No. It's you."

"Me?" I laughed again. "You need to add a little more detail to that statement."

"All of this is so very familiar to me. No, let me finish," he said when I opened my mouth. "I know you're not your brother and this isn't the same situation, but you obviously care about Katy. She's not like the other human girls you've had…relations with."

Huh. I had no idea Matthew kept that close of an eye on me.

"Katy is different to you, and you're different around her. You threatened us to protect her, and that's all the evidence that I need to know this situation could escalate very quickly. None of us took a stronger hand with Dawson, and look where that ended. I cannot allow that to happen to you."

Looking away, I slowly shook my head as I watched a tiny brown bird hop along one of the narrow branches. Kat was different. I couldn't deny that. "I can't keep her away from Dee."

"Dee's not the problem," Matthew informed me.

A muscle began to tick in my jaw, and then I laughed again for the third time. "I was thinking that it might be smart if Dee and I left. If we found another colony and moved there. Dee wouldn't be happy with that, but…"

"That's not what I want to hear, and I hope you're not so…invested in this girl that leaving here—leaving us—is the only viable option. That means things have already gotten out of control, and that is not you."

Was it the only option? If it was, then what did that say? I shook my head. "It's not."

Matthew clamped his hand on my shoulder and squeezed. "You are like a brother to me, Daemon. I trust you with my life, and I know you're going to make this situation right. You're going to help get that trace off as her as quick as possible, using whatever means necessary," he said, his blue eyes sharpening. "You're going to take care of this and none of us are going to have to worry about history repeating itself. We're going to move on from this and take care of the Arum, and then everything…everything will be okay. Can you do that? For Dee? For all of us, but most importantly, for you and for *her*."

"I'm not—"

"You don't need to lie to me, Daemon, and I don't even need you to confirm or deny what is beginning to start between you and Katy, but you know—you know more than anyone if you continue down this path, it's not just your fate you're sealing. It's Katy's fate also." Matthew withdrew his hand, his expression somber. "You don't want to be the reason she disappears or is killed. I know you don't. So take care of this. Soon."

# 22

Matthew's words haunted me throughout Saturday and into Sunday morning. Man, he'd nailed it all on the head, hadn't he? Things were already getting out of control between Kat and me, and nothing had really happened between us. At least not physically, if I wasn't counting yesterday morning, but there *was* something between us.

And neither of us liked it.

I did a lot of thinking, even when I went out on patrols Saturday night. Matthew had been right. I needed to get this trace off Kat as soon as possible, and then once I took care of the last Arum, things…things would be normal.

Things had to get back to normal.

Leaving really wasn't an option, at least not right now, and the likelihood of the DOD approving something like that was slim to none. So I needed to take care of this. I couldn't allow myself to think of anything else.

Dee was with Adam, and I figured now was no better time to start getting that trace off Kat. After all, she didn't want to be at risk or a danger to anyone else. Before I left, I grabbed the piece of obsidian from my bedroom. Rain poured down as I darted across the lawn, moving fast enough that the sheets of chilly rain barely hit me. Her mom's car was gone, as usual. I knocked on the door.

A few seconds passed before the door inched open, revealing a very…sleepy-looking Kat. She squinted up at me, brows knitted together. Her hair was a mess of waves, falling haphazardly over her shoulders. She was in pajamas and I was pretty sure she wasn't wearing a—

"What's up?" She broke the silence.

"Are you going to invite me in?"

Her lips formed a thin line as she stepped aside. I walked in, scanning the rooms. "What are you looking for?" she asked.

"Your mom's not home, right?" Figured I'd better double check before we started getting down to business.

Kat shut the door. "Her car's not outside."

The claws were out today. "We need to work on fading your trace."

"It's pouring outside." She stalked past me, grabbing the remote to turn off the TV. I beat her to it, flipping it off before she could hit the button. "Show-off," she muttered.

"Been called worse." I frowned as I faced her, finally getting a good look at what she was wearing. I laughed. "What are you wearing?"

Her cheeks burned bright. "Shut up."

I laughed again. "What are they? Keebler elves?"

"No! They're Santa's elves. I love these pajama bottoms.

My dad got them for me."

My laugh faded off. "You wear them because they remind you of him?"

Kat nodded.

The green and pink bottoms were ridiculous looking, but I understood why she wore them. It made me think of something I remembered hearing the Elders say. "My people believe that when we pass on, our essence is what lights the stars in the universe. Seems stupid to believe in something like that, but when I look at the sky at night, I like to think that at least two of the stars out there are my parents. And one is Dawson."

"That's not stupid at all." She paused as the hostility faded from her expression. "Maybe one of them is my dad."

I looked at her and quickly looked away. "Well, anyway, the elves are sexy."

She snorted. "Did you guys come up with another way to fade the trace?"

"Not really."

"You're planning on making me work out, aren't you?"

"Yeah, that's one of the ways of doing it."

She plopped down on the couch. "Well, there isn't much we can do today."

I arched a brow. "You have a problem going out in the rain?"

"When it's almost the end of October and cold, yes, I do." She picked up a checkered afghan and placed it in her lap. "I'm not going out there and running today."

I sighed. "We can't wait around, Kat. Baruck is still out there, and the longer we wait, the more dangerous it is."

"What about Simon? Did you ever tell the others about him?"

I'd actually forgotten about him until Saturday evening. "Andrew is keeping an eye on him. Since he had a game yesterday, it faded most of his trace. It's very faint now. Which proves that this idea is going to work."

She fiddled with a ragged edge on the quilt, peeking up at me. Reaching into the pocket, I pulled out the obsidian blade. "This is another reason why I stopped over." I placed it on the coffee table. "I want you to keep this with you, just in case. Put it in your backpack, purse, or whatever you carry."

Kat stared at it a moment and then lifted her gaze. "Seriously?"

I focused on the blade. Matthew would flip his shit if he knew I was giving it to her. "Yeah, even if we manage to get the trace to fade, keep this on you until we finish off Baruck."

"But don't you need it more than I do? Dee?"

"Don't worry about us."

A moment passed. "Do you think Baruck is still here?"

"He's still around, yes." No point in lying to her. "The beta quartz throws off our presence, but he knows we're here. He knows I'm here."

"Do you think he's going to come after you?"

Her question caught me off guard. "I killed two of his brothers and gave you the means of killing the third. Arum are vengeful creatures, Kitten. He won't stop until he has me. And he will use you to find me, especially since you came back. They've been on Earth long enough to recognize what that can mean. That you would be a weakness to me."

Her nose did that cute wrinkling thing whenever she was perturbed. "I'm not a weakness. I can handle myself."

Damn straight she could.

Kat glanced up at me, and I realized I was staring at her

like a freak. I glanced around the room. "Enough talking. We have stuff to do now. I don't know what we can do in here that will make a damn bit of difference. Maybe jumping jacks?"

Her response to that was to open her laptop. Nice. Good to see she didn't even attempt to pretend to listen to me. Her nose did the wrinkle thing again and she gave a little sigh as she eyed something on her screen.

"What are you looking at?"

"Nothing." She went to close the lid, but I wasn't having that. I kept it open. She glared up at me. "Stop using your freaking object thing on my laptop. You're going to break it."

Amused, I walked around the coffee table and sat beside her. On the screen was a girl…with pigtails. "Is that you?"

"What does it look like?" she grumbled.

A slow smile crept over my face. I'd seen these things before on her blog, but I couldn't let her know that. Nothing like adding cyberstalking to what seemed like real-life stalking. "You film yourself?"

Kat took a deep breath, and it took every ounce of my self-control to not check out her chest when she did that. "You make it sound like I'm doing a live perv show or something."

I choked on my breath. "Is that what you're doing?"

"That was a stupid question. Can I please close it now?"

"I want to watch it."

"No!" Horror filled her voice. You'd think there was an Arum in the room.

I cast her a sidelong glance, and her eyes narrowed as she turned back to the screen. The little arrow moved over the page and clicked on the play button.

"I hate you and your freaky alien powers," she muttered.

A few seconds later, the video started and there Kat was, showing off books, talking in an excited way I'd only heard her do a few times. While the video played, she sat beside me, her jaw locked down and her face the color of blood. It was obvious she filmed the video either last night or this morning. It ended with her smiling broadly at the camera.

Dammit.

She was such a…freaking nerd—a *hot* freaking nerd.

"You're even glowing in the video," I said, and my voice sounded rough to my own ears.

Kat nodded.

"You really have a thing for books." I closed the lid on the laptop. "It's cute."

Her head whipped toward mine so fast I worried she'd strain a muscle. "Cute?"

"Yeah, it's cute. Your excitement," I said, shrugging. "It was cute. But as cute as you are in pigtails, that's not going to do anything to fade the trace on you." I needed to focus. Standing, I stretched my arms above my head. When I glanced down at her, she was eyeing the section of skin that was exposed when my shirt rode up. "We need to get this trace off you."

She was still staring at my stomach.

I lowered my arms. "The sooner we get the trace off you, the less time we have to spend together."

And that got her attention. Her eyes snapped to mine. "You know, if you hate the idea of being around me, why doesn't one of the others come over here and do this? I actually prefer any of them to you, even Ash."

"You're not their problem. You're my problem."

Her laugh was harsh. "I'm not your problem."

"But you are," I said, and that was the truth. Probably

could say it a little nicer, but oh well. "If I had managed to convince Dee not to get so close to you, none of this would've happened."

She rolled her eyes. "Well, I don't know what to tell you. There isn't much we can do in here that's going to make a difference, so we might as well count today as a loss and spare each other the pain of breathing the same air."

I shot her a bland look.

"Oh, yeah, that's right. You don't need to breathe oxygen. My bad." She shot to her feet, knocking the poor quilt to the floor. "Can't you just come back when it stops raining?"

"No." I moved back and leaned against the wall, folding my arms. "I want to get this over with. Worrying over you and the Arum isn't fun, Kitten. We need to do something about this now. There are things we can try."

Kat was two seconds from losing it, and I loved it. Her hands curled into tiny fists. "Like what?"

"Well, the jumping jacks…an hour or so should do it." I was only half serious when I made the suggestion, but then my gaze dropped over the front of her shirt. Suddenly, I wanted nothing more than to see her jump around. "You may want to change first."

*Please say no. Please say no to changing.*

She took a deep breath. "I'm not doing jumping jacks for an hour."

And that was a damn shame. Crimson stained the tips of her cheeks. A sure sign she was angry. I couldn't help myself, so I pushed at her again. "You could run around the house, up and down the stairs." I met her eyes and grinned. "We could always have sex. I hear that uses up a lot of energy."

Her mouth dropped open. "That will never happen in a million years, buddy." She took a step forward, raising her pointer finger at me. "Not even if you were the last— Wait, I can't even say last human on the face of this Earth."

"Kitten," I murmured, sort of offended.

"Not even if you were the last thing that looked like a human on the face of this Earth. Got that? *Capiche*?"

I tilted my head to the side and smiled. She was really on a roll now. Eyes bright and face flushed. Part of me hated to admit it, but she was amazing when she was like this. Absolutely amazing.

"I'm not even attracted to you. Not even a little bit. You're—"

I was in her face before she had a chance to blink. "I'm what?"

"Ignorant," she said, taking a step back.

"And?" I matched her steps, compelled. Compelled by what? I didn't know. I came over to work the trace off of her and instead we were arguing with each other after a moment of nice conversation.

"Arrogant. Controlling." She took another step back, but I didn't let her get far. Oh no, I was all up in her face, sharing the same air. "And you're...you're a jerk."

"Oh, I'm sure you can do better than that, Kitten." And I knew she could. Kat had a mouth on her. Speaking of which, my gaze dropped. Her lips parted. Dammit. "Because I seriously doubt you're not attracted to me."

She laughed—the sound low and husky. Sexy. "I'm totally not attracted to you."

I took one more step, and her back was against the wall. Staring down at her, I think I may've forgotten to force my lungs to inhale and I definitely forgot the whole point of coming over here. There was only one thing I was thinking about. "You're lying."

"And you're overconfident." She wetted her lips, and heat pounded through my body. "You know, the whole arrogant thing I mentioned. Not attractive."

Man, she was so full of it. She'd say anything to keep arguing. Placing my hands on each side of her head, I leaned down, my mouth so close to hers I could almost taste her. I doubted her lips would be sweet. More like one of those red-hot Fireball candies.

I really, really liked that candy.

"Every time you lie, your cheeks turn red," I told her.

"Nuh-uh," she said.

I slid my hands down the wall, stopping beside her hips. "I bet you think about me all the time. Nonstop." As much as I thought about her, which was...nonstop, so it only seemed fair and right that she did the same.

"You're insane." She pressed back against the wall, her chest rising and falling sharply.

"You probably even dream about me." My gaze dropped to her mouth again. *Fireball*... "I bet you even write my name in your notebooks, over and over again, with a little heart drawn around it."

She laughed this breathless sound. "In your dreams, Daemon. You're the last person I think—"

Tired of arguing, I kissed her...just to shut her up. And yeah, I'd keep telling myself that. Just keep right on with that train of thought. That's why I was kissing her. No other reason.

But the moment our lips met, a shudder rolled through my body and I half growled, half moaned. Because I was right—her mouth was like a hot-as-hell Fireball.

Kat wasn't arguing anymore.

No, she was shivering.

Kissing really wasn't necessary anymore and I should stop, needed to stop, but then she pushed off the wall, fitting her body against mine. Her fingers sank in my hair and she moaned against my mouth.

This was so not about shutting her up.

Something came unhinged in me. Like a lock that had been turned. Or a dam that burst. Or, hell, it was like being struck by lightning, run over by a truck, and then shocked back to life. I was moving and doing without really thinking.

My hands gripped her hips, and I lifted her up. Her legs went around my waist and she was kissing me right back with a passion that almost startled me, and I was hoping she didn't notice that my hands were trembling. Hell, my entire body was shaking. There was a fire under my skin, and I was out of control. Seconds away from going full Luxen on her and what good would that do?

Aw hell, it didn't matter. Not when I pressed into her and she made this beautifully feminine sound that really had my blood pounding. And I could feel it building in me. Pure power—and it had nowhere to go but out. This had been building for months. Maybe always leading to this.

I never wanted someone as much as I wanted Kat.

Then we were moving along the wall. A lamp toppled over. Kat didn't seem to mind, thank God, because I was beyond the point of caring about anything other than who was in my arms.

Kat.

Vaguely, I was aware of the TV switching on and off. I tried to rein it all back in, but her hands went to my collar and then she was wiggling down, pulling at the buttons. I could only obey her silent command. I moved back and let her take off my shirt.

I'd pretty much let her do anything at this point. Kind of scary…and all kinds of hot.

I captured her cheeks, pulling her back to my hungry mouth. Man, I couldn't get enough of her taste, of how she gave it right back to me on all fronts. Her hands went to the button on my jeans.

There was a cracking sound in the house. Most likely something had just gone up in flames. But we were moving toward the couch and then we were on it, our hands everywhere, tugging on clothes, on each other. Our hips were molded together like our lips.

Kat whispered my name, and I was crushing her against me one second and then the next, I was giving up space to explore—for me to explore. Sliding over her arm, down the front of her shirt and lower, and her shirt was off. I don't even know how, but it was.

"So beautiful," I said, because she was beautiful. Damn, she was, and that flush I'd seen yesterday did spread everywhere. It took me a long time to lift my gaze, but when I did, I kissed her again. Kissed her until I knew she needed air, claiming her mouth as long as I could.

My body took over completely, rolling against hers, but something else clicked inside me. Another hidden door was opening. I slowed down, taking my time. Where everything had been so frantic and crazed, it was now more tender and controlled. I was still shaking, though, on the verge of…

Of not being able to stop—not wanting to, of needing her more than I should.

*You don't want to be the reason she disappears or is killed.*

I stilled and forced my lungs to work like hers. Inhaling ragged breaths that weren't enough, I lifted my head and opened my eyes. I knew they were glowing, speaking a thousand things I couldn't say and she'd never understand. Probably not want to hear, either.

Our gazes locked. The look in her eyes, the way her body melted into mine, I knew she'd let me do…anything. But if I didn't stop now, I wouldn't stop ever. And even though I was prone to moments of "great dickdom," as Kat would say, it wasn't right. Not under these conditions. Not on a freaking couch.

Not when her life was in my hands.

And I kept messing up with her. I was the one who traced her and led an Arum to her at the library. I was the one who pissed her off and all but chased her into a street. I was the one who exposed our kind. I was the one who was repeatedly putting her in danger.

So I said the only thing that came to mind. The only thing I knew that would snap both of us back into a cold, harsh reality.

I forced my lips into the half smile I knew always got under her skin and said, "You're barely glowing now."

# 23

After all this time, I'd finally succeeded in keeping Kat away from Dee. Instead of feeling satisfied about that, I felt like shit.

I was such…such an asshole.

Since Sunday afternoon, Kat kept to herself. I made the mistake of poking her with my pen in class Monday and the look she gave me shriveled up very important body parts. All she had said to me was that I blew up her laptop, and then she didn't speak to me. She didn't come over to the house to spend time with Dee and by Wednesday, my sister was super suspicious of what had happened.

Not like everyone wasn't already suspicious over how quickly Kat's trace had faded. No one asked. Except Andrew. He'd asked if I had sex with Kat.

I'd punched him Monday after school, hard enough to break his nose.

Andrew had laughed, and of course his nose had healed immediately.

*You're barely glowing now?*

As if that had been the sole reason why I'd kissed her, why I got my hands on her or got her on that couch, under me and topless. Use any means necessary, Matthew had said, but I doubted he'd meant that. And I was real with myself. I'd gone over there Sunday to work the trace off her. I was prepared to make her go running in the rain or up and down the staircase inside. I hadn't planned on kissing her.

I hadn't planned on any of that happening.

I was a dick, but I wasn't that big of a dick.

What had happened between us was because I wanted her and she *had* wanted me back. It had nothing to do with the trace, nothing to do with who we were. It didn't matter in those moments that it had been wrong or that we spent more time fighting each other than anything else. The only thing that had mattered was how she'd felt, how she'd tasted, and the way she'd whispered my name.

But it had been wrong.

Wasn't it?

Needless to say, my mood was knee-deep in Shitville, and it being Halloween didn't help. In class, I'd overheard Lesa and Kat making plans to give out candy at the former's house. Although Kat's trace was barely there, I didn't like the idea of her being out there when Baruck was still roaming around.

Without a trace, an Arum wouldn't be drawn to her, but Baruck had seen Kat. He would be able to recognize her, so like a creep, I'd followed her to Lesa's house and watched over her. I stayed down a block, and when I saw her leave in her Camry, I headed back home, beating her there, since I'd gone the Luxen route.

Dee had the front porch decked out with carved pumpkins that had tiny lights in them. I was surprised she hadn't broken out the string ghosts and bats like she normally did.

The moment I stepped into the house, I smelled something weird and burned. Frowning, I headed into the kitchen. Dee was hovering over a baking sheet. There was another on the kitchen counter. Dark, burned specks covered that sheet. "What are you doing?" I asked.

"Baking pumpkin seeds," she replied, brow furrowing as she placed her hands over the sheet.

"You know, you could just use the oven."

"What fun is that?" She twisted toward me, eyes narrowing. "You need to leave."

"Excuse me?"

"You need to leave," she repeated. "Kat is on her way over here. We're going to watch a bunch of stupid horror movies."

Leaning against the counter, I poked at one of the charred pumpkin seeds. "Sounds like fun."

"It's going to be a ton of fun, but you need to go. I don't know what went down between you two."

"Nothing," I murmured, glancing at the window beyond the kitchen table.

Dee snorted. "Yeah, that's what she said, and I don't believe her. I don't believe you, and whatever happened made her avoid me for days. So I don't want you here, because you will ruin the night."

"Ouch." I placed my hand over my chest and faked a wince.

Dee shoved me. "Whatever. Go hang out with Adam."

I was planning to do that already. Adam and Andrew wanted to see if they could lure Baruck out, but there was an irresponsible part of me that wanted to stay here until Kat showed up. I wanted to see her even though I knew she was going to ignore me, but after what I'd done, that took dickdom to a whole new level.

Pushing off the counter, I dropped a kiss atop Dee's head. "I'll be with Adam and Andrew. We're going to try to lure the Arum out."

Fear flickered across Dee's face, and then she steadied herself. "Be careful."

"Always," I replied.

Eyeing the baking sheets one more time, I hoped she didn't try to make Kat eat any of them. Yikes. Snagging my keys off the counter, I headed out and met up with Adam and Andrew in the parking lot of Smoke Hole Diner. They'd come the fastest way possible.

Andrew swaggered up to the driver's door. "What's the plan? Same as the last couple of nights?"

I glanced at Adam, who hung back a few feet. "Yep. Light up in the woods closest to the roads. Run away and see if you can draw them out. I'll drive around and see if I can sense him."

We'd been doing this with no such luck since Sunday, one of us taking turns doing the driving, which was by far the most tedious of assignments. I'd rather get out there in my true form than sit behind the wheel.

"I'll head toward town," Adam said.

Andrew shot his brother a look. "I guess I'll go away from it."

Smirking, I shook my head as I pulled out of the parking lot. The streets were still pretty busy. Parents taking their kids back to their homes after trick or treating in town. Others were on their way to parties. At a red light, I saw a Ninja Turtle in the driver's seat of a car next to me.

Heh.

I cruised up and down the highway, circling back through town a couple of times and killing almost two hours before my cell rang. It was Adam.

"Talk to me," I said.

"We spotted him." Adam was breathing heavily. "Baruck. He's heading toward the colony. Andrew is coming, but I've lost track of him."

"Shit." Glancing up in the rearview mirror, I saw the road was empty behind me. I yanked the wheel to the right, spinning the SUV around. Tires spun out on the gravel along the road as I hit the gas. "Get there now."

"On it."

Hanging up on Adam, I immediately dialed Dee. She answered on the third ring, exasperation dripping from her tone. "This better be good, Daemon, because—"

"Baruck has been spotted. He's heading toward the colony."

"What do you mean?" she said.

My hand tightened on the phone. "He's going toward the colony and he's going to pass right by our house. We're on our way. Is Kat still with you?"

"Katy is with me, but her trace is barely noticeable!"

I hit the gas pedal to the floor. "It still can be seen. Just stay inside, Dee. Keep her there."

"Okay," she whispered. "Be careful. I love you."

Fury roared through me. The son of a bitch probably had no idea how close he was actually getting to the colony or to where Dee and Kat were. With the beta quartz so close by, it would throw him off, but it was too close for comfort. I needed to ditch the wheels, but I was too close to town and too many cars were around to do it without drawing attention. Andrew and Adam were fast. They'd get there before—

My cell went off again, this time from Dee. A knot formed in my gut as I answered it. "What?"

"It's Katy," she said, voice shaking. "She made me trace her—"

"What?" I hit the brakes, nearly causing the van behind us to rear end. "She did *what*?"

"She made me trace her and then she left, trying to draw the Arum away from here. She's going where the field party was. Daemon, she's *glowing*."

My heart lodged in my throat. Fury and horror slammed into me like a punch to the chest. I wanted to reach through the phone and strangle my sister. How could she let Kat do this? But there wasn't time to yell at her. That would definitely come later. My head started working quickly. "Get in touch with Adam and Andrew, but text me her number now."

"Daemon—"

"Dammit, Dee, text me her number now!" I shouted, my heart pounding as I hung up. Why would Kat do this? It was suicide. Why? A second passed and then Dee's text came through. Hitting the numbers, I waited as the phone rang.

"Hello?" Kat's voice was another hit to the chest.

I lost it.

"Are you out of your freaking mind?" I yelled into the phone, swerving around a slow-moving sedan. "This has to be the stupidest thing—"

"Shut up, Daemon!" she screeched. "It's done. Okay? Is Dee okay?"

Is Dee okay? Did she not realize what she had just done? Kat was insane!

"Yes, Dee's okay. But you're not! We've lost him, and

since Dee said you're glowing like a goddamn full moon right now, I'm betting he's after you."

There was a pause. "Well, that was the plan."

"I swear on every star in the sky, I'm going to strangle you when I get my hands on you." I was literally going to do it. "Where are you?"

"I'm almost to the field," she said. "I don't see him."

"Of course you don't see him." Good God... "He's made of shadows—of *night*, Kat. You won't see him until he wants you to. I can't believe you did this."

"Don't you start with me!" she yelled back. "You said I was a weakness. And I was a liability back there with Dee. What if he came there? You said yourself he'd use me against her. This was the best I could do! So stop being such a damn jerk!"

No.

Oh no.

For a moment, I didn't even see the road in front of me. The horror nearly consumed me. "I didn't mean for you to do *this*, Kat. Never something like *this*."

Her deep breath was audible. "You didn't make me do this."

I pressed my lips together. "Yeah, I did."

"Daemon—"

"I'm sorry. I don't want you hurt, Kat. I can't—*I can't* live with that." Once those words were out, there was no taking them back. They were the truth. "Stay on the phone. I'm going to find a place to ditch the car and I'll meet you. It won't take more than a few minutes to get there. Don't get out of the car or anything."

"Okay," she said and then, "maybe this wasn't the strongest idea."

I barked out a short, harsh laugh as I spied the last of the headlights disappearing in the rearview mirror. I pulled over. "No shit."

"So, um, the not living with your—" She broke off suddenly as I killed the engine and threw open the car door. "Daemon?"

"What?"

"I think—" A scream cut her off.

My skin chilled. "Kat?"

Nothing.

"Katy!"

No answer.

Oh no. No. No.

Tossing the phone into the SUV, I slammed the door shut and then took off for the wooded line, switching into my true form and picking up speed. I ran faster than I ever had before, my form barely touching the ground. Scenarios swirled in my head. Kat beaten. Broken. Dead. I couldn't get the thoughts out of my head.

Only minutes had passed, maybe two by the time I reached the clearing, but it was more than enough time for Baruck to have seriously injured Kat or worse. I flew past the burned-out remains of the bonfire, nothing more than charred logs and scattered ash. Through the trees, I spied a bright white light rise too far in the air to be Kat unless…

I dug in, clearing the first stand of trees, and then I saw him—I saw *Kat*. The Arum held her up in the air with a hand around her throat, and his other was *inside* her chest. He was feeding on her. Rage tasted like metal in the back of my throat. I shifted into my human form as fury erupted out of me in a roar.

The Arum's shadowy head turned over his shoulder just

as I slammed into him, breaking his hold on Kat. She fell to the ground in a messy heap and she didn't get up. I landed in front of her in a crouch, the Arum several feet away.

I rose as the Arum did, both of us eye to eye.

"You've come to die with her? Perfect," Baruck said in his human form, rapidly moving from left to right. "That makes this so much easier, because I think I might have broken her. She tasted good, too. Different somehow," he taunted. "Not like a Luxen, but still worth it in the end."

Launching myself at Baruck, I threw him several feet away with one powerful blast of the Source from an outstretched arm. "I'm going to kill you."

Baruck rolled onto his back, choking with laughter. "You think you can take me, Luxen? I have devoured those stronger than you."

I hit him with another blast of light, drowning out the rest of what Baruck was saying. The ground trembled with the impact of all that focused energy. The hit had knocked Baruck down, but I knew he wouldn't stay there. Shifting into my Luxen form, I rushed him. We collided like thunder and hit the ground rolling, brawling like two humans, but our blows would've killed a human with one shot.

Pinning Baruck down, I slammed my fist into his throat, but at the last minute, he shifted and pulled his legs back, kicking me off to the side. I landed and rolled, popping to my feet just as I saw Dee race past the Arum, heading for Kat. There was no time to even process my sister's presence.

Bright, orangey balls of fire formed on the tips of my hands. They shot out past Baruck, fizzling out before they slammed into trees, turning the world amber and gold. Heat blew back, tossing crackling embers into the sky.

One slammed into the Arum's shoulder, spinning him

around. He ducked the other, and it hit the tree behind him, burning a hole deep into the truck. Over the chaos, I heard Dee begging, "Katy, talk to me. Please talk to me!" Then she screamed my name. "Daemon!"

My heart stopped.

I turned just as Baruck did. Dee had Kat in her arms. The Arum released his own essence. A dark bolt slammed into Dee, knocking her back from Kat, who slumped to the ground. I shouted as Dee sprang to her feet. Her eyes burned an intense white and then she flew forward, aiming straight for Baruck.

Spinning back, I released another blast and then another, but Baruck dodged my attack and went straight for Dee. I raced forward, but it was too late. He caught Dee, and for a heart-stopping moment, darkness swallowed her. She hit the ground, her body twitching.

I charged Baruck, tackling him. Branches shook, scattering leaves to the grass. I rolled atop Baruck, summoning the Source as I lifted my hand just as I saw Dee push to her feet. The moment of distraction was all it took.

Everything happened so fast.

Dee flickered in and out, blood trickling from her nose as she squared her shoulders and started toward us. Under me, Baruck lifted his arm and released another blast, shooting it straight at Dee.

Kat crashed into her at the second the blast hit them, knocking her aside a second before darkness surrounded them, and there was a scream. I couldn't tell if it belonged to my sister or Kat.

Everything was falling apart.

Both of them crashed to the ground. Kat was on her back and the front of her shirt was washed with a dark substance.

A metallic scent filled the air. Blood. Dee was beside her, on her side, her limp arm fallen across Kat's. Dee slipped into her true form.

Never take your eye off your enemy.

The blast caught me in the back, sending me through the air, ass over teacup. Pain made it difficult to hold form, and I felt myself slipping back and forth. My thoughts were consumed with my sister…and Kat.

Kat stood no chance against Baruck.

I smacked into the ground, stunned as I heard the Arum's voice in my head. *Three for one ssspecial.*

Trying to maintain one form, I twisted and my gaze cleared. Kat—I was next to Kat, so close I could touch her. She was alive. Her chest rose and fell in shallow breaths. She was staring at me, her lips moving, but there were no words. I tried to sit up, but aftershocks forced me down. My muscles spasmed. It was like being hit by a supercharged Taser.

*It'sss over. All of you will die.* Baruck advanced.

I turned toward Kat, saw the tears blurring her eyes. This wasn't right. She didn't deserve any of this, and I'd brought it all to her—everything.

Our eyes locked. I wanted to tell her I was sorry. I was sorry she moved here and met us. Not in the way she'd think—that it was her fault, but that she had no idea what she was stepping into. I wanted to turn back time, stop her from going to the library and erase the spaghetti incident, because without that, we would've never talked in the woods that night and she would've never walked out in front of that truck. So many mistakes.

Kat would be safe right now, watching stupid Halloween movies, maybe even in the arms of some guy who would never hurt her or put her in harm's way. *She would be safe.*

Out of my reach, but safe nonetheless.

Most of all, I wanted to go back and change the way I'd acted toward her. Because now, as she shuddered on the damp ground, as death loomed over us all, I was willing to acknowledge the one thing I'd been hiding from. The one thing that had truly terrified me.

I never wanted to push her away.

As selfish as it was, I was glad she had moved here. It was too late for us, but I cared for her…more than I should, but I did. It was too late.

Too late to tell her how I felt, to touch her, to just hold her, to make up for every terrible thing I'd done and said. It was too late for me.

But she was going to walk out of here. She was going to live if it was the last thing I did.

Letting my human form go, I was at my most vulnerable, but I was going to need everything. I extended an arm toward her and she reached out, her fingers disappearing in my light.

I focused everything into that touch, sending a jolt of energy into her body, knowing that whatever was in us would do its thing, healing her from the inside out. It would give her a chance to get away. Hopefully Baruck would be more focused on me.

A sob rocked her body, and I squeezed her hand. Then I saw her eyes flare with realization. She knew what I was doing, what it meant.

"No." Her voice was a hoarse, tired whisper.

She tried to pull away, but I held on, ignoring the desperate panic in her eyes. I squeezed her hand. I wasn't letting go. Not now.

Not ever.

Suddenly she sat up and grabbed my sister's arm while

she still held my hand. A pulse of light went through me, shining so bright that Baruck seemed to disappear. It arced high in the air, crackling and spitting. It went down into Dee. Her light connected with mine.

Baruck's shadow halted.

The arc of light streamed above and shot *down*, right into the center of Kat's chest. A second later she was above us, slipping free from my grasp, and she was above me, hovering, her hair flying out around her. Power built among the three of us, kicking the regenerative abilities into high gear. As it sparked, Dee and I slipped back into our human forms.

Dazed, I pushed to my knees, reaching for Kat. What was she doing…?

I could feel her pulling the particles out of the air, holding them close to her. It wasn't possible, but power coiled inside her, a tremor of the very same power shuddering deep inside me. This…this wasn't possible.

Screaming, she let it go.

Climbing to my feet, I stared in awe as it smacked into Baruck's chest. The air pulled tight and snapped. Intense light flared, and I threw my arm up, shielding my eyes. When it receded, Baruck was gone and Kat…

Oh, God.

"Kat?"

She was on her back and her chest…it barely moved. The scent of death was in the air. I shot to her side, dropping to my knees. She let out a rattling breath and raw panic exploded in my gut.

All of this… We came this far—I saved her and she took everything I'd given her, and instead of getting the hell out of there, she used it to save us.

She scarified herself for us.

I didn't deserve that. No way did I deserve this from her.

I pulled her into my arms, and she felt as light as a breath, as if a part of her that made her whole was already gone. "Kat, say something insulting. Come on."

Dee stirred and rose to her feet, panic filling her voice. I didn't take my eyes off Kat. Moving my fingers along her face, wiping away the traces of blood...but there was so much. Under her nose, the corners of her lips, her ears...and even pooling under her eyes.

This wasn't right.

I knew what I had to do. "Dee, go back to the house now."

"I don't want to leave," Dee protested, wrapping her arms around her waist as she stumbled closer. "She's bleeding! We have to get her to a hospital."

Kat's eyes fixed on me, but she didn't move. Horror climbed through my chest, digging in with claws.

"Go back to the house now!" I yelled, and then forced myself to take it down a notch. Dee couldn't know what I was about to do again. "*Please*. Leave us. Go. She's okay. She...she just needs a minute."

I turned my back on Dee, pushing the tangled waves of hair out of Kat's face. When I was sure Dee was gone, I let out a ragged breath. "Kat, you're not going to die. Don't move or do anything. Just relax and trust me. Don't fight what's about to happen."

There was no sign she'd heard me, but I wasn't giving up. No way. Lowering my head, I pressed my forehead against hers. My body faded out, and I slipped into my true form. Heat coursed from me into her.

*Hold on. Don't let go.* I knew she was beyond hearing me, but I kept talking as I cradled her head. *Just hold on.*

Focusing on her, I felt myself slip inside her. Then I

could see it all: bones knitting, cuts healing closed, torn muscles repairing, and blood flowing through her veins fast, but flowing without obstruction. She had been a mess, and it killed me to know what kind of pain she had endured.

I felt something click inside *me*. For a moment, I felt a strange feeling—a fluttering in my chest, next to my own heart, like our hearts were one, beating in sync, but then... then something else was happening. There was a tearing inside me, a rendering of my being—splitting into halves.

Her lips brushed mine. Colors swirled around me—bright reds and whites. It was like there wasn't *me* or *her*...it was us, only us. And I could feel an indiscernible pull toward her, a give and take. This was forbidden—healing her as many times I had, but this...this was more, because she had been on the verge of the unknown, teetering into oblivion and I'd pulled her back.

*What am I doing? If they find out what I've done...but I can't lose her. I can't. Please. Please. I can't lose you. Please open your eyes. Please don't leave me.*

*I'm here*, she said, but not out loud, and opened her eyes. *I'm here.*

Shocked, I jerked back, the light fading out of her. But something...something had been left behind. I could feel it. I didn't know what exactly, and I didn't care right then. She was alive. We all were alive, and that was what mattered.

"Kat," I whispered, and she shivered in my arms. I sat back, nestling her close to my chest and holding her up.

Her eyes were filled with wonder and a dose of confusion. "Daemon, what did you do?"

"You need to rest." I paused, bone-tired, weary to my core. Even I had my physical limits, and I'd blown past them tonight. "You're not a hundred percent. It will take a couple of minutes.

I think. I haven't healed anyone on this level before."

"You did at the library," she murmured, spreading her hands up my arms. Like it was the first time she'd ever touched me. "And at the car…"

I smiled tiredly. "That was just to help with a sprain and bruises. That was nothing like this."

Kat turned her head, staring over my shoulder. Her cheek brushed mine slightly, but it felt like a thousand soft-as-silk touches to me. I felt her stiffen.

"How did I do that?" she whispered. "I don't understand."

Good question. I buried my head in her neck, breathing in her vanilla and peach scent, committing it to memory. "I must've done something to you when I healed you. I don't know what. It doesn't make sense, but something happened when our energies joined. It shouldn't have affected you—you're human."

My words didn't seem to calm her. No shit. They weren't calming me much, either. My hand shook as I smoothed a strand of hair from her face. "How are you feeling?"

"Okay. Sleepy. You?"

"The same." But I felt amazing in a weird way. I ran my thumb over her chin and then her lower lip. I kind of felt like a kid going to Disney World for the first time and that was odd, because I'd never been to the land of mouse ears. Never wanted to go.

"I think, for now, it would be best if we kept this between ourselves—the whole healing thing and what you did back there," I said. "Okay?"

She nodded but otherwise remained still as my hands traced the lines of her face, removing the smudges and dark spots. Our gazes met and I smiled, really smiled in a way I hadn't in a long time.

And I stopped thinking.

Splaying my fingers across her cheeks, I kissed her softly. Keeping it gentle and slow, something I never really practiced before but wanted with her. Parts of me, places hidden from most, opened up. I tipped her head back and it was like the first time—was the first time, because this was what I wanted, perhaps even needed. The innocent touch left me breathless—a first.

I pulled back, laughing. "I was worried that we'd broken you."

"Not quite." Full of concern, her eyes searched my face. "Did you break yourself?"

I snorted. "Almost."

She took a little breath, her lips forming a faint smile. "What now?"

My lips responded to hers, and I breathed in the late-night air, the scent of damp grass, and rich soil. I breathed in *her*. "We go home."

# 24

Colonies were all the same.

Human. Luxen. Arum. Ant.

Nothing but a whole ton of crazy Kool-Aid I didn't want to come within five miles of, and I wouldn't be, but they had something I needed—that Kat needed.

She really owed me for this.

Picturing some of the ways she could repay me for this visit…that movie would never end. I kicked back in the sterile living room. All white—couches, carpet, walls, and pillows. It was like they had something against color. It made me want to spill something on purpose.

When Ethan Smith returned, he carried a small leather pouch in his hands. He took one look at me and his dark brows arched over eyes the shade of violets. "I know you're not the most patient of our kind, but it does take time to craft these things."

Yeah, almost three whole days of my life I'd never live again. Most of it had been spent searching the state for more

Arum and an entire day looking for the perfect piece of obsidian, but I was itchy to get back to Dee…and Kat. I didn't like the idea that she was glowing like a disco ball on steroids.

Ethan didn't hand the bundle over. Of course not, because that would be too easy at this point. "May I ask why you need this?"

"May I say no and you'll drop the conversation?"

A small, tight smile appeared on the older Luxen's face. "Your arrogance will one day be your downfall."

That among other things, not that I was mentioning any names or anything.

Irritation flashed across Ethan's face. "Not that I don't appreciate all you do for the colony, but your—"

"Personality could use an improvement," I cut in, thinking of Kat. "I get it. Trust me."

Ethan tipped his head to the side. Hair was starting to gray along his temples. "I hope so. It would be a shame to our race if something unfortunate happened to you."

I met his odd, amethyst-colored stare with my own. "I'm sure it would be."

The other Luxen was the first to break contact. "Does this have anything to do with the light show over the weekend?"

"Yes. I killed a couple of Arum and lost a few blades in the process, so I wanted something for Dee to wear just in case another happens." I sat forward, dropping my hands between my knees. "It's the same thing I told all the other Elders, Ethan."

"Hmm, I do believe it sounds familiar." He handed over the bundle, and the weight of the obsidian felt familiar. I slipped it in my pocket, ready to bounce the hell out of there. "Though, I must say I have never seen such a display of power. It was remarkable."

Unease trickled down my spine as I stood. There was something about Ethan, a quality I could never put my finger on, that sort of gave me the creeps. "Well, I am just friggin' awesome."

"Yes, you are." Ethan rose fluidly and straightened his pressed shirt. "Still, I am positive the Department of Defense will question it."

I stopped at the door, turning back to him. "And if they do?"

"We'll tell the DOD nothing if they ask, like we normally do, but if you bring them to our doorsteps too often, you won't just have them to worry about. Do you understand what I'm saying?"

Anger replaced the unease and I gritted out, "Yeah, I get what you're saying."

"Daemon?"

Facing him once more, my jaw was clenched so hard I was going to need to see the dentist. "Yes?"

Ethan clasped his hands together and smiled. "One more question."

I was going to throw myself out a window. "Go ahead."

"This human girl your sister and you have been associating with?" Ethan said, and I stiffened but wasn't surprised. The Elders were as bad as the DOD, if not worse. "Will she be a problem?" he asked.

"No." *But you will be if you mention that "human girl" again.* That I didn't say out loud or in our language, but the look on my face got the message through loud and freaking clear.

Ethan nodded and didn't stop me again.

Switching into my true form, I only took a few seconds to leave the colony and reach the cluster of houses. Not knowing if Kat's mom was out roaming about, I flipped back into human form before I stepped out of the woods.

The strangest damn thing happened as I headed up our driveway. Warmth shot over the nape of my neck, followed by an almost pleasant tingle between my shoulder blades. Along with that weirdness, another sensation prodded me. A feeling of completion. What the hell?

I think I needed a nap.

As soon as I hit the porch, a weird, warm shiver crawled along the base of my neck and I knew Kat was inside. I couldn't explain how I did or why, but I knew it in my core.

Pushing open the living room door, I headed through the foyer and my eyes found Kat before anyone else. She was sitting on the couch, thick lashes lowered, hiding those gray eyes. Her hair was down, falling around her face, over her shoulders, and down her back.

I stopped there, incapable of moving, too quick for her to notice. Seeing her, well, it did things I hadn't been ready to delve into before. Hell, I really didn't even know at what point I had become ready.

Probably happened somewhere between when I thought she was dead and when she wasn't.

I dropped onto the couch beside her, watching her. I knew she was aware of me on this intrinsic level. The faint blush creeping across her cheeks confirmed it.

"Where have you been?" she asked.

Silence fell as Dee and Adam turned to her. I arched a brow, fighting a laugh as the heat raced across her cheeks and down her throat. "Well hello, honey, I've been out boozing and whoring. I know my priorities are pretty off."

Her lips thinned. "Dick."

My sister groaned. "Daemon, don't be a jerk."

"Yes, Mommy. I've been with another group, searching the whole damn state to make sure there aren't any Arum that we're not aware of," I said, offering a better explanation.

Adam leaned forward. "There aren't any, right? Because we told Katy she didn't have anything to worry about."

My gaze flickered to him briefly. "We haven't seen a single one."

Dee hooted happily and clapped her hands. She turned to Kat, smiling. "See, nothing to worry about. Everything is over."

Kat smiled. "That is a relief."

I filled Adam in on the trip, leaving out most of the conversation with Ethan Smith, but the whole time my attention was more focused on Kat. Hyperaware of every small movement she made, every muscle that twitched and then relaxed, and every breath she took.

"Katy? Are you even here, right now?" Dee asked.

"I think so." Kat smiled again, but something was off about it. My eyes narrowed.

"Have you guys been driving her crazy?" I sighed. "Bombarding her with a million questions?"

"Never!" cried Dee. Then she laughed. "Okay. Maybe."

"Figured," I muttered, stretching out my legs. A second later, I glanced at Kat. Our eyes locked. Tension filled the room, and I wondered what was going on behind those eyes.

Dee cleared her throat loudly. "I'm still hungry, Adam."

He laughed. "You're worse than I am."

"True. Let's go to Smoke Hole. I think they're having homemade meatloaf." Dee hopped to her feet and kissed my cheek. "Glad you're back. I've missed you."

I smiled up at her. "Missed you, too."

When the door shut behind Dee and Adam, Kat turned

to me. "Is everything really okay?"

The urge hit me right then. I wanted to hold her, because she must've been worried to ask that question, and it seemed like the right thing to do. Of course it was. How many times had I held Ash when she was upset? Or, in a different way, Dee, when she was upset?

"For the most part." Before I knew what I was doing, I reached out with one hand, running my fingers over her cheek. A shock transferred to my fingertips, much like static, but so, so different. "Hell."

"What?" Her eyes shot wide.

I sat up and scooted close enough that our legs touched, not ready to go into what I suspected had happened between us when I healed her. "I have something for you."

Confusion flickered across her face. "Is it going to blow up in my face?"

I laughed as I reached into the front pocket of my jeans, pulling out the leather pouch. I handed it over to her, watching as she tugged on the little string and carefully turned the pouch upside down, like she was afraid a grenade would fall out. But when she saw the obsidian pendant, her lashes swept up and she was clearly surprised.

Pressure clamped down on my chest as I smiled. A different feeling, like when you're about to get on a roller coaster. I really never felt that way before. "Believe it or not, even something as small as that can actually pierce Arum skin and kill them. When it gets really hot you'll know an Arum is nearby even if you don't see one." I picked up the chain, holding the clasps. "It took me forever to find a piece like this since the blade turned to crap. I don't want you to take this off, okay? At least when... Well, for the most part."

The look of surprise hadn't faded as she twisted around

and pulled her hair out of the way. As soon as I got the tiny hook clasped, she faced me. An earnest pull to her expression had replaced the shock. "Thank you. I mean it, for everything."

"It's not a big deal. Has anyone asked you about your trace?"

She shook her head. "I think they're expecting to see one because of all the fighting."

I nodded, relieved that was one less thing to worry about for now. "Hell, you're bright as a comet right now. The sucker has got to fade or we'll be back to square one."

Kat stared at me a moment, her eyes sharpening. "And what is square one, exactly?"

"You know, us being...stuck together until the damn trace fades." Well, that kind of sounded like crap.

"After everything I've done, us being around each other is being stuck together?"

Oh crap.

"You know what? Screw you, buddy. Because of me, Baruck didn't find your sister. Because of what I did, I almost died. You healed me. That's why I have a trace. None of this is my fault."

"And it's mine? Should I have left you to die? Is that what you wanted?"

"That's a stupid question! I don't regret that you healed me, but I'm not dealing with this hot and cold shit from you anymore."

"I do believe you protest too much with the whole liking me part." I grinned, knowing the claws were about to come out. "Someone sounds like they are trying to convince themselves."

Kat took a deep breath, causing her chest to rise. "I think

it would be best if you'd stay away from me."

"No can do."

"Any of the other Luxen can watch over me or whatever," she protested. "It doesn't have to be you."

Yeah, that wasn't going to happen. "You're my responsibility."

"I am nothing to you."

"You're definitely something."

She looked like she wanted to hit me. I kind of wanted her to try, and honestly, I don't know why I liked to mess with her so much. "I dislike you so very much."

"No. You don't."

"Okay. We need to get this trace off me. Now."

One idea came to mind. "Maybe we can try making out again. See what that will do to this trace. It seemed to work last time."

Her cheeks flushed and a certain light filled her eyes. "Yeah, that's not going to happen again."

"It was just a suggestion."

"One that will never. Happen," she said. "Again."

"Don't act like you didn't have as much fun—"

Kat smacked me in the chest—hard, too. I couldn't help it. I laughed, and she made this cute little sound of disgust as she started to push away. Her small hand moved across my chest and it took everything in me not to grab her hand and do... well, other stuff with it.

I arched a brow. "Are you feeling me up, Kat? I'm liking where this is heading."

Her lips parted as she continued to press down. My pulse picked up a little as I watched her. Blood drained from her face. "Our heartbeats...they're the same. Oh my God, how is this possible?"

"Oh crap." Not how I wanted to start off this conversation.

Our eyes locked, and I placed my hand over hers and squeezed. I suspected as much. This only confirmed it, but what I knew about my kind healing humans was so limited, and what I did know was more like whispers and rumors.

"But it's not too bad," I said. "I mean, I'm pretty sure I morphed you into something and this whole heart thing proves we must be connected." I grinned. "Could be worse."

"What could be worse exactly?" Her voice had risen.

"Us being together." I shrugged. "It could be worse."

"Wait a sec. You think we should be together because of some kind of freaky alien mojo that has connected us? But two minutes ago you were bitching about being stuck with me?"

"Yeah, well, I wasn't bitching." I just had a moment of really bad word choice. "I was pointing out that we are stuck together. This is different…and you're attracted to me."

Her eyes narrowed much like a pissed-off cat. "I'll get back to that last statement in a second, but you want to be with me because you now feel…forced?"

I shifted. "I wouldn't say forced exactly, but…but I like you." Kat didn't immediately respond, and I prepared myself. "Oh no, I know that look. What are you thinking?"

"That this is the most ridiculous declaration of attraction I've ever heard," she said, standing. "That is so lame, Daemon. You want to be with me because of whatever crazy stuff that happened?"

I rolled my eyes as I stood. "We like each other. We do. It's stupid that we keep denying it."

"Oh, this is coming from the dude who left me on the couch topless?" She shook her head, sending locks of brown hair flying. "We don't like each other."

"Okay. I should probably apologize for that. I'm sorry." I took a step forward. "We were attracted to each other before I healed you. You can't say that's not true, because I've always...been attracted to you."

And it hit me then how freaking true that was.

From the very first time I'd seen her standing on my porch—the first argument, the first time she called me a douche, and from the very first time I realized how strong and brave she truly was, I'd been attracted to her. I'd wanted her.

Perhaps I had protested too loudly this whole time.

"Being attracted to me is as lame a reason to be with me as the fact we're stuck together now."

"Oh, you know it's more than that." I paused, sort of dumbstruck by the fact that a year ago I would have died of laughter if someone had said I'd be where I was right now, saying what I was. "I knew you would be trouble from the start, from the moment you knocked on my door."

Kat laughed drily. "That thought is definitely mutual, but that doesn't excuse the split personality thing you've got going on."

"Well, I was kind of hoping it did, but obviously not." I flashed a quick grin. "Kat, I know you're attracted to me. I know you like—"

"Being attracted to you isn't enough," she said.

"We get along."

She shot me a bland look.

I couldn't stop the grin that time and tried for a, "Sometimes we do."

"We have nothing in common."

"We have more in common than you realize."

"Whatever."

I caught a piece of her hair and wrapped it around my

finger. "You know you want to."

She hesitated a moment before she snatched her hair free. "You don't know what I want. You have no clue. I want a guy who wants to be with me because he actually wants to be. Not that he's forced to be out of some kind of twisted sense of responsibility."

"Kat—"

"No!" Her hands balled into fists as she drew in another deep breath. "No 'sorry.' You have spent months being the biggest jerk to me. You don't get to decide to like me one day and think I will forget all of that. I want someone to care for me like my dad cared for my mom. And you aren't him."

"How can you know?"

She stared at me a moment and then turned toward the door as if she planned on leaving. This conversation was so not over. I moved faster than she could track, appearing in front of the door.

"God, I hate when you do that!" Kat shrieked.

I stared down at her. "You can't keep pretending that you don't want to be with me."

She stared back with a look of fierceness I found incredibly sexy and...and yeah, I respected her for that, too. But then that look faded as she pressed her lips together. Sadness had crept in her eyes. "I'm not pretending."

Bull. Shit.

There had been hesitation before she had said that. There had been so much more that powered her words other than anger or frustration. She was afraid and she was sad. I got that. I had been a dick to her. There really wasn't an excuse in the world to make up for that, and like I'd realized when I'd been holding her in my arms in the field, I didn't—couldn't—let her go. "You're lying."

"Daemon."

I placed my hands on her hips and tugged her forward. The warmth of her body cascaded over mine, and I closed my eyes briefly, taking in a deep breath that tasted of Kat. "If I wanted to be with..." My hands tightened on her hips, and she swayed a little closer, until our legs brushed once more, proving that her words were at odds with what she wanted. I dipped my head and she shivered. "If I wanted to be with you, you'd make it hard, wouldn't you?"

Kat lifted her head. "You don't want to be with me."

Oh, I had to disagree with that. My lips spread into a smile. "I'm thinking I kind of do."

A pretty flush moved down her neck, and I wanted to chase it with my lips "*Thinking* and *kind of* aren't the same thing as knowing."

"No, it's not, but it's something." It was more than anything. "Isn't it?"

Shaking her head, she pulled away. "It's not enough."

I met her stare and sighed. Her stubbornness was something I loathed and was incredibly attracted to, which I guess made me sort of twisted. "You are going to make this hard."

She didn't say anything as she sidestepped me, and I let her get to the door this time.

"Kat?"

She faced me. "What?"

I smiled, and saw her gray eyes light up. "You do realize I love a challenge?"

Kat laughed softly and turned back to the door, giving me the middle finger. "So do I, Daemon. So do I."

Watching her leave, I had to admit that she looked just as good walking toward me as she did walking away.

I did love a challenge. And I never lose.

# ACKNOWLEDGMENTS

When I was first approached about writing Oblivion, I thought it was a great opportunity to give the Lux fans a little bit more of Daemon. I didn't plan on actually writing Obsidian, Onyx, and Opal (which is available in the digital version of Oblivion), but that was what happened. So you don't get just a taste of what it's like in Daemon's head. You get a whole heaping of it.

It really does take a village to finish a book. A huge thank-you to the following people for making it possible — Kevan Lyon, Liz Pelletier, Meredith Johnson, Rebecca Mancini, Stacy Abrams, and the team at Entangled Publishing. Thank you to K.P. Simmon and my assistant/BFF, Stacey Morgan. A special thank-you to Vilma Gonzalez for helping me work through Oblivion.

None of this would be possible without you, the reader. Because of you, this book happened. There aren't enough thank-yous in the world.

**Want more Lux? Collect the entire series by #1 *New York Times* and *USA Today* bestselling author Jennifer L. Armentrout**

## OBSIDIAN

There's an alien next door. And with his looming height and eerie green eyes, he's hot…until he opens his mouth. He's infuriating. Arrogant. Stab-worthy. But when a stranger attacks me and Daemon literally freezes time with a wave of his hand, he lights me up with a big fat bull's-eye. Turns out he has a galaxy of enemies wanting to steal his abilities and the only way I'm getting out of this alive is by sticking close to him until my alien mojo fades. If I don't kill him first, that is.

## ONYX

Daemon's determined to prove what he feels for me is more than a product of our bizarro alien connection. So I've sworn him off, even though he's running more hot than cold these days. But we've got bigger problems. I've seen someone who shouldn't be alive. And I have to tell Daemon, even though I know he's never going to stop searching until he gets the truth. What happened to his brother? Who betrayed him? And what does the DOD want from them—from me?

## OPAL

After everything, I'm no longer the same Katy. I'm different… and I'm not sure what that will mean in the end. When each step we take in discovering the truth puts us in the path of the secret organization responsible for torturing and testing alien hybrids, the more I realize there is no end to what I'm capable of. The death of someone close still lingers, help comes from the most unlikely source, and friends will become the deadliest of enemies, but we won't turn back. Even if the outcome will shatter our worlds forever.

## ORIGIN

Daemon will do anything to get Katy back. After the successful but disastrous raid on Mount Weather, he's facing the impossible. Katy is gone. Taken. Everything becomes about finding her. But the most dangerous foe has been there all along, and when the truths are exposed and the lies come crumbling down, which side will Daemon and Katy be standing on? And will they even be together?

## OPPOSITION

The world changed the night the Luxen came, and now Daemon will do anything to save Katy…even if that means betrayal. For Katy, the lines between good and bad have blurred, and love has become an emotion that could destroy them all. As it becomes impossible to tell friend from foe, and the world crumbles around them, they may lose everything—even what they cherish most—to ensure the survival of their friends…and mankind. War has come to Earth. And no matter the outcome, the future will never be the same for those left standing.

## SHADOWS

The last thing Dawson Black expected was Bethany Williams. As a Luxen, an alien life-form on Earth, human girls are…well, fun. But since the Luxen have to keep their true identities a secret, falling for one would be insane. Dawson is keeping a secret that will change her existence…and put her life in jeopardy. But even he can't stop risking everything for one human girl. Or from a fate that is as unavoidable as love itself.

*In the* **LUX** *series...*

**CONTINUE YOUR LUX JOURNEY WITH *SHADOWS*,
A PREQUEL NOVELLA**

# AVAILABLE NOW IN
# EBOOK AND PAPERBACK

HODDER

In the *Covenant* series...

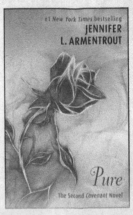

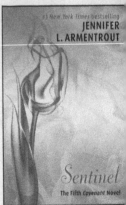

# AVAILABLE NOW
# IN EBOOK AND PAPERBACK

HODDER